MW01488234

NOW, I'M EIGHTEEN

DENNIS

ELIZABETH GRACE JUNG

abbott press®

A DIVISION OF WRITER'S DIGEST

NOW I'M EIGHTEEN
DENNIS

Copyright © 2013 Elizabeth Grace Jung.

Edited by Dr. Dennis Hensley (Taylor University)

All rights reserved. No part of this book may be used or reproduced by any means,
graphic, electronic, or mechanical, including photocopying, recording, taping or by any
information storage retrieval system without the written permission of the publisher
except in the case of brief quotations embodied in critical articles and reviews.

Abbott Press books may be ordered through booksellers or by contacting:

Abbott Press
1663 Liberty Drive
Bloomington, IN 47403
www.abbottpress.com
Phone: 1-866-697-5310

Because of the dynamic nature of the Internet, any web addresses or links contained in
this book may have changed since publication and may no longer be valid. The views
expressed in this work are solely those of the author and do not necessarily reflect the
views of the publisher, and the publisher hereby disclaims any responsibility for them.

Any people depicted in stock imagery provided by Thinkstock are models,
and such images are being used for illustrative purposes only.

Certain stock imagery © Thinkstock.

ISBN: 978-1-4582-0730-2 (e)
ISBN: 978-1-4582-0731-9 (hc)
ISBN: 978-1-4582-0732-6 (sc)

Library of Congress Control Number: 2012923417

Printed in the United States of America

Abbott Press rev. date: 03/25/2013

Also by Elizabeth Grace Jung:
College: In Sickness and Health....*Kaitlynn*
But God, I'm only Eighteen....*John*

T O ALL THE TEENS who found a home in our house, in the words of Grenville Kleiser written before 1910, "your degree of success is not measured by what you say and promise, but by what you attempt and achieve. The world awards its prizes not for excuses and explanations, but for performances and results. Intelligent men read you like an open book, and accurately appraise the kind and quality of your success. The creative, planning, aspiring power within the realm of your mind, coupled with earnest application and industry, is sufficient to place you in the front rank of men. **Life is rich with opportunities and possibilities** for the ambitious and persevering. Successful men in all departments of life have been characteristically hard workers. **There is a place of distinction for you,** if you emulate the example of great men," (and women).

As parents we have appreciated each of you and your uniqueness for who you are, and what you have become. Even though times were rough for each of you, life has been a learning experience for us as well as you. You brought to our home your own personalities, talents, and faults. Thanks for the time you spent in our home.

INTRODUCTION

D ENNIS MOORE IS THE second son and third child of the John Moore family. Dennis has an older sister, Kaitlynn, who is married to Matthew Davis, and they live in St. Louis, Missouri. His older brother, John, is a policeman. Because Dennis's father died in a farm accident, Dennis and his siblings had the responsibility of keeping the farm productive and profitable while their mother worked at the local railroad office.

Dennis's mother has precarious health. She operates on one kidney transplanted from her twin sister. His youngest brother, Paul, had a relapse with his leukemia and the family is concerned for him. Other younger brothers are Steve and a foster brother, Glen.

As a senior in high school, Dennis must make a decision regarding what he will do after high school. Do I go on to college, if so where, and what should my major be? The question—what does God want me to do with my life is a major concern. The story begins with his mother reminding Dennis to write his concerns in his journals.

CHAPTER 1

"I KNOW, MOM. I HEARD you. You don't have to tell me twice. I heard the same thing every time you told Kaitlynn and John. Now, I've heard you say the same thing to Steve, and Paul, too. 'Go get your journal and start writing. Why do you insist on cluttering your mind with the things that are bothering you?' Okay, Mom, I'm going. Besides, I've already filled enough pages to write a novel about my life."

"You're probably right, Dennis. If you ever become a leading citizen in the community or go into politics, there might be book publishers clamoring to get the book-rights to your life-story. Why don't you go back through your journal and start a best-selling book? Who knows... you may have a nice savings in the bank before Steve does."

My brother Steve is sixteen now, and he brags every time he puts a dollar in his savings account. He thinks he's going to be rich someday, but I'll wager he loses it all when he gets his first car or truck.

I went upstairs to my bedroom desk and looked at my older brother's police uniform hanging on a hook on our bedroom wall. John doesn't want it in our bedroom closet. He says I cram things in too tightly, and it gets all the creases messed up after he irons it.

Maybe I do. I try to be careful.

I sat at my desk, just thinking for a moment. I thought about what Mom said downstairs and about how she encouraged each one of us to write our thoughts and feelings on paper. My journals *would* make interesting reading, *if* I should ever become a leading citizen in our community, or go into politics. Mom is right. I looked at the police uniform again and thought, *I more or less promised John I would go to the Police Academy at the Southeast Missouri University as soon as I graduated from high school.*

Oh, well. Right now, I'm not sure of any direction I should take, except to stay on the farm and help Mom with the animals and all the planting and harvesting in the crop season.

I opened my lowest desk drawer to get my journal and pulled out my newest journal and one of the older ones. I had to laugh about some of the things I wrote when I was thirteen. Some of it would make no sense to others, but what I had written on my thirteenth birthday about being a teenager was typical of an immature kid. I chuckled and closed that one and opened my latest journal. I should label them on the front by ages. I could see how a few years later, my thinking and perspective on things had changed. Now, I'm the one in the transition time of my life, and I have to make decisions regarding what I am going to do after high school. Mom told me that my journals would often give me clues for the future by looking at the preparation I've had in high school and through my experiences in the past.

She said, "Dennis, please look at your journals, and while you are at it, think about what you feel are your best talents. Your life up to this point, and for the next few years, is the time of preparation for your future."

When my sister, Kaitlynn, and my brother, John, were seniors, I heard the same thing from Mom. So, the question was always in my mind, from my high school sophomore year, until now: what should I do as an occupation or profession to support myself the rest of my life? Now that I'd become a senior, I wasn't sure what I was supposed to do after I graduate.

I opened my journal and reached for a pen. Since I started thinking about my future, I thought again about what Mom said, and I said to myself, "I *should* make my life into a novel. Maybe it will sell really well, and I can pay for my college education. That's *if* I go to college."

I guess I should or would start a book by telling something about myself. I looked over at the police uniform again. I had to pray, "God, did you allow John to hang that uniform on that hook just as a reminder that I should consider the Police Academy?"

I was a little amused and dated the page in my journal and started writing. "I'm Dennis the third child and second son, born to the John and Bonnie Moore family in Chaffee, Missouri. I am eighteen years old now and a senior in Chaffee High School. My sister Kaitlynn is twenty-two, and she is married to Matthew Davis. They live in St. Louis. My older brother John is twenty, and he is studying criminal justice at the university in Cape Girardeau, Missouri. He went through the Police Academy and works part time on the police force in Chaffee. Chaffee is our mailing address, although we live on a farm outside the city of Chaffee, Missouri. Besides my parents and grandparents, John is the biggest influence in my life. Well, God is really the one who influences me most, but he uses my parents and John, and the Bible, too, of course. I try to read my Bible every day and memorize verses, too.

I have two younger brothers, Steve and Paul. We're all less than two years a part in age and being so close in age has helped our ability to work together on the farm. We had to learn each other's jobs, and I think it made us more like close friends. Each of us experienced some health or other serious problem, and our concern for the one with the health issue made us closer as a family. We are supportive of one another, and we appreciate each of our different abilities or talents. Yes, we argue sometimes as siblings do, but usually we don't have the *time* to waste on bickering. Besides, Mom would intervene very quickly and give us some nonsense chore to do, if we didn't stop and evaluate the other person's opinion. We get even with each other through some harmless revenge, and then we have a good laugh out of it. Humor keeps us from wasting time feeling sorry for ourselves with all the issues that have plagued our family—Dad's farm accident and death, Mom's kidney failure and kidney transplant, Paul's leukemia, my reaction to bee stings, weasels killing our chickens, and other things less serious. Through all the crises, our family has grown stronger and God has been faithful to help all of us. Those two things give me confidence in life.

I closed my journal and just sat on my desk chair thinking about our family. I had many thoughts going through my head and that's exactly what they were doing, *going through* my mind. I thought about our brain and memory and all that stuff. Sometimes I can recall things in detail just like that police uniform. All the stitching on the pockets are the same and they are probably the same on every uniform designed. I should tell John to put his uniform somewhere else, so it won't distract me.

I opened my journal again and started writing about Kaitlynn and John. I wrote: Both Kaitlynn and John have written about their lives, and I have been encouraged to do the same. It helps us to keep perspective in our thinking when negative things happened. Mom has encouraged us to write. I can hear her, now, telling one of us or all of us, "don't clutter you minds with details that worry you. Write them down and you can refer to them anytime you want. Besides, while you are writing, the details get evaluated, and often don't seem as trivial as you thought at first." Mom was right about that, too.

People have said we are *mature* kids. I owe that to Mom and to

Dad too, before he died. Some kids think they are mature because they have the *facts* about life, meaning all about sex, but I think assuming responsibility and consideration for others is being mature and not the process of mating in humans. Grandpa lived with us, and his wisdom was always given in such a way that I always felt as though I had more understanding about life. John said the same thing. He probably wrote that in *his* journal. My parents and Grandpa taught us to look to God for answers when there didn't appear to be any. Grandpa used to say, "People will fail you, but God will *never* fail you." Then he would burst out in the chorus of the song "Jesus never fails." It was written by A.A. Luther, and copyrighted in 1927. I can hear Grandpa's voice in my mind. He had a baritone voice, and he would sing the words to "Jesus never fails" after having a discussion with us on friendships.

The first verse says, "Earthly friends may prove untrue, doubts and fears assail; one still loves and cares for you: One who will not fail." Then Grandpa would put his hand on my shoulder or arm to make sure I was listening, and sing the chorus. "Jesus never fails, Jesus never fails; Heaven and Earth may pass away, but Jesus never fails." That keeps my thoughts positive. John was always repeating to me what Grandpa had told him. Sometimes I felt like I was getting a triple dose of something that Grandpa had said. Grandpa would say something, Mom would say almost the same words, and then John would repeat it to me. I wonder if I then repeated the same things to my younger brother, Steve.

One day I heard Grandpa singing a different verse, and I wondered who he was singing to that time. I went and looked, and it was Mom. She was standing by a kitchen counter, and he was sitting at the table with a cup of coffee in front of him. Mom must have been feeling bad about something because Grandpa belted out-loud, "Tho' the sky be dark and drear, fierce and strong the gale, just remember He is near, and He will not fail." I must have been around ten or twelve years old. Grandpa looked at me as I pulled out a chair at the kitchen table and sat. He placed his hand on my arm and continued singing, "Jesus never fails. Jesus never fails."

Then he spoke the last words, "Heaven and earth may pass away, but Jesus never fails."

Grandpa glanced at me and then Mom and said, "Your husband and his dad may have passed away, but Jesus is still near us."

He looked at Mom with a very serious face. He said, "Daughter, remember that!"

Then he looked at me and said, "Dennis, do you understand the words in that song?"

I said, "Yeah," and left the kitchen. I don't know why that scene just went through my mind. Now that I'm older, I understand why Grandpa used the words in many songs to get a message into our hearts and minds. All of us in the family needed encouragement from time to time, and God used the songs, written long before we were born, to give us some stability in our lives without Dad.

I should get back to my journal and write again. My mind was wandering to memories of Grandpa and many other things. I clicked my pen a couple of times and started writing. I wrote: Our family has worked together in just about everything. We worked together at the Chaffee Café when Mom was the owner. Now, we work together to make our farm prosperous, and we play our musical instruments and sing together. Mom and Dad insisted that we pray together over family problems, and we go to church together.

I laid my pen down because I knew I was writing the same things that my older sister, Kaitlynn, and my older brother, John, had already written.

➤ ⟵

Last Fall I started working one night a week with my older brother in Cape Girardeau at a youth center. The work is a crime prevention program that Officer Harrison started. He has six young teen-aged boys meet at the youth center once or twice a week after school. Officer Harrison is on the police force in Cape Girardeau and teaches in the Criminal Justice Department at the Southeast Missouri University and the Law Enforcement Academy, too. John attends college there and I will in September. I guess, I will. I sort of promised John I would go.

It's been more than a year since Officer Harrison called my brother John to help, and he came home and asked *me* to help. Now, we have another program out on the farm giving the boys an opportunity to help themselves and their families. There is a lot of work, heartache, and reward seeing six boys, ages thirteen to fifteen, from poor, dysfunctional families, turn themselves into hard-working productive kids with hope for the future. It's rewarding to see attitudes changed and school work become a priority.

I took on the responsibility for the planning and seeing that each boy would feel special when he came to the farm. It was rewarding to me. I'm not much older than the boys in the program, but my brother John was in the midst of spring planting when Officer Harrison called or talked to John at the university. John tried to tell the officer that he had a full workload on the farm, and his studies for classes at the university took all his available time, but it didn't come out that way. God put words in John's mouth, and he said, "The only way I can do it is to have the boys come to the farm and work for me."

Officer Harrison thought it was a great idea. I thought it was, too. Everyone but John thought the boys would be a project that the whole family could do. My idea was to give the boys the use of three acres to make gardens and produce vegetables and fruit for their families. Anything extra, the boys could sell at a roadside stand. It seemed like a good idea to me, but John needed encouragement.

God had already given us extra help on the farm, when Paul's orthopedic doctor, Dr. Lynn, retired and purchased the farm adjacent to ours. Dr. Lynn's son, Brian, came back from a university in England and was experienced at keeping machinery in repair. He stepped in to help with our tractors and other farm equipment as well as on Mr. Jenkins's and Dr. Lynn's farm, next to ours.

Then Paul's home nurse's husband, Mr. Webster, was laid off work, and he took up the job of painting all of our out-buildings—the barn and the shed, and he even used masonry paint on the cinder-block chicken house. He painted our house, too. He taught the boys in the prevention program to paint. They were afraid at first, but after they got the hang of filling in holes and using the brush, and painting in only one direction they were very proud of themselves. I heard one of the older boys telling another boy, "In jest two or three years, I'm gonna get me a job paintin'. All the houses on 'ar street needs paintin' jest like the Moore's barn. It'd sure look better. I think I'd be most proud to live on 'ar street if'n the old houses look as good as this 'n."

I told the boy, "That's a good idea. You hang onto that. I think I might even pay for your first two-gallon cans of paint. You do a good job here, and I will even get you some business cards."

He asked, "What's a business card?"

I explained, "It's a little card with your name, phone number, and the title of your painting business. You can give them to the people on your street. They might call you to paint something for them. Then, if they like your work, they'll tell others to call you. So, do a good job here, and maybe I'll find a business that will hire you to help them.

You would have thought the boy, who was almost sixteen,

had just been handed a platter of one-thousand dollar bills. He looked at me for 10 seconds. He was thinking. He finally said, "I be sixteen in three months. Do ya think I kin quit schoolin' 'n work at a paintin' job?"

I said, "No, don't quit. Stay in school as long as you can or until you graduate from high school."

He wanted to know why. "I know how ta paint now."

I had to quickly think of a logical answer. I said, "If you can't figure out how many gallons of paint you will need for a certain size job, and figure out how much to pay your helpers or to save to pay taxes, you might not have any money left over for yourself."

One of the other boys said, "Yeah, Martin, that's why we have to take math. You're good at math."

I said, "That's good, but we won't get *this* job done, if we stand around and talk."

I turned to wipe my brush off and place it in a brush cleaner bucket, and I heard a third boy's voice say, "Aw Marty, youse jest dream'n agin."

He was about fifteen feet away from me, but he'd been listening to the conversation I was having with the other two boys. I wiped my hands off and looked at him. He said, "I'm paintin.' See, I did all this yere. I'm faster'n them are."

He waved his brush around to show me where he had painted. I saw drops of paint go through the air and I wanted to fuss at him, but I got my thoughts organized, and said, "Yeah, Buddy, you are all doing a good job, but did you know that dreaming sometimes turns into an invention? Take the farm truck sitting over there. That used to be just a dream in someone's mind. Have you ever heard of Henry Ford? Well, Mr. Ford and his friends got tired of riding on horses, and invented something that they say has more horse power than six or eight horses. They dreamed about that until they finally did something to make their dream come true. Don't be afraid to dream and then *do* something to make your dream come true, especially, if it is something helpful for people."

The boy looked at the other boys and then down at his brush and then put it down in his paint bucket to get more paint on it. He said, "Yeah, s'pose youse right."

I went on in the house, smiling to myself. John wanted to know what put the big grin on my face. I said, "Well, John, I just learned that a few chosen words at the right time can encourage your boys to be dreamers of something good."

I laughed and told John about the conversation. I said, "It makes me glad Mom and Dad gave us a project that we were responsible for."

I went on upstairs and jotted down some notes, used the bathroom, and went back outside.

—▶ ◀—

The farm painting projects were all done last week. And we've had little time to relax and do things with our projects. My brothers and I have worked at different projects to put money in our family account, and it has taught us responsibility for something, and for each other. My brother Steve is sixteen now and my brother Paul is eleven. Paul is finally in remission from Leukemia, and we are praying that he stays well.

When Dad died and then Grandpa died, John and I stepped right into their shoes and assumed responsibility for the farm. Then my mother married Dr. Marshall Lynn last June. Dr. Lynn grew up on a farm and began sharing responsibility just like Dad would have done.

Mom's wedding was a big affair. Dr. Lynn's daughters and my sister Kaitlynn planned the whole wedding. Dr. Lynn lost his first wife to cancer, and he was a widower for three years. He met our family at Saint Francis Medical Center when Paul broke his arm, and Dr. Lynn did surgery on it. Something clicked mentally and emotionally for him, with all of us. He lost his nine year-old son to leukemia, and Paul became his little boy again. Mom was an added bonus. For Mom, it had been a couple of years since Dad had died in the farm accident working on our antique combine, so they both were given a second chance at love. It was interesting how God matched and meshed our two families. We're a good fit.

—– —

I graduated from Chaffee High last week, and I've been busy with my project, which is ten acres of soybeans and helping to take care of our two milk cows. The boys in the crime prevention program have their gardens, and that keeps me busy, too.

When my brother John called Officer Harrison at the Cape Girardeau Police Department, he told Officer Harrison, his *family* made the decision to help with the boys *for* him. Well, I don't know that we did that, I just thought it was something that would be helpful and sort of a ministry that our family could do. I've wondered how I got to be the one to manage or oversee the project. I guess John thought the family motto *all for one and one for all* meant *all for the boys* and somehow he was left out of the equation. The boys did become a family *and* a neighbor project, too. John was encouraged after the family took some of the load of concerns from him. Actually God did, as I reminded John of Isaiah 40:30 and 31. "Even the youths shall faint and be weary, and the young men shall utterly fall, but those who wait on the Lord shall renew *their* strength; they shall mount up with wings of eagles, they shall run and not be weary, they shall walk and not faint" (NKJV).

I told John we would all work and help him. I said, "You don't need to think you need to be responsible for everything. We all get tired at times, but God still wants us to rely on him." We were going to bed when I said that to John. I pulled my covers up and thought, *Maybe I should be a preacher.* I didn't remember anymore, as I woke up to a rooster crowing and the smell of coffee.

→ ◄—

This past year in high school was extremely busy, but Mrs. Miller, our high school counselor, stopped me one day in the hallway and said, "Dennis, you need to stop by my office. Now is the time to get your college applications filled out and submitted."

Mrs. Miller said she would be in her office until four o'clock, so I went that afternoon right after school. She had a file full of admissions applications from most of the colleges in our area. I told Mrs. Miller the same thing that John had told her, and she was looking at me like, *where have I heard this story before?* But it was all true. John and I had talked about it several times. With Mom's kidney infections and then her kidney transplant and my youngest brother Paul's leukemia being in remission for only a few months, it always seemed easier for one of us to stay at home and keep the farm running smoothly. Especially, since Kaitlynn married and lives in St. Louis, and John carried such a load with the farm while going to the Law Enforcement Academy, it just seemed like one of us should stay home and work the farm. Now he's going for a Criminal Justice degree, too, and he's helping Officer Harrison after school one afternoon a week while working part-time three afternoons as a policeman in the Chaffee Police Department.

When we started working with the boys in the crime prevention program out on the farm, I felt like God had something in the program for me to do, and I just went for it. God had given me a second chance at life when I was stung by some bees under our apple trees. I had a severe reaction, so I can at least show my gratitude by working with the boys. I almost died when my throat began swelling and I couldn't breathe. I would have been gone, if it had not been for John's quick thinking to give me cough medicine with an antihistamine in it. Then Dr. Lynn showed up at the farm right at the very moment we needed him. He gave me a shot of epinephrine. God sure knows ahead of time what is going to happen and sends help when we need it. I spent two days in the hospital because Mom wanted the cardiologist to see me while I was there. Last year Dr. Lynn heard a heart murmur when he gave me a sports physical, but the cardiologist declared me healthy enough to continue to play basketball my senior year.

I was rambling on and on and the school counselor was grinning at me. She stopped me and said, "Dennis, you have taken your family and your responsibilities seriously. That's what I've appreciated about your family, but there comes a time in life when *you* must make decisions for *yourself* and *your* future. Yes, consider your family and their needs, but one day, you'll find yourself needing a back-up job for an income, and now is the time to prepare yourself with an education for that job or profession. I suggest you do that this week."

She handed me some admissions applications for Southeast Missouri University and for the police Academy, too. "Are there other colleges or universities you have thought about?"

I said, "No," and took the applications that she'd laid on the corner of her desk. I had a knot creep up in my stomach, and I felt tense. I asked, "Do I bring these back to you, or do I send them somewhere else?"

She said, "I've attached an envelope to each one of them, so you can send them to the university yourself."

I stood and said, "Thanks, I'll do that."

The counselor stood and said, "Dennis, remember—one week."

That was weeks ago perhaps two months. I did sign up to go to Southeast Missouri University, and also the Police Academy. I sort-of felt good after mailing them. I felt relieved about finally making the decision to further my education. Now, I can think of other things. It seems like there have been a lot of changes in my life during the last six months. For one thing, Mom and Dr. Lynn married, and that was the biggest change for the family. We see a lot of his son, Brian, and Dr. Lynn's sister, Miss Susan, who is a widow. She requested that we call her Aunt Susan. Brian and his Aunt seem like real family to us, now. We did start calling her Aunt Susan.

Mom found her biological family and they have become important to us, too, but having Brian and Aunt Susan close by on the Jenkins farm has been like a close extended family. I've liked that. Brian Lynn enrolled in the university in Cape Girardeau and he plans to go there for a couple of semesters. He is hoping to transfer to the university at Rolla, Missouri after this year. It's a good mechanical engineering school, too, and Brian's major is engineering. He's been dating Kaitlynn's friend, Chelsey. He probably thinks by going to Rolla, Missouri, Chelsey will be closer at her university. Mom enjoys watching that romance grow. She likes Chelsey. Her dad was Mom's lawyer, and he was the person who was so helpful to Mom when Dad and Grandpa died.

I'm still debating what to do this fall. I know I enrolled in the Southeast Missouri Law Enforcement Academy, which I sometimes call the Police Academy, but maybe I won't go. Mom told me, "Dennis, if you are still having doubts, maybe you should step out in faith and go. God will show you immediately if you have made a mistake."

She reminded me that Satan is the author of confusion. The day I filled out the college application papers, I left Mom sitting at the kitchen table, reading something. I thought *Mom is right, so just think about what's on your schedule today.* I had written down what I wanted to do for my day's schedule, and it included my thoughts on the garden projects.

I've been accused of always having something on my mind. I guess I do, but John asked me to put in writing all about the garden projects with the crime-prevention program boys, and I have attempted to do that. John thinks I have insight or discernment into other people's thinking and feeling. He said, "You'd do a good job talking with the boys about their problems."

We had agreed that I would enroll in the Police Academy once I graduated from high school. John talked his girlfriend's brother, Robert Weber, my brother, Steve, and me, into becoming policemen. After what happened to Robert and his sister Janet, John told us, "There's a right way and a wrong way to go after law-breakers, and we especially need to replace that bad cop, Officer Blair, with some good moral policeman."

Robert had a bad attitude and some vengeance in his heart for the beating that he had, and his sister's rape, but John changed Robert's thinking while he was still in the hospital. So Robert, Steve, and I have always had it in our minds that we would go to the Police Academy, but now... I'm having second thoughts. I need to get my thoughts on what is on today's "Things to do" list, but somehow my mind won't shut down and relax. I'm still wondering if becoming a police officer is right for me. It's that uniform hanging on that hook on the wall that keeps reminding me. I took it off the hook and hung it in a hall closet. I left a note. "John, your clean uniform is in the hall closet." I came back to my desk, but was still thinking.

I guess, as a police officer like Officer Harrison, I could work with him and keep the prevention program going. I could minor in psychology, and that might be helpful, too. I really need to keep praying for God's direction and wisdom. I know God sent help with the farm for John, and he will for me, also. But, not knowing when the help will come, makes me want to stay here on the farm and work. As Mom said, "Dennis when God's intentions are not clear, you must step out in faith and follow your instincts. God will use whatever steps you take and redirect you if necessary."

She is right, but I'm eighteen, and sometimes it's a struggle to make decisions that take me out of my comfort zone. I'll continue to pray and ask God for guidance. In the meantime, I guess I will follow through with the Police Academy. The professors were always proud of John, and Officer Harrison told me that the professors at the academy were happy to see another Moore brother on their list of new students. John was happy that I finally enrolled in the program. I'll continue to farm and work with the boys and their gardens as long as I can, or until God gets more specific on what He wants me to do.

I have been thinking—that's almost funny, I'm sorry, but I can't stop thinking. I was looking back over Officer Harrison's prevention program, and since John asked me to keep records of what we did with the boys, I started writing them down. Perhaps, I should write a book or some articles about that someday. Before the boys came to the farm for the first time, I used to lie awake at night and think about all the details. I thought about the different garden tools Mom had in the shed and which tools we would have to purchase. I thought about the name we were calling the gardens. I called it *God's dirt* and realized the boys might think *they* were being called dirt, so I changed the name to "God's soil." The project would be God's project, and, in a sense, God would be planting ideas in the soil of the boy's minds and hearts each time they came out to the farm to work in their gardens.

I wrote a note in my notebook that Paul was anxious for the boys to come to the farm, so they could learn all about chickens. He wanted to send home a dozen eggs with them each Saturday.

Steve was hoping that an extra boy might come, so he could get him interested in raising good beef cattle. Then Dr. Lynn came home one day with six new hoes and rakes and six notebooks with spread sheets in them for recordkeeping. I couldn't believe he had done that. Especially, since I hadn't said anything to him. It surely was a God thing. I asked him for the receipt because I thought it would be good for each boy to do the math and figure out cost of equipment, seeds, fertilizer, and all that. It would help them in school with their math word problems. I'm glad Dad, Mom, and Grandpa did that with us. We sure learned to keep good records of everything. It helped with our spending, too.

I, also, had written a note about the water bottles that Dr. Lynn had for the boys. The bottles were plastic water bottles with an insulated cover on them. Each bottle had a hook to put on the boy's belt, but some boys didn't even have a belt. Mom remedied that by finding belts that were mine or my brother's and were too small for us, or too worn-out to wear to church, but could be worn while the boys worked in their gardens. The insulated bottles came from different drug companies and had advertisements on them. Dr. Lynn said, "I got them at different medical meetings. The bottles were free."

The boys thought they were really hot-stuff wearing the bottles. You could see the pride written all over their faces. Mom was glad to have them because the bottles kept the boys from wanting to stop and run to the house for drinks. When we stopped for lunch, Mom refilled their bottles with ice water from the refrigerator.

The first year that the boys worked in their garden plots, Mom and Steve worked in the kitchen as hard as the boys worked in the gardens. Miss Susan… I mean Aunt Susan, and our neighbor, Mrs. Molly Jenkins, took the vegetables from three of the gardens and taught the boys how to wash and prepare the vegetables for canning and freezing. Mom and Steve took the other three boys and their vegetables and taught them.

I tried to have the boys keep records, but it got to be haphazard because they were so busy in school and other activities; also, because Steve and Mr. Jenkins and I went through the garden during the week to get tomatoes that were ripe and made sure the bugs weren't devouring everything. I found it interesting that each boy had gotten about two bushels of potatoes. They wanted to sell one bushel at the stand that was set up along the highway and keep the rest for their families.

When Dr. Lynn married mom, he sold his house and most of his furniture, but Mom suggested that they should keep *his* refrigerator, and it really came in handy to store the extra potatoes and corn from Mom's garden and the boys' vegetables, too. Mr. Jenkins bought a used refrigerator, so they could do the same.

At the end of the season, according to my records, as poor as they were, each boy had picked five quarts of strawberries. We figured next year as the strawberry plants expanded on their own, there would be more. They had at least seven cantaloupes apiece, and the watermelon crop was different on each plot. We couldn't figure that out. One boy had three nice watermelons, while another one had eight. We thought someone might have been stealing watermelon at night.

Every week, Aunt Susan, Mrs. Jenkins, and Mom would bag up enough potatoes, corn, green beans, tomatoes, and a cantaloupe or two, to feed a family of seven, and she would have each boy's name on everything. Officer Harrison brought his wife out to our farm one Saturday to help freeze extra plastic bags of corn and green beans. Another weekend two mothers came out and helped. Mom didn't say anything, but I caught her taking things from her own garden and giving them to the ladies. I know one lady had some apples that we had in the freezer. I figured God would bless Mom, though it sure made my record-keeping hard.

I insisted that the boys give money into the program, so there would be seed money for next year. I only required them to pay back two dollars, which didn't cover the cost, but I wanted them to also be accountable for expenses. One boy said, "But, I won't be in the program next year, so why do I have to give?"

I reminded him that someone had given for him to plant his seeds and he, in turn, should do it for someone else. He said, "Oh."

The boys did keep records of the food they sold at the stand. We gave each boy marked baskets, and they recorded what came out of whose marked baskets. The IGA grocery store gave the boys plastic bags. The manager of the grocery store came by one day and bought a lot of potatoes and corn. He told the boys, "This looks better than what I sell in the store."

That one remark did a lot for the boy's sense of pride. Anyway, after the season was done we figured that each boy had earned around eighty-five dollars off the highway stand. We asked them to give God something, too, because God provided the sun and the rain. The money, also, gave them enough to buy some school supplies when school started. We insisted that they decide where the money would be used so it wouldn't be blown away on candy or gum. They agreed that all their work was worth more than candy or gum. On the boys' last day at the farm, Mom rewarded the boys with pencils and pens, note books and paper from the Dollar Store, and she included a little candy, too.

———

Officer Harrison came out to the house one afternoon during the week, and Dr. Lynn, Mom, John and I were all taking our traditional afternoon break, which we hadn't been able to do for a long time. We were sitting at the kitchen table drinking iced tea when Officer Harrison knocked on the back door. We hadn't even noticed him drive down the farm lane or driveway.

He wanted to evaluate the crime program from our perspective. Of course, my mind started running full speed ahead with what I thought. Officer Harrison said, "From *my* viewpoint and what I have seen from the families in town, it was a huge success. Before the boys were out of school for the summer, teachers were asked to evaluate behavior and grades. Each teacher said she could tell a big difference in the boys. They all said in almost the same words, "The boys had a subject that was dear to them, and they talked about it to other kids. They wrote about their gardens in themes and their math grades improved. Even their attitudes were more positive, and they hadn't skipped school while they were in the prevention program."

Dr. Lynn was amazed. He said, "Who knows, one of them may grow up to be a doctor."

I laughed. "Guess we had better add science to our teaching next year."

John said, "We did teach them science. I heard Mr. Jenkins explaining photosynthesis to a couple of the boys. He told them that photosynthesis was one of the things that kept the plants growing in the sun and the weeds *not* growing where the straw was so heavy covering the soil. The sun couldn't get through the straw. Then later, I heard one of the boys explaining it to another one. He was really quite funny because he repeated the big word as often as he could to impress the other boy."

Mom asked if any of the boys had complained that on occasion we slipped in the fact that God loves them. I looked at Mom and Officer Harrison. He said, "No."

I added to what Mom said, "We tried to explain that sin started in a garden, and since that time Satan tried to put weeds, not only in their gardens, but in their lives as well—weeds like cheating, stealing, disobeying parents and teachers."

Officer Harrison didn't get a chance to answer us, as Steve came in from the barn, and was washing his hands in the kitchen sink. He added, "I heard what you were talking about. That's interesting because I overheard one of the boys saying as he was hoeing his weeds, 'take that you ole devil.' I asked him why he was saying it and he said, 'Because your Ma 'n Mr. Dennis said, 'sin in ar lives are like the weeds. If'n we let 'em stay, they take over dis whole garden just like sin'll take over our whole life and it be all 'cause of the ole devil.'"

I asked Steve, "What did you answer back to the kid?"

I just told him, 'Mom and Dennis are right,' and went on to check the next boy's work."

Officer Harrison said, "When we meet with the boys for an hour on Tuesday evening—we require them to check-in with us, even when they aren't in school—one of the boys thought he would tell on another one." He chuckled, but said mimicking the boys, 'He's gonna' get a bad repootation, if he hang around older gang kids in the neighborhood. Ain't he, Officer Harrison?"

I almost fell off my chair when another boy spoke up and answered for me and said, 'A reputation is valuable, but character is priceless, ain't it?' I had the opportunity to explain the difference to all the boys. As the boys were leaving, I asked the one who had come up with such a profound statement, where he learned it. He said, 'Dennis Moore taught it to me.'"

I had to look at Mom and say, "Thanks, Mom. I remember you telling us that you had seen the statement on a church sign and you thought it was good. God reminded me of that statement when the boys were talking among themselves about some kid not in the program. At the time, I wasn't sure when I explained the meaning, that the two boys understood. I guess we need to thank God, huh? A good seed was planted, and it took root."

Another one of Mom's quotes came in handy when two of the boys were out in the gardens arguing over something silly. I could see anger in their eyes. Mom taught us well when she said, 'The only people you should try to get even with are those who help you.' I told the two boys they had thirty seconds to get in their own garden and back to work. I told them I would be back in ten minutes for each of them to explain what I meant. I walked off thinking...*that quote is not exactly right because the Bible says,* 'Love your enemies, do good to those who hate you.' So, I had the opportunity to tell them that we should never try to get even with anyone for wrong doing, because God said, 'Vengeance is mine. I will repay.' And... if we only did good things to those who are good to us, or help those who help us, this world would never improve. I explained that we didn't know the boys in the program. They had never helped us, but so they would learn what it means to be kind and good, we were helping them, anyway."

Officer Harrison said to Mom, "God must follow you around as you teach your sons. I have never known boys as young as yours to have such mature thinking."

Dr. Lynn answered for Mom, "Officer, you're right. Bonnie has had a lot of tragedies in her life and these boys have, also, but Bonnie's relationship with God is what has sustained her, and she has taught her boys to follow her example. This maturity, as you call it, struck me between the eyes on my first meeting with them. I was so impressed I had to get to know the family better. I'm glad some of their philosophy is rubbing off on the boys in the program. As far as your original question—do we think the program has been a success? You and the teachers can better evaluate that, than we can. It was work, and more work for some of us, but it gave meaning to several folks that we hadn't expected. My sister, Susan, lost her husband and her children to a disease, and our elderly neighbors, Mr. and Mrs. Jenkins, who live on the farm adjacent to ours, became involved with the boys and it gave them a new motivation for living. They got as much out of working with the boys as the boys did their gardens. It gave them a reason to look forward to another day."

John was standing near the table rather quiet. He got up and got some ice and the tea pitcher and refilled everyone's drink. Steve walked noisily out of the kitchen. "Mom, I'm going to haul some chocolate chip cookies out of the freezer."

She said, "Fine, but don't eat too many. It's getting pretty close to supper."

When John pulled out his chair and sat, he finally spoke up. "Officer Harrison, when you called and asked me to work with you on this program, I could *not* see how I could possibly have anything else in my life to do. I felt overwhelmed with going to school and all the farm responsibilities. It just seems like every time my days get full and I can't do anything more, God would give me something else to do or to think about. I sometimes feel like a wimp inside this great big body of mine. I couldn't make the decision to help you in your program. My family made the decision, as though God had asked *them* to do it? I can see now that it really was to become their endeavor and not mine. But, you didn't know the rest of the family, so you asked me. I couldn't believe all the ideas they were coming up with... before I ever called you back. Dennis, especially, sounded as though this was to be his work, and I think that's the way God meant for the family to work it out—through him."

Dr. Lynn reached over and knuckled me on the upper arm and said, "Yeah, Buddy."

I had to laugh, as Dr. Lynn had picked up on the way we

talked to each other. He's been our step-dad for a year, so I guess, we influenced him, too.

I thought back to the first time I came in contact with Officer Harrison's boys. John came home from the university and said, "This afternoon, Dennis, you are going back to Cape Girardeau with me to visit with some street kids." I responded with, "Oh, I *am*, am I?"

John still had on his mind passing his constitutional law exam and getting the winter wheat harvested, but I was ready to go. The winter wheat was on my mind, too, but I thought, *oh, well, I might as well go and see what John is doing with the street kids.*

I went with John, and was actually looking forward to doing something different than our chores. I even took a little pocket notebook with me to write down the kids' names. I asked them each to tell me something about themselves or their families. I figured the first thing they would say might be something they cared about. I'm so big and tall compared to those street kids that I supposed they thought they had *better* answer, or I might get them in a head-lock or something. That's the kind of stuff they experienced in their families and on the streets. Actually, what they put on paper was sad, yet I had to chuckle. The spelling was not good. The grammar was bad, and one of them said, "My dad hah three girlfriends. One come on Thursdee to wash our shirt 'n pant. Duh one I like, come on Sundee and go to church wid us, but duh one who come on Tuesdee, I like hah "cause she duh one me dad marry las yeer. She talk wid me and tell me, I wud a good kid, but she ain't gonna stay, and fer me to hab onlyest one wife, and no lady friend forever. She be the bestest one.!"

The other boys had notes with terrible spelling, too, but they spelled words just like they talked and probably *hear* all the time. We're working on that, too.

The first week we visited at the youth center, Officer Harrison had food ready for them. Someone had made some really thick sandwiches, cups of Jell-O and milk to drink, According to Officer Harrison, some kids had only crackers and milk until the next morning when they were given breakfast at school. Notebook paper, dictionaries, pens, calculators, and things like that were provided and in the room. John and I helped them from four to six with homework. We often stayed until eight o'clock, but we had to get someone else to do the evening chores at home, if we stayed too late.

I was impressed with the way Officer Harrison handled the boys. Every minute was accounted for, and if the homework wasn't done, they were required to come back directly after school the next day. The boys often came back a couple of times anyway because they knew they would be able to get at least a snack before going home.

The second week we visited, John and I had fixed up six care packages for the boys. The care packages were large baggies filled with two toothbrushes in plastic boxes, a plastic box with a bar of soap, two combs and some deodorant. John commented on the way home the next week that the boys smelled better and their hair was combed. I was glad we had done it. We figured in two weeks we had better give them more soap and toothpaste, as their families probably used up the first. John suggested we give the same items…even more combs. Maybe some shampoo, too.

Mom interrupted my thoughts, "Where's Paul? I haven't seen him since Officer Harrison arrived and he went upstairs."

We all realized that it had been more than an hour and none of us had seen him. We all jumped up. Officer Harrison didn't know what was happening, but he stood up, too. Steve made it upstairs first and into the bedroom he shared with Paul. We were right behind him.

Paul had gone to sleep with a book in his hand. Dr. Lynn felt

Paul's head and he woke up. Paul looked at us like, "What's going on?"

Mom said, "You scared us. We didn't know what had happened to you."

Paul smiled. "All for one and one for all, huh?"

Dr. Lynn asked, "Paul, do you feel okay? Do you feel sick at your stomach, headache, or feel weak or dizzy?"

He had Paul's wrist, taking his pulse as he was asking. Paul said, "Why should I? I was resting and having a nice dream when you woke me up."

I noticed Dr. Lynn's glance at Mom. Mom said, "Well, son, it's getting close to suppertime. You need to get up."

John said, "Officer Harrison probably wonders if a skunk stepped into the kitchen the way we all disappeared."

When we came downstairs, he was standing in the doorway with a questioning look on his face. I told him, "Paul went to sleep with a book."

Dr. Lynn was behind me. "You guys keep an eye on that boy. Being tired to the point of taking a nap is a little unusual for Paul and could be a symptom of the leukemia coming back."

He had an anxious look on his face. We all said, "Yeah," or "Okay," or "We'll watch him closely."

Officer Harrison said, "I must be leaving and hope all goes well."

I walked the officer to the car and told him if Paul's leukemia should be coming back, and if the boys needed to come out to the farm for anything, please call *me*. Mom and Dr. Lynn may be out of the picture for helping with the boys. He said he would let us know in advance.

I went back in the house, and Steve was already getting something out to fix for supper. He said, "If you guys don't mind waiting, I'll put together a meat loaf real quick."

"That sounds good. Mom would probably appreciate that," I said.

I had a quick thought about Steve assuming so much responsibility for cooking and said, "Steve, you're getting to be quite a chef. Did you know that?

He looked at me with an expression on his face like he was thinking… *You just gave me a compliment. What am I going to have to do for you?*

"I mean it, Steve. I don't like to cook, so I'm glad you do."

Mom walked in and said, "That is unusual for Paul." She paused and said, "Maybe one of you guys better close up the chicken house for him this evening."

John said, "I'll do it, Mom. Don't worry."

Dr. Lynn asked, "Where is Paul? Didn't he get up?"

Mom answered, "Yes, he went to the bathroom. I told him to go ahead and get a bath or shower and get ready for bed. Someone would do his chores for him this evening."

Dr. Lynn looked apprehensive or worried, so I told him, "I'll go up and check on him."

I knocked on the bathroom door and there wasn't any answer. I yelled, "Paul," three times and still no answer. The bathroom door was locked. I went to my room and got a long nail that we used to put through the hole in the doorknob to open the door from the outside. We're big kids now, but we still accidently lock a door when there is no one in the room. Mom said it was a safety measure from when we were toddlers and would accidently lock ourselves in a room.

I called for Paul one more time before I opened the door. He was on the floor behind the door. Mom, John, Dr. Lynn and Steve had already come upstairs when I was yelling at Paul. I pushed the door open and moved Paul with it. He was as white as a sheet, and he moaned when I moved him. I picked him up and carried him across the hall to my bed. He still had his underwear on, and apparently had passed out when he was undressing. John turned off the shower and picked up his pajamas. Steve was right behind him with a cold wet washcloth. Dr. Lynn felt his head again. "He's a little warm. Where's my bag?"

Fortunately, he still kept his medical bag in a place where he could quickly get it if one of us or the boys who work in the gardens should get injured or stung by bees. For some reason, I made a mental note that it was on the music cabinet by the piano, so I said, "I'll get it."

When I got back upstairs, Dr. Lynn was trying to talk to Paul, but he was just moaning. Dr. Lynn shook his head negatively and said, "I'm not sure what is going on… I think we'd better head for the hospital."

John had already given Mom his pajamas and Dr. Lynn put the top on him and wrapped him in my blanket. Steve said, "I called 911. They're on their way."

I didn't think it was necessary, but Dr. Lynn said, "Thanks!"

Mom sat quickly on John's bed, as white as Paul. I said, "Here we go again! Mom is going to be a patient, too."

John patted Mom's shoulder. "Mom, Paul's going to be okay. Let's go downstairs and find you something to eat or drink. Dr. Lynn will take you up to the hospital with Paul. Just don't faint on us."

"I'm *not* going to faint," she said.

I went back downstairs and looked in the refrigerator. Steve was behind me and said, "Just give Mom a glass of juice and get her blood sugar up. I'll save her some meatloaf."

John came downstairs carrying Paul with Dr. Lynn and Mom right behind him. Paul was awake and was saying, "I'm okay… I'm o—kay. I can walk."

Dr. Lynn said, "Just the same, young man, you're going to the hospital and will be checked over thoroughly. A person just doesn't pass out on the floor or fall asleep abnormally for no reason."

Paul looked up at John. "Do I have to go? I was just tired this afternoon."

Mom answered for John, "Yes, Paul we need to have some tests run to make sure your leukemia is not back."

He groaned again, "John?"

"Sorry, Paul, Mom's right. I suspect they will let you come home tomorrow. I'll take care of the chicken house for you."

The ambulance arrived and Dr. Lynn greeted the paramedics outside and apologized for the call. He told them the problem and said he could drive Paul up to the hospital, if they would check his vital signs. One paramedic said, "We can take him. We haven't had a call in three days. That's good, but sitting around waiting was getting boring."

I watched them put Paul in the ambulance, tell Dr. Lynn what his vital signs were, and then I just stood there until the ambulance drove off with Mom and Dr. Lynn following in the car.

I couldn't help but think about the many times 911 had been called by someone in our family. If nothing else, we sure supported the North Scott County Ambulance Service.

It seemed as though it had been four or five times. John asked me what I was thinking about and I shook my head. "I wonder if God has us in training right now to get us accustomed to lights and sirens, paramedics, and emergencies."

Steve put a dish in the sink and turned to us. "I think I'll be a paramedic fireman or a paramedic policeman. Maybe I'll get a higher salary than you guys."

John laughed. "That's our business man for you."

Steve was taking potatoes off the stove to mash and I couldn't help saying, "Steve, the firemen and paramedics would welcome you as their chef. They'll make you stay behind and cook for them while they make their runs."

I had to add, "That's if John and I don't keep you at home cooking for us."

Fun-n-y!" Steve said.

I got up and cleared the table of all the glasses and the cookies from earlier and set the table. John was still sitting and thinking. "John, I'm the one who always meditates about everything and doesn't talk about what is bothering me. What is going on in that head of yours?"

John looked at me. "You guys are joking right now, and I understand your coping mechanisms, but our little brother just went off to the hospital, and we are about to sit and eat a good meal."

"Yeah, John, but if you think about it, we have to be Mom's strength for her and Paul, too. It's more helpful to her if we carry on here with the chores and housework, so Mom doesn't have anything except Paul to worry about."

Steve added, "I think Dr. Lynn does enough worrying for all of us. Did you notice the expression on his face when Paul wouldn't wake up? He was probably reminded of his own little boy who died with leukemia. I wonder, after being married to Mom for a little more than a year, if he views all of us as his own sons instead of step-sons. I think he would be as upset as the rest of us if Paul should die."

With Steve's last remark, I felt very uneasy and looked at John. He swallowed and said, "Dennis, Steve, I think we need to stop and pray for Paul." He paused and said, "And Mom and Dr. Lynn."

Steve put the food on the table, and John asked me to pray. I immediately thought of God's response to Job and had to voice what I knew, so I said, "Father God, you put all the planets in space, and you cause the sun to rise and set. You have given us light at night with the moon and stars. You cause small seeds to spring forth into giant trees, and I know that you can take care of Paul. Help us to be thankful that you are with Paul and Mom, yet are with us, also. Give us wisdom and guidance as we do what needs to be done here at home. And Lord, thank you for Steve's talent in food preparation and thank you for this food. We pray in Jesus' name, Amen."

I couldn't help but chuckle, when I looked at Steve and John' faces. John said, "I'll say Amen to that! Pass me the potatoes."

Steve handed him the potatoes. "Thanks, Dennis, for reminding me that God is good, and he's still the master of everything. Did you know you prayed like you were a preacher or some teacher? We're *not* normal kids, I guess."

I had to add, "Well, most *normal* kids haven't had all the responsibilities that we've had—at least not with the family or farm *problems* that we've had."

John said, "I used to think that, too. But, after working with Officer Harrison and all those street kids in his crime prevention program, I've changed my thinking a little. Those kids seemed to have more crises than we do, but they lack the kind of parents and training we've had. By the time they're 10 years old, and sometimes before, they start searching for something good in their lives. Often it's in the wrong places and with the wrong kind of kids. Officer Harrison has some college students working with some kids who are younger than the boys we work with. He just found an older college student to work with the same age girls as the boys we have on Tuesdays. I sometimes wonder if the man ever goes home."

We finished supper and cleaned up the kitchen. I went out to the barn to milk the cows and feed the cats. Steve asked if I would check on his Hereford cattle because Cousin Stacy would be out for two cobblers in the morning, and he would check and make sure there were enough clean eggs for her, too.

John said, "I'll put up the chickens and collect eggs. Dennis, I'll be out to the barn as soon as I lock up the chicken house."

As I headed to the barn and John went to the chicken house. I thought about how our lives were so wrapped around the chores of taking care of the cows and chickens. I wondered if my brothers ever got tired of the same thing every day—mucking (cleaning) out the stalls, watering and feeding the animals, cleaning the floor of the chicken house and collecting and washing the eggs, and that's not to mention all the field work with the crops and garden.

I brought the milk cows in and tied them in the stall to the feeding trough. I put feed in the troughs and realized what I was thinking. God has the earth and sun rotating on his schedule, and it's just as routine as our chores. If God ignored the natural laws that he put into place, this world and this universe would be in chaos. I had to say, "Thank you, Lord, for these jobs that you have given us to do."

I didn't hear John come in the barn when I was milking the cow and he said, "*John,* are you praying out loud again?"

I had to laugh at John, because that's what we always said to him. He followed up with, "Dennis, I have to thank God, too, for the chores, because if I didn't have them to do, I might be like some other irresponsible kids who are out on the streets this time of the evening, not doing anything to make this world a better place. I get tired sometimes, but God always comes through with a blessing. We have the milk, butter, and eggs to sell or give away, and that money covers a lot of expenses. Because God has given us so much work we have paid off our loan at the bank, and each of us has been able to save for our own vehicle to drive, and for our college education. Thinking about that, how are you feeling about starting school in just a few weeks?"

"It doesn't feel any different from any other year. I have never been out of school for any period of time, except for the summer and holiday vacations. Right now, I can't think of college until we hear something positive about Paul and his health."

We waited for Mom or Dr. Lynn's call. It was almost ten o'clock, and I was ready to go crawl in bed. The phone finally rang. It was Dr. Lynn. He said, "I'm sorry, boys, but Paul's leukemia is back and his white count is at a dangerous level again. We're making arrangements to fly him back to St. Louis. Have you called your sister and Pastor Bishop?"

I told him, "No, we ate supper and then went out to the barn and henhouse and did the chores, but we would call them."

The next five minutes were spent calling Pastor Bishop to start the prayer chain, and Aunt Susan. John took his cell phone and called Kaitlynn and Matthew in St. Louis to let them know Mom and Dr. Lynn would be up. John, also, called Marianne. She's still living at her university in St. Louis. He's been calling Marianne a lot lately.

I felt better knowing so many people care, and they would be praying, again, for Paul and all of us.

The next time I looked at the clock it was a little after ten, but I decided that I should call Robert and Janet and their parents. They had become like *our* family since that awful day when that bad cop, Officer Blair, almost destroyed their family. I called and Mr. Weber answered. I told him Paul's white blood count was at a dangerous level and Mom and Dr. Lynn were at the hospital making arrangements to fly Paul back to St. Louis. He wanted to know when this happened. I told him only about three hours ago, Paul passed out, but Dr. Lynn called twenty minutes ago to let us know what was going on. I apologized for calling so late, but we didn't know what was going on with Paul."

He said, "Oh...ah... will you need Robert and Janet to come out and help with the chores?"

I told him, "Maybe in a couple of days. Right now, we have to wait on the reports from St. Louis."

I could hear Mrs. Weber talking in the background and I heard what she said, "Tell them we will be out in the morning"

It's been so good to have the support of other people. I know that's what God wants of us, too. We *should* help others who have a need. John will be happy married to Marianne someday and get another family like the Weber family as in-laws.

CHAPTER 2

Paul had been in St. Louis for two weeks and when Mom called last night she said, "Paul is finally responding to a different chemo-therapy. He doesn't feel quite as sick this time."

I told Mom, after chores on Saturday morning were done, we're going to go up and see Paul. Steve and I decided to give more blood just in case they decided Paul needs it.

Mom said, "I'm planning to come home and work at the railroad office. Dr. Lynn will stay in St. Louis with Paul. If you are coming up, I'll go home with you and leave my car with Marshall."

Uncle Al, Mom's retired doctor brother had offered his car to Dr. Lynn to use, however most of the time Dr. Lynn just stayed with Paul. Mom doesn't want to take any more sick days off work unless she has to. She's had to take so many days off work already and doesn't want to lose her job at the railroad office.

The next morning, Mom walked in the door. She said, "Since Paul was feeling better, I decided to come on home and go to work. I left Paul in good hands and I felt secure with Paul in Marshall's hands."

Sometimes I wished it was me instead of Dr. Lynn. I guess that would be a natural feeling when it's your little brother who is sick.

The Law Enforcement Academy starts in another week. I think

I'm ready. We have our fields planted in winter wheat, and my soy beans won't be ready for a month. John harvested his corn and Mr. Jenkins' corn last week. Between Dr. Lynn, Brian, Mr. Jenkins, John and I, we kept the combines and trucks going all the daylight hours we could squeeze in. Robert and Janet came out and helped Steve with the barn and chicken house chores. Mrs. Weber and Aunt Susan kept up the house work and cooking while Mom was at work and in St. Louis with Paul.

I spent about two hours on the three acre gardens Officer Harrison's city boys use, checking out what needed to be plowed under and putting more straw between the strawberry rows. There were a few cantaloupes, and watermelons left. I got them and put them at the end of each garden and then went back later for them. I divided them between Mrs. Weber, Aunt Susan and Mr. Jenkins. I told them there were still a few late green beans that came on the pole beans. If they wanted them, they could get them because I was planning to plow everything under for the winter. Aunt Susan said, "I don't want to look at another green bean until next spring." She laughed, and Mrs. Weber said, "Sounds like a job for Janet and me then."

The next day, Janet and Mrs. Weber were out in the gardens before 8:30 a.m. I guess they realized field work can get mighty hot in the sun. They got a whole bushel of green beans off all six of the boy's gardens. Mrs. Weber said, "I'm going to freeze them and then give some of them away. There isn't any sense in leaving them in the field when someone can use them." I agreed. It was good to see Janet a second day, too.

I asked Mrs. Weber how Robert was feeling about starting at the university next week, and I asked if she was still okay with him going to the Law Enforcement Academy. She didn't have a chance to answer because Steve walked into the kitchen with Robert, so I asked Robert how he was feeling. He said, "Well, if you can say a person is obsessed, I'm obsessed. I've thought of nothing else since graduation. I did well on my SAT/ACT exams and that put me in good standing at the university. I'm trying to test out of English and history, and I hope that I pass the tests so I can spend more time on my other subjects. I really can't wait to get started. I've been thinking about this for a little while. I'm going to go for a Criminal Justice degree, too."

Robert and I are both still eighteen, but we're almost nineteen. I will be nineteen in another ten days, and Robert's birthday is soon after that. Janet and Steve are sixteen… almost seventeen. Her birthday is the day after mine, but we are two years apart in age.

I still keep having feelings for Janet, but after talking to John, I'm trusting God for my future spouse, so I put Janet in His hands. I would like to take her out on a date, but something in me keeps saying *no*. Maybe she is in reserve for Steve…who knows.

Janet has been taking voice and piano lessons for the last two years, and she has a lovely voice. Steve sings, too, so maybe she is a better match for him. Steve has never said anything about girls. His cattle are all the girls for him right now. I suppose I should talk to him about Janet sometime.

———— ◆ ————

School started this morning. Mom swapped her car for Grandpa's truck, so we could pick up Robert and go to the university in Cape Girardeau together. Robert and I are in most classes together. He did test out of history, but not English. I would have flunked history and passed English. We had a lot to talk about on the way home.

John completed his basic training at the Law Enforcement Academy, and he was offered a position as a policeman. He decided to go on for a degree in criminal justice, too, this fall, so he took the job as a part-time job. He figured there wouldn't be much farm field work, except for soybeans in the fall, so he could carry a heavier class load and a lighter load in the spring

Robert and I are taking the required courses for our major, and the classes aren't as easy as I thought they would be. I'm glad I learned to study while at Chaffee High School.

John introduced us to his classmates. He acted proud of Robert and me. Robert said later, "I hope we don't embarrass your brother and make him regret those introductions." I told Robert to be himself and not worry about impressing anyone or living up to John's reputation. I thought about John later when I was leaving a class that caused me to have to take more notes than I ever had to take in high school. I realized just how much pressure John had been under.

Last night Mom called and said that Paul would possibly come home in just a few days. Dr. Lynn thinks he can watch him pretty closely at home. She said, "We'll just have to see in the next few days, how he does." She also suggested that we might consider changing bedrooms around. I figured when Mom came home, she would have us busy moving furniture. I was right.

On Saturday, she had us all busy moving furniture. She wanted Grandpa's queen-size bed taken upstairs to Steve and Paul's bedroom and the twin-sized beds moved to the downstairs bedroom off the kitchen for Paul to stay downstairs, and she would sleep in the room with him. Three days later Dr. Lynn brought Paul home. It was good to see him. He was pale and didn't have very much energy. Dr. Lynn said, "Paul still feels poorly from the chemo treatment. He usually feels that way for two or three days after each treatment. According to lab tests, his leukemia is doing better."

Paul said, "I'm so tired of not being able to go to school and feeling yucky."

I don't blame him. Anyway, Mom thought if Paul could be downstairs, he could be in on a lot of the family time, and we could take turns sleeping in the room with him at night.

Dr. Lynn will stay with Paul, so he doesn't need a home nurse coming to the house. A teacher will come, three mornings every week, until Paul is feeling well enough to go back to school. The teacher suggested that when Paul feels good, she would combine his lessons with another student who she sees in the afternoons. Perhaps the boys might find a sense of companionship and not feel so isolated from other students. Dr. Lynn suggested that one day a week might be better, but he would wait and see. He wanted Paul to really feel much better.

I've been going to my room immediately after coming home from the university and studying. John goes to Kaitlynn's room, now our guest room, instead of Grandpa's room like he used to do. On the way home today from the university, John and I decided we should go by the humane society and get a dog for Paul. We had promised him another dog after our dog, Jack, died. We talked it over with Dr. Lynn, and he thought it would be a good idea. "Every boy needs a dog," he said.

We found a small dog Paul could have in the bedroom with him. It probably won't go after the weasels in the hen house, but I plan to take him out with me whenever I do the chicken house chores. Paul was excited about the dog and wanted to name him *Jack the second.*

The little dog is perfect for Paul. It takes his mind off how he feels. After two days, Paul said, "Jack thinks I'm his mother already."

— ◆ —

My soybeans are ready to be harvested. Mr. Jenkins said he would do them for me, but I told him, "You can help, but I will do them, too."

I have more than ten acres of soybeans since Dr. Lynn bought the Jenkins' farm. We can use both combines and the truck and and have the beans done in one day. We watch the weather report every night because so much of what we do on the farm depends on the weather. The five-day forecast said it would be clear through Monday, so Friday afternoon will be soybean harvesting day.

I knew I shouldn't trust Mr. Jenkins *not* to do the soybeans. Dr. Lynn said as soon as we left for school at 7:15 a.m. Mr. Jenkins backed his combine out of the machinery shed and went to work. He had Aunt Susan out there helping him. Dr. Lynn said, "My sister called me and asked if the coast was clear, and when I asked why, she said, 'because Jenkins and I are going to harvest soybeans, and Molly is going with me in the truck.'"

Dr. Lynn chuckled and said, "My sister sounded like an ornery little girl giggling and about to do something behind our mother's back."

Anyway, when we came home around 1:30 p.m. Mr. Jenkins was just finishing up the last acre. I don't know which person was happier, Mr. Jenkins and Aunt Susan for doing it, or me for seeing the job done. He had a big smile on his face when he saw me drive up to his farm house. I thought I would scold them a bit, but I couldn't help responding to his grin with one of my own. I gave him a big hug and Aunt Susan, too. Miss Molly came out of the house. "I accept hugs, too," she said, so I hugged her.

I asked Mr. Jenkins what was left for me to do. He said, "Well, since everything is now harvested, we need to clean up the machinery and get it ready for next year."

"I'll do that," I said, but behind me was a voice. "No, you

won't! I keep that machinery in tip top shape, and I don't want anyone else messing with it."

Brian Lynn, Dr. Lynn's son, was living at the Jenkins farm, too, and he had come out of the house and heard our conversation. I turned around. "Well, there should be something I can do."

Aunt Susan said, "The truck is loaded and ready to go to the granary. You can do that."

Brian added, "I have about an hour before I have to hit the books. I'll go with you."

Mr. Jenkins handed me his truck keys. I had never driven a truck as large as his truck, but I thought, *there's always a first time for everything,* so Brian and I got in the truck and headed to the Granary. I called John on my phone to let him know that I was going to the granary and Brian Lynn was with me.

I questioned Brian about an appropriate gift to show my gratitude to the Jenkins and Aunt Susan. He suggested a couple of good old fashioned Hallmark videos. They love the old movies and perhaps a big container of popcorn from a movie theater to go with it. It was a good idea.

We were half-way back from the Granary when John called. Brian answered my phone. I could tell from his side of the conversation something was wrong, and the Moore-Lynn family was about to have another crisis. "How bad is it?" he asked. "What is the street? Do you know the road? Okay. Three blocks from the high school. Okay. We're on our way."

All I could think to do was look at Brian and say, "What? What happened?"

"It's Steve. A car didn't stop at a stop sign and hit him on the driver's side. Then a kid from the high school wasn't paying attention and plowed into him from the rear. Steve says he's okay, but he's shaken up a bit. He had Janet Weber with him in the truck. She had asked him to take her home, but she's not hurt."

I knew the area and the particular corner. People were always going too fast through there. When we arrived minutes later, the police were there, and an ambulance had just arrived. Dr. Lynn pulled up from a side street as we came from the opposite direction. Steve was sitting on the curb with his arm around Janet's shoulders. He was white around the mouth, but not noticing anyone around. I thought *He looks just like Mom when she's about to faint.* The paramedics were assessing the injured and checking the two older ladies in the car that hit Steve. Dr. Lynn talked to the two boys in the pick-up truck that hit Steve from the rear. It looked like they had a whip-lash neck injury and one had a cut on his forehead. They hadn't worn seat belts and the passenger hit the windshield.

Brian pulled me back and said, "After the police talk to Janet, let me take her on home and explain to her mother."

I stooped down beside Steve. "Brother, you need to lay down here on the ground. Brian is here. He'll take Janet home and explain what happened to her mother."

I stood up, and a policeman was coming toward us. I asked, "Is it okay for this young lady to go on home?"

He said, "Yes. I wished your brother, John, was here to help. We could use an extra hand today."

I said, "I'll tell him."

Steve swallowed hard, and I could tell he was in pain, but he said, "Janet, I'm sorry. Tell your mother, I'm sorry."

Janet patted him on the back and said, "Steve, it wasn't your fault."

He said, "Tell her anyway."

Brian helped Janet up off the street curb and said, "Can you get in the house, when you get home?"

I heard her say, "Yes, Mom said she was going to be late, to find a way home, but she should be there now. I do have a key somewhere in my purse."

I was relieved that she was on her way, so I could concentrate on Steve. Dr. Lynn was beside Steve, feeling his neck and down his back. "Steve you took quite a lick. I want you to go to the hospital and have some X-rays done. We don't want any permanent injuries."

An ambulance took both ladies away, and a tow truck pulled their car away from Steve's truck. Steve groaned. "All that work with my cattle and it's down the tubes with that truck."

Dr. Lynn squatted in front of Steve. "Insurance will cover it, but don't worry about that right now."

Two more ambulances came from somewhere. The two kids in the rear car left in it, and the tow truck pulled *their* vehicle from the back of Steve's truck. The truck's tailgate was mashed way in.

Dr. Lynn said, "Dennis, see if the truck is drivable."

I walked around the truck and decided the gas tank or something had been ruptured, and I shouldn't try to turn on the motor. Something was leaking under the truck. It might start a fire. Dr. Lynn went to the tow truck driver and asked for a truck with a wench on it to take Steve's truck to a car repair body shop in Cape Girardeau.

A paramedic from the South Scott County service had come and was putting Steve on a backboard. Dr. Lynn said, "I need to go to the railroad office and talk with your mother. Will you go to the hospital with Steve?"

"Yes, but Brian just took Janet home with the Jenkins grain truck. I'm stranded here unless he comes back soon."

Dr. Lynn looked over my shoulder. "Here he comes now." I turned around to find Mrs. Weber, Janet, and Brian walking across the street. Janet was limping. I turned back to Dr. Lynn and said, "Go get Mom and take her to the hospital. I'll go home and tell John and Paul what happened."

I waited a moment and let Dr. Lynn talk to Mrs. Weber and Janet. He questioned Janet to make sure she had no injuries. She said, "Only my knee. When the truck hit us from the rear, my seat belt broke or came loose, and I scooted forward and hit my knee. It'll be okay, though. I can walk."

Dr. Lynn said, "Janet sit down. He pointed to the curb."

He felt around on Janet's right knee and twisted her leg a little. Janet grabbed her knee, and he frowned. He looked up at her mother and said, "Better to be safe than sorry. You need to have your knee X-rayed. I'm sure Steve's insurance will cover it. If not, I will."

It was time for me to leave, and go home to John and Paul, but Mom came down the street. Dr. Lynn said to Mrs. Weber, "Take Janet up to Saint Francis Medical Center Hospital. That's where I told them to take Steve. Dennis, you head home, too."

Brian handed me the old grain truck keys and cell phone, and Dr. Lynn handed *his* car keys to Brian. Mom hopped out of her car and grabbed Dr. Lynn. "What happened? Someone said you were in an accident over here and came by the office to let me know."

About that time, the tow truck pull up, and Mom saw Steve's truck that had been pushed down the street. Her face got white. I said, "Mom, stop. Steve is okay. Dr. Lynn will take you to Saint Francis Medical Center. That's where they took everyone."

Mom's eyes got big and she raised her eyebrows, "Everyone?

Janet said, "Two elderly ladies didn't stop at the stop sign and hit us from the side, and then kids from school weren't watching and hit us from behind."

Mrs. Weber patted Mom on the arm. "The kids are lucky. God was with all of them. Janet we better go get that knee checked. Let's go."

Brian said, "Let's go home, Dennis. We've had enough surprises for one day. Good and bad."

I grabbed Mom and gave her a kiss. "Now, you be good for your husband and don't faint on the way to Cape Girardeau.

She laughed a nervous laugh. "I won't. I guess we had better be on our way."

I walked the half block back down the street to the Jenkins' old dirty grain truck and said out loud, "Okay, what else is going to happen today?" Then a voice from nowhere said, *in all things give thanks.* I remembered the verse was from the book of James in the Bible. I had memorized it, and Mom had quoted it to us often. I thought about Steve's accident and prayed, "Lord, I don't know why you allowed this to happen to Steve, nor do I know the other kids and the two ladies, but I know that you want me to say *thank you* for something in all of this, so I'm going to say thank you for sparing Steve's life and Janet's life. Please bring healing to both of them. And Lord, give Steve a testimony for the kids that hit him… and the older ladies, too."

My mind wandered for a moment, and I realized that I was headed down our lane with Mr. Jenkins' truck. I had to say *thank you* again to God as I had forgotten to call John. It would be better to talk with John and Paul face-to-face. They were both standing at the door waiting to hear something. I told them, "God spared Steve and Janet and everyone else in the accident, but Steve's truck is not in good shape. Mom and Dr. Lynn went to Saint Francis Medical Center Hospital. Dr. Lynn wanted Steve to be checked over well, to make sure there wasn't anything hidden that could cause long term injuries. Janet went home, but she came back with her mother and Dr. Lynn told her to go get a knee X-rayed."

Paul looked out the door at the truck and asked, "Why are you driving that old truck? Isn't that the Jenkins's old truck?"

I looked out the door and chuckled. "Brian and I took the

soybeans to the granary. We were on our way back when John called. Brian took his Dad's car, and here he comes now...."

We all watched Brian get out of Dr. Lynn's car with a serious face. I said, "Mom and Dr. Lynn have Mom's car. I'll ride back over to the Jenkins' house with Brian and bring back grandpa's truck."

Paul was looking up at me and then back out the door toward the old truck. He said, "Geez, what a complicated mess with all the trucks and cars."

I had to laugh and say, "You know what Paul, God is a God of details, right? He worked it out, so every drivable vehicle got where it was supposed to go with a driver, and to finish it up. I'm going with Brian, as soon as he comes in for the truck keys. I'll go in the Jenkins' old truck to get our old truck."

I felt in my pocket for the keys and they weren't there. I must have left them in the truck. Paul pulled out a chair to sit at the kitchen table and said, "I'm glad I don't drive yet."

John was smiling, "I'm glad too, Paul."

Brian came in, and we sat at the table with Paul and had a Pepsi. Brian said, "I sure hope this accident doesn't leave Steve with a lot of apprehension about driving. To be hit twice within seconds can emotionally unnerve a person."

Paul looked at Brian and very seriously said, "Brian, that's when we have to trust God, isn't it?

Brian didn't answer for a second or two and then said, "What do you mean, Paul?"

Paul hesitated and looked at me and then John as if we would answer for him, but he said, "Well, none of us knows when God wants us to leave this earth and be with him. We just have to get out of bed in the morning and live each day like it's all we've got, but God has a plan for us on earth or in heaven with Him? Aren't I right, John?"

He sipped his drink and we all were just looking at each other amazed at what Paul had just said, but he went on and said, "Steve has to get into his truck. Well, not his, 'cause it needs to be fixed, but he has to drive somebody's truck and trust God for it to keep him safe. Isn't that right, Dennis? I'm right… aren't I, John?"

John reached over and gave Paul a hug from the side and said, "Buddy, you are right on… right on."

I couldn't help saying out loud, "Thank you, God," again. I looked at Paul suffering with his Leukemia and realized that he—more than any of us—understood what he had just said. Brian was getting emotional, having lost his own little brother to Leukemia, and I could tell he wanted to say something. He finally swallowed and said, "Paul, how old are you now?"

"I'm gonna' be twelve, but I'm still eleven for two more months?"

Brian reached over and patted his arm and said, "Paul, you're very wise for thinking like you do, and I want you to know that I'm proud to have you as my brother, even if it's only a step brother. You're right. None of us know when we will take our last breath or how it will happen, but God knows, and we have to trust him, don't we? When Steve comes home, be sure to tell him what you just told us. Would you do that for us?"

Paul took a zip of his drink and said, "Sure!" He said it like it was something we should have understood or a statement of fact. Brian patted Paul's arm again and got up from his chair. "Well, I have studying to do, so I better get back over to the Jenkins and all the oldies that pamper me."

We laughed. It felt good to laugh. I said, "I left the keys in the truck."

I left Paul sitting at the kitchen table with John and rode back over to the Jenkins farm with Brian to get Grandpa's old truck. Aunt Susan was already coming out the door, and Mr. and Mrs.

Jenkins were following her. They must have heard the truck as it pulled into their farm drive. Their faces told that they had heard about the accident. They wanted to know about Steve. When I told them, they were relieved. Mrs. Jenkins said, "I think I know those two ladies. I hope they're okay."

Mrs. Jenkins is a sweet old lady, and I could tell she was worried. "Mrs. Jenkins, I'll see what I can find out for you, okay?"

She patted my arm and said, "Bless you, son."

I climbed in Grandpa's old truck and headed for our farm thinking about Miss Molly's dementia. She must have needed a good diet, rest, and whatever medication she is taking now. Aunt Susan has been taking good care of Mr. and Mrs. Jenkins. I couldn't help thinking how much younger Miss Molly looked. Aunt Susan must be helping her with her hair and make-up. Mom will be pleased the next time she sees Mrs. Jenkins.

When I got home, I parked the truck by the barn. I was chuckling to myself as I got out of the truck. I said, "I guess since I noticed all that, I should say, *thank you*, Lord, again."

John was just coming out of the barn. He laughed and said, "What is it you say to me, 'John, are you praying out loud?' "

I laughed and said, "I'm getting just like you, John."

I told him I was thinking about Mrs. Jenkins and how good she looked since Aunt Susan has been caring for her. She talks coherently and seems happy."

John smiled, "Yes, I noticed she is doing better, too. We really do need to keep an attitude of thankfulness because if we don't, I would think we were living under a dark cloud that just wouldn't go away. I have to fight a doom and gloom attitude sometimes, and the only way I can fight it is by talking to God and being thankful for what *is* and not what could be or what might have been. Paul is right-on in his thinking, isn't he?"

We walked to the house together. John said, "I checked on

Steve's cattle and their water tank. Steve must have freshened the water this morning. I spread out a bale of hay and threw another one down from the loft. Steve probably shouldn't do any lifting for a while. Remind me to check the hay on the ground this evening. By the way, has Steve said anything about one of his heifers looking like she is in season?"

I didn't remember him saying anything, but I thought Steve would be glad to know that he has another heifer to breed. He has his stock up to eight now, and he wants to sell a couple of them. He likes getting that money so he will be glad to hear the news. I said, "Yeah, Steve *will be* glad to hear about his heifers."

John chuckled and said, "Our business boy, Steve, will have his mind spinning on how much he can get from a calf to make a down payment on another truck. His truck was less than a year old, and he'll get a good insurance payoff on it, so he should be able to get another truck fairly soon. He has two calves that are pretty well weaned. One of them should meet his insurance deductible."

We walked into the kitchen, and Paul was sitting at the table waiting on us. He said, "I'm hungry, and do you guys know that our chief cook is not here."

We laughed, and John said, "Well, Paul, you be sure to tell Steve how much you need for *him* to cook for you. What time is it anyway?"

I looked at the kitchen clock. It was already 4:30 p.m., and we had not heard from Mom or Dr. Lynn yet. I was beginning to get a little concerned.

John grabbed his books from the bottom stair-step and started upstairs, so I went to the refrigerator and looked for something I could get started for supper. I didn't see anything I knew how to fix except for slicing up some tomatoes and stuff to make a salad. I went to the freezer on the back porch to see if there was any meat that didn't require a long recipe. I told myself, *I need to learn how to cook, too.*

The phone rang. Paul grabbed the kitchen phone and was saying, "Un-huh, un-huh, un-huh."

My nerves made my muscles tight. I almost said, "Give me the phone." Instead, I hurried to Grandpa's room—I mean Paul's room—and picked up the extension phone. It was Dr. Lynn. John was on the phone upstairs. I said, "I'm on the phone now. Can you back up and repeat what you said?"

Dr. Lynn said, "I was telling your brothers that so far Steve has checked out pretty well for the hits he took. He took a side hit and then a back hit, so he has some vertebrae that have some bruising around them. He will have to wear a Thompson Collar for a while on his neck, but we're thankful for his good physical condition. His strong neck muscles protected his neck somewhat. There is a good size bruise on his left arm and a bump on his head from the whip-lash he took. He must have hit his head on the door window in a come-back movement."

I asked, "Will they be keeping him in the hospital for another day?"

I could hear Paul breathing heavily, and he finally said, "Tell Steve the nurses will be nice to him."

"Paul, I will. I will," Dr. Lynn answered Paul, but went on to say, "I've looked at all the x-rays, and I don't think we have missed anything, but I recommended to Steve's doctor that he be kept for 48 hours."

John asked, "How is Janet's knee?"

I was thinking the same thing and wondered how the two ladies and the other kids were?

Dr. Lynn said, "She has a giant contusion on both her knees. I'm surprised she was able to go home and then walk the half-block back to the accident scene. Her right knee cap has a hair-line fracture, but no chips or other broken bones. We put an elastic knee brace on, and she is to stay off the leg, so she'll use crutches until it's better."

Paul asked, "What's a con-tu-sion?"

Dr. Lynn answered but I was glad Paul asked because I was wondering *is that the same as a bruise.* I thought it was.

John was upstairs doing something and the noises were coming through the phone loudly, but he said, "I think I need to call Marianne and Kaitlynn about this."

I answered. "Let her mother call Marianne first."

"Yeah, I'll call Kaitlynn, but Mom may have already called her."

Dr. Lynn added, "You might want to start the prayer chain for all the people involved in the accident. The two ladies are hurt, but I haven't been able to check on them. I've been with Steve and Janet."

I told Dr. Lynn, "Mrs. Jenkins said, she knew the ladies and wanted to know how they were. I told her I would find out. So tell Mom to check on them."

Paul was still listening on the kitchen phone. He asked, "How's Mom? She didn't faint, did she?"

Right now she is talking with Mrs. Weber. Steve has been sedated and has drifted off to sleep. Janet is sitting by his bedside here in the room. She's half asleep, too, from pain medication."

Since we were on the extension phones, our voices sounded like we were speaking into a microphone. Paul said, "You guys talk too loud. You about broke my eardrum. I'm hungry, and Dennis can't cook."

Dr. Lynn said, "Well, Paul, I'm happy to hear that. You must be getting well. You tell Dennis to call Cousin Stacy and order a big dinner. I'll tell Mom to meet you there at 5:30 p.m. Would that be okay?"

I looked at my watch, and it was already 5:05 p.m. I said, "John, what do you think?"

He was making noises again and said, "I don't care. I just got my books open and I really need to look at a couple of pages before we do the chores."

I thought, *That's what all the noise was. He was getting his backpack and books.*

Paul said, "That sounds good. We'll wait at the Café' for her, but who's going to stay with Steve?"

We let our eleven-year-old brother make the decision for us. I guess we've done that a lot since he's suffered with his Leukemia, but I heard a little chuckle from Dr. Lynn, and I knew what he was thinking. Paul had been so sick, but now he is caring for someone else, and that is good. He said, "Paul, I want your mother to come home and rest this evening, so I am going to stay here with Steve."

Dr. Lynn said, "I'll be home in the morning to stay with you, and perhaps I'll bring you up to see Steve. Would that be okay?"

"Yeah, Dad, that would be great."

I was glad Paul couldn't see me smiling. Paul hasn't seen Dad since he was six years-old, when Dad died. Paul needed Dr. Lynn, and Dr. Lynn needed Paul. I thought... *That's another thank you, Lord.*

John said, "I appreciate your call Dr. Lynn. Tell Steve we'll start the prayer chain for him and send Mom on her way. We'll wait for her. I'll call Cousin Stacy and let her know we are coming."

John put the phone down upstairs with a clunk. Talk about a broken ear-drum.

John called Pastor Bishop on his cell phone, and I called Cousin Stacy on the house phone. She had heard about the two ladies in the accident, but didn't know it was Steve that they hit. She was surprised and wanted details. I guess folks had come into the Café and told her. Chaffee is a small town, and word gets around quickly.

———➤ ➤———

Two weeks have passed since Steve's accident. He missed three days of school, two of which were spent in the hospital. Janet went back to school the next day, but was on crutches. Steve was very lucky. One of the ladies in the car that ran the stop sign is still in the hospital.

They say, she had a lot of bruising and suffered a stroke from a blood clot. The other lady was released after five days. The two kids who hit Steve apologized several times. They were given a ticket for careless and reckless driving, and they had only the minimum insurance on their old truck. They had to get a new radiator and front bumper. They, also, had to pay some of Steve and Janet's hospital bills. Their parents weren't very happy, but Steve had the opportunity to let them know that he had no hard feelings, and life was far more important than any vehicle, so they should use the accident as a learning experience and never follow too closely to any car.

Steve gets a lot of respect from his high school peers. He's passed up John in height and is now six-feet, four-inches tall with a rugged, muscled body. I'm proud of him because he isn't conceited—at least I don't think so. He's like me, though. With all the farm responsibilities and family crises, we haven't dated a lot. The girls fall all over themselves to be sweet to Steve, and he's nice to them, but that's it. I think the guys look up to him and especially appreciate him for not chasing after *their* girlfriends. I look back and see that the same things were happening to me with the girls. I'm glad God blinded my eyes, as I could have fallen for several of them and lost my focus on what my priorities are.

Now that I'm nineteen and in college, I wouldn't mind having a date now and then. I did go to the prom like John, but the girl had to ask me, and I only went to the prom to be part of what was going on at school. I don't even remember the girl's last name. Her first name was Becky. She gave me her address, so I could pick her up. I'm embarrassed. I'll probably meet her somewhere. I hope I remember her last name by then, and I hope I don't run into her on campus.

Mom tells me, in God's time, the girl who is to be my spouse will just fall from heaven, and I'll know she is my angel. She teases us boys about that, but no one measures up to my sister, Kaitlynn, and John's friend, Marianne, except maybe Marianne's sister, Janet. Someday, maybe Janet will go out with me. I should pray about that. Well, like I said, Robert Weber, John and I are all attending Southeast Missouri University in Cape Girardeau. So far I have not had any problem making good grades. The professors give study guides, and I take pretty good notes.

My soybeans have all been harvested, thanks to Mr. and Mrs. Jenkins and Aunt Susan, so I don't have to worry about that. Other than my normal chores, I just have to study.

John saved all his notes from his freshman year, and I try to not use them, but on occasion I've had to go to them or ask John for an answer. He usually knows the answer before using his notes. It's difficult to decipher John's abbreviated words. He can barely read his own writing.

Once a week, John and I stop by the youth center to help with Officer Harrison's Prevention Program for the 13-15 year old boys. Robert is now attending, too. He said, "I can help you guys or walk home. You're my ride."

I wondered why Robert didn't have his own car, so I asked him. His answer surprised me. He said, "My Dad grew up in a big city. The kids didn't have cars unless they worked and paid for the car and the insurance. I have worked at paying jobs very little, so I haven't been able to save very much toward a car. Dad tells me it is cheaper to buy the gas for your old truck than it is to buy a car. He told me when I start working as hard as you guys for everything, then he would consider paying for half. In the meantime, carpooling is the way to go."

My first thought was he must be a tight-wad, but then I thought about Cousin Stacy who is always looking for reliable help. I thought about the cards on the bulletin boards on campus in the different buildings looking for student help.

"Robert, I think we can help you."

John chuckled. "We can?"

If I find a job that will suit you and where you live, will you consider it, even if it is cleaning chicken manure out of the chicken house and cow manure out of a stall?"

Robert laughed. "You guys had me doing some low-down dirty jobs didn't you? I appreciated having something to do, and it did teach me humility."

He laughed again. "Besides all the top-level influencing you were doing, it was really good for me."

John said, "We did do that, didn't we?"

"Yeah, John, but that was over two years ago, and now I've learned to set goals, priorities, and I've lost my feelings of vengeance. Those times were tough, but good. I even quit looking at the girls because you guys weren't dating, and you were liked by everyone anyway. So, here I am nineteen and in college. Who would have ever thought? It sure beats hangin' out on the Food Giant or IGA parking lot... right, John?"

John looked over at me and then said to Robert, "How do you know about that?"

"Because, I was one of the guys leaning on the car, watching the whole thing," Robert said, with a chuckle. "If my parents had known where I was, I would have been carted off to a juvenile detention center. I heard what you said to the kids and what you said to Officer Blair. After you left, I said to the guys, 'I'm out of here.' They didn't care whether I was there or not. They didn't even say good-bye or see-ya. That alone made an impression on me."

I decided to ask John about that later. I wondered what he was doing on the Food Giant grocery store parking lot, but figured John had a good reason for being there. Man, that was four years ago. Grandpa was still alive then. Oh well, right now, I have to think about a job that will give Robert a paycheck.

I went home that evening and thought about what kind of job would be good for Robert. I realized, *Hey, I'm in the same boat. I don't have a car and haven't saved enough to buy one yet.* John has always taken me wherever I needed to go and Mom lets me borrow her car. I should ask Mom what I have deposited in the family account.

After thinking it through, I asked God if I should use my money for another truck. I decided that I should wait until Steve gets his truck replaced and see if Mom needs any extra money for the medical bills for Paul and Steve. Besides, Grandpa's truck is getting old, and it may need to be replaced.

The same afternoon Dr. Lynn went after Steve at the school. They both came in smiling. Steve was still wearing his Thompson neck collar. I asked, "What put you two in such a good mood?

Dr. Lynn said, "W-e-l-l,"

He looked at Steve and Steve just grinned, so Dr. Lynn said, "The insurance company called. They've totaled Steve's truck, and they're giving him full replacement value."

I was pleased to hear that and said, "Wow! What about the medical bills?"

Steve was still grinning, "The ladies who hit me first had good insurance, and they paid everything, plus a fee if I signed a waiver never to sue. For signing the note, they gave me a check for five thousand dollars. I guess they figured as hard as I was hit and considering the injury I have, they might be in for a long haul for years to come. Dr. Lynn told me it was optional, but I figured by staying in therapy for a while, and considering how young I am, my neck should heal up nicely."

Dr. Lynn said, "But there is always the chance that a neck injury can plague a person for a lifetime."

Steve added, "I chose to have them pay off all medical bills and pay for therapy for six more months, plus the fee for not suing."

Dr. Lynn started laughing. "This brother of yours likes to barter for a good price. The insurance agent had a moment of silence when Steve suggested paying for therapy for six more months."

Steve said, "Yeah, they wanted to pay me only three thousand dollars, and I said, six months of therapy and five thousand, and that will be it. The man raised his eyebrows so high that he looked like he had a facelift."

Mom walked in the back door, "Who had a facelift?"

We all started laughing. John came downstairs from studying in Kaitlynn's room and bopped me on the shoulder. "Dennis, I thought you were going to check around for a job for Robert. What or who is everyone laughing at? Let me in on what is funny?" Steve and Dr. Lynn repeated everything to Mom and John. John was happy for Steve. He said, "That's our business man for you."

Mom asked, "What is this about you finding a job for Robert? Can't he find his own job?"

I looked at Mom like, *that's beside the point,* but I shared with her what Robert said on the way home from school. "I figured that while I was looking for him, I might find a paying job for myself, too.

"Steve was smart to save for a car. I figured Grandpa's truck would last forever, I guess, but one day John or I will have to replace it, so I might as well work part-time this winter and save up until the next soybean season. I need to tithe, pay the family account and then take care of my school bill."

Mom looked at Dr. Lynn and smiled, "Son, have you checked your account in the family account lately. You realize the mortgage and the loan have been paid off, and your soybean money has only gone to your education and tithe. You haven't purchased anything to speak of for a while."

I sat there thinking. "Well," I said. "The soybean crop was good this year, but I still had to pay for cow feed and help with the paint job on the house and seed for the boys' gardens. Plus I got new jeans and Nikes for school. I hope you have been using my money for things that I'm responsible for. You know, Mom, once we slack off and let you start paying for things, it will wind up being a mess. I'll pay for jeans and John won't, or Steve will buy cattle feed and I won't. We need to keep to the rules that we have set out."

Paul said, "But everyone else has been doing my job, and they should get paid for it."

He was so serious. I had to tell him, "No, Paul. When there is sickness or an injury, we all chip in so you will continue to get what you did before you got sick. Unless, it is a special circumstance, like when you shared egg money with Janet. Emergencies don't count either. John and I will continue to do Steve's jobs and your job until you both are well enough to handle it alone again. I expect the same from you, if I should ever get sick or injured. Anyway, I told Robert I was going to help him find a job where he receives a paycheck, so he can save for his own car. I don't think he know beans about looking for a job. Tomorrow I'm going to check on campus. Maybe there's something available in the Criminal Justice Office. Robert is nineteen, and he really needs to get a part-time job. It will certainly help his Dad feel like he isn't footing all the bills by himself. I thought Cousin Stacy might use us both for a couple of nights a week. Tips are always good on Friday and Saturday nights. I wouldn't even mind learning how to cook—well, maybe a hamburger or something like that."

Mom and Dr. Lynn glanced at each other, and he winked at her.

I finally said, "What's going on? What is so amusing between you two?"

Dr. Lynn put his hand on my arm and said, "God is one step ahead of you, Son. Your mother and I have discussed for several weeks that your grandpa's truck needed to be replaced before you get stranded on the highway between here and Cape Girardeau. The tires need replacing, and the mileage is pushing two-hundred and twenty. It needs a good overall tune-up, and we can do that, but we think you guys need something safer to drive to school. We should keep the truck, though, for working with the boys in the gardens. Back and forth on this farm and to the Jenkins is about all it is good for. Besides, if you think about it, I think you would want something nicer to take a sweet girl out on a date."

Steve laughed. "That'll be the day the sun falls out of the sky. Unless Dennis opens his eyes and notices Janet. All she can talk about is Dennis, Dennis, and Dennis."

I was shocked. "Steve, I thought you had feelings for Janet, so I decided until the Lord told me something specific, she was hands-off."

I looked around at everyone, and they were waiting for me to comment. I know my face was getting hot. I finally said, "Well, Steve, I hadn't noticed Janet having any vibes for me. Maybe it's because I thought she was your age and into music and would be a better match for you. I used to have feelings for Janet, but she was too young to even think about dating her back then. Besides that, I thought she needed to overcome that traumatic rape and get on with her life. I didn't want her to fear a guy every time he looked at her, or asked her for a date. She needed time and space." Steve poked me on the arm with his index finger. "I need to bust those scales you've had over your eyes. Yes, she's my age, and, yes, she is into music, but for some reason she's become my Kaitlynn, my sister. I would have no ill feeling, about her becoming my sister-*in-law*."

Mom and Dr. Lynn were laughing and Dr. Lynn said to her, "Aren't we glad to be sitting at this table right now, hearing these boys converse about a girl—especially a girl we like."

I couldn't help it. I had to laugh. "I guess I should check my account, if I am going to get a vehicle and start dating. I hear girls can be costly."

Dr. Lynn looked around at all of us and said, "We need to finish this conversation after supper. Your mother has worked all day. She needs to eat something, and Paul needs to keep his appetite satisfied, too."

Steve, the chef, jumped up and said, "And I know what I'm fixing."

Mom got up, too. "Well, Steve, don't I get to fix what I want?"

"Sure, Mom, it won't hurt to have two main courses, but I'm going to fix some good old fashioned stew with the beef that's already cooked and frozen. Give me twenty minutes and the micro-wave, and you'll have a generous portion of beef stew with carrots, potatoes, and corn bread on the side. Maybe I'll throw together a chocolate pie for dessert, too."

Mom sat back down, "Steve, you win."

We all laughed at Mom, but John got up from the table and said, "While you are fixing supper, I'll go start the chores. By the way, Steve, did you know you have a heifer in season?"

The look on Steve's face showed surprise. He said, "Let me get the stew on, and I'll be right out.

He went to the pantry for some potatoes, got out the potato peeler and slammed the drawer. He was peeling so quickly Mom had to tell him to slow down, or he was going to cut himself. He ignored her.

"I've got to breed that heifer before it's too late," Steve said. "Her calf will bring a good price."

Dr. Lynn got up, took the potato peeler out of his hand, and said, "Steve, go check on that heifer. I'll peel the potatoes and carrots."

I got up and cleared our drinking glasses off the kitchen table and set it for supper. I said to Mom, "Before Steve gets back teach me to make cornbread quickly."

I know I was grinning because Steve thinks I can't cook anything, and here was my chance to cook something. Paul was listening and said, "I know where the cornmeal is in the pantry. I'll get it if you go get some eggs and milk."

Mom added, "Get two eggs and bring in some butter."

I went out to the refrigerator on the back porch, and Mom got up, got a bowl, and turned the oven on. She handed me a long pan and the butter and said, "Butter the bottom of this."

I looked at her and thought, *Are you for real?* "What do you mean?"

I had the pan in my hand and some butter, and I couldn't figure out why I should butter the bottom of the pan. She looked at me in time to see me looking at the outside of the bottom of the pan. Paul, turning the pan over, said, "She means the bottom in here, Silly."

Mom sat down in the chair, laughing, and she couldn't stop. Dr. Lynn kept saying, "Bonnie, you are going to have a heart attack."

Paul was laughing, too. Now, I know why Steve thought I didn't have any talent in the kitchen.

Finally I said, "Paul, help me." He handed me the cornmeal and a cup. "It's only a one measuring cup and the directions say two cups of cornmeal, so put cornmeal in the cup, two times. That will give you two cups." I wanted to say "duh," but didn't. "Dump the cornmeal in the bowl."

He then handed me a fork and said, ""Break up the lumps."

I did. "What's next?"

Mom settled down and said, "Give me those two eggs, and you measure out a cup of milk."

I did it while she cracked the two eggs and put the contents in the bowl. Both Mom and Paul said, "Now stir it up."

I took the wooden spoon that Paul handed me and stirred ever so lightly.

Paul reached for the bowl. "Dennis, gimmy that." He took it right out of my hands and started stirring like the bottom of the bowl needed punishment.

He handed it back and said, "Now dump it all in your greased pan." I did that, and he took the spoon and made sure the pan bottom had the batter all over.

"Now, put it in the oven before Steve gets back in here."

I did that, too. Then I couldn't wait to see how it turned out. Dr. Lynn said, "The potatoes and carrots are half-done and the meat is simmering. It looks like we'll have everything done about the same time.

I said, "Not quite. What about that chocolate pie Steve mentioned?"

I no sooner said it, when Steve came in the barn talking to whoever would listen. "That heifer will produce an awesome calf."

Paul looked at me and thought I was going to say something about the pie, but because I hesitated, he said, "Well, my stomach needs chocolate pie for dessert, not a calf."

"Oh, I forgot," Steve said. He hurried to the freezer for his pie crust that he makes up ahead of time already in a pan ready to go. He was getting in Dr. Lynn's way in front of the Stove, but Steve got out a pan, poured in milk, sugar, cocoa, cornstarch and vanilla all together and turned a burner on under it. He said, "This isn't the way to do it, but I'm going to take a short cut and hope it turns out okay."

He let the mixture comes to a boil and simmer until it was thick and then poured it over his pie crust. I was watching him closely to see how he did it. I thought, *I can do that, too.* Then Steve broke-open several eggs, dropping only the egg whites in a mixer bowl. He turned it on and let it beat the egg whites until they got really white and stiff. He put a couple of drops of vanilla in it and some sugar and then ran the mixer again. Then he dumped the whole mixture on top of the chocolate already in the pie-crust and swirled it around.

When Steve opened the oven door, there was the corn bread ready to come out. It looked good. The first thing Steve said was, "Who made the cornbread? Paul?"

Paul was kind. He said, "Dennis did."

Mom started laughing again, but Paul looked at Steve, and said, "He did! He tried to do exactly what Mom said, and it turned out right, didn't it, Mom?" Steve looked at Dr. Lynn for an explanation.

"If Dennis made the cornbread, I'm not sure what is so funny."

Mom said, "I haven't enjoyed my boys like this in a long time. We've gone from money in the family accounts, to truck replacements, to Janet's feelings for Dennis, to heifers in season, to measuring cups, corn bread and chocolate pie, and all in the space of thirty minutes. I enjoy my family."

Paul gave Mom a hug and said, "Mom, we like you, too."

The food was on the table when John finally came back. The stew was really good. We were all hungry.

Steve said, "John, Dennis made the cornbread."

John didn't look up from his stew bowl. "Didn't know he could."

Mom started laughing again, and Dr. Lynn asked, "What is *so* funny?"

She looked at Paul like, *You better not tell either*, but he blurted out, "Mom told Dennis to butter the bottom of the cornbread pan, and he asked her if she was for real."

Steve glanced at me, "So…? I always butter the bottom of the pans."

I said, "Okay, Paul. You don't need to tell anymore."

He started laughing, "Yes, I do. Dennis thought Mom meant the outside of the bottom of the pan—*not* the inside. She said, 'Butter the bottom of the pan,' and he couldn't see why she would do that. That's not all…"

Paul, stop!" I said.

"No, because I learned I was smarter than you in some things. Dennis couldn't figure out what Mom meant, when she handed him a measuring cup and said, 'Measure two cups." He said, 'Paul, help me.' I think he thought Mom meant to measure the cups. Get it?"

Everyone was laughing including me because I *did* think that for an instant. Dr. Lynn chuckled. "I missed all that right behind me while I was fixing the stew.'

John was laughing, too. "That's okay, Dennis. You're a whiz at the criminal justice courses. I've heard glowing reports from my professors. They think you should teach in the system someday."

I was glad the subject changed, but I was surprised to hear John's comment. I said, "Really? I hadn't thought of that. I really think, though, that professors ought to have some hands-on-work, so to speak, out on the field *doing* what they teach first."

"That's what I mean, Dennis. You have the gift of discernment, and you can come up with ideas that are right-on."

"Well, I don't know about that, but I have been thinking lately on some other ideas that I'll have to talk about with Officer Harrison."

We finished supper, and all of us boys cleaned up the kitchen. Mom and Dr. Lynn went to the living room and turned on the television. They flipped channels for a moment and then turned the T.V. off. It reminded me of what Brian said about getting some really good Hallmark videos for the Jenkins and some popcorn from a movie theater. I put my dish towel down and went to the living room. Mom glanced at me as I sat down in a chair opposite her. "Mom, Brian suggested to me that perhaps I could repay the Jenkins for doing the soybeans with some Hallmark videos and theater popcorn. What do you think?"

Dr. Lynn smiled. "That sounds like Brian. He's always able to come up with unique, appropriate gifts that are satisfying for a long time."

Mom added, "Dennis, I think that's a wonderful idea. Get a big barrel of popcorn with a lid on it, and it would be good to go."

I sat there for a moment and then asked, "But, where would I find Hallmark videos?"

Mom didn't answer right away, but said, "I believe I saw a set in the Hallmark shop in Cape Girardeau."

I had not thought about that. The Hallmark store would be the logical place. I wondered if there might be some place in Chaffee. Mom said, "I'm going in to Cape Girardeau, Saturday, and I will pick them up for you. Do you want me to get the popcorn, too?"

"Yes, take the money from my account."

Paul came in the living room, hearing only part of the conversation. "I want some, too. What is it you are getting?"

We all started laughing again. Dr. Lynn said, "Boy, sit down here beside me."

As big as Paul was getting, he snuggled up under Dr. Lynn's arm. I noticed how much they had bonded as father and son. I think Dad would be happy about that.

"Your mom is going to get some Hallmark videos for the Jenkins and Aunt Susan for helping Dennis with the soybeans. It was Brian's suggestion to get the videos and some theater popcorn. What do you think?"

Paul looked at me, "Do you think they will let us look at them when they are done with them? I'd like some popcorn, too."

Mom answered for me. "I supposed they will let you see them. However, we'll have to check your diet to see about the popcorn."

"I wish this stuff in my body would go away!"

Dr. Lynn took on a serious look and gave Paul a hug, "That's what we're praying for, Paul. I wish I could take it from you, but God has his reasons for allowing it to be with you. We just have to trust Him for healing. Are you doing that?"

"I trust God *and* the doctors, Dad."

Dr. Lynn looked at me and raised his eyebrows and then at Mom. She smiled, so I know she wasn't offended. I had a little twinge hit my emotions, but I knew it was coming.

Dr. Lynn looked down at Paul. "Paul, do you realize you just called me Dad?"

"I did?"

Paul looked at me and then Mom. I didn't know if he was wanted our approval or not. I answered for Mom.

"Paul, Dr. Lynn is not your biological father. Your father had you for six wonderful years, and we all loved him and still do, but God has him in heaven now. You have been without a Dad for almost six years, and you've needed one. Dr. Lynn is God's gift to you be a Dad for you. It's okay to call him Dad. I sometimes want to call him something else besides Dr. Lynn all the time, too.

Mom said, "Thank you, Dennis. I'm glad you feel that way. It makes me feel good about my marriage to Marshall. He has been good for me, too."

Dr. Lynn put his other arm around Mom and pulled her close and kissed her, then he kissed Paul and said, "Paul, you feel like you are my son, and I'm proud to have you as a son. I hope I can be a good Dad to you."

Paul giggled. "You already are."

I sat there for a moment and finally said, "I don't feel comfortable calling you Dad or Marshall, and Dr. Lynn seems too formal. Would you mind if I call you Pop or Pa?"

Dr. Lynn started to answer when Steve came into the living room and flopped on the shorter couch across the room and said, "Are we getting pop to drink now? I thought Mom said we didn't need to drink all that sugar. Frankly, I don't see any difference in putting sugar in iced tea and the sugar in soft drinks like what's in a Coke."

It seems like lately, someone is always getting in on the tail end of a conversation and coming up with something they *think* they heard, and it is always way off-base and often funny. I said, "Steve, the pop we are talking about is not something to drink. How would you feel if we called Dr. Lynn Pop or Pa?"

John joined us, leaning on the door frame. He said, "I don't know about that. I sort of like having a doctor around."

Dr. Lynn and Mom laughed, and Dr. Lynn said, "I felt like this conversation would come up at some point in the future when I married your mother. I really expected you to talk with your mom long before now, but I was not going to push you guys into calling me anything other than what you want to call me. I know you have great memories of your dad. I don't want to replace him in your hearts. I can replace some things he did in his role as a father. Maybe not as well, but I can try."

Steve's humor surfaced. "Well, you may not be as sweet as a can of pop, or the sugar I put in my tea, but Pop sounds good to me."

We all chuckled, and I had one of my meditating or thinking moments, but Mom noticed. "What are you thinking, Dennis?"

I had to say what was on my heart. I looked at Dr. Lynn and then John. "Dr. Lynn, I'm 19 years old, and John is 21. Both of us had our Dad longer than Steve and Paul. Grandpa filled in for Dad and was like a Dad to us after that. Now, you are here, and I want to say that for the last year and a half, I have not had any question in my mind about you being placed in this family by God. The two families have been meshed together like we have always been one."

I wasn't expecting what happened next. Dr. Lynn broke down and cried. He kept saying, "I'm sorry. I'm sorry."

I looked at John, and he said, "Well, Dennis, you started it. Now, what are you going to do?"

Mom and Steve had tears running down their faces, and Paul was saying, "Mom, what's wrong? Mom, what's the matter?"

Dr. Lynn turned to Paul with both arms and hugged him. By then, Dr. Lynn had regained his composure and said, "Dennis, I grieved for my son, and there was a hole in my heart. Then my wife died, and there was an even bigger hole. I lived in a daze and functioned as though only my brain was at work, but then I met you and your family, and somehow the emptiness began to fill. Tonight, my heart has caught up with my mind. I can finally put my wife and child in the past. God has given me four wonderful boys to fill my son's place. I feel like Job in the Bible. God replaced his family, and he has replaced mine so beautifully. Thank you Bonnie, for giving me four wonderful guys as my sons."

Steve has no reservations about doing or saying anything when the moment is right. He got off the couch and took the few steps to Dr. Lynn and held his hand out for a high-five. "Put it there, Pop!"

Dr. Lynn stood up and gave Steve a hug.

I said, "Yeah, Pop," and gave him a hug, too. John was still leaning on the door frame watching the whole scene and thinking when Dr. Lynn looked at him. John put a silly grin on this face and said, "I already think of Brian like a brother, so I guess that makes you my Pop, too. And, by the way, I was impressed with your daughters. They will be great sisters, too."

Dr. Lynn didn't hesitate to hug John even though he was at least six inches shorter than John. John started chuckling, "I want you to remember one thing. I'm bigger than you!"

When Dr. Lynn sat down, he said, "John, in more ways than one, in more ways than one!"

John laughed as he walked through the room to the stairs. He stopped on about the second step and said, "I don't agree with that." He hesitated than said, "Pop!"

Steve said, "No, Pop, you have had a head start on John, being a man."

He looked at John and laughed, "But, you're a close second, John."

I looked at my watch and realized both cows needed to be brought in and milked. It was pushing 7 p.m. I yelled at John before he hit the top step on the stairs. "John, what has to be done in the barn?"

He stopped. "Oh, I really need to study. I spread hay for Steve's cattle, brought the cows in, and fed the cats. We still need to close up the chicken house and milk the cows. I would sure appreciate it if you milked the cows tonight."

I yelled upstairs, "Okay."

Pop got up. "Well it looks like I need to learn how to milk cows and put up the chickens, so Dennis can study, too.

I smiled at him . "Let's go!"

CHAPTER 3

I T WAS GOOD FOR us to go out to the barn together. It gave Dr. Lynn—I mean Pop—and *me* time to be alone together. He apologized for falling apart. "I unloaded all the grief that I've been storing up for the past five years. I want to thank you for expressing your feelings in the house tonight."

"No problem. I figured, like you, that we would have had that conversation long before we did. I think being so busy with farm responsibilities, with Paul's leukemia, and the work with the prevention program, we just haven't had a relaxing evening together."

He agreed with me. I showed him how to milk the first cow and to be firm because the cow knows when someone new is at her side. For being in medicine all his life and very intelligent, he caught on pretty quickly, so I went to the other cow and milked her. With both of us working, it took only twenty minutes. Dr. Lynn was amazed at how much milk we had. The buckets are four gallon buckets, and both cows gave over a gallon. I showed him how to put the milk through a strainer and collect it in sterile bottles. Then it had to be refrigerated. We put half of the milk in a refrigerator in the barn and took the rest to the refrigerator on the back porch of the house. Sometime during the day, someone would separate the cream from the milk and make butter, or save some of the cream for whipping cream or baking. We use large gallon pickle bottles to hold the milk.

As we walked back to the house, Pop said, "We started to talk about replacing the truck earlier, and we never did come to an agreeable solution."

"Yeah... Well, I need to sit down with Mom and see what's in my account. I really do think it's time for John to have his own vehicle and for me to have my own. John is hesitant to use what he had built up in his account because, for so long, he felt like the bread-winner of the family—especially when Mom was so sick. There was always that gnawing fear on both our parts that something would happen to Mom, and we would both be responsible for the mortgage, and the rest of the bills, too. John used to say, "I would rather put $500 in the old truck to keep it running, than to put $5000 in another one, and still have to keep fixing things. Now that the mortgage is paid off, that burden is lifted."

As we got to the porch, Dr. Lynn said, "Well, I think it is time you, your mother, John, and I, sit down and discuss this more. I'm concerned about you driving to Cape Girardeau every day in the old truck."

When we walked into the kitchen, Steve was sitting at the table. Paul had already climbed into his bed in the room next to the kitchen. He was reading something, and he set it down and said, "Good night, everybody."

Pop said, "Let me go pray with Paul. I'll be back."

Steve looked up from his calculator. "I've been waiting for you guys to come back."

John came downstairs and was getting a cookie out of the metal cookie container. "Dennis, we need to talk about the truck."

Steve adjusted his chair and reached for more paper off Mom' kitchen desk. "That's what I want to talk about."

Pop came back to the kitchen, pulled out a chair, and said, "We need to talk about the truck."

We all started laughing. Pop looked at us like he had missed something again. "What's so funny?"

Steve said, "Because I was waiting for you and Dennis to come in from the barn, so we could talk about the truck—Grandpa's old truck. Then John just came out here and said, 'I need to talk to you about the truck.' And now you just said, 'I need to talk to you about the truck.' Apparently God put a subject on all of our minds. Let me guess first what it is—the word is truck."

John scooted his chair back. "Well, I have been thinking, since I'm not making mortgage payments anymore, perhaps I can swing car payments. If Dennis can get that part-time job—although I wouldn't recommend it his first year at the university—he can save for his own wheels one more year."

Steve said, "Wrong on both counts. Since I'm going to be a businessman, and perhaps a banker, I might as well start right now. I have a check for $5000 in my possession, and I'll be getting another check for around $18,000 from my totaled truck. That's $23,000. You guys can borrow money from me to add to your amount in the account and get your own vehicle. None of us needs to get another brand-new truck. We only need one pick-up truck on the farm. I'm sure you both can find a half-way decent car for a low price.

Mom came back to the kitchen from the dining room. She had been listening to our conversation. "Wrong song, my dear son, Steve," she said.

To start with, you still owe the bank for your truck, even though it has been wrecked beyond repair. That insurance money must pay off the note at the bank and you must start all over again yourself with whatever is left.

"I admire your generosity, Steve, but brotherly love often goes out the window when there's money involved. You might feel at the moment, that the money would be good for John and Dennis, and in their hearts, they wouldn't think of not paying you back. But... often circumstances arise that make it impossible to pay some or all of it back. That's why civil courts flourish—friend against friend, brother against brother. I don't want my sons at odds with each other over money. So far, you've all functioned very nicely with the family account, and the rules we set up. Marshall and I sat down and looked over each account, and we justified every expense. You all have been very obedient to tithing and paying into the family account for the farm's needs, your own needs, and emergencies, too. I couldn't be more proud of you.

"For that reason, Steve, you are to put your money in a savings account, and you will only keep out what is needed for a down payment. That's after you pay the bank off for the other truck. Perhaps there will be enough left for a year of payments. By then, you will have sold another calf or heifer, and you can put that money into a checking account with interest to pay off the following year's payments. If you want to go for another *new* truck, that would be okay, but let the interest on your savings make a couple of payments for you. Is that agreeable with you?"

Steve looked at Mom. "I thought I was the businessman in the family. Now I know where I get my business sense. Yes, Mom, that would be agreeable. But let's see what these other guys say."

John said, "Mom's right, Steve. You worked hard at earning and saving your money, and you should use it for your vehicle."

I was listening and chuckled, "No, I want a loan for $10,000."

Mom was standing behind me and grabbed my shoulders hard. "Dennis, you better be kidding."

I laughed. "I am! I am! But, I need to know what I have in my account that can be used toward *my* wheels."

Dr. Lynn finally spoke up. "Now this is where I come in. I'm willing to do for you boys exactly what I did for Brian and my daughters. They had to come up with half of the price, and I came up with the other half. Brian still had some of his mother's insurance left, so he used that money, and I paid the other half. He was able to get a late model used car and pay a year's insurance, too. He's doing odd jobs for Mr. Jenkins and Aunt Susan for his room and board, so he gets $20 a week. It gives him his gas money and pays for a lunch at school. I pay him for keeping the Jenkins' farm machinery clean, greased, and in good repair. It is mine now, so I pay him."

John interrupted. "He seems to have a talent for machinery. Our tractor has never worked as well, as it has, since Brian has been keeping it tuned up."

Pop said, "Yeah, you're right. Your Mom has been paying him $5.00 an hour, when he works on your farm machinery. We actually pay him minimum wage, but the extra is for social security. We consider the work on the tractors and equipment to be his project, just like you have yours. He's started paying into the family account with the rest of you. He doesn't have much yet, but it is a savings program for him. He is happy to have his money work for him this way.

"Your Mom's idea, or your dad's idea, was great for teaching you boys how to handle money. I wish we had done it years ago. Now—in looking over your accounts—it appears that you Dennis, can spare at least $5000 and you, John, as much as $8,000. Your mom has continued to put ten percent into the family account from her salary, and it has built up during the last year.

"So, I have decided one thing. Your Mom's car is going to be traded in, and I am buying her a new car. I can pay for that out of my savings, so she won't have to use any of her money."

Mom gasped. Apparently, he had not said anything to her.

Pop went on talking, "It will not come out of the family account. I have been thinking about this for quite some time. My car still doesn't have high mileage, so if one of you would like to purchase your mother's car and one of you purchase mine; I'm willing to go for it, if your mother is agreeable.

"Tomorrow we will check at the bank, or one of you can go on the internet and see what the blue book value is for both cars. I think your Mom deserves a new car. Don't you guys, think?"

We all looked at Mom and she was smiling. She said, "Even though my car is an older car, it's still not a high mileage car, and it's still in good shape. It should go for another 50,000 or 75,000 miles. I really haven't put that many miles on the car in the seven years I've had the car."

Pop added, "Your Dad did well when he bought her a good car. I want your Mom to have a new car to drive back and forth to St. Louis with Paul, and if I need to go to Cape Girardeau or further than the Jenkins, I'll use your Mom's car. Just driving to the Jenkins' place or in town here, I can use the old truck. What do you guys think?"

I shook my head. I couldn't think of what to say. I could tell by Mom's face our conversation made her happy. She looked at Pop and said, "Marshall, thanks for being so generous. I never thought about our older cars being a solution for the boys." Mom walked around the table and gave Pop a hug.

I finally said, "John, you deserve the better car or the newer one. I still have time to save, so I will buy Mom's car. Perhaps in a year, Robert Weber will be looking for an older car that's still in good shape. Maybe he can buy Mom's car from me."

Steve's mind was running ahead when he said "John, why don't you just buy Pop's car because Dennis won't be using it often anyway. Keep Mom's car as a second for Pop. In a year, Dennis will have saved enough to buy a car or a truck with lesser mileage than Mom's car. You all ride to school and go to the prevention program together, anyway—right? If there's some time you both have to be coming home at different times, then I'm sure Pop will let you borrow Mom's old car, or if Dennis breaks down and asks Janet for a date, he can borrow your car or Mom's old car—right? I really think there needs to be a good running car here at the farm at all times, especially until Paul is out of the woods with his leukemia."

Dr. Lynn said, "Steve, you're right again. Mom, I sure am glad your boys know how to think and are problem solver young people. John, my offer still holds on going half, even if it's my car. I'll call the bank tomorrow and get the blue-book price."

I could tell John was happy, when he said, "Sure. That sounds great to me."

It was getting close to 9 p.m. and I hadn't opened a book all day. I got up and kissed Mom.

"Mom, this all sounds good to me, too, but I need to get upstairs and study. May I be excused for the night?"

"Sure, son."

"Goodnight, Steve, John."

I looked at Dr. Lynn and smiled. "You too, Pop."

He said, "Good night, Dennis. I'm headed for my bed upstairs, too. I'm tired. Thanks for teaching me how to get milk out of that cow."

We all laughed and one by one went upstairs, except for Steve. He was taking his turn sleeping in Paul's room with him for a week.

CHAPTER 4

THE SUN WAS SHINING just above the horizon this morning, when I woke up with a start. Someone was throwing something at our bedroom window. My feet hit the floor the same time John's did. We both were frowning at each other. "What was that?" John asked.

I opened the drape fully and saw one of the younger boys in the prevention program. He was down under the window with Blake Hegel, a boy who used to go to our youth group at Calvary Church. If I remember right, the younger boy's name was Glen. Both John and I put our pants on and rushed downstairs. How did they know which window to hit? Had they hit other windows and not gotten a response? Mom heard us and came out of her bedroom tying the belt on her blue robe, with Dr. Lynn close behind her with his grey flannel shorts on and a white tee shirt. Mom said, "What's going on?"

"I don't know. Blake is outside with Glen," I said. "I can't imagine how they got all the way over here from Cape Girardeau."

We were virtually running down the stairs. Mom closed Paul's bedroom door off the kitchen, and John opened the back door to two, tired, and very cold boys. Glen was shaking. The temperatures had dropped in the upper forties during the night. John said, "Come in here and let's get you boys warmed up."

Mom turned on the tea kettle. "I'll fix some hot chocolate," she said.

The boys looked at Dr. Lynn very apprehensive, so he said, "Boys, I am part of the family now, and I'm not going to hurt or tell on you boys, but you need to come clean with John and Dennis about why you're here."

Glen's whole body seemed to be shaking, but he said, "I ran! I didn't know where to go, so I ran to Blake's house.'

Blake said, "And I didn't know what to do except to get him out of town. I told Mom that I was going for help and would call her as soon as I could."

I asked, "What do you mean… out of town?"

Blake said, "Call Officer Harrison and see if the coast is clear. There must have been twenty-five policemen at Glen's house."

Glen started crying and hadn't even thought to sit. "He killed them—all of them. He killed all of them. I got away."

He started crying hysterically and Dr. Lynn took him by the arm and said, "Sit down here, Glen." He pulled out a chair from the table and Glen sat on the edge of it. Both boys weren't making too much sense.

I reached for the phone and called Officer Harrison. His phone number was on a card by the kitchen phone. His wife answered, so I asked for him. "He's not here. May I call him for you?"

She wasn't about to tell me where he could be reached. I said "Yes, this is Dennis Moore. Tell him to call John or Dennis Moore. It's an emergency with one of the boys named Glen."

She paused. "Well… he's gone over to Glen's house now. Do you still want him to call?"

"Yes, tell him that John and I have Glen and Blake sitting here at our kitchen table. He will know where that is."

Mom gave the boys their cups of hot chocolate, but I noticed Glen was still shaking and Dr. Lynn had left the room. He came back with two of his flannel shirts and gave one to each of the boys. He also had his medical bag and he opened it, took out his blood pressure cuff and put it on Glen. He started crying again. "He shot them all."

The phone rang and I grabbed it. It was Officer Harrison. "You have Glen with you—Blake, too. How did they get that far?"

I don't know, but Glen is in a pretty high emotional state. Dr. Lynn is checking him over right now."

Officer Harrison said, "Um-m, can you go to another phone? I need to talk to you. I'm home now, so feel free to talk."

I handed the phone to John and said, "Hold this... okay." I ran upstairs to the extension in Mom's room. "Okay, I am here. What's going on?"

Officer Harrison cleared his throat. "It appears that someone shot Glen's mother, two sisters, and his elderly grandmother. There is a bulletin out for Glen right now. He's the only one missing from the family, and someone suggested that he might have been the one who did it."

I said from the phone upstairs, "John, don't say anything down there in the kitchen, let me talk up here. Officer Harrison, Glen has been crying since he got here, and acts like he's in shock. All he says is 'He shot them all. I got away.'

"He has been shaking like a leaf either from the cold or from the shock of whatever happened. Blake said he came running into his house and kept saying, 'He shot them all. He shot them all.' So, whoever is the person he refers to as *he* is the one who did it. Blake said that his mother told him to somehow get him to us here on the farm where he would be safe. Blake's mother called the police. If you don't mind, Officer Harrison, since both John and I have classes this morning, would it be okay to have Dr. Lynn keep them here and perhaps give both boys a sedative. The boys look like they've been walking all night. Why don't you come out around noon time? That will give the boys time to sleep. John and I should be home by twelve-thirty. If you find out anything before noon, you can reach us at the academy. Or, you can call Dr. Lynn and talk to him.

"We have morning chores to do, and then have to get to our eight o'clock classes, so just know Glen is in good hands here. He won't be going anywhere. See if you can pull that bulletin. I don't want the local Chaffee police showing up here because someone saw the boys walking up our lane or across a field."

Officer Harrison said, "I'll do that, but I'll have to bring a homicide detective with me to question the boys."

John said, "That will be okay. The boys will be safe here."

"John, I asked you not to say anything down there."

Dennis, I'm sorry, but let's get on those barn chores, okay?"

Okay, I'll be down in a minute. Officer Harrison, I know that you care about these boys. They know that we care, too. That's why they came to us. We'll honor that. In the meantime, do what *you* have to do to protect Glen, and we'll see you at noon."

I went back downstairs to the kitchen, and Dr. Lynn glanced from me to John. "What shall we do, boys?"

"Officer Harrison said it would be okay to give them a sedative, so they can get some rest and sleep."

Glen's face and eyes took on fear again. "He's not going to come and get me and take me home, is he?"

"No, but, after you get some breakfast and some sleep, Officer Harrison will come out here at lunch time just to talk with all of us."

Mom had started the coffee pot, and it was beginning to smell good. She made the boys some toast with jelly on it. She said, "I don't want these boys eating too heavy as their bodies might not tolerate food with their tiredness and stress."

Dr. Lynn closed up his doctor's bag, "John, Dennis, I think instead of a sh-h…, I mean injection, I will just give them some of your Mom's Tylenol P.M. One pill should take the edge off and send them off to slumberland."

He handed each of the boys a pill with a glass of white grape juice. Blake took the pill. "I hope we aren't too much trouble."

Mom gave Blake a hug from the side. "Nonsense, we're glad you came to us. That's what God wanted you to do, and I'm glad you did."

Mom looked at the boys and then at us. "Take them to Kaitlynn's room. We'll let them use her bed. Blake, you don't mind staying with Glen, do you?"

"I've spent the last ten hours with him walking and running, I guess I can rest with him, too. Besides, he isn't going to be any good at all if he doesn't get rest, so I'll stay with him. Thanks for taking us in. I would appreciate it if you would do one thing for us though, if you can? I told Glen about Pastor Bishop, and how he used to help me out with my stepdad. Can you call him later and ask him to come over to see Glen?"

I answered before anyone else could. "Of course… we'll call him. Pastor Bishop can, and he will pray for you both. Glen, was it your stepfather who did this to your family?"

He started crying again and said, "Un-huh" while nodding. I couldn't help myself. "Well, Glen, he will pay for his bad deeds, just you wait. I will see to it. That's why John and I are studying to become policemen—to get bad guys like him. Do you know why he did it?"

Glen looked at the wall as though he was seeing right through it. He was thinking through the catastrophe that had taken place in his home last night. He just shook his head and picked up his napkin and wiped at his cheeks.

Blake turned to me. "He told me, the man came home so drunk, he thought his older sister was his wife and wanted her to go to bed with him. She wouldn't do it, and when her mother tried to stop him, he went after the little sister. She's only ten. Then the grandmother got angry and told him to get out of the house and not to come back until he was sober. He left for about twenty minutes and came back and shot them all."

Blake had turned seventeen and not in the prevention program now, but he and Glen had been together in Officer Harrison's program when Glen first started after his thirteenth birthday. They lived next door to each other, so they were neighbors, too. Blake went on to say, "Glen apparently heard the shots and went in the house just after the man shot his grandmother. He aimed the gun at him, and it didn't go off, so he threw it at him. He ran to my house."

I asked Glen, "What is your step-father's name? Glen just looked at me glassy-eyed and shaking.

Dr. Lynn said, "Carry him upstairs and get him in bed."

John picked up Glen and he didn't resist at all. For a fourteen year-old boy, he wasn't much bigger than Paul, but then we are all big tall guys. On the way upstairs, I heard him say, "Bud won't find me here, will he?"

John caught the name and said, "No, Glen, Bud will never find you here. Does Bud have a last name?"

"Williams," Glen quietly said.

I heard John say, "Glen, you go to sleep. We will get Bud Williams and put him behind bars. He will never hurt you here. We big Moore guys will protect you."

According to John, Glen's eyes went closed and he started breathing deeply before he could get out of the room. I had to say, "Thank you, God," again.

John and I went to the barn and the chicken house and did the morning chores. We hadn't lost any time, because the boys had us up earlier than usual. Mom had a breakfast of pancakes and sausage, and I had to make myself eat. Dr. Lynn handed John his car keys and said, "Go ahead and drive my car. See how it drives. You may like it."

"Thanks. I hope you won't need it today, with extra boys in the house."

Mom added, "The boys will sleep until noon, and I will be home then. My car will be available. Leave the truck keys, though."

John handed the truck keys to Dr. Lynn. "We're out of here. Robert will be waiting."

We both kissed Mom good-bye when Steve walked into the kitchen ready for high school.

"What *is* going *on* around here? You all sure made enough noise early this morning. I wanted to get another minute or two of sleep. All the talking got me up."

John and I walked out the door as Mom was explaining. We were quiet on the way to Robert's house. I was trying to think over the previous hour and wondered what would become of Glen. Just before we reached Robert's house, John asked, "Do you know if Glen has any relatives in the area? Someone is going to have to take custody of him. He's still a minor. He certainly won't want to go back to his house, with no one there."

I said, "John, it's interesting that you and I were having the same thoughts. Let's see if Mom will let him stay with us until arrangements for the family and for him can be made. He knows us and seems comfortable around Mom and our family. We can work with him the way we did Robert and Janet Weber in overcoming the tragedy they experienced. If no one comes forth, he surely will go in a foster home anyway."

I don't know why I thought of what I said next, but I said, "He can have the lawn mowing job and be taught to be a landscaper for a project, since the rest of us all have a project to earn our keep."

John smacked the steering wheel. "Good—that'll work. I just mow the lawn because it's one of those things that need to be done, and I don't particularly enjoy it. Dr. Lynn would probably work with him on that. He goes over and mows the lawn at the Jenkins's place when Brian or one of us can't get to it."

We stopped in front of the Webers' house, and Robert was waiting with his heavy backpack. Janet was with him. My heart skipped a couple of beats and I prayed, *Lord, Janet is only seventeen. Please, help me to hold off my feelings for her.*

Janet walked toward the car with Robert. She said, "Good morning, Dennis… John… Do you think you can drop me off at the high school on your way? It doesn't have to be at the front door. A couple of blocks away would be fine. Mom had an early doctor's appointment in Cape Girardeau, and she couldn't wait on me."

John said, "Janet, anytime. We go right by the high school. It's no problem."

Janet giggled her funny little laugh, and said, "I was planning to walk, but Robert said he would hold me on his lap in the truck. I told him, *no.* The accident with Steve was one accident *too* many for me, and for your family, too. Now, this morning you show up with a car. That must have been a God thing. I figured that I could go the five blocks on these crutches, but Robert was adamant about me squeezing in the truck with you all."

John chuckled. "See, Janet, God knows what we need before we ask. Dr. Lynn wants me to buy his car from him, and he handed me the keys this morning and said, 'Drive my car and see if you like it. What do think? Do you think a Buick Riviera is a little too plush for a farm boy?"

Robert laughed. "For you—yes, but my sister, Marianne, will love it."

Janet added, "I don't know about Marianne, but I sure do. It beats having to ride in your old truck."

I couldn't help myself. I pulled a Kaitlynn whenever she was around Matthew before she got real serious with him. I said something stupid. I asked, "Janet, now if I were driving the old truck of Grandpa's and asked you for a date, would you ride in the truck?"

There was silence in the back seat and Robert started laughing. I realized how it sounded, and Janet did, too. She said very meekly, "Dennis, are you asking me for a date? If you are, then the answer is *yes*. If you aren't then the answer is… I might!"

I remembered what Steve said about me having scales over my eyes where Janet was concerned, and I couldn't think quickly to answer her. I felt John's elbow in my ribs really hard, so I said. "Janet, I would love to take you out on a date, but right now our family is in the middle of another crisis, and, hopefully, it'll be settled in about two days. Would you mind if I call you… say, tomorrow night?"

John interrupted, "Janet, if my brother, Dennis, doesn't make arrangements for a date—I will make them for him."

Robert added to it by saying, "And if John doesn't do it, I will. It's about time you two quit avoiding each other when you know you have feelings for each other."

Janet said, "Tha-n-ks… Robert!"

I said, "…and thanks, John!! I think Janet and I will rely on the Lord's timing. Right, Janet?"

We stopped at the high school, and I jumped out and opened the back door for Janet. I held her crutches until she could put her backpack on and then get the crutches situated under her arms. "Thank you, Dennis," she said. "I'll look forward to your call, but don't let my brother and yours push you into something you don't want to do."

I shut the back door and said, "Janet, I think the Lord just gave us a shove, and he used our brothers. I look forward to talking with you."

She smiled her radiant smile and said, "Thanks!'

I hopped back in the car and both Robert and John were laughing. "John, how can you be laughing, at a time like this?"

"I'm laughing because I know God is still working in our lives. He *ain't* done with us, yet. And I know, also, that the situation at home *isn't* going unnoticed by God either. You just wait until we get home. You'll see."

Robert was quiet for the next few minutes on the way to the university. He finally said, "Well, John and Dennis, it sure would be nice if you would share with me the crisis that is going on in your family. After all, both my sisters may be part of your family one day, and you'll be part of mine."

John cleared his throat, "I'm sorry, Robert. I was just thinking through some things. Dennis and I had a real shock around five o'clock this morning."

I said, "And Robert, I apologize. I was just thinking about asking one of my professors to delay my test for a day until we can get what is going on at our house straightened out. I can't seem to think of anything else except Glen. He's one of the boys in the prevention program."

John added, "Do you remember the boy, Blake Hegel, who used to live in Chaffee?"

"Vaguely—why?"

"Well, Blake and Glen showed up at our house this morning around five. They were tired and cold. Apparently, someone had killed Glen's entire family. All we could get out of Glen was the person killed his sisters, mother, and grandmother and tried to kill him, but the gun didn't fire. Glen ran to Blake's house. If Glen was right in his incoherency, it was his step-father who did it. Blake's mother told him to take Glen to us. She said that he would be safe at our place. Mom gave them a little breakfast, and Dr. Lynn checked Glen over briefly and gave him something to help him go to sleep. Officer Harrison is coming out at noon to talk with the boys."

"Man! I heard on the news this morning that they were looking for the fourteen your-old boy, and here you had him at your farm."

I quickly added, "And, please, don't tell anyone. He needs to feel safe at our place. Blake called his mother to let her know that they made it to Chaffee. I hope *she* doesn't say anything to anyone. Officer Harrison is supposed to be looking for Glen's stepfather and putting a block on the news about Glen. Apparently, there are some eager reporters out for any news they can get. Anyway, Robert, John and I were thinking about something, and we are going to pray about it. We would appreciate it if you will pray, also."

I had to think for a second as John pulled onto Highway 55 and headed toward the university. I have a habit of watching the traffic for John, as though I was the one driving. I stopped talking and looked both ways for on-coming traffic. When John had gotten on the highway, I said, "We haven't said anything to the family, but if some relative doesn't come up to take custody of Glen, he will be put in a foster home. I think our family can handle having him stay with us. We talked about having Glen take over all the lawn and landscaping as a project. We were thinking that Dr. Lynn and Brian would be good teachers for him, for our lawn, and over at the Jenkins' farm, too. We could give him some space to grow bushes of different kinds and perhaps boxed flowers to sell in the springtime. He will need some kind of project to make him feel like he *can* do something. He would need to be able to contribute to the family account and to tithe. That reminds me, Robert, have you thought any more about a job?"

"I have one this Friday and Saturday evening from four to nine. Those are dating night, but since I need a car to date and don't have one, I'm free to work. So… believe it or not, I took a chance and called your Cousin Stacy, and as God would have it, she was looking for someone. It will be temporary, but it could become somewhat long term. She told me, 'Tips are good on Friday and Saturday evening. I could make as much as seventy-five dollars in one evening. That would work out well for me. Then I could study during the week. Dad said…." Robert started laughing. "Dad said, 'Robert, I'm glad you are able to start at the bottom and take whatever job you can get. That's spunk in my book.' He looked at me for a second like, *Son, are you dense.* Then I said, Oh, spunk. I thought you said skunk and it was a real put-down. I wondered where the word *spunk* originated. Anyway, If I can make a minimum of one-hundred twenty-five on a weekend, times four weekends, I should be able to save up at least four-hundred a month. I know Dad compares me to you guys, so I want to show him I can do it."

➤ ◄

John parked the car where he normally parks the truck in a university parking lot. He realized the car didn't have a sticker for the parking lot. He said, "Dennis, I don't have the right sticker on this car. I'll get a ticket for parking here."

I didn't see it as a problem and pulled out a sheet of notebook paper, I wrote…*Security Guard—this Buick belongs to Dr. Marshall Lynn. The car is parked in the normal lot for the truck belonging to John and Dennis Moore. John is driving the car today as a replacement for the truck. He will take care of the transfer of the sticker from the truck to the car this afternoon.*

Eight o'clock to twelve o'clock classes prohibit us from doing it this morning... unless you would like to do that for us. Thank you, Dennis Moore.

I handed the note to John and he read it, "Do you think it will work?"

"If it doesn't, I will pay the ten dollar fine."

John said, "Okay," and put the note under the windshield wiper.

We hurried on to the Criminal Justice Building. John went one way, and Robert and I headed to our first class, but first we looked at the bulletin board. We read all the posted notes. I spotted one that looked interesting. The note said, "*Wanted: Student Assistant—Ten hours a week. Call B-U-R--G-L-A-R, or see Dr. S. in the crime lab department. Minimum wage.*

Robert said, "Here's another one." *Wanted: Student Assistant-Fifteen hours. Minimum wage. Must be computer literate. Call: Officer Harrison at 334-J-o-b-s.*

Robert said, "Man, Officer Harrison must never sleep. Do you think this is the same Officer Harrison we know?"

I couldn't help chuckling and shook my head. "I don't know. Which job do you want to check out?"

Robert looked at me, "Well, since I told your Cousin Stacy I would take her job, I think I had better check out the ten hour job. What do you think?"

"Sounds good to me, I said. "Let's hope God has been there before we get there and the jobs will be ours."

We walked into the classroom together. Several students were talking about the quadruple murder in Cape Girardeau the night before. One student said, "They're looking for the kid right now."

Robert and I both shook our heads---like *they don't know what they are talking about,* so I whispered, "I need to talk to the professor before he lines up all the evidence against Glen and lectures on why all evidence points to him."

I shoved my way to the front, "Excuse me, Dr. Stone. I need to see you privately for a moment. Can we go to your office? It won't take more than one to two minutes."

Several students looked at me like, *Moore, you have your nerve.* I didn't care.

"Dr. Stone, it is urgent… before class begins."

"All right, Moore, this better be good."

We went two doors down the hall into Dr. Stone's office. "I apologize for the delay in the class, but I needed to tell you the boy, Glen did *not* kill his family, and he was almost a victim himself only the gun didn't go off. He ran. He ran all night until he reached our farm. Officer Harrison has the boy in his prevention program, and he's aware of where he is. A Detective and Officer Harrison will be talking to him this noon. So, please don't allow the students in the classroom to believe what they heard by some misguided news-reporter who was anxious for a tiny tidbit of news. It looks like the man who did this despicable thing was the boy's stepfather. We don't know that for sure, but we have the boy sedated and before he went to sleep he said, 'please don't let Bud find me.' John asked him if Bud had a last name and he said, 'Williams.'

"Since this all happened last night, and because he didn't show up at our farm until five this morning, and because any student in the class could be related in some way to the man, I would appreciate it if you would wait until tomorrow to have the class talk about evidence. At least wait until Officer Harrison and the detective have a chance to talk with the boy and the search for Bud Williams gets underway."

Dr. Stone said, "Dennis, aren't you a freshman this year?"

I was puzzled, but answered, "Yes."

Then he asked, "How do you know Officer Harrison?"

I wondered where he was going with his questions, but I said, "Because my brother and I have worked with him for two years in his crime prevention program, and I oversee the garden projects the boys do on our farm."

"Are you John Moore's brother?"

I'm sure I hesitated longer than I should, because he went on talking, "If you are, I've been keeping abreast of the program, and what a fantastic job you've been doing and the positive results that are happening with the boys."

I didn't answer his question about John. I just said, "It is a lot of work with no pay, but I've enjoy it and the rewards it brings. Since it doesn't pay, I am looking to work ten or fifteen hours a week. You wouldn't happen to know whose phone number is Burglar, would you?"

He laughed, "We have to get back to class. You are hired."

He walked out of his office with his back to me. I stood there a couple of seconds, and he turned back and said, "I said, you are hired. Start tomorrow afternoon at one o'clock"

My thoughts suddenly went to Robert who wanted the job. I said, "Thank you, Dr. Stone," and followed him back to class and prayed… *Thank you again, God. You go before me, don't you? Thank you.*

The class went smoothly and the professor did bring the murders up, but said, "Class, what you hear on T.V. may not be the truth in the case of the four murders last night, and we will not discuss it today. Tomorrow we will see if more evidence comes in."

Someone had to ask, "But what about the missing boy?"

Dr. Stone glanced my way. "To start with, he is not missing. Secondly, he may have been a victim, also. Don't believe everything you hear on the news. This class looks at facts, and if the news commentators are giving out information before the police or detectives know anything… then be careful. And, I believe we were to have a quiz today. Is everyone ready?"

The professor was handing out his test sheets while looking at me. He said, "How about you, Moore. Are you ready?"

I must have had a negative expression on my face as Dr. Stone said, "Did you hear me, Moore?"

I had to answer something, so I said, "Well, sir, I am *not* quite ready. My mind has had some rather serious matters saturating it for the last twenty-four hours. I should have stayed out of classes today and tended to them, but, sir, I would like to go ahead and try. A fifty grade is better than a zero in figuring up my average." Some in the class were already looking at the quiz, but others were looking at me and some chuckled.

I took the test that was handed to me, and I could see right off that I knew several of the answers, so I prayed a silent prayer. *Lord, a lot these questions are common sense. Give me your wisdom and help me to apply it to the test today, and, Lord, help me to entrust Glen totally to you during this hour.* For the next thirty minutes, I answered all but one of the questions. Some of them, I didn't remember studying, but I did remember John discussing them with me. I was glad for that. Hopefully, I can pass the test.

Students were handing their tests in and leaving the room. Robert left about five minutes before I finished. He's a good student. When I handed the test to Dr. Stone, he said, "Let me grade it before you leave. There is no sense concerning you with one more thing today."

He took the test and started making it with red check marks. I couldn't believe that I had gotten those questions wrong. He put an A-minus at the top of the page and asked, "What were you worried about?"

I looked at the test and said, "I thought your check marks meant the answers were wrong."

He said, "No. That means I have read that one. If it is wrong, it gets a slash and a note. You only missed one question."

"Whew! Dr. Stone... are you sure you are grading *my* paper?"

"Dennis, didn't you think you could do it. You got them all right, except..." He was looking down the paper. "You missed the one you left blank."

I looked back at the class and the last student was going out of the door. He said, "You left blank... "When a policeman comes upon a situation that looks suspicious does he: A. Unsnap his holster. B. Proceed with caution and observe the surrounding. C. Call for back-up. D. All of the above.

"Dr. Stone, I remember reading that. My mind was on Glen between every question. The answer to that is D, but I'll take the A-minus or even a B-Plus. I am happy with that."

He just said, "Keep up the good work, Dennis."

I know I must have had a little boy smile on my face when I said, "Thanks" and turned toward the door. Officer Harrison came rushing into the room and nearly bumped into me. "Just the one I'm looking for."

Dr. Stone got up from his desk, "Me or Dennis?"

"Well... I was looking for Dennis, but you can be privy to the information. Dennis, Bud Williams was found at the Golden Rod Bar. He was drunk and blabbing his mouth off about getting that no good stepson of his who got away. The bartender asked him if he knew anything about the two women and two girls who had been shot last night. He was stupid enough and drunk enough to talk. He said, 'They deserved it. Do you want me to shoot you, too? This place ain't big enough for me and those bossy women. I wasn't gonna hurt those two stupid girls. They needed to be taught how to make love to a man, and he uttered a big hearty laugh.' Fortunately, your call this morning allowed us to put a tail on him and one of our plain-clothes-men had already located him and heard him blabbing his mouth off, so he sat on the bar stool right beside him. Bud was arrested and went without incident.

"Now, Dennis, we have a problem. What to do with Glen? We still want to talk with him, but we'll wait until he wakes up. I'll call Dr. Lynn in just a few minutes and let him know not to wake the boys up at noon.

"What I need from you, Dennis and John, is to be a big brother for about four or five days… at least until we find a family member who will take custody of him or the right foster home. Do you think your mother and Dr. Lynn can handle having him under your roof with Paul's health for a couple of days?"

My mind was swimming at that moment with all kinds of thoughts, so I said, "Officer Harrison, I can only ask them. However, I think God is ahead of us both. John and I discussed this very thing this morning on the way here. Do you think the Division of Family Services would approve our home as a foster home if no one steps up to claim custody of Glen? That really won't be necessary though, if we can get John appointed legal guardian. I'm only nineteen. However, John has been declared a legal adult since he was seventeen. He's twenty-one now. What do you think?"

Officer Harrison looked at Dr. Stone, "What do you say? We test this kid out of everything and put him on staff here or the police force. He not only has discernment, but a gift of serving or service."

I said, "Thank you for the compliment, but I have another class to get to."

"Before you go, there is one more thing I really need to talk to you and John about. The police department has a social worker who will help Glen with a funeral, but Glen knows you best of all. He needs to feel he has a place with you before we take him back to his house or plan a funeral… even if he goes elsewhere with family."

"Officer Harrison, I know a lot has been dumped in your lap because Glen is in your program, but let's not make decisions right now. Let me talk with my family. Dr. Lynn and Mom will be parenting Glen if he stays with us. They'll help Glen with the funerals, and we have a super pastor and church that'll help. Besides, surely Glen's stepmother had a family somewhere, and they might surface pretty quickly."

Students were wandering into the classroom, and I began edging my way out. Dr. Stone said, "Remember, Dennis, one o'clock tomorrow, the department offices."

I reached out my hand to shake Dr. Stone's hand, and he didn't know for a second if that's what I meant to do. I guess it isn't a customary thing for students to shake the professor's hand. He did take my hand and I shook it. "Thanks, Dr. Stone, for the job."

Officer Harrison's eyebrows went up. "Dennis, I didn't know you were looking for work. I would have hired you."

Dr. Stone laughed. "Sorry, Harrison. He's mine now."

I remembered Robert. "Officer Harrison, Robert Weber is looking for a job. He needs to get a vehicle to drive and needs a job to make payments. John is going to purchase Dr. Lynn's car, so we'll have something reliable to go back and forth from Chaffee to the university here. Grandpa's old truck is about to fall apart. Robert can't depend on us all four years of the university here, so he's looking for a part-time job on campus."

I looked at my watch and it was one-minute before the next bell. "I'll talk to you later, Office… call Dr. Lynn, would you?"

He pulled out his phone as he walked out of the classroom with me. My classroom was two doors down the hall. I walked in as the bell was ringing. I took my place and took notes all during class, but I had the worst time trying to concentrate. The next class was better. I finally prayed and asked God to quiet my heart and thoughts and to give us wisdom and peace about Glen.

I left my last class at ten till twelve and met John and Robert at the car. Sure enough, John found a notice on the car—Dr. Lynn's car. The notice said, *This is a warning. You have twenty-four hours to purchase this car and take care of the transfer of parking permits. I'll give you $200.00 for your old truck. Call security T-i-c-k-e-t-s. Ask for Jud Redman.*

John was laughing and said, "Do you think the truck is worth two-hundred dollars or is it worth more for us to use on the farm?"

Robert interrupted, "He probably looks on the truck as a classic vehicle and will restore it. Does your Mom have any sentiment attached to the truck because it was her dad's truck?

John said, "I hadn't thought of that. Mom is home for lunch. Let me call her."

He pulled out his phone and was dialing. I reached for his phone, "Let me talk to her. You drive." He handed the phone to me as it was ringing.

Dr. Lynn answered, "Pop, did Officer Harrison call you?"

"Yes, about an hour ago. We're glad Glen has been cleared, even though *we* knew he wasn't guilty. He woke up around eleven this morning… wailing. It was like a sick animal. Harrison said to let him sleep. He told me about the influence you and John have had on Glen, and he suggested Glen stay with us for several days. I need to talk to your mother, but what would you say if I decided to seek legal custody of the boy?"

I know I must have paused a long time, because he said, "Dennis?"

I said, "God is one step ahead of us again. I had thought

maybe John could become his legal guardian, but… you… that's even better. You asked me what I would say. I would have to say, 'Thank you, Lord, again.'"

John said, "The truck, Dennis!"

"Oh, I need to talk to Mom."

Mom came to the phone, so I asked, "Mom, how sentimental are you over the truck, since it was your dad's?"

She chuckled. "You mean that thing out in the drive with four wheels and a brown fender, green doors and rust on the bumper? My heart would weep for joy to see it gone, but you guys have to decide what to do with it."

"Well, here, talk to John. He's had an offer on the truck."

Mom apparently told John to do what he wanted with the truck. Grandpa left it to him. John either didn't know that, or didn't remember it.

"Okay, Mom, we're going over to the Traffic Office to change over the truck to the car for our parking lot permit. Then we'll stop somewhere for a hamburger and then come on home. I have a heap of studying to do… Okay… Bye."

That was the gist of the conversation. John put his phone away. "I wish we had Steve with us to negotiate the price."

Robert asked, "Why?"

We both laughed. "Because the security man wouldn't know what happened before Steve had five-hundred dollars out of the man."

Robert has an allergy cough and he coughed and said, "Well, ask for five hundred. He can't do any more than say *no*. He may come back and say three-fifty… bargain with him."

"John, let's do it," I said.

I was all for trying, anyway. We parked the car and walked to the university's traffic office and took care of the parking sticker and then went to the security office. The man was about ready to leave. John looked at the man's badge and name tag. "Officer Redman, I'm John Moore. My old truck is yours for five hundred. It's worth that much to use on the farm. I can't imagine why you would want an old multi-colored truck with high mileage."

"I need it to restore another one… three-fifty. Take it or leave it."

John looked at Robert and said, "Four-hundred and it's yours this afternoon."

There was a slight look of disbelief when he looked at Robert and me, but he said, "We'll have it here for you in the morning. Where would you like me to park it?"

The security guard smiled from ear to ear, "I'll come and get it… four-thirty this afternoon. Where's it located?"

I answered, "It's on our farm on route seventy-seven, Chaffee. I'll put a bandanna on the mailbox. It is exactly two miles south of Chaffee."

John said, "I would prefer a money order or cashier's check, if you don't mind."

I could see by the security guard's face that he was surprised at John's request. He said, "That's fine, but I'm not sure I will be able to get to a bank before closing time. Are you sure you won't take a check?"

John smiled. "A check will be fine as long as you give me permission to print your name on a bill board or the front page of the newspaper if it bounces."

He laughed. "You have my word. Do you always do business in such a hard-nosed fashion?"

I laughed, too, and said, "He doesn't usually, but he's learning from our brother Steve, who drives a hard bargain on everything." John looked at me like… *I can answer for myself.*

We got back in the car and headed south to highway 74 and on to Chaffee. Robert was quiet for a while. He sat back and leaned his head against the top of the back of the seat like he was thinking. He sat forward quickly. "Dennis, I saw Officer Harrison in the hall and he approached me about the job he had posted. I understand Dr. Stone hired you for the ten-hour-a-week job."

"Yes, I would have preferred the fifteen-hour job. I asked Dr. Stone whose phone was Bur-Glar… he said, 'why, are you looking for a job?'"

"I said, 'Yes,' and he said, 'You're hired.' He started walking off and turned around and said, 'I said you are hired. It's time to get to class.'"

Robert cleared his throat, "Well, Officer Harrison hired me. I took the job, but I'm not sure I can handle fifteen hours."

John turned to Robert, "Robert that's only three hours a day— Monday through Friday. What do you have to do beside home chores and study?"

I thought John's tone of voice sounded a bit harsh, so I said, "Robert, I can check with Dr. Stone and switch jobs if you'd prefer. It makes no difference to me."

"Let me try it for a while. I may be able to get whatever needs to be done in ten hours. Ten times five is fifty dollars a week or two hundred a month. I should be able to find a car for that amount for a payment each month. I'm not going to look to Dad for any help. Now… if he should offer…."

I could not help feeling that God had placed us in the job that He wanted us to have, so I said, "Robert, let's work the jobs the rest of this semester and see what happens. I think God has been staying one step ahead of us, for whatever reason, and we both got a job at the university, *today*. Let's thank God for the jobs and see what happens."

━ ━

We drove on toward Chaffee, and Robert said, "I thought we were going to stop for a hamburger, I'm hungry."

We were within two miles of Chaffee, when John remembered, "Oh, guys, I had so much on my mind, I forgot. Do you want to stop somewhere?"

Robert said, "No, Chaffee only has the Café' and I don't feel like being waited on by some old lady who looks like she needs a cane and probably takes her teeth out at night… and, yes, I know she was kind enough to give me a job and she is nice and all that."

"John, the boy's blood sugar is low. Give me your cell phone." I dialed Cousin Stacy at the Café and said, "This is an emergency. Can you prepare three hamburgers, hold the onions, and have them ready to go in…" I looked at my watch, "…in ten minutes?"

She said, "Dennis… how about fries and a chocolate shake to go with it?"

She started laughing. "My boys are hungry, right?"

I had to laugh. "You know my voice like God knows it, huh?"

She yelled the order back to the cook and then said, "I not only know your voice, but I want to see your face once in a while. Say, Dennis, I hired Robert Weber for Friday and Saturday rush time, I need someone to come and train him? Do you think Steve would be willing to come in tonight and tomorrow evening to train Robert? I don't know if I can reach Robert, but I would like for him to come in for an hour this evening and tomorrow evening and learn the ropes before the dining room gets busy on Friday and Saturday."

I said, "Cousin Stacy, for the price of that hamburger, I will deliver Robert to you in five minutes."

She laughed and said, "Oh, one of the hamburgers is for Robert, huh?"

Comin' right up served on our finest platter—Dr. Lynn's car."

She laughed her jolly laugh again and said, "See you in just a few minutes."

Robert asked, "What was that all about?"

John said, "Sounds like you are going to be served as something or for something. Reckon it's a paper to appear in court?"

Robert wasn't in a good mood for some reason. I told him Cousin Stacy would like for him to come in for an hour this evening and tomorrow evening for training and she wondered if Steve could come in and train you.

Robert didn't say anything. John parked the car, and we walked a half-block up to the Café.' Cousin Stacy was waiting for us with her usual jovial persona. When she saw Robert, she said, "Just the person I want to see. After I talked to you the other day, I realized that it would be difficult to train you when we're so busy, so if you can, would you come in an hour this evening and tomorrow evening and Steve can come in to train you. It would be great if you can. Those Steve's trained have been the best employees."

She sat us at our usual table and a waitress was beside her already to take our drink orders. Cousin Stacy said, "What will you have to drink today?"

As we each said what we would have to drink, the waitress wrote the order on her pad. Cousin Stacy said, "By the way, this is Susan Harris. She's new in town. Her grandparents bought the old Comstock place down the road from you. She's working here in the daytime and going to the university in the evening."

Cousin Stacy pointed to each of us. "This is Robert Weber, and my cousins, Dennis and John Moore."

She smiled a radiant smile and said, "Glad to meet you. I'll get your drinks."

When she walked off toward the kitchen, Robert said, "I'll take *her* to train me." He laughed for the first time.

Cousin Stacy said, "She's a very sweet girl. I hope she can continue to work for me for a long time. But Robert, she won't be able to train you. Her classes begin at six."

John asked, "How old is she? She looks awfully young to be a university student."

She *is* young. She's sixteen and taking three classes at the high school in the mornings and then two classes in the Excel program in the evening at the university. She'll be seventeen in just a few days, but she's very mature for her age. She's had a pretty tough time growing up... lost both her parents and a little brother in a car accident. She moved here with two younger brothers to live with her grandparents."

She walked up behind Cousin Stacy with our drinks and hamburgers. She placed them in front of us like a pro. Cousin Stacy said, "Enjoy! I've got to get back to work."

As the waitress walked off, Robert said, "I think I just found my next project."

John quickly added, "And you had better remember your priorities while you are working the project. Growing in your relationship with the Lord is your *first* priority. The second is your family. Your studies are next and then your job, and then if you have time—a girlfriend. Only when you marry do the priorities change. Then, your wife takes second place after the Lord. Your job is a necessary part of your life, but God is still the director over you."

Robert said, "Such a killjoy you are!"

By the time we left the café, Robert was in a better mood. I thought, *Tomorrow I am going to make sure he has eaten breakfast, even if we have to stop at a McDonald's for a biscuit.* As we were leaving, Robert told Cousin Stacy, "I'll be here later this afternoon."

I added, "If Steve doesn't come, I'll be here."

We dropped Robert off at his house on our way back to the farm. As we drove up the lane, I could see several vehicles in the drive and in the yard. Mom was home from the office already, and

Steve was home from school. Officer Harrison was there with a detective and *so was* a television crew. I could tell by Mom's face, not a person was coming in the house without her permission. Mom's lawyer drove in right behind us.

John said, "What a mess! How am I going to get the truck cleaned up without someone standing over me asking questions or poking a microphone in front of my face?"

He looked at his watch and then at me. I answered his question for him.

"Tell you what… I have to go get a bandanna to put on the mailbox. Let me get some grocery sacks while I am in the house. Take the truck down to the mailbox and clean it out down there."

We both got out of the truck and started to go toward the house. John just seemed to be bewildered with everything. The news lady was heading our way with a cameraman, and I was the first one she reached. She put the microphone in front of my face and said, "I understand you have been harboring a criminal here on the farm."

Anger went all through me and I said, "May I hold the microphone?"

Without thinking she said, "Yes," and handed to me.

"Come with me," I said. John was looking at me like… *What does he think he's doing?* "John, …the truck, Com'on." He followed me, as did the cameraman.

When we reached the truck, I reached over the side and took John's tool box with one hand and handed it to John. He reached over for a shovel, too. I walked to the other side and took out a rake and another shovel and handed them to the news lady. "Here, take this and follow John."

We cleaned out the back end of garden tools, while I kept the microphone. The cameraman was *very* annoyed, but was polite to his partner. "Adrienne, we have a deadline to meet."

John looked at me, "Dennis, what is *our* deadline?" I looked at my watch and it was already two-twenty p.m.

I know I had a smirk on my face, but I couldn't help it. "John, we have only two hours and ten minutes. Shall we get the stuff from the inside?"

I had given myself enough time to get over a little anger and think about what to say to them. I said, "On this farm we are all involved in a crime prevention program. We work with kids during the planting season on through the harvest. Two of us are attending the Southeast Missouri Law Enforcement Academy. With the love we have for kids in impoverished families and our dislike for crime, do you think we would harbor a criminal? If you are looking for the murderer, who murdered the two girls and the two women, you are wasting time here in Chaffee. The murderer has been caught, arrested, and is jail in Cape Girardeau. Here's your microphone. You had better be on your way, if you want to be first with the news."

The news gal asked, "But what is Officer Harrison doing here? We followed him. It was our understanding he *works* with the boy who is missing, and *he's* a suspect? What is Officer Harrison doing here, and the detective, too? We followed them."

John stepped up behind me and said, "Officer Harrison has come to this farm… what would you say, Dennis, forty times?"

I laughed and said, "Well, maybe not forty, perhaps twenty. Shall we go in and see if he's staying for supper."

The man with the camera was talking on his cell phone or I-phone, whichever it was, and said, "Let's go! I just called the courthouse and, yes, they have their man. We're sorry to have bothered you."

The lady introduced herself, then added, "Yes, I'm sorry to

have bothered you, but I would like to do a story on the crime-prevention program and the boy's gardens. Would you allow us to come back and talk with you again?"

John looked toward the house, but said, "Yes, but you'll need to wait until April or May and then talk with Officer Harrison or the other administrators in the program."

The cameraman had loaded up his equipment in the trunk of his van and said, "Let's go."

The lady said, "Thank you for your time. We're sorry we bothered you."

As she walked to the passenger side of the T.V. van, I heard her say. "I know there's a story here. My instincts tell me that kid is here."

She climbed in the van, and they took off down the lane. I thought *If they wanted something to do… I could have given her my bandanna, and had her put it on the mailbox.*

John was out of breath. "We need to hurry."

I ran into the barn and found two plastic bags in the feed room and took one to John. He said, "Don't leave anything behind. There might be something of Grandpa's that Mom might want."

I started on the passenger side and took every scrap of paper and anything that didn't belong to the truck. I reached under the seat and pulled out everything there. I almost stood on my head to reach under the seat and behind it, also. There was something with a metal clasp on it, but I couldn't see what it was. I asked John to check from his side to see if he could see it. We finally decided time or not, we would take the back of the seat out of the truck

John said, "Here take this. I found it in the tack room." It was an old deteriorated scarf. It must have been Dad's or Grandpa's scarf.

John said, "Take Dr. Lynn's car. Here's the key. Take the bandanna down to the mailbox and I'll work on this. We've been home thirty-five minutes and haven't even been in the house yet, and I'm getting eager to see what's going on."

I took Dr. Lynn's car and went back down the lane to the mailbox and put the bandanna on the mailbox flag and came back.

Steve came out of the house, "Mom wants you both in the house just as soon as you can come in."

John said, "Steve, we need to take the back of the seat out and get every item out of here. We sold the truck and the man is coming at four-thirty to pick it up. There is something under the seat that we can't reach, and I want to make sure that it isn't something Grandpa or Grandma lost in the truck. Mom may want it."

There was a small latch and between Steve and John the back of the seat came right out. John was able to get the item and it was a bracelet that was Grandma's. She had hoped to give it to Mom, but she had lost it. I remember Grandpa commenting about the bracelet to Mom once.

He said it had at least two carets of small diamonds on it. Steve looked at the bracelet and said, "Man, this could be worth more than two old trucks."

I said, "Thank you again, Lord. This will make Mom happy."

It took another few minutes to get everything out of the truck. I took the plastic sacks and put them in the barn. John had the bracelet in his pocket. He said, "I'll wait until everyone is gone from the house so Mom can enjoy the discovery more."

We all went into the house. Blake and Glen were eating a sandwich and Mom had placed a plate of cookies on the table. Paul was sitting at the kitchen table with the two boys. Officer Harrison, another man, who was a detective, and Mom's lawyer were at the dining room table with Mom and Dr. Lynn.

Steve sat at the kitchen table and promptly took two cookies, saying, "I baked these cookies. I can show *you* how to bake cookies like these."

Blake said, "Maybe someday," but Glen didn't answer. It looked like he was having trouble getting the sandwich to go down. On my way past his chair, I stopped and squeezed his shoulders and said, "Buddy, we're here for you. You have a place at our table anytime or for all the time."

He swallowed and choked back tears and said, "Thanks."

John and I went on into the dining room and sat. I apologized for not coming right in. I told them Officer Redman from the university security office was coming after the truck. For some reason, he wanted it this afternoon. Officer Harrison said, "The man deals in classic cars and trucks and has an antique car show coming up in three months. I've seen some of his restorations. He's quite good at it."

I laughed. "Robert replaced Steve at the bargain table. Redman offered John two-hundred dollars and Robert said, 'Tell him five and he may come back with three-fifty.'"

"John told the man, 'I'll take four and you can have it today.' Redman said 'Sold.'"

Mom looked at John, "Good for you, John."

Mom's lawyer and Dr. Lynn were at the other end of the table from Officer Harrison and Mom, so I asked, "What's goin' on?"

"They're drawing up papers for Dr. Lynn to take legal guardianship of Glen and to have physical custody of him. My lawyer is going to take the papers to a judge to see if he can get the papers signed as soon as possible.

"Marshall and I have discussed it with Glen. He said, 'I don't care... I don't care about anything.' We feel he needs some real loving right now, and to be put in a half-way house or a foster home would be adding damage to injury. He needs to develop some coping mechanisms to get him through the next day or two. We want to help him get dresses for the girls and everything else ready for the funeral. I think it will be something he can do for them as a final closure on his family. Some of the church ladies will be going into the house and cleaning it after the detectives get through. Pastor Bishop came by about thirty minutes before Officer Harrison arrived and prayed with the boys.

"The funeral home called, also, and they said they would wait another two days for Glen to be able to make some decisions."

John was just sitting there shaking his head. I asked him what he was thinking. He said, "I just never thought we would become so involved with the boys, but I can see that our kind of program prevents kids from growing up and becoming just like Glen's stepfather. They need some substance in their lives. Some sense of belonging to something good and a desire to make life better for themselves and others."

I looked at Officer Harrison and said, "I'm concerned with what happens to all those boys who turn sixteen and are no long eligible for the program."

Officer Harrison raised his shoulders and back down again, and shook his head negatively. "Dennis, do you have any suggestions?"

"Yes, but... you will need some volunteers to oversee the program... that will...." I didn't get to finish my sentence.

Our conversation with Officer Harrison ended when Mom's lawyer asked her to come to the other end of the table and sign some papers. I watched Mom and Dr. Lynn sign the papers. The lawyer said, 'You realize now that extended family members can step in and say no to you, and say they want the boy."

Both Mom and Dr. Lynn said, "We are aware."

Officer Harrison was still thinking and waiting for me to finish answering his question. I looked at him. "Oh, I'm sorry.

This day has been anything but normal and I'm having a mental problem staying with one subject. Tell you what… let me pick Blake's mind and see if he agrees or disagrees with my idea, then I'll write it down and work out the details with you. I would have to do some checking on some of the details, too."

Our attention went to the dining room when the lawyer and Dr. Lynn stood and shook hands. He was leaving. Officer Harrison and the detective stood and shook both Mom and Pop's hands, too. They left, but as they went through the kitchen they each stopped and patted Glen on the back or put a hand on his shoulder and said, "Glen, we're here for you. Make us your family now."

He just looked at the plate of cookies on the table and said quietly, "Okay."

I asked the detective if he had cleared Glen of everything. He said, "Yes, the perpetrator was consistent in what he said he did, and with what Glen has said. We just hope Glen can get strong enough to testify against him."

Officer Harrison decided he could take Blake home. His mother was concerned about him, and she had called twice.

The phone started ringing again, and Steve grabbed the phone. It was Cousin Stacy asking if Steve had agreed to come in and train Robert Weber. I had forgotten to say anything to Steve.

John said, "Tell her yes, I will take you in town. How long will she want you there—two hours as usual?"

Steve said, "Yes," to Cousin Stacy and shook his head *yes* John. When Steve hung up the phone, John looked up at the clock on the kitchen wall and said, "Well… Steve, go out and check on your cattle and check the water level and put some feed in the outdoor trough under the canopy. They've only had hay for two days."

John sounded like Dad or Grandpa ordering Steve to do something but Steve asked, "Is Robert going to need to be picked up?"

John said, "Call him."

I could tell by John's voice that this day was another one he wanted to mark off the calendar and none too soon.

The phone rang again, while it was in still in Steve's hand. He smiled really big and looked at John. Then he asked, "Do you need me to pick you up? …Okay. …I'll tell him that."

"John, Robert has a surprise for you, and I'm supposed to tell you that."

He turned back to talking to Robert. "I'll see you in about twenty minutes. My girls out in the pasture need me." Steve left the room laughing.

On the way out of the kitchen, Steve stopped and said, "Blake call me anytime, okay? Come to me if you need me. I have big shoulders and can handle most anything. Glen, I'm here for you, too, Buddy. I really look forward to some good times together. Please think about what Mom and Pop talked about. I could stand to have a brother between Paul and me."

Paul's face took on a negative expression for an instant, but he changed it immediately and said, "Glen… me, too. Steve sometimes seems *way too* old for me. It'll be nice to have someone closer to my age."

Steve said, "I gotta go. Those girls in the pasture are waiting' on me."

It was about 4:10 p.m. when Officer Harrison, Blake, the detective, and the lawyer left. Officer Redman drove in the drive about ten minutes later. I was glad they hadn't all been there at the same time. John had the truck title ready for the man, and Officer Redman gave him a check. Dr. Lynn and Glen were left alone in the house as John, Mom, Paul and I went out to see the old truck leave the farm for the last time.

Mom said, "Part of my past just left, and it's a part I don't mind seeing go."

John chuckled. "You would have, if Dennis and I hadn't cleaned it out and found this."

John reached in his pocket and handed Mom the diamond bracelet that had been missing for fifteen or more years. Mom's face was a picture. She was totally surprised. I thought she was going to cry. "Mom's bracelet! After all these years, and it was in the old truck. Oh, Momma, if only we had found it for you before you died."

Mom swallowed and she looked at the bracelet in silence.

As we walked back to the house, I said, "God has a blessing for us even in such a day as this. Thank you, Lord."

Mom said, "Yes, thank you, Lord, for giving me such great caring sons and for helping us all to love and help Glen."

Paul heard what we had said. "Mom, let me help with Glen, too."

I was surprised at his request, but Mom said, "Son, Glen needs all of us—*all* of us. He especially needs the Lord, right now. Let's stop right here in the yard and pray."

We all stopped on our way to the house and Mom prayed. "Dear Father, God, we need you right now. We need your wisdom and guidance in our lives every day. Especially right now, we want to lift Glen up to you. He will be lost without his family. Fill that huge void in his life and give him strength the next few days. Help him to make decisions for his family. Help us to support him at all times. Forgive us for our failures, and... Lord, Thank you for my mother's bracelet. It gives me something tangible here on earth of my mother's. Help Glen to choose things from his family to keep memories alive for him. We will love him as you have loved us. Thank you, Lord, for your love. We pray in the name of Jesus, amen."

Steve walked up behind us, "Are you all praying? That's what I was doing out with those Hereford girls."

Paul said, "Let Glen sleep in my room tonight, please, Mom."

I put my hand on Paul's shoulder. "Paul, let Glen decide. He may want to sleep in Kaitlynn's room again. He may feel a part of that room already."

Paul meekly answered, "Okay."

We went on to the house and just as we entered the back porch Paul said, "I have something I want to tell Glen."

I tensed up, thinking Paul might say something inappropriate for such a tension-filled time as today had been. I under estimated my youngest brother, who was almost 12 years old. Dr. Lynn was still sitting at the kitchen table with Glen.

Paul plopped himself down hard in a chair beside Glen. The chair scooted on the kitchen floor in Glen's direction. Mom frowned at Paul. "Slow down, son, that's a good way to break a chair."

"I'm sorry, Mom."

He reached over and put his hand on Glen's arm and said, "Glen, our family has a motto. It's *All for one and one for all.* That means that when one of us has a problem or a hurt of some kind, the whole family helps that one person. Right now, I feel like God wants you to be part of our family and we're going to help you. You are the *one* now and someday, you will be the one that does things for *all* of us."

John was standing closer to Glen and Paul than I was, and he put his hand on Glen's shoulder and Paul's and said, "Agreed!" I couldn't help myself. I reached over and put my hand on the back of Glen's hand that he had on the table and said, "Agreed." Dr. Lynn put his hand on mine and then Steve and Mom put their hands on top of his. We all said, "Agreed." Then Dr. Lynn said, "What do you say, Glen? Will you unite with us as one and agree?"

Glen's head came up and his eyes swept quickly from Dr. Lynn to Mom and then to Steve and Paul. I shook my head in a *yes* fashion and Glen said quietly, "Agreed."

Paul yelled, "Y-e-a-h! Let's celebrate with some ice cream."

Mom nixed that as it was supper fixing time. Mom frowned and said to Paul, "Just as soon as we eat something more substantial."

John was looking at the kitchen clock, but turned to Steve. "Steve, you need to scoot and pick up Robert."

He looked at the clock and said, "Oh, I just came in from the barn. I'll need to shower and shave. Can you take me into town?"

Mom said, "You told Robert, you would be there in twenty minutes. You'd better call him first."

"Yeah, Mom, I'll call him on the upstairs phone. I'll be out of here in 15 minutes or less."

John looked at Mom with a sigh, and Mom said, " Steve, hurry and get your shower. You can take my car."

Steve yelled as he hurried upstairs, "Thanks, Mom."

Paul looked over at Glen and said, "We aren't old enough to drive, but we will be someday, and that is what 'all for one and one for all' means. Steve's truck got wrecked, so Mom is letting Steve drive her car, and this morning Dr. Lynn let John drive his car. Someday, when we have to go somewhere, then we get to drive someone's car. At least until we get our own wheels."

Glen looked at Paul like... You're crazy.

I had to come to Paul's aid and say, "Glen, in this family, it works that way."

Mom glanced at the clock, "Steve will be coming through this kitchen at sixteen minutes before five and he will be saying, 'Mom, where's your car keys?' I'm going to put them right here on this countertop. Don't any of you forget. Let Steve know where they are."

I said, "Okay, Mom, since your number-one cook assistant is going to leave, would you like for me to help you fix supper?"

Dr. Lynn did a little humpf sound, "I'll tell you what... Let's all pile in my car and go in town to the café after Steve leaves. Let's do it quickly while Steve is picking up Robert, so we will be all seated when they arrive at the café."

Mom looked at Glen and back at Dr. Lynn, "Oh, I don't know. That might make Glen a little nervous being out in public so soon."

John was putting his books on the dining room table and said, "I have to study. Just bring me back a plate of Cousin Stacy's good meat loaf if she has any tonight."

I started laughing and said, "Let's do it. Paul, are you with us?"

"Yeah, Let's go."

Mom nixed it, "Not so fast, Paul, Steve is still here."

Glen turned in his chair and got up. "I need to go to the bathroom, and I think I look awful. I've had these clothes on since yesterday morning."

I remembered something. "Mom, that box of clothes sitting in the corner in Paul's room... they were Steve's and my clothes that you were waiting for Paul to grow into. Something may fit Glen, or they may all fit him now."

Mom's eyes lit up. "Glen, come with me." They got up and went to the bedroom off the kitchen and I heard Mom saying, "In this family, we don't throw anything away. From John... Dennis gets his clothes... then Steve gets them from Dennis. Then if it is still wearable, we wait for Paul to grow into them. Now, it looks like we have the perfect person to step into them."

I followed Mom and Glen to the bedroom and lifted the box

onto the bed. I pulled the tape off and pulled out some pocket T-shirts and underwear from the top. Glen reached for a green T-shirt. The sizes all looked like they were a sixteen and would be just perfect for Glen. Mom lifted out several pairs of jeans and said, "Here's a fourteen. I think that should be your size."

Mom pulled out a smaller box from the bottom of the closet. It had a large baggie of socks and a good pair of tennis shoes that Steve had purchased. A month later, he complained that they were getting too small. Mom made him stop wearing them because he was going through a rapid growth spurt, and there was no sense in ruining the shoes.

She handed Glen a pair of socks and the tennis shoes, and said, "Go to the bathroom in here and wash from your waist up and then put these things on. You can take a shower before you go to bed. You can try the other things on for size, later. If the shoes don't fit, just leave them here and wear what you have on."

Mom left the room and I got a washcloth and towel for Glen. "Glen, if you don't feel like going and want to stay home, I'll stay with you."

Glen hesitated, but said. "No, I have to make myself live. I'll go. I may not eat anything, but I'll go."

"Okay, Glen, remember we're with you. Hurry, because Steve is going to be leaving in about three minutes."

I left the bathroom and shut the door. I went back to the kitchen, but I was thinking, *this is not a good idea for Glen to go out.* Mom looked at me as I pulled out a chair from the table. "Mom, do you think Glen will come to feel like he is one of us, and do you think he should stay home? I'll stay home with him."

Mom had a serious look on her face. "To answer your first question, left to himself, *no,* but, with our prayer, God's help, and our patience and love, I think he will do okay. We will have to think of a project for him, though, so he will feel some worth around here and not just dependent on all of us."

I couldn't help myself, I almost felt giddy. "Mom, John and I came up with an idea. "We'll teach him to be a landscaper. He will learn to use the riding mower and do the landscaping. Aunt Susan can help him with learning about different fertilizers and teach him to take cuttings. We can give him a piece of ground, and it'll be his to start a nursery. If that isn't where his talents lie... he'll change the course for us, but I suspect that he will enjoy it like he did when he was doing his garden with the crime prevention project. He seemed to have a natural interest in how things grow and how his garden was doing. When he starts making money for his work, he'll get into it. What do you want to bet, he will spend time with his plants and find some comfort with God there."

Dr. Lynn came to the kitchen, "Dennis, where do you come up with these ideas? I think that's a wonderful idea, but let's not say anything until after all the big decisions are made and there's a little grieving time. I suspect there are a lot more tears that need to come to the surface. There is some anger, too, that he will process, also. Tomorrow, we have to get everything expedited, so the necessary funeral decisions can be made."

Mom said, "I plan to go into Cape Girardeau with Glen tomorrow and get the girls some new dresses for burial."

Pop was listening and had a thoughtful look on his face, "Let me go with you. He will need to make decisions for the caskets and all, so I'll help him with that. I suspect he will need a man to lean on at that time."

Steve came downstairs and said, "Mom, Where're your car keys?"

I said, "Right there on the countertop, where Mom left them for you. Tell Robert hello, and I hope he likes the job, okay?"

Steve grabbed the keys. "Bye Mom, Pop and...." Glen was

standing in the doorway of the downstairs bedroom looking real spiffy. The shirt and pants and even the shoes were a perfect fit. There was a faint smile on his face.

I noticed Steve's expression of surprise when he glanced up at Glen, "Well, look at my new brother. He looks better in those clothes than I did."

Steve started toward the back door, but turned back to Glen. "I'll see you when I get home, Glen."

Steve did a little wave of his hand and hurried out the back door to Mom's car. I couldn't help smiling and saying, "Glen, you do look pretty darn good. I hope you're feeling better, too."

Pop said, "Well, is everyone ready?"

We watched Steve drive down the lane and we all headed out to Dr. Lynn's car and John yelled. "Make that meatloaf with a baked potato. Forget everything else"

As we were getting in the car, I said, "Mom, ask Cousin Stacy to fix two plates. Make one with raw broccoli and bean sprouts, if she has them. We'll give that plate to him first."

Dr. Lynn said "There is nothing wrong with enjoying a little humor when the stress is high. In fact it helps the body to relax."

We were about five minutes behind Steve getting to the Café when Glen quietly said, "I need a truckload right now."

I realized then, that my humor in front of Glen might not be appropriate and said, "Glen, I'm sorry. I hope I didn't offend you with my remarks on fixing John's take-out plate."

"No, when this is all over, I hope to enjoy a lot of humor. I know Mom, Grandma, and my sisters are probably enjoying a lot of humor in heaven right now. I have to keep thinking about that. I suspect they met Dad and he's telling my little sister why the sky is blue and telling Mom to help me do what is right on earth."

I was surprised that Glen was able to verbalize his thoughts in his emotional state. Mom said, "Glen, what a wonderful way to look at it. I never knew my real mother. She died right after I was born. I never knew my real Dad either, until a little more than a year ago. Both my adopted parents are gone, too, now. I like to think they're all communicating and talking about me. Perhaps that is why I have done so well with my new kidney... do you think?

Glen didn't answer. I did and said. "Well I know God watches over us boys. He has shown himself to us in so many ways. Just like the truck sale and Robert and I getting a job at the university, and it's all in one day."

No one said anything else because, we saw Mom's car pull in the back parking lot of the Café, and we had just a couple of minutes to get in and get seated. Steve and Robert would be going into the Café through the back door stopping in the kitchen area and washing up. That was the first thing Steve would teach Robert. "Always stop and wash your hands with water as hot as you can make the water." So, we knew there would be at least three minutes for us to get in and be seated.

The next item was to make sure there was enough napkin wrapped silverware for the dinner crowd. A waiter or waitress was supposed to fold napkins, if all other jobs were caught up. The next thing was to make sure the ice-maker was not clogged up and there was sufficient loose ice to fill the water pitchers. Robert would be taking notes on a little spiral bound pad that Steve had provided. (He told me one day that he bought several of them and he told those *he* trained to write notes, even if it was something ridiculous as *fill water pitchers.)* The next thing was to fill all the water pitchers and then fill glasses with ice as soon as there were at least eight people in the Café. After that, Steve was to show Robert how to make coffee and tea. I felt like I knew the procedure for training someone as well as Steve.

Cousin Stacey had seated us, and we told her what we were

doing. She put us in a very conspicuous spot and gave us our menus. Another new waitress was being trained and she was farther along than Robert, so Cousin Stacy sent her to get menu requests, but not the drinks. She then went and told Robert that there was a family of five seated in the dining room who had requested Robert Weber to wait on them.

I knew what Steve was saying to him. "Here's your order pad. Go request their drinks first. Both Robert and Steve walked out from behind the drinks bar and we grinned as big as we could. Dr. Lynn said, "I hear there is a new waiter in the Café. Do you think you can have him wait on us?"

Steve didn't answer the question when he said, "What do you think you are doing?"

Robert said, "Its okay, Steve. These folks are big tippers, so we'll give them service they won't forget. Right?

Steve glared at me, but said to Robert, "If you think you're ready?"

"Of course, "I'm ready. Mrs. Moore, what would you like to drink?"

Mom said, "I believe I will have water with lemon." Robert wrote it down. Steve looked over his shoulder and asked, "What are you doing?"

On the pad of paper, he had made a rectangle and in Mom's position he had written, WwL.

Steve asked, "What is that supposed to say?"

It was almost too funny for words. Robert said, "Water with lemon."

Then Robert looked at Dr. Lynn, "Sir, what would you like to drink?"

"I believe decaf coffee and water will be fine this evening, Robert." He wrote by the rectangle on the pad, W, dcf.

Next he looked at Paul. "I'll bet the young man on the end will want some kind of drink…what will it be tonight?"

Paul looked at mom and said, "Mom, is it okay for me to have a Coke?"

She shook her head *yes*, so Paul said, "Thanks, Mom, I haven't had a Coke in a long time." Robert wrote down Cke.

Glen didn't know what to say, Robert said, "Whatever you would like, Glen, I'll get it."

Glen very meekly said, "Coke will be fine."

Robert looked at me and said without cracking a smile, "Dennis, how nice to see you again, today. What may I get for your drink?"

I thought I'd be funny, too, so I said, "V-8 over ice, please." I figured at his home that would be one of the "never drink the stuff" items for him, and he wouldn't know what it was, but he wrote V-8 with a slash mark under it, and then under the slash he wrote *ice*.

Robert then turned to Steve, "Come, I'll never get trained just standing here staring at this nice family."

We all burst out laughing, but Steve was glaring at us.

Paul said, "Looks like we embarrassed Steve, and he doesn't know what to do with us."

Dr. Lynn said, "We'll leave two tips."

Mom agreed. "Robert doesn't need any training for drinks, anyway."

Glen said, "Wait until he brings the drinks. You had better sample them before you drink them."

I laughed. "Yeah, Robert was too confident and nice to us."

Cousin Stacy came to the table and pulled up a chair from the table nearby. "What's going on with Steve and Robert? I thought Steve would be a natural to train Robert, but it looks like tension is brewing."

We laughed, but Mom said, "It was our intention to pull a fast one on Steve and Robert, and show up here this evening and ask for them to wait on us. Robert apparently realized this is what we were doing and decided to play it cool and act like a real professional waiter. He was super nice to us and didn't give Steve a chance to tell him what to write on his pad. I think Steve felt Robert was being too confident and didn't need his help."

Cousin Stacy said, "I'll take care of that. Your drinks should be ready in a minute."

She walked back behind the drink counter. Our drinks were ready on a tray. She apparently told Robert to serve them and told Steve to come with her. I saw Steve follow her into the kitchen as Robert was walking toward us. He served us our drinks and went back to the kitchen.

They were gone for twenty minutes. I can only imagine the fun Steve, Cousin Stacy, and Robert, too, when he joined them, were having in the kitchen because Robert came back with a tray on his shoulder. Steve probably taught him to do it, while they were back there. Steve was behind Robert with a tray stand and he unfolded it for him. We had already ordered our food, and Steve had finally cheered up. Robert set our drinks down and took the tray back to the kitchen.

When our food arrived, the plates had covers on them. Robert served those of us on one side and Steve the other side. They walked off quickly saying, "Enjoy your dinner!"

Mom said, "What are we supposed to do with the lids." We all lifted the hot lids.

Paul said, "Mom this isn't what I ordered."

The rest of us lifted our lids. Mom's plate had a raisin on top of a note. The note said *fruit,* a small cube of cheese that was labeled *protein* and a tiny spinach leaf with a yellow wax bean on it. The label said *leafy green and yellow vegetable.*

Dr. Lynn had an apple ring with a dollop of whipped cream in the center of it. It said, *fruit and dairy.* There was a slice of a boiled egg for *protein* and a very small pickle for *green vegetable.* I had a small round piece of Pepperoni, sort of like what is put on a pizza for *protein,* an artichoke heart for a *vegetable* and a grape for *fruit.* Glen's tears were so near the surface that he laughed, but his tears were running down his cheeks, also. His plate had three little macaroni's with cheese for *protein,* a green bean and three strands of hash brown potatoes for *vegetables.*

We were all laughing so hard, others in the Café were looking at us, when Paul said, "Mom, I don't think our food will keep us healthy enough to get home."

Dr. Lynn let out a loud laugh. Paul's plate had a cube of beef about the size of a cube of cheese for his protein, an asparagus tip and one single slice of a peach.

Steve came back to the table and asked, "Would you folks like dessert?"

Robert then joined Steve and asked, "Did you folks enjoy your dinner? Can I get you something else?" Neither guy cracked a smile.

I thought mom would be sick, if she didn't quit laughing. Cousin Stacy came up behind Steve and said, "Did they enjoy their appetizer? We have their dinner ready."

Steve and Robert took our plates and lids from the table and took them back to the kitchen laughing. Cousin Stacy, chuckled and said, "There's nothing like a little humor to change a mood. I had better go and see if they get your dinners right."

She left us and went back to the kitchen. I noticed that Glen had gotten very quiet. When Steve and Robert delivered the food we had ordered. Glen said to me, "This is more than I've had for supper many a night because I gave my food to my grandmother."

I had real guilt feelings for being in the restaurant when it had only been about a day and a-half since his family was taken from him. I said, "Glen, I'll bet your Grandmother is looking down on us and the food that you have, and she's feeling so happy because you won't have to share your food with anyone. What do you think?"

Cousin Stacy started taking the plates with the lids off our table and Glen didn't answer because Cousin Stacy said, "Here, Steve, put these in the cooler for the next unsuspecting customer."

Robert served us our food. We all had generous portions on our plates. Mom asked Robert to fix a meatloaf plate with a baked potato to go for John. When we left the restaurant, we left a tip for Robert, and Dr. Lynn gave Cousin Stacy a ten-dollar bill for Steve at the check-out counter. He said, "Tell Steve his tip is for his sense of humor."

Glen was quiet on the way home. When we went in the house, John was still sitting at the table studying. I remembered a quiz that I was to have the second hour in the morning. I went upstairs and got some notes to go over while I milked the cows.

Mom asked Glen if he would prefer the room upstairs that he slept in last night or the twin bed in the room with Paul.

"I don't care," is all he said.

Pop said, "Glen, we have two more big days in front of us. I want you to get a goodnight's sleep."

He looked at Pop and meekly said, "I'll sleep upstairs."

I figured it would be upstairs as I suspected he needed to be alone, so he could cry in peace without someone saying something to him. It was pushing seven-thirty, so I told John that I was going to the barn.

He said, "No need... I went out and milked the cows and threw hay out for Steve' cattle. I brought the pregnant heifer in.

Steve's not going to get much sleep tonight. She's in labor. You can go out with Paul and take care of the chickens."

I said, "Good," as I sat down at the dining room table, "I need to talk to you."

"Can it wait until we go to bed or tomorrow? I have two big tests in the morning."

I said, "Sure."

I went on out to the chicken house. Paul and Dr. Lynn were already out there closing up the henhouse. Paul had his old dirty pick plastic bowl with three eggs in it. He had to show them to me. I left them and went back to the house and went through the kitchen. Mom was loading the washer, so I stopped at the laundry room door and said, "Would you like for me to read a verse of scripture with Glen and pray with him?"

Mom looked up at me and said, "I don't deserve my sons."

She hugged me. "Yes, that would be nice."

I don't suppose I will ever get too old for her hugs. I left Mom folding clothes in the laundry and went on upstairs to my room with my books and thought about Glen. He would never get a hug from his mother or grandmother again. I decided that Isaiah 43: 1 and 2 would be appropriate verses for Glen.

Glen followed me upstairs. I sat on the chair at my desk and Glen stood in the doorway. I said, "Glen, come on in. I want to read something to you."

He flopped down on my bed and I read the scripture to him. 'Trust in the Lord with all your heart and lean not on you own understanding.' Glen I'm only five years older than you, and in our family we have had one crisis after another. Sometimes I think I can't take any more heartache, but God has become so real to me. He is not going to let anything swallow me up emotionally or mentally."

Glen was silent for a moment, and I hesitated to say more.

Everything was still in the mental image stage, and so very real that it was hard to think of anything else, especially when our family was going on with normal activities. His life was anything, but normal, and it would never be what it was before.

I asked, "Glen, do you feel overwhelmed and just swallowed up by everything that is happening.

He said, "Yeah," and sniffed again, and then I was the quiet one. I didn't know what to say next, so I said silently, *Lord, help me. Give me wisdom and knowledge and remember I'm nineteen and not always appropriate.*

I hesitated, but said, "Glen, would you do me a favor. I took four sheets of paper and wrote Grandmother at the top of one, stepmother at the top of one, eldest sister, and youngest sister at the top of the other two. I handed them to Glen and said, "This is the favor, I want you to do for me."

I handed him a pen. "Go to your room and write. Take the mother sheet first and write everything about her you can think of. Write the good and the bad. If you should start thinking about another one, just take that page and write something on her page. Here... Here is more paper. If you need more, come and get it. We keep lots of notebook paper here in the desk. I took some folders out of my second desk drawer and said, "Use a folder to put your pages in. No one, but *you*, needs to see your papers. They are *your* memory sheets.

"Tomorrow I'll find something better for you to keep the papers in. Perhaps we can find some pictures to put with them. I heard another sniff, and he slowly got up from the bed as I moved to my desk chair to sit again.

He said, "I don't know if I can do this. My writing isn't very good."

"No teacher is going to grade your papers. They are yours and yours alone. You don't have to share them with anyone. If Pastor

Bishop does your fu…. the services, he may ask you about each one of them. It would be helpful for him to know something about each one—your sisters, your stepmother, and grandmother, too. I would be glad to help you spell words if you don't know the spelling. Don't be afraid to ask me."

I took his hand and said, "I want to pray for you, will it be okay?"

I prayed and asked God to give Glen strength for the next week and to give him an extra measure of comfort and a good night's rest.

He took the papers and folders, said, "Thanks, Dennis," and slowly walked back out of the room. He was like an old man weighted down with years of responsibility and heartache. He went across the room to my sister's old room. I knew he must be carrying a heavy load.

I studied until almost ten o'clock and got hungry. Five-thirty or six was going to come awfully early in the morning.

Dr. Lynn, I should remember to call him Pop or something else, came upstairs and poked his head in our room. John was still studying at the dining room table. "Still with the books, huh?"

"I'm just finishing up."

He looked across the hall. "Glen's light is still on. Do you think I should say anything more to him tonight?"

I don't know. I gave him an assignment this evening with paper to write on. I asked him to make his own memory book and to write down everything he could think of about each of his sisters, mother, and grandmother. I suspect that is what he is doing."

Glen must have heard us talking, because he opened his door and asked, "What am I going to do about school. They will count me absent, and I can't be absent too many days, or they will make me repeat my grade."

Pop said, "Glen, you won't be counted absent for any of the days you miss this week. You have an excusable absence. I'll be happy to take you by your school and get your assignments from your teacher. I, frankly, do not want you going to school all week."

He said, "Okay… That will be a relief."

Glen looked at me. "I've written four pages."

"That's good, Glen. I'm going to put my papers and books away and hit the sack. I'm tired, how about you?"

"I'm tired, but… I think I'm hungry, too. Do you suppose your mother has any cookies left?"

I looked at Pop and he had a big smile on his face. He saw an opening for him to have a moment with Glen. He said, "Son, let's go down and see what we can find to eat. My stomach is telling me it's hungry, too.

They went downstairs, and I decided to *not* go down, although a bowl of cereal would sure go down mighty good. Mom came out of her room and looked in Kaitlynn's room and came to my room.

"Where's Glen?" She had one of the kits in her hand that she had made up for the boys in the garden project. It looked like she must have added a few things to it. The big baggie had a comb *and* brush, a soap box with soap in it, a plastic toothbrush box with toothbrush, toothpaste, a couple of men's hankies, a small box of tissue, nail clippers, and she had added some pre-shave and after shave lotion and a couple of razors and some shaving cream.

She said, "I have to get in bed. I'm feeling exhausted. Would you give these to Glen when he comes back upstairs?"

"Sure, Mom, but I'm not too old for a *goodnight* hug, too." She grinned. I took the baggie from her, gave her a hug and took the baggie downstairs to Glen.

CHAPTER 5

W E WOKE UP AT our usual time. John and I had taken a shower the evening before to get the day's sweat and barn dirt off us before getting in bed. Glen was still asleep. When I passed by Steve's bedroom, his room was empty and it looked like his bed had not been slept in. An alarm went off in my head, but then I remembered what John said, *I brought Steve's heifer in, she's in labor.*

I went on down to the kitchen and saw the vet's truck outside the barn. If the vet had been called, I knew there had to be trouble. Steve hadn't gone to bed at all. Mom was fixing breakfast and she said, "Marshall was concerned last night and called the vet around midnight. I thought about Pop being downstairs with Glen, and I wondered if Glen went out to the barn last night, too. Mom interrupted my thoughts. "Steve needs to come in the house and get some sleep before school."

John came through the kitchen and said, "I'll go get him... oh, here he comes now. Mom, tell him to eat, take a shower and sleep for three hours. He can make it in school for the rest of the day. He can catch up on sleep as soon as he comes in from school this afternoon."

Dr. Lynn came out of the barn with the vet. He shook the vet's hand and headed to the house. He looked awfully tired. He looked around at us and asked, "Where did Steve go?" and headed to Grandpa's bathroom and washed up.

John said, "He was coming in just before you came out of the barn, but he never came in."

I said, "I'll go look."

John went to the refrigerator on the back porch and looked in. I guessed he was checking to see if anyone had dated a box for today's eggs. He said to me as I was going down the back steps, "Open up the chicken house on your way back in."

Steve had made a detour and was sitting in Mom's car. I walked up to the car, "Steve, what's going on?"

"I lost the mother. The calf was too big. When I get married, I'm never going to get my wife pregnant."

I stood there for a moment and finally said, "Remember, Steve, when you go in the house. The cow was not your mother, grandmother and sisters. Glen may not be able to have any understanding for how you feel about the cow and calf. Read Isaiah 40: 29-41 before you go to sleep. Mom said for you to come in and eat, shower, and go to bed for three hours. Did you sleep at all during the night?"

"Yes, I lay down in the tack room and slept from one something till four this morning. Pop slept from about eleven-thirty until a little after one, when the vet came."

"Well, you're good to go then. No moping around the house. Glen doesn't need it. He's lost his entire family and doesn't need more sorrow added to it."

Steve looked over to the barn and swallowed. He said, "Okay," and got out of the car.

We went on in the house and Mom said, "Steve, I'm sorry."

"I'll get over it," he said. "I'm headed for a shower and will be back down in a few minutes to eat."

Mom had finally gotten a warming oven and it was really handy with her four boys and husband coming and going every ten minutes or so in the morning. She never complained, because she knew morning chores were a necessity and sometimes the animals didn't want to cooperate and do things on our time schedule.

Dr. Lynn… I mean Pop came out of Grandpa's bathroom, now Paul's bathroom, and stopped at Paul's bed. He was sound asleep. I could see him from where I was sitting at the table. He put his hand gently on Paul's head and then took his pulse. I could see his lips moving and knew he was praying. I got up and went into the bedroom and looked at Pop with a curious look. "How is he?" Paul stirred.

"I believe he's fine. I'll keep an eye on him today."

Paul opened his eyes, looked at us and sat up, "What's goin' on?"

Pop asked, "How are you feeling, son?"

He said, "I'm feeling fine, but my stomach… he put his hand over his mouth and I grabbed the waste can by his bed. Pop went to the bathroom for a cold washcloth and came back saying, "I was afraid of that. He ate pretty heavy last night and he's not used to it. Then last night he came back to the kitchen and ate a couple of cookies."

After losing the contents of his stomach, Paul flopped back on his pillow and said, "Wow, I feel better already. I'm ready for some pancakes and sausage."

Mom had joined us, "I don't think so, Paul. It's hot tea and chicken noodle soup all day for you."

He sat up and put his feet over the side of the bed, like he was going to get up, ready for the day. He glanced at Mom and said, "Aw, Mom… I just ate too much last night."

Pop frowned, "Just the same, Paul, your body is trying to get over something really devastating and we don't need to make it work overtime trying to digest food. I want you to lie back down for another twenty minutes."

We left him and went back to the kitchen table. Mom put

my plate in the microwave for thirty seconds and warmed it up. "Thanks, mom, but you have a stressful day coming up. You need to sit here with me and eat."

Mom looked at John and then at me. "Dennis, are you feeling ready to take over in John's place in telling us all what needs to be done?"

She laughed a little when she said it, and I realized that I did tell Mom to sit down with a little authority in my voice. I said, "Not, yet, Mom. He can have the job awhile longer."

Mom fixed herself a cup of coffee and said, "I got up at five-thirty and had the first pancake off the griddle, so I'm fine. You're right about the day. We need to stop right now and pray for God's blessing on it."

John had joined us. He was getting a plate from the warming oven. I looked at John and chuckled, but he said, "What are you all talking about? While we are praying, let's pray that Marianne can come home and play for the funeral and Kaitlynn and Matthew can come to play their violins, also. I need to see Marianne. I'm getting so lonely for her that I feel like dropping everything down here, marrying her, and transferring to some other school."

John was deep in thought about something and had missed what Mom had said about me taking over for John telling people what to do. Then Pop said, "Let's pray." He prayed for each one of us by name. When he got to my name, he prayed that God would give me wisdom in planning a program for older boys and to bless the communication between Glen and me. I was surprised at that and decided to ask him later about the program for older boys. Officer Harrison must have mentioned it to him, or he had heard some of our conversations before.

When Pop was done praying, I said, "Dr. Lynn, thank you. If I haven't told you before, I appreciate you and your concern for each one of us."

He grinned from ear to ear as though my comment was one he needed. He said, "Thank you, Dennis, but I thought I was *Pop*."

I laughed and said... "I'm getting better at it."

John looked at the clock, and I followed his eyes and did the same. It was 6:36 a.m. John said, "Let's get out to the barn, Dennis, and get those cows milked. Where's Steve? Do we need to do anything with his heifer?"

Dr. Lynn said, "No, the vet called the packing house and they should be on their way out. Steve said to give her meat to the Salvation Army. The Vet milked a lot of colostrum and gave it to the calf."

I asked, "Where's the calf?"

"He's being wet nursed by another one of Steve's cows. She accepted the little one right off. The bigger calf didn't like it, but she was eating mostly grasses and feed anyway. I'll go check on the calf later."

I got up from the table and placed my plate and knife and fork in the sink. John followed me and did the same. We headed out to the barn. John said, "Dennis, when you get up in the morning do you ever wonder what the day is going to throw at you?"

"Not really, John, most of the time, I just go with the flow. You've had more of the family responsibility on you since Dad and Grandpa died. I've always pitched in and worked, but mentally I could just trust you, Mom, and God to make things turn out right.

I've learned to pray and trust the Lord for you and for myself, too, that all things will work together for our good. Paul's not out of the woods yet, but he's making progress toward a remission or healing of his Leukemia.

Steve still needs to go with the flow, but he's learning, too. Mom is happy with Pop, and that's important. But you, John, after you said what you did, this morning about seeing Marianne, I'm concerned about you."

We both did the usual things—tying the cows in the stalls, putting feed in the troughs, getting the milking stools and buckets. We were done in twenty minutes and let the cows back out to pasture and cleaned up the stalls. Dr. Lynn joined us and helped put the milk through the strainer and into the new milk cans. He really came out to talk to John.

I heard what Pop was saying to John. It made a lot of sense, and I needed to hear it, too, for me. He said, "John, a man is not complete in life without a wife. The scriptures tell us that, and I've experienced it. I really missed my wife when she died, and your mother filled the big vacancy I felt. You've been very patient and committed to your family and your education and helping with the crime prevention program, but when you start having feeling of throwing everything to the wind, then it is time to start making plans with Marianne. You're in your third year of college and are doing well. May I make a suggestion? Marianne will be graduating this spring. I'm certain she feels like she's in limbo with you, also. Seal your commitment to her."

As I was listening to the conversation, I began thinking about Janet. It would be nice to have a double wedding on the farm, but I haven't even had a date with her. I decided that after the funeral of Glen's family, it would be time for me to make a date with Janet. After all, I'm not going to be nineteen forever, and she isn't going to be seventeen forever. She's a senior this year, and she will be considering college. I would not stand in her way if she chose to go away to a university, but I would miss her. I suspect that she would want to stay close to home though. After being raped at age fourteen, she doesn't date very often. I think she may be afraid. I'm glad she sees us Moore guys as the type of men she thinks men should be. I'm not perfect, but I do have feelings for Janet, and I know she will have problems being married to any man. Knowing all about what happened to her will be helpful. I know the devastation and physical hurt she felt. Well, I don't really, but I can imagine, so I would have to be very patient with her on many levels. I need to call her, and soon.

John interrupted my thoughts when he said, "You're right, Pop. I'll take care of that issue right away. In the meantime, I need to take care of purchasing your car and getting another farm truck. I don't want you to be stranded here without a vehicle when Mom takes the car to work."

Pop said, "I think this next weekend Steve and I will go look at trucks... especially with an insurance check burning a hole in his pocket from his other truck."

I thought about Steve's accident and asked. "Has Steve had his neck checked lately?"

"Monday at four, Steve has an appointment with my partner. Well... ex-partner now that I'm retired. He'll take X-rays again. Steve is wearing his Thompson Collar less and less, and that's a good sign. I haven't heard any complaints of his neck hurting, and that's a good sign, too, that he's healing.

"About the car, John, let's wait until next week after we get everything settled with Glen. Or... if you want to get it off your mind, we can settle up this evening and the car will be yours. Come to think of it, we may need a truck to clean out Glen's house. The lawyer is trying to expedite all the legal work, so that I can become his legal guardian. Obviously, Glen will own everything left *in* the house. I don't know about the house. His stepmother may have been just renting... the lawyer is checking out everything. His grandmother may have something to pass on to him, also. I would prefer Glen not worrying about anything except what is normal for his age... if that could ever happen again."

I asked, "What will you do with all the stuff in the house?"

"Well, I'm not sure *I'll* do anything with it. Personally, I think Glen should have a say in everything. It also depends on who owns the house. As soon as the law releases the house, then the ladies will go in and clean. Then we'll take Glen back in for whatever he wants. Your Mom thinks we should clean the house out of everything and put it in a storage unit for Glen when he's grown. He and his wife can go through the stuff or sell it and use the money for whatever the need is."

I didn't answer. It was getting time for John and me to go pick up Robert and then go on to Cape Girardeau and our classes at the university. Pop handed John his car keys. He said, "Try it out again. See if you like it. John took the keys and said to me, "Thanks, Let's go, Dennis."

After yesterday, it was a normal day for us at the university. John said he thought he did well on his two exams, and I felt confident on my quiz. Robert never says anything about how he feels or thinks about his classes, or his tests. I asked him about his training session at the Café. He said, "Well, if I have any more evenings like last night… I will enjoy being a waiter. When your Cousin Stacy hauled out her plates from the cooler with the labels on them and Steve lightened up his attitude, I really enjoyed the two hours. It wasn't too busy. Even so, I still made thirty-six dollars in tips. This morning having cash money in my pocket sure feels good."

I thought about our parents' teaching and said, "Robert, do you know why God blesses financially?' I didn't wait for him to answer before I added. "It's because we give back to God what He has given to us… even though we worked hard to attain it, we need to allow God to be in control of everything. We can only do that, by giving God a minimum of a tenth, and use what is left wisely and with his direction."

John added, "I'll say amen to that, Robert."

"So, what you are saying is I should give three dollars and sixty cents to God and ask his direction on what I should do with the rest?"

"That's the way it works," I said, "Try it for a year and see if God doesn't somehow, someway, increase what you have over and above what you give to him and what you earned."

"I'll try it... I'm willing to give him an old truck and get a shiny Buick Riviera."

John said... "Um-m, you are right. God did bless me with a car and I didn't even have to go looking for it."

The thought never had entered John's or my mind that we might purchase Pop's car or even Mom's until Dr. Lynn brought it up. Mom was promised a new car. I wondered when she will get that. I suspected soon.

—■ ■—

As I was leaving my Criminal Law class, Officer Harrison was coming in. I was looking straight ahead and in deep thought, wondering if the police were done with Glen's house and if he was able to get in and get anything. Officer Harrison grabbed my arm and I almost tripped over my own feet. He said, "Whoa there, Dennis. Where're you going? Don't you have a job to go to?"

I stopped. "You're right. Both Robert and I have jobs. I guess we'll have to find John and get him to take us somewhere for a lunch and get back here by one. I wonder where Robert is... oh, here he comes."

Robert came bouncing down the hall in a good mood. He said, "I just saw John and he said he would be right out."

Officer Harrison looked at me. "Why don't I take you all over to the University Center for a quick lunch? You can tell me what you have in mind for the older boys who have graduated from our program."

John came toward us listening to someone on his cell phone. He was frowning and my inner radar went sky high wondering who and what was going on.

He hung up when he reached us and said, "Robert, Dennis… I'm sorry, Officer Harrison, hello."

John reached out his hand and shook Officer Harrison's hand. I was looking at John with a huge question expression, but Officer Harrison said, "John, I hope everything is fine on the home front."

John laughed. "We don't know what normal or fine is at our place."

I was glad John laughed, but he still had a concerned look on his face.

That was Aunt Susan. She said Molly Jenkins woke up this morning and didn't know where she was. She didn't feel well when she went to bed. This morning Molly is just lying in the bed looking around. Aunt Susan was looking for Dr. Lynn. I told her to go ahead and call 911, but to try to give her some aspirin in case it's a stroke. She said she already had, but she won't respond. Mr. Jenkins is beside himself, and Aunt Susan can't handle them both. I think I'll head on out for the Jenkinses'. Get some lunch somewhere, and I'll come back at four for you both."

Officer Harrison said to John, "You go on and don't bother to come back. I'll see that the boys get home. I'm going to be in my office most of the afternoon, and my wife isn't expecting me until five."

"Thank you. I had better get out of here."

I watched John walk down the hall and wondered if I should forget about the job this afternoon and go with him, but Officer

Harrison spoke interrupting my thoughts, "Let's walk across campus. I need the exercise."

I had not walked around the campus that much. It was a nice walk over to the university center. We had never thought to eat in the cafeteria before going home. Robert and I got a hot plate, and Officer Harrison just got a salad and a sandwich.

I thought over what I had decided in my mind would be a good extension for the younger boys' crime prevention program. "Officer Harrison, someone has to do some legwork in order for the program that I have in mind to work. Someone will have to do some record keeping, also. It can be the same person, if he or she has a love for the boys. I did talk with two people to get opinions, and they were positive, but again… legwork has to be done.

"The program I am suggesting is that when a boy turns sixteen the boy is given a birthday celebration of sorts—not a big deal, but a rite of passage from one program to the next. Just have one celebration for those turning sixteen even if the birthday comes at an odd time. I would like to see an employer there at the meeting who will give the boy a job two hours each evening and six hours on Saturday. Pay him minimum wage, but the employer must pay into program twenty-five cents for each hour work, and the kid will pay twenty-five cents for each hour into the program, also. This will cover some of the costs if we have to hire someone to take kids to a job and pick them up, too. The boy will still get to take home almost five dollars an hour after taxes.

"I talked with Blake Hegel and asked him what he thought of the idea. His response was, 'I will work one hour free and one hour for me each evening, if I can work at a job each evening and Saturday. Blake thinks he's good at math. He stood there looking at me and said, 'During the week I would make a minimum of twenty-five dollars and the six hours on Saturday would give me another thirty. I'd be glad to work for fifty-five dollars a week. I could give Mom some money to help with groceries.'"

Officer Harrison chuckled. "He'd be really surprised then to find out he had made about that much during the week."

I thought about my conversation with the manager of Chaffee's biggest grocery store. "I did talk briefly with the Food-Liner manager and he said, 'I would be willing to try the program.' However, all the boys are from Cape Girardeau, I think a grocery store or some other business up here would be better."

Officer Harrison sat there thinking as he usually does before answering, so I asked, "What do you think?" Do you have very many boys who have gone through the program and are out of it now?"

He still sat there eating his sandwich and thinking. It made me think my idea was a dud. I said, Officer Harrison, if you think this is a dumb idea… you won't hurt my feelings. I'm sure I could come up with another idea."

He laid his sandwich down. "I think your idea is a good one, and I think I know just the right person to head up the program. Let me think on it for a few days and I'll get back with you. We could possibly get a grant to subsidize the program. Lest we get confused let's call this the Senior Program and the weekly younger group the Junior Program."

Robert had been sitting at the table eating and not saying a word. He was listening to us talk and finally he said, "That sounds like a winner."

I didn't know if he meant the title of the programs or the programs. We finished our lunch at the university center and walked back to the Rosemary Crisp Hall and our new jobs. Robert would be working for Officer Harrison and I would be working for Dr. Stone. All the offices were in one central location, so we were not far from each other. Dr. Stone had given some papers to me and I was to record the grades in the computer. It helped having them in alphabetical order, which a student worker had done during the noon hour. She went as far as she could and left a note that the last forty papers were out of order. I did that before recording the grades in the computer. My quizzes were already in the computer. In Dr. Stone's class, I had an average of a B-plus, which made me happy. Just a little more and I could bring it up to an A.

I worked for my two hours and wondered if I should go on or let the next student worker finish up. No one came in, so I went on working. I had to wait for Robert anyway.

About twenty till four o'clock, Robert peeked in and said, "I'm done. Are you?

I looked up and said, "I have three more grades to record and then I'm done."

I piled all the papers neatly according to the class period and looked around for Dr. Stone. He was not in the office complex. Officer Harrison came out of his office and said, "Ready to go?"

"Yes, but how do I sign in and out, if Dr. Stone is not here?"

"He didn't show you?"

"Show me what?"

"He should have a sign-in and a sign-out sheet somewhere. You put your name and the time in and out on it."

The sheet was hanging on a wall behind me. I went ahead and signed out and left with Robert and Officer Harrison. We were in the car and headed for Chaffee by four o'clock. I used my cell phone and called John to let him know we were on our way. He didn't answer... Paul did. Paul sounded sick. I asked, "Who is with you?"

He sounded so disgruntled, "My teacher has been here all day long."

"Well, where is John?"

"I don't know, he said he was going over to the Jenkinses, but he hasn't come back."

"Paul, don't worry about John. I'm on my way home, okay?"

He said, "I'm tired and I'm going to sleep for a minute or two?"

"Fine, boy, take a good nap and get well."

It puzzled me why John didn't relieve the teacher and where Steve, Mom, and Dr. Lynn could be. Steve should be home from school, and Pop should be back with Glen. I told myself not to worry about things beyond my control. I realized that I was going to have to find a car pretty quickly as this kind of thing might happen often. John couldn't always be my chauffeur. I would have to talk with Mom and check my account again.

Robert was sitting beside me quietly and said, "You know, Dennis, we can't always depend on John to be our chauffeur, we need to be looking for a car." I smiled and thought, *Lord, you are here and are one step ahead of me, aren't you? He's thinking my thoughts.*

I said, "You're right," but a verse of scripture came to my mind, so I added it to what I said to Robert. "'Seek ye first the kingdom of God and His righteousness and all these things shall be added unto you.' I'll have to look that up when I get home because I don't think I quoted it right. But anyway, the verse is talking about our needs. God knows my needs and he knows yours, so let's trust God for a car and just know he will come up with something. We don't need any big fancy car… just something in good shape that will get us back and forth to the university."

Robert was silent for a moment and then said, "Oh, but… it would be nice to have an MG or a Thunderbird." He laughed. "God knows my wants, too."

I agreed, but I wondered if Robert would be satisfied with just anything. Maybe I shouldn't be either.

Officer Harrison said, "Which one of you would like to buy this car?"

He pulled over to the side of the road, "Why don't I take this exit and head back to Cape Girardeau? This car is going to be traded in. My wife thinks it has too many miles on it, but I say it's just broken in. If one of you would like to buy this car, I'd be glad to sell it to you and not trade it in on a new one. My wife has a nice car, so she can take me to see a car dealer or dealers this evening."

I could tell Robert didn't have this kind of car in mind when he said, "Isn't it a bit big for a college student? What kind is it?"

"It's a Lincoln Town Car, and it's six years old... and, yes, it is a might big for a college student and would make a better family car. But, the price is good and the car is still in good shape."

I was still thinking about us sitting on the side of the road and Paul not feeling well and wondering where Mom and Pop and John were.

I said, "Robert, if you aren't interested, I'll be glad to at least take it home and let Dr. Lynn look at it. What are you asking for the car?"

Officer Harrison pulled back on the road and took the Dutchtown exit to turn back to Cape Girardeau. He said, "I probably can get maybe fifteen thousand out of the car as a trade in, but I would be glad to sell it to you for twelve."

"That may still be out of my league, but I won't say no, until I have Dr. Lynn and Mom's opinion."

We took Officer Harrison home in the Woodland Hills area and I drove the car back to the highway. When we reached Highway Seventy-Four, I asked Robert if he would like to drive it the rest of the way.

"No, I'm more interested in getting a small more fuel-efficient car. These big cars are nice for long distance traveling, but all I need is something economical for back and forth to the university and for an occasional date."

"Okay, Maybe Mom will be interested in the car. Dr. Lynn wants to get her another car. I don't mind driving her car. We'll see.

I dropped Robert off at his house and Marianne's car was there. John was there, too. They both had a radiant face. They were outside leaning on Dr. Lynn's... now John's car. When we drove up with Robert in the good looking creamy-colored Lincoln, the look on John' face was... well, I should say... interesting. It was a big question mark as well as a surprise.

Robert jumped out and said, "Don't you think a young college kid looks out of place in a big Lincoln Town car?"

I rolled the window down and said, "How about two college kids."

John looked in the window of the back seat. "This looks like Officer Harrison's car."

"It is. He offered to sell it to Robert or me and not trade it in. He gave us a good price, and I thought just maybe Dr. Lynn would be interested in it for Mom."

John walked around the car. "Could be, could be." He said.

"John, I called home and Paul was there by himself with his teacher. He said you had gone to the Jenkins' house and would be back. I suspect the teacher is getting anxious to get home."

I nodded to Marianne. "Marianne, I'm glad you're home. John-Boy, here, hasn't been worth anything lately because ...as Dr. Lynn says, 'Man is not complete without a woman in his life.' John has been acting like an incomplete term paper—not good, but not bad. John, you know what else Dr. Lynn said, so... get with the program."

I chuckled and said, "I'm out of here."

I went on home and parked in the drive behind the house. Mom had come home with Glen and Dr. Lynn. Dr. Lynn came out the backdoor to see who was driving up. When he saw it was me, he said, "Well, well, well, what do you know? Is this Dennis or a chauffeur?"

I laughed. "Officer Harrison tried to get Robert or me to buy this car. He's going to trade it in on a new Lincoln. He told me or one of us to drive it home. Robert isn't interested. I thought maybe you might be interested in it for Mom. It has seventy-six thousand miles on it and is six years old. He quoted twelve thousand, but thinks he could get fifteen as a trade-in. That's a big difference. I guess God made him put his foot in his mouth when he quoted twelve to us."

I got out of the car and Dr. Lynn sat in the driver's seat. Mom came out of the house and said, "What a beautiful car. Dennis, I like this car. Is this the car you're going to buy?"

I looked at Pop and he said, to Mom, "What do you think of a Lincoln Town Car?"

"I think it's a beautiful car... all leather interior. Wow! Doesn't Officer Harrison have a car something like this?"

"Mom, don't you recognize this car? This *is* Officer Harrison's car. He was going to trade it in on a new one, but he offered it to me for a good price. I'm not sure that I need a big family car. I need something more practical to go back and forth to school in. What do you think?

Pop said, "Bonnie, if you like this car rather than a new one, we'll buy it for you. You can drive it for two years and then trade it in. Come on... get in. We'll take it down the road a mile or two and see how you like it."

"Paul had come out of the house. Glen followed him. Paul said, "I want to go, too."

Glen said, "Me, too."

I just stood there. Somehow the idea of Robert or for me to buy the car was lost in a matter of a few minutes. I watched Dr. Lynn pull out of the driveway and head down the lane. I couldn't help, but smile again and think, *Thank you, Lord. Mom needed a boost in her spirit today. I'm glad to see her smile, and I wouldn't mind driving her older car.*

Steve came out of the barn and wanted to know who it was who brought me home. I said, "I brought myself home."

"Well, who was that in the car that looked like Officer Harrison's car… it sure didn't look like him."

"It is Harrison's car, but I drove it home. Pop and Mom and the two boys took it for a spin down the road a piece. Officer Harrison thought I might like to buy it. It's a super nice family car, but I'm like Robert, who nixed the car, by the way. I need something more economical to drive… something that gets really good mileage. I probably should go look for a small or mid-sized truck to use during the spring garden planting time. When are you going to replace your truck?"

"Just as soon as I get the time," Steve said, as he washed his hands in the back porch sink. "I'm thinking of going and looking this coming Saturday. Want to go with me? Pop said he would go with me, and you might as well go and look, too."

I looked back out the side of the back porch to see if the car was coming back down the lane, but it was not there. "Let me think about it." I went on in the house and Steve followed.

"Did I tell you Marianne is in town? I saw John over at the Weber's house when I dropped off Robert. Are you going back in town to the Café to train Robert this evening?"

Steve was thinking and didn't comment on Marianne and John. He said, I thought I would, for an hour. Robert has to have a way over to the Café. His Mom can pick him up or his Dad can later. Last night he made around thirty-six dollars in tips. He was happy about that. Hopefully, he'll do as well tonight. It sure made him feel good to earn his own money. When he works Friday and Saturday night, he should do very well with the tips. However, being on his feet, having to move quickly, do things right and be courteous the whole time, might make him happier to be going home at closing time than the amount of tips he earns. We'll see, though. When he can pay for his own car, he'll see the value in work and the value of setting a goal and working toward it. I'm glad mom taught us so well with the family account and saving. I'll say this… we sure have learned the value of work. Don't you think so, Dennis?"

"Right, Steve. I agree."

Steve opened the refrigerator door and got out the pitcher of ice water. I looked back out the kitchen door and glanced toward the lane. Steve said, "A penny for your thoughts."

I didn't realize I was off in space somewhere. I looked at Steve and said, "Why?"

"Your face showed your mind was off in the blue somewhere thinking."

"Am I that transparent?"

"Not usually, but we both have had hectic schedules and things have happened lately that cause us to do a lot of thinking."

"Right, Steve. God seems to be honoring our commitment to Him, and I keep wondering why it is that He keeps blessing us with our needs. …often before we ask and yet, Robert has given his life to the Lord and he doesn't recognize that it was God who was present today when Officer Harrison offered his car to us. I was willing to take the car and Robert refused it right off. I see now that it was the car for Mom and not really for me—or Robert. But who knows what God had in mind if Robert had been willing to take the car.

"I can't wait for Mom to come back. She certainly fell in love with the car at the first sight of it. Mom had not asked for a car, but God had already instilled the idea in her mind that she would be getting a car, even though it was Pop that had said, 'I'm going to get you a better car.' With Paul's health and running back and forth to St. Louis for check-ups, she really needed a more stable car... at least for the next two years, and this car will fulfill that. By taking a used car, Mom will be setting an example for us that we can make do with a good dependable used car for our needs at the present time. And I find it interesting that God used me to bring it about."

Steve was standing by the kitchen counter with his glass of water, just looking at me like he wanted to say something, but he didn't say anything. I said, "What?"

"Are you saying that it was wrong of me to save and buy my *new* truck, and God really didn't want me to have it, because I should have been willing to take whatever God wanted me to have?"

I couldn't believe what I was hearing from Steve. I had to pray, *Lord, help me. I don't know what I have said.* I know I frowned and lost a second or two before answering. "No, Steve. That decision had to be between you and God. The new truck was super nice. You'd saved for it for years and I liked the truck, but you have to decide now what the meaning of the accident was that took it away from you. Maybe you had too much pride in it.... or else God had something in mind for all the people involved in the accident. I don't know, Steve. I would be only guessing.

"You have all that money back again, plus a second check over and above the amount of the truck. I wonder why that happened as it did. You're getting over your injuries. What do you suppose God wants you to do with all that money? Does God want to use it someway or somehow? I don't know, Steve, only you can answer those kinds of questions. Don't underestimate God's ability to bless us, but… He wants our honor and allegiance over every*thing*, and you know what, Steve? That kind of commitment to the Lord is reflected in what we do with our money or in the lifestyle that we live. Don't you think?"

Steve didn't have time to answer because Mom drove up in the driveway grinning from ear to ear. They all piled out of the car. "Well, Mom…?"

"I really like this car. Marshall thinks it should last another five years and be good for at least one-hundred fifty thousand miles. It has only a little more than half that right now. It even has heated seats. It'll be great for when I have to transport you kids to the doctor with a fever and chilling."

Mom handed me the keys and Pop said, "Let me talk to Officer Harrison, Dennis. Do you really feel you need something smaller and more economical?"

I didn't answer Pop. I looked at Mom, "Then Mom, you are saying you want *this* car. You know your husband has offered you a brand new car….?"

She interrupted me and said, "Yes, I know, but I think we can use the extra money somewhere else. Who knows what tomorrow will bring? We may need the money for something or… someone else may need it more. In five years' time, at least three of you boys will be out of our home and on your own. Then perhaps that will be the time for a brand new car.

"God knew that my heart and mind would be saturated with Paul's health, Steve's accident and now helping Glen, He brought me a car that is dependable without me having to go looking or making decisions on money and all that. Isn't God wonderful?"

I noticed Glen wandered off toward the house. Steve said, "Mom, the car looks like one you should be driving. You're an elegant lady, and it fits you."

He started laughing, "Boy, I know how to flatter, don't I?"

Mom chuckled and looked toward Glen. Steve took a few steps toward the barn laughing at himself. "Well, I need to go check on that new calf."

He walked off and I silently prayed, *Lord, speak to Steve' heart while he is out there. All things are to be for your glory... old, used or new.*

"Mom, before we go in, tell me about your day with Glen."

Mom looked toward the house and Glen, who was just going into the back porch, so she said, "Well, the first thing we did was to have an emergency hearing with the judge to grant Marshall temporary custody of the *said minor,* as they called Glen, and they gave Pop power of attorney, also, so he can sign anything for him. There was a lot of legal language, and I think Glen was overwhelmed by it all. The police stated to the judge that they have all they needed from the house for evidence. They have the gun and have ten pictures, and they have Glen as a witness. The judge asked Glen a number of questions about relatives and if he would prefer to go somewhere else besides here. "Glen said, 'I'll stay with Dr. Lynn... for now, anyway.'

"The judge said, 'How about we make it for four years. That won't be too long will it?' Glen didn't realize that in four years he would be eighteen and wouldn't need anyone to sign any legal papers for him.

"After leaving the judge's chambers, a package containing a house key was given to Pop, so we went by Glen's house. I got some clothes for the girls and grandmother to wear if Glen chooses to buy them in their own clothes. His mother's clothes were mostly uniforms of some kind. I couldn't find anything dressy for her, so I'll find something of mine or go buy a dress. I don't think he wants to make any decisions on such things right now. He wouldn't go inside the house. A detective had gone inside the house and looked for any rental contracts, check stubs or receipts that indicated that they were paying rent. Apparently, the house belonged to the grandmother. There was a house deed with a name on it, and he didn't know yet if it was Glen's dad's name or his grandfather. They're still checking that out. It was a different last name from Glen's. Marshall is going to see if the stepmother had been married twice or the grandmother had more than one husband. We don't know at this point about the house… at least we know they were not renting.

"We took Glen by a cemetery and picked out some plots. He didn't want to go by the funeral home and see his family, but Marshall and I think he should. When I get the clothes ready for the funeral director, then we will insist that Glen go see them, before there is a public viewing or service. He will do better at the funeral if he does that. I'll take the clothes in tonight and then perhaps tomorrow he can go see his family.

"We talked to Pastor Bishop and he asked Glen about the girls and his stepmother, and I realized that the papers that he had been carrying in his pocket were what he had written last night when you asked him to do the assignment. He gave them to Pastor Bishop."

I asked Mom when and where the funeral was going to be. She said, "It will be at Ford's funeral home on Mt. Auburn Road at ten Saturday morning. Today is Thursday, so we have a little more time for Glen to adjust. We also went by his school and talked to the principal. She had Glen's records and from the looks of them he's been a fairly good student, especially after being in the after-school prevention programs. He was a strong B student the spring semester. He had some C-pluses and a couple of B's and a couple of A's. I was pleased. The principal said he had a good attitude, too."

I said, "Well, we had better get in the house. I'm hungry even though I ate a good plate lunch at the campus University Center. I hope I'm not going through a growth spurt."

I laughed because I remembered getting so hungry and eating and eating and then found my clothes were getting too small and I had grown another inch in height. Mom smiled and said, "I remember those days. Each one of you got ravenous for food and then you seem to outgrow everything in a week's time."

We went into the house. Pop was at the kitchen table with a cup of hot cider. Paul had gone to his room and was lying down to rest. Glen had gone upstairs. I thought I would get a cup of hot cider and take it up to him. I wanted some myself. I didn't want him feeling like he would like to have some, but was afraid to ask.

Pop asked, "Where's John?"

"Marianne is in town… does that answer your question?"

He chuckled and said, "Sure does."

Oh, Pop, did Aunt Susan find you around one o'clock?"

"No, we've been gone all day and didn't get home until around three. "Why?"

I stood there looking at him and picked up the phone and called John's cell phone. He answered. "John, what was going on at the Jenkins' house when you checked in over there? Pop and Mom don't know anything."

"I left a note on the dining room table."

I turned to Mom, "Mom, look on the dining room table for a note from John."

She hurried to the dining room table and didn't see a note… she said, "Wait a minute. Steve put his books down on it."

Mom read the note and kept saying, "Oh, my, Oh, my." She handed the note to Dr. Lynn.

He read, "1:32 p.m. Molly Jenkins… had a stroke. Can't find Dr. Lynn. I had Aunt Susan call 911. She was taken to Saint

Francis Medical Center Hospital by ambulance. I checked in over at the Jenkinses and the ambulance was just leaving. Marianne called. I'm going over to the Weber's. Pop, a plan has to go into action. Call Aunt Susan on her cell phone. …don't know the number."

"Mom found it, John. See you later."

I handed the phone to Pop, and he dialed Aunt Susan's number. She was home with Brian.

"Sister Sue, what's going on?" Pop kept saying "Uh-huh, uh-huh. That's a shame. Do I need to go up there right away? Okay… I'll wait until after dinner and then stop by and pick you up…. Bye…. Love you, sis."

Mom and I both asked in unison, "What happened?"

He shook his head negatively and said, "Apparently, Molly thought Sue hadn't given her night-time medicine to her, and took some from a bottle of medicine that she had. Sue puts the medicine in a divided box. Mr. Jenkins looked in the box and thought today was Saturday and Molly hadn't had her medicine, so he gave her some, too."

"Sue said, "When Molly said, 'I took my medicine,' then I knew there would be trouble. I called the pharmacy to see what side effects there would be. The bottles looked like she had taken only one out of each one. She acted just fine for several hours, but this morning when I checked on her she was just lying there looking around and couldn't seem to speak. That's when I called John."

I shook my head negatively, too. I said, "I know God has a blessing for us in this day. We need to find it."

Pop looked at me with a curious look and said, "Dennis, your wisdom sometimes amazes me. You're right. What are our blessings from this day?"

Glen had come back downstairs and heard Pop's explanation

of what happened at the Jenkins' home. He went to the sink for a drink and said, "I have a new home, four brothers, my own room, clothes that I can change every day if I want, food at every meal time, and a Mom and Dad who will love me for the next four years."

Glen was at my back and I stood up quickly and turned around, "Glen, our love doesn't turn on and off with time. God ordered us to love even our enemies, and you are *not* an enemy, so we will love you as God loved you and gave his life for you. You are family now, so that's the blessing that I put at the top of the list for today, and it will also be forever."

Mom added. "And I put you there, too."

Pop said, "I put you there as soon as I met you and you will stay there until we get through the funerals, and when you are settled in as one of our boys, you will stay a top priority along with my wife and all the other guys in this house—four years, ten years or forever."

Mom said, "The next blessing is my car. I love it, too. God just drove it right to our door. Well… not God but he used Dennis to bring it to me."

I laughed. "For a minute there, Mom, I thought you were calling me God."

Steve came in the kitchen and said, "What are you all talkin' about?"

Pop said, "This has been a stressful day, and we were counting our blessings."

"Well, I have one. That calf that was born is a dandy. She is eating well and is strong. The new substitute mom has taken to her like she is her own, and I'm pleased."

Glen said, "I guess that calf and I have a lot in common."

Steve looked at Glen, "Would you like to have her? I'll let you raise her. You can learn all about the beef business. Who knows, you may be able save enough for a truck by the time you're sixteen, too."

Glen smiled a faint smile. "I don't know beans about cows."

Pop patted my arm. "Hand me the phone, Dennis, but first dial Officer Harrison. Would you, please? If your mother has the car on her blessing list, I had better make it permanent."

I dialed the phone and handed the phone to him. Glen came on to the table and sat. I looked up at the clock, "Mom, what can I help you do for supper? I have a hungry brother here."

Mom said, "How hungry? Pizza hungry… roast and mashed potatoes hungry, or…"

Steve came through the kitchen and said "or… Café hungry with a big tip hungry… Mom, I'm out of here. Do I take the Lincoln or the old car?"

Mom smiled at Steve, "Here's the keys—see which car they fit."

He recognized the old keys and said, "Aw, Mom," then he kissed her, "I'll see you in about an hour and twenty minutes. Save some of your good pizza for me."

Mom laughed, and said, "Well, I guess it's pizza."

Glen said, "Ditto."

Pop was listening to Officer Harrison telling him about the car, but he put a thumbs-up motion to Mom. I didn't know if he was saying 'Ditto' about the pizza or he was happy to hear what Officer Harrison was saying about the car.

Paul came to the door from his bedroom and said, "Ditto, what?"

Glen said, "Pizza."

"Then double ditto. That teacher thought I should eat more chicken noodle soup this noon and I'm tired of chicken noodle soup. I don't even want to think about my chickens outside. The next time I go out there, I'll probably see a Campbell's label on each hen."

I got up. "Mom, turn the oven on. I'll go get some from the freezer."

Mom always made up fresh pizza crusts on the pan ready to put filling on. Or whenever there was a store special she'd buy several. The freezer always had one or the other in it. I first looked in the pantry and, yes, there were several cans of pizza sauce, so I went to the freezer on the back porch and brought in two pizza crusts and one ready-made pizza. We had plenty of shredded cheese of several kinds.

Mom added, "I can brown hamburger and add onions and green pepper… what else sounds good?"

"Leave one cheese and pile the works on the other."

She said, "Okay."

Pop said loudly, "Sold! …Bonnie you have yourself a Lincoln. Congratulations to the new owner."

"Oh, Marshall, I'm looking forward to driving it to work and showing it off. Thank you. Thank you."

I whispered to Mom. "What did you do with all those Campbell's soup labels that you have been saving for Paul's school?"

Mom looked at me like she thought I had just lost my mind, but she said, "They're in the junk drawer, why?"

I whispered, "…because I'm going to cut some of them up and stick them on Paul's chickens with double faced tape, but I'll wait until late Sunday afternoon or I'll see how the mood is when I do it or maybe one day next week, and I'll get Glen to help me."

Mom laughed and Pop said, "What is all the conspiring going on over there on the other side of the room?"

I turned around. "We need to take Glen shopping and get him a new suit and some dress shoes before Saturday morning."

I was proud of my quick thinking, but I knew my face showed

some ornery feelings. Paul asked, "What day is today anyway? I can't get my days straightened out with so much going on."

"This is Thursday evening and as soon as we eat supper, I need to go up to Cape Girardeau and check on Molly Jenkins at Saint Francis Medical Center Hospital. Tomorrow morning early, I'll get a cashier's check for the car and if Glen wants to go with me, I'll take him to the Mall and get that new suit."

Mom said, "First we need to check the suits that were purchased for Kaitlynn's wedding. I suspect there is a brand new suit upstairs in the hall closet that will fit perfectly. All of you need to find what you are wearing Saturday, just in case we need to take several of you boys shopping. After supper, that's an order... nothing else until I approve of what you are wearing to the funeral."

I whispered to Mom, *May I take the Campbell's soup labels upstairs with me.*

"That's enough, Dennis, Get the table set." Mom can be a sergeant when she wants to be, but I knew that I could get her to come down from her high-horse, if she relaxed, so I said, "Okay... Okay! I just wanted to make sure an old hen had a new suit, too."

"Dennis... Set the table!" Then she laughed.

Marianne stepped into the kitchen from the porch as Mom was sternly telling me to set the table. John was behind her. Both of them had smiles on their faces like something had happened. I thought maybe they were laughing because of the way Mom told me to set the table, but when Mom said, "Marianne, how good to see you. How are you?"

Marianne answered Mom with, "One hundred percent better than I was about two hours ago. John wanted me to come over and show you this."

I knew the smiles weren't because of my conversation with Mom on the Campbell's soup labels. Marianne held up her hand for us to see a sparkling diamond engagement ring on her finger. Mom's expression was priceless. "John, you've been holding out on us. When did you have the time to think about a ring... much less buy one? Oh, Marianne, I'm so pleased that you two have finally... that... Oh, Marianne, you really are going to be legally a part of our family."

Marianne hugged Mom and then John hugged Mom. Mom's stressful day finally was released of its tension. Mom grabbed a dishtowel to hide her face and started crying. John grabbed Mom and Marianne at the same time in a big hug. Pop said, "Wait a minute, I need to be in on this."

John turned around and reached out his hand to shake it, but Pop said, "No, I want a hug, too."

Pop hugged Marianne, too, but Glen was sitting at the table watching. I noticed him get up and leave the room. Pop said, "Shall we add this to our list of blessings for this day. Congratulations, John, you have chosen well."

John said, "Thanks for the shove!'

I laid the three pizzas out on the counter on thick place mats and stacked some dishes at one end. "Pizza's ready. Line up at the end of counter number one and would the cook please put some pizza back for the number three son when he comes home, while I go find number five son who has walked out of the room?"

Pop looked around. "I'll go after him. After all, he is as of today, legitimately my son... something I hope to change soon for a few others."

Glen came to the kitchen door, "I'm here."

John reached out his hand to Glen. "Come here, Glen, you are the newest member of this family. I want you to meet Marianne, my fiancé. She will be the next member of this family."

Marianne held her hand out to show Glen the ring and he did

a little bow and kissed her finger like he had done it many times before. "Congratulations," is all he said.

There were several eyebrows raised. I had to say, "Glen, what's with the kiss?"

He looked embarrassed. "Grandma said if a girl reaches out her hand palms down, I should do a little bow and kiss it."

Pop came to his rescue, "...and what a nice gesture she taught you."

We all turned our attention back to our supper because Paul had picked up a plate and said, "Aren't we going to eat?"

Mom had made a salad to go with our pizza and had taken out one of Steve' famous apple cakes for dessert. It was all consumed within twenty minutes.

Steve came home from the Café, and said... "Well, look what I have been missing here at home. I hope someone saved me some pizza."

Mom got up and opened the refrigerator for his salad and told him his pizza was in the warming oven. He looked at Marianne, "What's this Robert tells me... that he's losing a sister to me?"

She lifted her hand. "It's true, see!"

"Wow, John. You've been keeping secrets. How many wheat harvests did that set you back?"

Mom said, "Steve, don't ask... John don't tell."

Steve laughed, but I thought about Janet and wondered if I should call her. *Call her.* I felt like John. He was always saying God spoke to him. I reached for the phone and said, "Excuse me. I have a phone call to make."

I went to the living room, punched in the Weber's phone number and Mr. Weber answered. "Mr. Weber, this is Dennis Moore. Congratulations, you will finally get John as a son-in-law. I didn't think he would ever feel he was free enough of some of his other responsibilities to make Marianne his wife. Dr. Lynn finally had to tell him his feelings and frustrations would be better if he had a wife beside him to support and help him. That was all it took. He had been holding out on us with the ring. We are ecstatic out here on the farm."

My mouth was running off a mile a minute. Mr. Weber finally said, "Dennis, did you just call to congratulate me."

I know I must have taken a deep breath and he probably heard it. I meekly said, "No... I really wanted to talk to Janet. Is she there?"

"She is sitting here at the table and just maybe her mother will excuse her from clearing the table and let me do it, so she can talk with you."

He handed the phone to Janet and she quietly said, "Hello."

"What's the big idea taking my brother and making him yours?"

I heard her giggle—her famous little giggle. "Isn't it neat? Her ring is beautiful. Did you help John pick it out?"

"The ring was a complete surprise to all of us. He had really been hiding it—not a hint of it. Not a word!"

"Well, I guess that makes it more precious to Marianne. It's a surprise to everyone who sees it. Dennis, how are you? I haven't seen or heard from you since the day you all took me to school. Goodness, that was three weeks ago."

I know I hesitated, but Janet can really make me nervous. "I'm fine, Janet. How are you doing with the crutches and the knee?"

"I have an appointment with Dr. Lynn's associate first thing in the morning. Well, ex-associate now that Dr. Lynn has retired. I'm really glad he insisted that I go get that X-ray. I've been very faithful to wear the elastic band and use the crutches. I can tell when I try to put a lot of weight on it, that it's not quite healed, but I think a lot of it is just from lack of use. I guess he'll tell me tomorrow morning. He'll probably prescribe for me to go to one of those gym places for some knee rehabilitation."

I was listening to the melody in her voice and thought about her voice lessons and just responded with an un-intelligent, "Yeah." I had to think quickly. "Are your music lessons doing as well as your leg?"

She paused, "I guess. We just had the Music Festival at the university and I received a superior rating. I was pleased with that."

I thought about the youth program at church and how often she had participated. The only time she is in the music program at the church is when Marianne comes home. So, I said, "Janet, have you ever thought about how the Lord can use your talent?"

She paused again, "What do you mean?"

Then I paused. "Well, Janet, God is the creator of everything and when he creates a person he gives one person this ability and or talent and certain gifts such as teaching. He gives them to us to give *him* pleasure. We were created for his glory. Satan does an on-going job of messing it up, but we who know God recognize the work of the devil. Even so, God still wants us near and dear to him and whatever we do by developing our talents or abilities should bring honor and praise to Him. Do you understand what I am saying?"

I realized I might sound like I was preaching. Janet said, "Yeah, but.... "

I almost said, *no, yeah or buts about it,* but I didn't. She had paused and I said, "I haven't heard you sing, except in a trio. Do you think maybe we could get together and sing a duet sometime? I'm certainly not the singer you are, but I guess I could play the guitar for us."

Janet laughed. "Wouldn't Marianne and John smile about that—another Moore-Weber duo."

I had to laugh with her. "Who knows what the future holds… but I'm sure that the Lord would be pleased if we use our talents for him. Think about it. By the way, Marianne is here with John now. Would you like to come out and have a jam session? We haven't had one with the family for a long time and we could practice something for the funeral Saturday morning and then sing on Sunday morning, too. I can come get you if you would like to do that.

There was another pause and Janet giggled. "I would be glad to come out, if this is the way I get you to call me for a date. Let me check with Mom and Dad."

She left the phone and I could hear the conversations. Robert had come in and was thrilled with his *forty-two dollars and twenty-five-cent tips* and it was just in two hours of training time. He was saying just wait until tomorrow night and Saturday night when the weekend crowd come in. "I should be able to make boo-coo bucks."

The sounds became muffled as Janet neared the phone talking to her mother, but I did hear Mr. Weber say, "Robert, with last night's tips and tonight's tips, you already have almost half a month's car payment."

Robert said, "Where else can you work for twenty dollars an hour? I might give up being a police detective and become a permanent waiter."

I felt a little uncomfortable listening to their conversation. Janet must have laid the phone on a counter or somewhere near them.

She picked the phone up and said, "Mom said it's a school night, so I have to be back by ten."

I looked at my watch. It was about six-forty, so I said, "I'll be right over. Come as you are, okay."

I yelled, "Mom, I'm going over to the Webers' house and pick up Janet. We are going to do some jamin' and anyone that wants to join us is welcome."

Steve said, "Good. I like singing with Janet."

"No, Steve, this time you are milkin' the cows. We are the duo this time."

Steve looked at Mom and then John, "Our brother is waking up. Janet is a good catch. Well, not like a fish catch, but she's a good girl for him."

I asked Mom, if she minded if I borrowed her car. She handed me the keys. "Hurry back."

As I passed by Paul's room, I noticed both boys were on a bed watching something on Grandpa's T.V. Mom left it in there for Paul. When he is sick with the chemo, it helps to take his mind off how he feels. Otherwise, the household policy is *no* television in the bedrooms.

I stopped and quietly said to Mom, "Did you find any sleeping shorts for Glen? He may want to get comfortable and just sleep where he is."

She looked in the bedroom, "I'll go check right now."

I went on out the door and leaped off the three back porch steps. I twisted my foot and something hurt, but I didn't want to stop and worry about the pain. I was so excited that things between Janet and me were getting friendlier.

I prayed on the way over to the Webers' house. *Lord, I don't know many girls... I really haven't been looking for a girlfriend. The girls at the university seem okay, but none of them has had any appeal to me, but Janet... Lord, I have a desire to meet her on several levels. But, Lord, she is still just a senior in high school and has four years of college. That seems like a long time. What if she goes away somewhere to college like Marianne did? I'm not sure that I can be patient like John has been.*

Like John, I heard a voice again. In my head the scripture

came to me, so loud and clear. *Be still and know that I am God… My time… not yours.* I said, "Thank you, Lord, I know that was from you."

I arrived at the Webers' house within eight minutes and knocked on the door. Mr. Weber answered and yelled for Janet. He invited me in. "So you are going to be doing some *jamin'…?* What is jamin?"

"Well, John and I play our guitars and mom plays the piano and Steve sings. When Paul is well, he plays the trumpet. Dr. Lynn joins us, too, on his guitar. Our music isn't loud because we are not electrified. God's music in nature is soft and subtle, so we try to be… with our acoustic guitars. We like it that way."

Mr. Weber was looking at me sort of strangely. I couldn't read his face. After a couple of seconds, he said, "That's nice."

Janet joined us and looked as sweet as she usually did. It occurred to me that Janet and Marianne might have gotten their music ability from their father. "Mr. Weber, when you were younger did you play an instrument or sing?"

He looked out the door that I had opened and was leaning on, "Yes, but I had to give it up when the children came along. Being out every night playing in a different club wasn't how to rear children as a father."

I know my eyebrows must have gone sky high as that was a bit of information that I would have never guessed. "What instrument did you play?"

"…Whichever one was needed."

"Well, Mr. Weber, you have just handed me a big surprise. When Dr. Lynn is able to join us… he has to go see Molly Jenkins tonight, would you join us?"

"It depends on what the family has going, but otherwise… yes, I would love to."

Mrs. Weber heard me say something about Molly Jenkins and asked, "Is Molly okay? Is she sick?"

"Yes and No, Ma'am. Something unfortunate happened. Aunt Susan gave her medicine to her, and Mr. Jenkins looked in the daily box and forgot that today was Thursday and thought Molly didn't have her medicine, so he gave it to her, also. Apparently with Molly's confusion and dementia, she knew she had taken it twice, but her mind was saying only the medicine part and she went to the bottles and got more, but apparently not much. She went to bed and Aunt Susan couldn't get her to respond this morning. She would just look around and couldn't seem to speak. Mr. Jenkins is a basket-case knowing what happened and that he contributed to it. He feels responsible. They couldn't find Dr. Lynn and called John at the university around noon. He had them call for an ambulance. They took her to Saint Francis Medical Center. Mom and Dr. Lynn were dealing with lawyers and all that for Glen today and didn't know anything about it until around four this afternoon. Mom is holding up pretty well with an extra boy. Surprisingly, Glen is, also. His first day, he wailed and cried all day, and was in and out of sleep. We're giving him all the hugs and love we can give him.

"We were talking about all the things that had happened today and decided God still had some blessings for us, in spite of everything that had happened, starting with losing a cow in the birth of a calf. Glen vocalized that he had found four new brothers and a Mom and Pop who love him and food at every meal time. I was surprised to hear him speak, but we have been trying to re-affirm that feeling."

I realized I was talking non-stop and standing on one foot and it was hurting. Mr. Weber said, "If you need any help holler. Then he laughed, "I'll bring my wife and Robert over to work."

Robert yelled from the kitchen. "I heard that!"

Mr. Weber laughed again, "Well, you kids be on your way."

I took Janet to the passenger side of the car and closed the door gently. On the way around the car, I realized that my shoe was hurting my foot and my ankle was *really* hurting.

"Janet, I may need to borrow your crutches."

"What for? You are kidding me, aren't you?"

"This day has not had enough things happened to give our minds and hearts pain, now my ankle and foot hurt. I took a leap off the porch steps to come and get you, and I felt a stab of pain but was too excited about coming after you and spending time with you that I didn't give it another thought until I got out of the car to walk to your door. When I was standing there talking to your dad, it was smarting something fierce, but I didn't want your dad to know it. I may have broken my ankle or foot."

Janet asked if Dr. Lynn was at home or if he was still at the hospital. She reached in her purse for her cell phone and dialed our home number. I took note of that… she had it memorized. John answered, "John, this is Janet. We're on our way to your house. Is Dr. Lynn at home?"

"No, he left to go to the hospital. He should be home soon."

We pulled up in the drive behind the house and Janet was still talking. "Can you come out to the car? I think Dennis has broken his foot or ankle. Don't bother your Mom yet."

John came out the back door. I guessed Mom and Marianne were talking because John came out alone.

I opened my car door and pulled my shoe and sock off. Man… did I ever sprain or break my ankle or foot. It was swollen and had already turned black and blue. John looked at it and said, "What did my big little brother do?"

I told him, "I jumped off the back steps when I went to get Janet, and I felt a stab of pain and a pop, but went on over to the

Webers' anyway. It kept getting worse. Now look at it. What do you think I should do?"

John said, "Well... the first thing we are *going* to do is call Dr. Lynn on his cell phone and see if he can meet us at the emergency room. If I go in and tell Mom, she'll pull a Mom stunt and faint."

Janet was looking at my face and she could see my agony. She said, "John... Dennis, you have to tell your mother. I'll go get Marianne and your Mom and I'm deciding right now that you are going to go have an X-ray. Marianne and John can drive us to the hospital. Your mother needs to stay here with Glen and Paul. So... let's get the phone call made to Dr. Lynn. I'm going in to talk to your Mom and Marianne. I have to be in by ten and if we leave now. We should be back. We can work on music tomorrow evening after visitation at the funeral home."

I looked at John and laughed. "Bossy little thing, isn't she?"

Janet went in the house and came back out with not only Mom and Marianne, but also Steve, Paul, and Glen. I felt like I was a specimen in front of a biology class. Mom said, "Yeah Dennis, I believe you did break something."

Paul was frowning, "Ooh, Dennis, that looks awful. Looks like my broken arm did."

Steve was shaking his head, "Well, big brother does this mean I need to milk two cows and close up the henhouse, too?"

I groaned because I had forgotten the evening chores. "It looks like it."

Glen was looking at Steve with a questioning look. "Steve, I thought you had already closed up the chicken house."

"Shhh, Glen, I want him to feel sorry for me."

"Steve, I feel sorry for *you*. Especially with the way your day started. You need to get in bed early tonight. You were up most of last night with the birth of your new calf."

I told Mom, "You need to get in bed early, also, and so does Pop. The girls can take me to Cape Girardeau, and John can stay here and milk the cows with Steve."

Janet took charge again. "Quit talking. It only takes fifteen minutes to get those cows milked. Get going, John and Steve. I'll try to reach Dr. Lynn again. What's his number?"

Mom told her. She still had the phone in her hand. I found it interesting that even Mom stepped back and let Janet take charge. She should be a nurse or doctor someday—maybe an administrator of some kind. When Pop answered the phone, Janet said bluntly, "Dr. Lynn, where are you?"

He must have said, "To whom am I speaking? You have a lovely young voice."

Janet answered, "Forget the lovely young voice. This is Janet Weber."

"Well, I just parked the car in the front drive in front of the house. Are you waiting for me somewhere?"

For some reason, Dr. Lynn had decided to park the Lincoln in front of the house. He was coming around the house when he answered the phone. He stopped to answer the phone and was watching all of us from the corner of the house. Janet looked around and saw him. So she decided to make it a big production.

"Well, Dr. Lynn, it's about time you showed up at your place. Don't you know that you have four boys, no five boys who need you? One isn't well, one has had a tragedy in his life and now one of them is lame with a broken ankle or foot."

"Marianne said, "Janet, be courteous, for Pete's sake."

"Well, how did the boy break his foot? Was he in a hurry to see you?"

"No, he wasn't in a hurry to see me... I was in a hurry to see him, so he hurried over and leaped off the steps of your back porch."

Dr. Lynn must have said, "Is that what you call a lover's leap?"

Janet started laughing and said, "No, it wasn't a lover's leap… Now get over here and take a look at Dennis' foot, p-l-e-a-s-e?"

Pop walked up behind everyone. "Well, Janet, move these people over and I'll look at your young man's foot. Everyone was so engrossed in looking at my foot that they hadn't bothered to look or hear Pop drive up or walk toward them.

Steve and John had gone to the barn to milk the cows, leaving Mom, Paul, Glen, Janet and Marianne gawking at my foot. Pop stooped and didn't even touch my foot. "Dennis, I hate to tell you this, but that ankle and foot need to be X-rayed. I'll go relieve John of the cow milking and you all go on up to Southeast Hospital or St. Francis Medical Center. St. Francis is closer. I'll call them and tell them you're coming. I've *got* to get some sleep. That cow kept me up most of the night. Do you mind?"

I looked up at Mom and she had that worried look again. I said, "No. Mom needs you here with her with the two youngest boys. You all go on to bed. We'll see you later."

I tried to put a sock back on over my foot. Pop said leave it off, but I had it already over my toes and foot and the pain actually felt better with the sock on. I looked up at Janet, call your parents and tell them you're going to Cape Girardeau with me. I don't want them thinking you're over here when you aren't. If something should happen on the way to Cape, I want them to know up front why you weren't here at my house."

"Oh, they won't care. I'll explain to them."

"No… explaining isn't necessary when they know up front why you won't be here. It saves a lot of time and heartache on their part and yours if something unforeseen should happen. How do you think they would feel if your dad suddenly had a heart attack and they wasted time calling here and there to find you?"

"Dennis, you're right. I'll call them. Let me use the cell phone again and I'll call them right now."

Janet was standing there looking at me like I had come from another world or something, so I said, "Janet, you do understand, don't you?"

"Of course, I understand what you said, but I just don't see what the matter is if we tell our parents now or wait until we get back, even if something should happen. They trust you, and they trust Marianne and me."

I guess I looked at her with a look of disgust or something, because she said, "Dennis, I trust you."

"Janet, it isn't a matter of trust. It is matter of courtesy and caring. When I tell someone where I am going to be, that is where I'm going to be. I don't want anyone in the position that Aunt Susan was in this morning—looking for someone... just anyone, when Molly Jenkins became so ill. It was hard for her to find the first person on her list to call for help. She called for Dr. Lynn's help, but he was in court and couldn't answer his phone... that was excusable. She called John at the university next, and because he was so far away and not able to tell what the problem was over the phone, he had her call 911.

"I called him to let Mom know that I would be a little late and she had not gotten back home yet, but she apparently arrived home shortly after I called. There was a young boy in the house not feeling well and very worried, because no one had shown up to relieve the teacher. The teacher had other things to do and places to go. When I dropped Robert off, there was John with you, Marianne. He had gone over to check on Molly Jenkins on the way home and slipped by your place. That was fine, but it would have relieved Paul and the teacher had they both known where John was. It would have relieved the lady to know that mom was about to drive into the driveway. You see, Paul trusts every one of them, but his anxiety level could have been greatly reduced if John had called him.

"Mom expected John to relieve the teacher, I expected Mom to be home with Paul, John assumed Mom would be home, and I assumed Mom would answer my call. I got anxious because Paul wasn't feeling well. The teacher could have gone on to wherever she needed to be or made some phone calls to let whomever was waiting on her to let them know why she wasn't there or they could make other arrangements. Aunt Susan could have called 911 immediately, which she probably should have done, but when you think someone is close by to help that isn't the first option you think of.

"When a life is at stake, it would have been appropriate for Pop to have called Aunt Susan this morning and said, 'I'm going to be unavailable all day long. If something should happen, call 911.' It would have been appropriate for John to have checked in with Paul first and then headed over to see Marianne."

I realized I was sermonizing again. "I'm sorry. I guess I need to shut-up."

Marianne said, "No, I'm sorry. I called John, just as he was leaving the Jenkins' farm, and we were so anxious to see each other, we didn't think about anyone else."

"Marianne, I'm not faulting you. I might have done the same, as badly as John wanted to see you. What I'm saying is… that it's a matter of courtesy to check in, and let people you care about and care about you, *know* where you are expected to be and *when* you are expected to be there. It saves a lot of anxiety and worry. It is a rare thing for Mom to have to say… *Where* have you been? It is a statement as well as a question and the tone of voice is full of worry.

And, Janet, I don't mean for this to be a sermon, but I have found the more that I have called Mom and said, 'I'm going to

171

stop here or there... I'm going to be late...' the more she trusts me. Because she knows that I care about her and her feelings for me."

I looked toward the barn. "Where is John? I thought Pop went out to relieve him in the barn. What's keeping him?

Janet smiled. "Ah, Dennis you just made your own point. Your anxiety level is up because you are feeling pain and waiting on John, whom you thought should be here by now to take you to the hospital."

Marianne said, "Can you get into the back seat? I'll drive us."

Janet started toward the barn, "I'll go see what's keeping John."

As I was getting into the back seat, John came out of the small front barn door with Steve and Pop. Janet turned around and headed back our way. She climbed back in the other side of the back seat and reached over and took my hand. "I didn't mean to cause you concern. I understand now where you are coming from and you're right."

—▶ ◀—

It took us fifteen or twenty minutes to get to Saint Francis Medical Center Emergency Room. Dr. Lynn had called in to let them know we were coming. A wheelchair was waiting by the door. Janet jumped out of the car and got the chair and brought it to me. It was nice having her help me. I told her she should go into nursing. She giggled again. "I've considered it—strongly."

"Remember, Janet, you have a knee that needs for you to be careful. You jumped out of the car and hurried for the wheelchair."

"Yeah, you're right. What a mess we both are."

Marianne went with John to park the car. A volunteer relieved Janet of the wheelchair. "You are Dennis Moore, are you not?"

"Yes, sir, I was told that was my name."

"Well, I'll tell you what, find your license and insurance card and try to convince the clerk that you are who you say you are. Dr. Lynn told us to give you the royal treatment, and that starts right here. Give this lady, with the badge on that says *Margie*, your insurance card and I'll wheel you on down to X-ray in just a few minutes. They are expecting you there, also. She'll take the papers to you there to sign. You are over eighteen aren't you? "

"Yes, almost twenty. I'm sorry I look so young."

He laughed and said, "That's your luck not mine."

He glanced toward the emergency room door. "Man... who is this man who looks to be another version of you. You aren't twins, are you?"

I turned to look where he was looking. John and Marianne were coming in the door.

"No, he's my brother, John, and he's almost two years older than I am. It's a shame he looks so young, too."

The volunteer chuckled. "Well, you can tell I'm three score and ten, but I can out-do many a twenty year-old. I *feel* young. Brought up on hard work and clean livin' as my wife used to say."

He wheeled me into the emergency room behind a curtain and a man in a white coat said, "We need to have you get up on the table if you can. The doctor will be in here in a minute."

He walked out leaving us on our own to get me out of the wheelchair and up on the table. Janet was still standing beside me. John and Marianne said, "We're going out to the waiting room. If you need us, that's where we'll be."

"First stop by the little office cubicle and get my insurance card from Margie and sign any papers, okay? I'm sure they want to know *you* will be responsible for the bill." I laughed. "No, I'll take care of it."

A nurse came in and said, "We need to get you up on the table. Can you stand?"

Janet answered, "He can stand. I'll help him."

She came around to the front and pulled up the foot flaps and said, "Hang onto me and put your weight on your good foot."

I was more than willing to hold onto her, but I'm so much taller than Janet that it was almost impossible to do. "Wait, Let me get closer to the table and I can do it. I don't want to hurt you."

The nurse was watching the whole procedure and said, "That's the way. A doctor will be here in just a few minutes. Just relax."

Janet was eager to help. "Would it hurt you if I pulled your sock off?" She was doing it anyway and I yelled *ouch!* She jerked it away so fast, "I'm sorry."

I started laughing, "I'm just kidding."

A paramedic walked past the door and glanced in our cubicle. He stopped and took a step back. "Let's see… you are John Moore of the bring-em-in-two-at-a-time Moore family and Dr. Lynn's step-son. Is that right?"

"Right, No, No, I'm John's brother, Dennis, except there is only one this time and I foolishly didn't go down our three back-steps at the house, but leaped down and something popped in my foot or ankle."

He started laughing. "I heard you took a lover's leap. Is this the young lady?"

I hesitated and thought…*I'm going to get Pop back for telling that,* but Janet answered and said, "I had better be the one."

She looked at me and smiled, showing the dimple in her right cheek and her even white teeth. *Man, she's beautiful,* I thought.

"Sir when you look at a young lady with a smile like that—wouldn't you say, 'she's the only one.'"

Janet blushed and the paramedic smiled. A man wearing a short, white coat came in. He didn't have a badge on. The paramedic did a little wave of his hand and went on.

The man was probing around on my foot, and it hurt like the dickens. I was frowning and said, "Doctor, I don't know what you're doing, but that hurts like hell."

Janet's eyebrows went way up and I said, "I'm sorry, Janet." I swallowed and knew I could cry very easily.

She patted my arm. The doctor said, "Well, let's get an X-ray and see what's going on."

He stepped out and I said, "Now, why didn't he do that first. If there is a break, he could have made it worse."

He was back in less than a minute and said, "Let's get you back in a wheelchair."

The older gentleman volunteer came in with a big grin. "Looks like I get to take you to get a picture taken of that foot and ankle. Dr. Lynn has already called and said he can't go to bed and sleep until he hears from us."

I looked at Janet, "The delay must be because Pop is that other doctor's enemy."

We passed the waiting room and Marianne and John were standing outside the room. I asked, "Is something the matter?"

"No, I just wanted to let you know that we're going up to see Molly Jenkins and see if Mr. Jenkins has had any relief. He may need to go get a bite to eat or something."

"Oh, …go on. You're right. He'll be glad to see you." They walked down the hall with us.

We were put in the X-ray unit's waiting room and we weren't there but maybe three minutes when someone came and got me. Janet looked so sadly at me. "I'll wait right here. I won't go anywhere."

"Thanks… that's courtesy in action."

"On second thought, I think I'll wander up and down these halls and play hide and seek with you."

"Funny! You wait right here. You are my comfort."

The technician was smiling at us. "Come now, you two can see each other in just a few minutes." We both laughed.

I wasn't back in the X-ray unit more than ten minutes, but, man, did it hurt to have my foot moved. I had to get up out of the chair with help. When I finally got back to the X-ray waiting room, Marianne was sitting with Janet. She had tears rolling down her face. I was about to ask Janet if she had some Tylenol or something in her purse, but looking at Marianne's face, I said, "Marianne, what's the matter?"

I reached over and took her hand, Marianne, where is John?"

Marianne swallowed, "He is upstairs with Aunt Susan, Mr. Jenkins, and Brian. We walked in just as a doctor said, 'I'm sorry, Molly is gone.' Mr. Jenkins needs John right now more than he does me. Aunt Susan is upset, as is Brian."

"Marianne, don't underestimate how much John needs you. John and Mr. Jenkins were very close. John isn't going to be any more level-headed than the others right now. You need to get yourself together and go back up there and do what you can for all of them. Okay?"

"Okay, I guess I could do some calling for them. Or I can have the hospital chaplain do it. He would be the logical one to call the Jenkins son and daughter."

"See Marianne, they probably haven't even thought of that. What room is she in? Ask the girl behind the counter to call the chaplain's office and go up there right now to that room?"

She got up and I could tell this was something Marianne had never done or anything like it, and needed just a little encouragement. I wheeled my chair up closer and said, "Be strong,

Marianne. God will lift you up with wing of angels. Let him do it."

I prayed out loud, "God be with Marianne and all those upstairs in Molly's room. Give John strength and wisdom."

An X-ray technician came out. "Dr. Copeland wants to see you. "I'll take you to him. Do your friends want to go, also?"

Janet answered, "Yes, if you don't mind." As we left the X-ray waiting room, Marianne went the other way. "Janet, do you think Marianne will be all right?"

"Yes, Marianne is usually calm during a crisis, but she hasn't experienced a death before. She'll do okay."

The technician wheeled me into a small consultation room which had a lighted X-ray board on the wall. The radiologist doctor was slipping my X-ray film behind the clips. He kept saying, "Um-umm, uh-huh, well, Dennis, you messed up your foot good. You have a crack right here and one over here and a ligament that looks like it might be torn. This X-ray doesn't show ligaments too well, but just the same we will treat it like one. What in the world did you do... to do such damage?"

"It wasn't what I did but *how* I did it. I didn't go down three steps off our back porch, but took a leap off the top step and went down at angle with all my weight. As you can see... six foot-two inches and two-hundred pounds doesn't do well on one small foot when it lands wrong."

"Well, I'll tell you what I'm going to do, since nothing is out of place. I'm going to wrap your foot to stabilize it and put a boot on you. If it is still giving you severe pain in a week, I'll want to do an MRI on it. I know Dr. Lynn very well, and I will tell him that you will not be working in the barn or the chicken house or driving a car for two weeks at least. If you should have to do your chores, make sure you have your crutches and do *not* put any weight on the foot. It will be at least six weeks before you can go without the boot. Janet, how is that knee?"

Janet looked at him surprised, "How did you know?"

"I remember you coming in with your mother. I was the one that looked at your X-rays. We were busy that day and one of our technicians put your knee brace on and got your crutches for you.... But who could forget your face."

When he made the comment he was looking at me, "Your girl is beautiful, but she seems to be beautiful on the inside, too. I waited for Janet to answer. She seemed embarrassed.

I looked up at her and almost answered the doctor, but Janet said, "I *am* beautiful on the inside. I gave my life to God and he made me beautiful. I had the older brother of Dennis here, take hold of me when I was fourteen and tell me that Satan may be able to destroy my body, but he couldn't touch my spirit as long as I have God in me and beside me. He told me to look in the mirror every day and say, 'God, this is Janet here. What can I do for you today?' It's been three years since someone came into our house and beat my brother and beat and raped me... my bruises have disappeared and my emotions have healed. I haven't forgotten that awful experience, but because of the friendship and love of the Moore family... my attitude changed. I know that all men are not animals. Some of them have such love for people and are gentlemen to the most unloving people that I, with God's help, can even love those despicable men who by the way, are now locked up where they should be. God loves them, I forgive them, and, hopefully, their discipline will be severe enough for them to never mistreat anyone again."

"My pain was so great without any medication that I bowed my head and covered my face and silently let tears roll down my face. Janet reached over and took hold of my wrist. "Dennis are you all right?" I raised my head and sniffed.

"Yes and no. I need some pain medication, but what you said is what I have wanted to hear for a long time. I needed to know that… that awful experience had not misshapen your view of all men. It also tells me that the work we are doing in the prevention program will give the kids we work with—hope. You need to work with us next summer and give a testimony of encouragement to the girls in their program. Even the boys need to hear it lest they think they will grow up to be like their fathers or other guys when they have witnessed such behavior."

The doctor was just standing there listening. Janet and I seemed to be in a world of our own for a few seconds and were oblivious to him.

He left the room and came back with some water and a couple of capsules and handed them to me. "Dennis, this is for your pain. I'm going to take you back out here and get you out of the wheelchair. You should have been put on a gurney when you first came in and the foot elevated and iced down and *not* put back in a wheelchair. Who was in the emergency room when you came in?" Both Janet and I had looked at each other. I had not seen a badge on the man.

Janet said, "I don't think he had a name tag on."

"Okay, I'll find out later. Right now, let's get you out of the chair and onto a gurney and I'll get the foot wrapped and the boot on so you can be on your way."

He turned and called for someone to come help me. I said, "Thank you, I would appreciate it."

John and Marianne were in the X-ray waiting room when we came out. They were both visibly upset. An orderly was waiting with a gurney. "Let me help you up here, young man."

I stood and the orderly looked to be about five feet ten inches and he said, "Well, on second thought maybe your twin here had better help you."

179

I looked at John, "That's the second time tonight that you have been referred to as my twin."

John smiled. "You didn't know you were so lucky, did you? What's going on?

I told John and Marianne that there were a couple of cracks in the bones in my foot and a possible torn ligament. "The doctor is going to wrap it and put a boot on it for tonight and then I'm free to go."

"Well, what's with the gurney?"

I told him the doctor didn't like the fact that I wasn't put on a gurney in the emergency room. Janet said, "…and ice on it anyway."

John helped me up on the gurney. "Dennis, your foot looks bad. Doesn't it hurt?"

Janet answered, "He said, it hurts like hell."

I chuckled. "I'm sure glad I won't have to experience hell, if the pain is anything like this. The doctor gave me a couple of pain capsules, so I might be sawing logs on the way home. What time is it anyway? We have a curfew to meet tonight, or my name will be mud with the Marianne and Janet's parents."

Marianne looked at her watch and the clock that was on the wall behind me. "It's almost nine o'clock, so relax. We'll make it home in time."

The orderly took me back down the hall and to the left—back to the emergency room. The doctor was waiting for us. Marianne and John stopped in the waiting room. A security man was standing out in the hall. He made me nervous—like something was going on.

The doctor wrapped my foot and ankle tightly. It hurt. Someone walked in with a boot. I wondered why they had asked for my shoe-size. The boot was slightly bigger than my shoes, though.

The doctor seemed a bit nervous, "Do you know Officer Harrison?" He asked.

"Yes, I work with him and he is on staff over at the Law Enforcement Academy."

"Oh. Well, then I am going to involve you in something, and I need you both as a witness."

I looked at Janet, "Janet, would you like to be excused. You can go to the waiting room with Marianne and John."

She said, "No, as long as there isn't any shooting, I'll stay. What's going on?"

"Well, we think we have a man here posing as a doctor on the staff. Those in the offices don't seem to know any different. So far, serious mistakes have not been made, but we want to prevent that. Would you recognize the man who posed as a doctor when you came in? The nurses are assuming he is a doctor and follow orders, but they are questioning what he does. We haven't verified *all* his credentials, but some of them seem to be fraudulent. What we are going to do is call for him and since you know what is wrong with your foot, would you ask him what your prognosis is and how long you will have to wear the boot?

"He may ask you if the X-ray found any broken bones or he may tell you… ask him any kind of question you want. We will be listening."

Janet asked, "What's prognosis mean?"

I answered for the doctor. "It means what can I expect as far as healing. It means what does the future hold for my healing."

She said, "Oh."

Doctor, my brother is in his third year at the Police Academy and is working toward a criminal justice degree. This would be a good experience for him. Would it be okay if he is in here to witness this? I will make a suggestion myself, though. Get that security guard out in the hall out of sight. Put him next door." I pointed to the area with the curtains drawn.

"We'll do that. I'll go get John and explain, and then I'll send for the so-called Dr. Woods."

He walked out and I told Janet, "There cannot be a hint of panic or suspicion of the man. If you have ever been an actress you must do it now."

The security officer walked in another door and slipped behind the curtain. I said through the curtain. "Just to be on the safe side… get up on the gurney and cover yourself with a sheet. He may pull back the curtain and look to see if anyone is over there. Close your eyes if necessary. Roll up your sleeve and pull the I.V. over and tuck the tube on the inside of your elbow. Bring your arm up to hold it there."

He laughed, "Have you ever been a stage manager?"

"No. I'm just a quick thinker."

John walked in and said, "So, we are going to do some first-hand police work tonight. You realize we have only about four hours until midnight and every hour this day has been filled with something. I hope this is the last."

Janet was looking at my foot, so John said, "Janet, sit on that chair right over there. I'm going to step back over and pretend to be talking to the other man… getting his insurance papers ready for him to sign. By the way, I took care of paperwork and signed for you. I'll step back in after he comes in and say, "Are you about ready to go home?"

Then you can ask as many questions as you can? I activated this recorder. Put it in your shirt pocket just in case the hospital isn't able to pick up anything."

I looked at John and almost asked where he got such a tiny thing, but decided we didn't have time to talk. I'd ask him later.

Janet said, "This is exciting."

I shook my head and wondered if we should send her out to be with Marianne, but I only said," Remember you are an actress."

"I'm cool, I'm cool."

We waited a few more minutes and heard the announcement for Dr. Woods to come to the emergency room. It took him about two more minutes to get there. He still didn't have his name tag on.

He said, "Oh, my patient is done and ready to go home, is he?"

"Yes, but I have just a few questions. A nurse or technician put this Ace Bandage on; do I sleep with it on?"

"You leave it on twenty-four hours a day… and avoid getting it wet. You just wash your body and legs. No showers or tub baths."

"Well, how about the boot? Do I need to wear it?"

"Yes, all the time except when you go to bed."

"How long do you think I will have to wear it? Two weeks, a month?"

He looked like he was thinking and said, "You may have to wear it for six months. Well, maybe… wear it until you can get your shoe on anyway."

Janet asked, "How about pain medicine? Does he need anything for pain?"

He looked at Janet, "You're supposed to be his medicine for pain."

I ignored that and asked, "Well, what can I take?"

"Oh, you can take as many Tylenol as you need. Just don't take any more than what is prescribed on the bottle."

Janet said, "I thought when you have a couple of cracked bones and a torn ligament, the doctor would prescribe something stronger than Tylenol. What do you usually prescribe?"

The man turned to Janet and laughed. "Sex three times a day with a girl as pretty as you."

Janet got indignant and said, "Sir, that comment was very unprofessional of a doctor. What medical school taught you to say things like that?"

The man couldn't keep his eyes off Janet, "No, I wasn't taught that in medical school... I wasn't speaking as a doctor, but as a man. I have known people to smoke a couple of joints of marijuana for pain. How does that sound?"

I was much bigger than this man standing three feet away from me and I wasn't going to keep my act going much longer, if he didn't start acting more professional and stop looking at Janet with his leering eyes. "Doctor, just write me a prescription for pain and we'll be out of here."

Janet was not intimidated. "No, Dennis, I may be young, but I'm not stupid. This man just recommended sex and marijuana for your broken foot. I want to know why. And I really want to know why you don't have a badge on or why you didn't introduce yourself earlier when we came in.

I saw an expression on the man's face that I didn't like, so I asked him, "Sir, I will need a prescription for pain. With my body size, Tylenol will not touch the pain. I only need enough for the next two days. After that, I think I should be able to tolerate the pain. What about crutches? Don't you want to prescribe crutches, so I can go somewhere and get some?"

"Go to Wal-Mart. They should be cheaper there. As far as the pain, I can give you some samples for the next two days. Let me see what I can find."

He left the room and the security man behind the curtain said, "Hang in there, Kids. He is going to trip up yet. Be sure and take the medication, and we will check it to see what it is."

The man was gone about five minutes and came back with a

regular envelope with about ten pills in it. He had written on the envelope. *Take two pills every four hours for pain.*

Janet said, "Dennis, let me put them in my purse, so you don't lose them." She reached for the envelope and he said, "No, you never want to give anyone else your prescription drugs."

Janet had all she could take of acting and said, "Sir, Dennis has a long way to go to get home. Give him one of the pills before we leave."

"No, wait until he gets home, that way he will be able to sleep longer before waking up with pain."

"Sir, I'm only seventeen years old, but if you are a real doctor, I am forty. I have been in this hospital several times and the doctor would always give me something for pain before I leave."

"Janet, you need to calm down. I will make it."

"No, give me that envelope."

She grabbed it out of my hand. She got a whiff of the envelope and said, "Dennis, You aren't leaving here without taking something."

She opened the envelope and took a sniff, "Oh, these are the good kind. They come in mint, orange, and cinnamon."

The man got nervous and said, "Yes, go ahead and take two now. They won't hurt you."

She got me a cup of water and whispered in my ear. "Tic Tacs."

"Oh well, honey, put them in my jacket. I left it on the chair in the other cubicle."

I got down off the table and held out my hand and said, "Thank you, Doctor. I know I'll feel better with Tic Tacs. At least I know that my breath will taste better.

"Tic Tacs? I had better check with the pharmacy and see what they gave me. Wait right here."

The security officer stepped around the curtain. Janet went

out the door with the envelope and gave the envelope to John. "You can go in now. I think Dennis' real doctor would like to have a word with the… the… whatever you want to call him. The jerk!"

The security guard put handcuffs on the man and John stepped back in the room to wait until the local police could get there. John was so much bigger than the security guard. The orthopedic surgeon came in and said to Janet, "Good work, young lady."

It all happened so fast that the pretend doctor was standing there looking at all of us with a look of hatred. The security guard asked the man if he had any identification on him. He didn't answer, so John put his hand on the man's shoulder while the security guard checked his pockets.

He had a couple of car licenses with pictures. One must have been his Dad, but he looked older. They had the same name and address. The orthopedic doctor was looking at him and shook his head. "Your father was Dr. James Woods, right?"

The man just looked at the floor. The surgeon just said, as though he was talking to himself, "Well, that will be easy to check out."

I couldn't believe one more thing had happened in my day. I prayed, *Lord, did you allow me to break my foot, so Janet and I could be here at the hospital to catch this imposter and did you put John upstairs just at the right time when Molly Jenkins died? Whatever you are doing in my life… give me a little more notice, please.*

I felt bad for thinking that way and prayed, *I'm sorry, Lord, I know you are with me every minute of the day and, Lord, you will have to give me your wisdom in all situations, because sometimes I feel like John did when he was my age and I want to say, 'Lord, don't forget, I'm only eighteen.' Well, I'm really nineteen, now.*

Like John, my mind heard a voice and it said, *"Remember David was but a youth when he slew the giant."*

I wanted to answer and say out-loud, "Don't send me any more giants tonight," but two Cape Girardeau policemen came in and took custody of the poor substitute for a doctor. The regular emergency room doctor came in and apologized for not being there for me as his wife was upstairs having a baby and babies just didn't want to come at a convenient time. "I have a son and all is well, so now I can go to work."

It was a good thing, too, because as we were leaving the hospital, there was an ambulance driving up to the emergency room exit. I asked John, "Did anyone call Mom and Pop to let them know about Molly?"

Marianne said, "The chaplain came up and he called their children. They will be here sometime tomorrow morning. Aunt Susan called your Mom. Dr. Lynn was asleep and she said, she wouldn't tell him until the morning."

Janet asked, "What time is it, anyway? I need to get home before my mother worries about me."

John looked at his watch, "It is… nine …twenty …three, if I'm reading my watch right in the dark."

I couldn't help thinking, *Ahh, Janet learned from my little lesson earlier,* but I said, "John, stop at McDonalds's on the other side of the highway and get us a shake. That pain medicine isn't sitting well on my empty stomach.

We all laughed at that, but Marianne. She had to be filled in on all the happenings in the emergency room because she was sitting in the waiting room reading and waiting for John and didn't know all the excitement that had taken place.

She said, "Is this the kind of thing that I'm going to hear about after we are married?"

John was very appropriate in his answer. "Honey, there are far worse things that happen in this life every day, and I'm going to be on the side of keeping *good* balanced on top. Don't ever think about my job negatively, or you'll get scared for me, or depressed and insecure. Always think that Robert, Dennis, and I are setting things right, okay? A more positive attitude will always keep your thoughts in perspective. I will always be careful, so you needn't worry. Besides, I may be a big man… but, God is bigger."

I said, "Here! Here! I agree—one hundred percent!"

We stopped at McDonald's and got our shakes. It was twenty five till ten and we were on our way home finally. Marianne and Janet made it home before Janet's curfew.

CHAPTER 6

WITH ALL THAT HAS been going on at the Moore-Lynn farms or with one family member or another, time has a way of escaping into oblivion and me with it. I was thinking about Glen and how much adjustment he has made. He is amazing. I thank God every day for him.

A little more than six months have passed since Glen's family was taken away from him in those brutal murders and he was completely wrecked mentally and emotionally. Mom and Pop insisted that he go to the funeral home, before anyone else ever went and spend time alone with each family member. She had asked him to write a note to each one that he could put in the casket to tell them good-bye. He did that. Mom stayed with him, while he was in the room, but she sat on a chair off to the side. He was overwhelmed, but Mom said, he stood by each casket and cried, but leaned over and gave each one a kiss good-bye and put his note in their hand. He is only fourteen years old, but very much a man.

There has been only one hearing that he has had to attend. The lawyers are going to try to keep him from testifying in a few months. It's been a terrific burden for him to talk with the lawyers, but we all assured him that he was *our* brother now and we were his family and we would be with him all the way.

Pop suggested that Glen spend two weeks with Paul's homeschool teacher before he enrolled in school at Chaffee to help him catch up on anything he might have missed. The teacher got work from the school he had attended and the eighth grade teacher in Chaffee, too. He really should be in the 9th grade for his age, but somewhere he must have missed too many classes and had to repeat a grade or something, because he is very bright and does well on all the assignments. Every paper has a "good work" statement or a "perfect" grade or some comment. Pop is going to check into why he is not a freshman in high school.

A real strange thing happened on the Monday two weeks after the funerals. Mom took the day off and two ladies from our church, Mrs. Weber, Aunt Susan, Mom, and Pop went up to Cape Girardeau to get Glen's house cleaned up. There was a moving truck there and two men going through stuff and taking what they wanted. Pop called Glen's lawyer and he promptly called the police. The police showed up first and then the lawyer with the detective who was working Glen's family's case.

The police asked for identification and the men gave it to him. They were a son and nephew of Glen's step-father. One man claimed that since his father was still married to the ole battle-ax, everything including the house still belonged to his dad and he had asked him to take care of everything.

The detective said, "I'm sorry, but the house belonged to someone else… not your father, and the personal belongings belong to the biological son and grandson. You can fight this out in court if you choose, but right now, you must unload what you have on the truck, and get out of here. If you insist, then we will have to arrest you for trespassing and theft."

According to Mom, they had gone through drawers and left things scattered everywhere. They had loaded a television and a table and chairs on the truck and a living room chair. They grumbled, but took them off. Pop saw one of them stash something on the front seat from the opposite side of the truck and Pop told the police that he had better take a look. He called for back-up and two more police cars came.

The men got really anxious. The detective told the policeman, the one who had been there from the start, to go check the cab of the truck to see what was there, and one of the other cops to check the status of the two men on his car computer. Pop chuckled again as he was telling us the story. "That cop got out of his car and bravely walked up to the two men who were about to lift the chair off the back of the truck and asked, 'Which one of you is Thomas Smart?'"

Pop was laughing when he was telling what the policeman said, "Why don't you live up to your name? You have a warrant for your arrest for theft, and your partner in crime here, is also wanted in three different states for related crimes, such as you were just caught in the act of doing. I'd say your name is Thomas Dumb!"

Pop said both men were hand-cuffed and taken away. They had even registered the rented truck under their real names. That was dumb, too, but then I guess they had to give them some identification in order to rent the truck.

I asked Pop what they had in the cab of the truck, and he said, "They apparently found a box with jewelry, cash, and some papers that were stocks and bonds that belonged to the grandmother. The detective said he had missed them when they went through the house. They had the same name on them that was on the deed of the house. I suspect the jewelry and papers belonged to Glen's grandmother and she had either forgotten them or didn't know what to do with them... or she had hidden them from her second husband. It's a shame because they could have lived very well, if she had remembered them or knew what to do with them. Who knows what or why she kept them secret. Glen's stepmother may have been a rebel in her younger days and the grandmother didn't want them squandered, but I suspect she didn't know where the papers were hidden."

When we came home from the university, Mom called all of us to the kitchen table for a family conference. She and Pop told us what had happened. Pop was standing behind Glen's chair, but I could see his face. He looked like he was going to cry. Pop patted him and finished Mom's story. "Glen, sometimes we don't see what God is doing and we question why he allows things to happen in such unexpected or an unbelievable ways. It seems like God uses Satan's mistakes all the time to accomplish His will. I suspect things were supposed to be done differently, but Satan is always trying to muddy the waters. So, God takes those things that happen and turns them into something good, not only for us, but for *his* glory. Today, those crooks found something that the detectives had missed. Only a thief would know how to look for things of value that are hidden. God knew, and he allowed the thieves to find a box of valuables belonging to someone, and God allowed for us to see the man put the box in the front of the truck. In the box were a lot of papers… certificates for stocks and bonds. We still don't know who the name on the certificates is, but the detective is working on it."

I asked, "What was the name?"

He said, "Arthur G. O'Malley… a very Irish name.

Glen put his head down on the table and started crying. Pop said, "What is it, Glen?

Mom interrupted and said, "I broke down and bought some Cokes today. How 'bout I fix all of us one?"

She got up and started getting glasses and ice out, when Glen said, "My name is Arthur O'Malley. My Dad's name was Arthur O'Malley. My Grandfather's name was Arthur O' Malley."

Leave it to Steve to not always be appropriate at a time of

tension. He said, "Well, what in the world are we calling you Glen Malley for?"

Glen didn't answer him. Pop sat in Mom's chair and said "Son, look at me."

Mom handed Glen some tissue and he blew his nose. Pop went to say, "It appears that there have been a lot of secrets that you have had to live with. Right now you are a part of this family and we are here to give you love and support. You don't need to hide who you are or anything else. No matter what happens with, for or *to* you, we are your family and we will stand by you. You are safe with us. Now… let's back up and you tell us all that you can think of about the O'Malley family, okay?"

Glen said, "I was born in Ireland and came to the country when I was four years old. My mom, dad, and grandparents came, too. My grandfather was with a government somewhere. He was some kind of spy, but I didn't know that until he was murdered here in the United States by some Irish Catholic misfit who didn't understand he had retired long before he came to the United States. Dad changed my name, but not legally when I started to school. The school accepted his explanation about the difference in my name on the birth certificate and the one they wanted me to use in school.

"Mom got sick and died and my grandmother raised me for four years until Dad remarried and used the name of Martin. My older sister was my stepmother's daughter, and my younger sister was my half-sister. Grandma remarried, but he ran out on her after two years. Grandma and Dad told me that I was to keep the bloodline going for the O'Malley family someday. Then Dad died.

My stepmother asked if Grandma would come to live with us and take care of us kids while she worked. They liked each other and my Grandma was happy to be with us. I don't know anything about the papers you found. Grandma did worry from time to time about her second husband stealing from her and leaving her a poor woman. May be she didn't know the stuff had been hidden. Maybe that's why the man married Grandma. He died in a car accident when I was ten. It just seems like everyone connected with me has died. I don't want anything to happen to this family."

Pop stood and let Mom sit back down and he said, "Well, Arthur Glen O'Malley... did you know your middle name was Glen?"

Glen wiped his nose with the wet tissue and said, "I thought it was, but I have never seen my birth certificate. Grandma said it was."

I was still sitting there taking this whole scene in and it sounded like Glen could write a book on his life already. It was interesting. I said, "Pop, you really ought to call the detective and tell him what you just learned. Perhaps he can get a new birth certificate from Ireland or something from a citizenship type form. Surely, they all became citizens of the United States. Glen really needs some validity as to who he is. I want that for him."

Glen looked at me with sad eyes, but a slight smile and said, "Thanks."

Pop shook his head like he was trying to shake a surprise off.

Pop said, "Hand me the phone." He called the detective and explained what Glen had just told us. We were hearing only Pop's side of the conversation and he was saying..."You don't say... Really? Well, I'll be..." He was smiling.

John reached over and put his hand on Glen's shoulder, "It sounds like good news, doesn't it, Glen?"

"I need some."

Pop shook his head like he was trying to shake something off his head he said to whoever he was talking to on the phone. "Wait until I explain this to Glen. He needs good news."

Pop finally laughed and said, "I'll tell him." He hung up the phone and was grinning from ear to ear and looking at Glen.

Glen said, "Well, what is it?"

"Glen, stand up. I want to shake the hand of Mr. Arthur Glen O'Malley born January 23, 1980 in Dublin, Ireland and became a citizen of the United States at the age of five. Your birth certificates, your parents' and your grandparents' citizenship papers were all in one of the files in that box. Those stinkin' thieves were going to use them to collect whatever they could of your inheritance. The detective has turned the papers over to an investment counselor and he thinks, Mr. O'Malley, that you are worth in the neighborhood of..." Pop paused like he had said too much, but he added, "Something in the seven or eight figure range."

I will never forget the face Glen made and the comment he made. We were all shocked at the amount he was worth, so the remark made it so much more meaningful.

"What is a million dollars *worth* when you grow up with the loss of everyone you love? What is it worth to be hidden away, while you live in poverty and have to be in a prevention program for at risk for crime boys? What is it worth to those who have died? They all had to leave every cent behind and I will, too. Having family, having roots, having a sense of who you are, is worth more than all the money in the world."

Glen paused. "Being part of this family is worth much more than money... how much is seven figures anyway?"

We all laughed and Paul said, "I think it's a lot."

Steve said, "It's more than what I have for my truck.... Man.... Glen, You can buy two trucks when you are sixteen."

Glen's next comment was about as good as the first on. "Maybe I can give some money to Officer Harrison to help more boys and put in more gardens. The food from my garden sure helped my family. Do you think some of the money can help buy the supplies for the garden next year?"

I was overwhelmed, but said, "Glen, the remarks you just made are what God hears and he will bless you abundantly for giving to him to help others."

Pop said, "I think God had a blessing in storage waiting for him all along."

He looked at Mom and Pop and said, "Does that mean I can?"

Pop was almost giddy from the look on his face. "It sure does. This is why we in the family say… give to God first and he will make your money stretch beyond what you ever dreamed. You haven't had money to give, but your time and labor in the gardens for your family was giving to their needs."

Glen looked at the rest of us and sheepishly said, "Thanks. When I was working in my garden last year, I wished that I could be the helper instead of the one being helped. When I went with home with vegetables and eggs the first time, Mom sat down and cried. She fixed us all an omelet with tomatoes and cheese in it. I never had tasted anything so good. Because you gave us home-made butter and I took home potatoes from my garden, some meals we had just baked potatoes with butter and slices of tomatoes. It felt like we were really eating a lot."

Pop said, "See Glen, you did give to the Lord when you gave your vegetables to others."

Glen said, "Yeah," but he added, "Grandma was always having stomach problems and I know it was because she was slipping her food to my little sister, so when I brought home eggs, I told her that three of them were for her and to boil them and make a sandwich every day."

Mom said, "Now you are talking about food, and you are making me hungry for a baked potato. How about we all eat a big baked potato in honor of Glen's grandmother? I imagine she is in heaven feasting at a banquet this evening and has all she wants. I'll make a lot of toppings to put on the potato... broccoli, cheese, butter, maybe even a little Chili. That sounds good."

Mom got up and got busy, and I said, "Well, if you *all* will excuse yourself from the table, I will set it for supper."

Glen said, "Let me help. It's about time I learned."

Everyone moved out of the kitchen except Mom, Glen, and me. I wiped the table and showed Glen where the dishes were... next came the napkins. I showed him where we keep dinner napkins and where to place them on the table. He commented, "Grandma insisted we use dinner napkins. She washed and dried them every day. She would always say, 'We don't have to be high class people when we are outside this house, but in here, we can have some social graces and cloth napkins.' She insisted on it, even when we had very little food. What are social graces, anyway?"

I looked at Mom for her to answer that one. Mom said, "There are several... one of them is... *how* we set a table. With cloth napkins and china plates, would be one of them. Having manners at the table is another one."

Glen said, "She insisted on that, too. We always had to help ourselves with the food in front of us and then pass it to the person on our left... or was it the right? Anyway, one way or the other, so all the food was passed in the same direction. Grandma said she used to send out invitations to parties and they had to be mailed on the right day or week before her party. Is that a social grace?"

The table was set and Mom added to the middle of it a small Lazy Susan tray with salt and pepper and extra napkins. The tray turn around so each person can reach what they want. Glen was looking at it like he had never seen one before. Mom said, "There now, you guys did an excellent job."

Glen smiled and asked, "Do you have a lot of studying to do, Dennis?

I told him, "Yes."

Mom didn't miss Glen's question, she said, "Well, Dennis get in the dining room and study."

I reached for my crutches and left Mom and Glen and the rest of the family, and went to the dining room and thought no more of Glen and his family. I had to shut out everything and everyone.

—▶ ◀—

I sat that evening in the dining room and tried to study, but I didn't accomplish as much as I wanted because my foot was hurting. John was sitting across the table from me with his books piled all around him. I started talking to him and he said, "Dennis, right now, I really need to study. You need hit your books, too, for about twenty more minutes or else supper will be ready, and you'll have no time to study later."

I wished that I could be as committed to my studies as John. I said, "You are right bro. Where did I put Criminal Law Book? I looked at my watch and realized I would have to hobble around again with the crutches to see what I had done with my books. I yelled, "Mom?"

She answered from the kitchen, "Do I hear one of my little boys calling me?

"I hate bothering you, but can you see if I left my backpack on the floor by Paul's bedroom door."

She yelled, "Yes, you did-d."

Glen picked it up and brought it to me. I said, "Thanks, Buddy, this is no fun trying to stay off this ole foot."

"Yeah." Glen was still very emotional, but he swallowed and said, "Why don't you sleep in Paul's room tonight? You won't have to climb the stairs. I heard you all talking about Pop's sister moving over here since Molly Jenkins died. If she wants she can have my room, I don't mind sleeping in Steve's room or with Paul down here."

I said, "Tell you what, while I'm hobbling around on crutches, you stay upstairs for a while until we see what Aunt Susan is going to do. In about a week, I suspect we all are going to make some changes in our rooms."

Steve came downstairs, "My room is *not* up for grabs. I have *too* much stuff in there to move."

I looked at him, "Sorry, Steve, if you are that fond of your room, John and I will move out and find an apartment, so Aunt Susan won't feel uncomfortable over there alone with Mr. Jenkins. She was there to take care of Molly and now Molly is not there. Do you have any suggestions?"

"Yeah, you and John take your beds and replace yourself in Aunt Susan's room over at the Jenkinses' house."

John was getting a little perturbed. "I'm trying to study, so you guys need to take your bedroom discourse somewhere else."

Glen said, "I'm sorry. I started it."

"You all are forgiven, but go somewhere else, please."

I shut up, and Steve said to Glen, "Com'n, Glen. I have something to show you.

They went through the kitchen to go out the back door talking about whatever was in the barn. Mom yelled at them. "Oh, no, you don't... supper will be ready in five minutes. Where is Pop?"

Those fourteen and sixteen year-old kids stopped in their tracks on the back porch, and I heard the ol' *Ah, M-o-m.* They both came back in and Steve said, "Do we need to do anything to hurry supper?"

"Yes, ice in the glasses and pour the tea."

John said to anyone who would listen. "I really need to study.

I don't want to get behind, so I'm going to sit on this end of the dining room table and study."

I had my stuff spread on the other end of the table and my books opened, but I couldn't get my mind on my <u>Introduction to Criminal Investigation</u> or my notes. My mind kept going to Glen and the loss of his earthly family, or Molly Jenkins death and John and Marianne's engagement, my broken foot, where Aunt Susan would live, Steve's new calf and the loss of its mother, Robert's job and my job... I leaned back in my chair and looked out the window. My mind was going from one subject to another. I thought Glen might even like to make a donation to the older boys program. Then I wondered if all those stocks and bonds had increased in value.

John looked over and me, "Dennis, you are studying more what is out that window and not the book in front of you."

I looked down at the book, and said, "Yeah, my mind is on all the things that have happened around here this past week." I laid aside my book and took my <u>Introduction to Criminal Corrections</u> book and notes and heard Mom yell, "Supper is ready!"

We know that if we are over a minute responding to Mom's call for supper or getting to the table, when we are *in* the house, we skip dessert, so we're always on time. When Mom says, "come," we go.

Mom said, "Dennis, "Where are you?"

"I'm coming, Mom."

"No, you aren't. You stay where you are. I want you to put some time into those studies. I'll bring you something."

Mom took my plate off the kitchen table and fixed me a baked potato, with chili and cheese on it, and a small side dish of broccoli. Steve brought me my silverware, napkin, and drink. "Big brother, enjoy this... you may be helping me someday."

I laughed and when I answered Steve, Dr. Lynn, I mean Pop, came down the stairs and passed through the dining room just as I said to Steve… "No broken bones in your foot, please,"

Pop's eyebrows went up. "Don't tell me someone else has cracked a bone."

Steve said, "No, Pop, I just told Dennis to enjoy being waited on because I may need him to wait on me someday, and he said he hopes it isn't for anything more than a cracked bone in my foot."

That really wasn't quite what I said, but it would do. Pop said, "Oh," and went on to the kitchen.

I watched him walk to the kitchen. He seemed bothered by something. I wondered what he was doing upstairs in the bedroom so long. I wondered if being up all night with Steve's pregnant cow caused him to be overly tired. I wondered if there was something else the matter and he didn't want to share it with us.

I heard Pop praying in the kitchen and bowed my head and thanked God for Dr. Lynn and for Mom and Glen. I wondered if Pop was worried about Mr. Jenkins, and if Mr. Jenkins would be able to keep up the duties over on Lynn Acres. I finally took a bite of my potato and said, "Lord, it seems like I am trying to borrow things to worry about. Help me to trust you for every member in this family and for Aunt Susan, Mr. Jenkins and Brian. And… Lord, your will be done with Janet and me. Thank you for Janet. In Jesus' name I pray, Amen"

Someone burped in the kitchen and Mom and Pop both laughed. Pop said, "John, was that your compliment for the meal."

He said, "No, I'm sorry. Excuse me… but you know, I've heard in some primitive societies that it's a compliment to the cook to burp."

Mom didn't let that pass. "Since I'm the only female in this house, I'm glad that I don't live in that kind of society, so I'll take a verbal 'Thank you.' Please."

I laid my books aside and decided I could stop and go out to the barn and help milk the cows. I said loudly enough for everyone in the kitchen to hear me, "There are chores to do, and there is a funeral home to go to tonight, so the quicker they are done, the quicker everyone can go in town to the funeral home."

I reached for my crutches, and I guess I made enough noise when I dropped one of them for Pop to react. I heard his chair scrape on the kitchen floor, and he suddenly became Dr. Lynn and he appeared in the dining room door way and said, "Ole Bessie may like you pulling on her udder better than when I do it, but you need to stay glued to your chair until you're done studying. You need to stay off that foot as much as possible. That's an order!"

He had a half smile on his face, and he said very seriously, "I realize you are very committed to the work here on the farm, but ten minutes worth of work in the barn is not worth you doing a downhill slide in your grades, if I can help it. And… you don't need to be in the barn for another two weeks. You will have to do enough walking on campus. Better yet, we should think about getting you a wheelchair for a while."

I gave him a dose of my pearly whites by making my smile as big as I could get it and asked, "Was that the word from Pop, a friend or from the orthopedic doctor, Dr. Marshall Lynn?"

He put his hand on the side of the door frame and said, "Dennis, I think I can take a little time and help you this evening and do for you as Pop, a friend and as Dr. Lynn. You're too big to pick up and love on when you get a skinned knee, but I can step in and do your chores for you when you need help."

He slowly walked over to the table and said, "Put it there, man."

I grabbed his hand and said, "Thanks, Pop."

"You are welcome."

Glen came from the kitchen and stood beside him and said, "I can take care of you, too. I want to learn how to milk a cow."

John was coming into the room from behind him and headed for his books at the end of the table. He looked at Glen and then Dr. Lynn and said, "How about tomorrow morning? Do you think you can be up and be dressed by six-thirty? That way, Pop can get a little extra sleep. Tonight Mom may need you and Steve to clear the table and take care of Paul's chickens. All of us need to pitch in and help while we have two sickies in the house. Remember the family motto, 'All for one and one for all,' only this time it is three of you that need to take time to recuperate—Paul, Dennis and you. You aren't sick, but you do need time to adjust to your new home and your new family. They all left me in the dining room alone, and I had nothing to do but sit and study. Later, Mom came through the door a couple of times, and each time she would pat me and say something like, 'Study hard, son,' or 'Make an A for me, son.' She didn't realize that every time she said something I lost my concentration.

I finally asked, "Mom, what time are you all leaving for the funeral home?"

She said, "Just as soon as the kitchen is cleaned up and the chores are done. I suppose everyone will be back in the house in about fifteen minutes."

I decided I would take a break and wait for them to leave. I asked, "Mom, how is John taking Molly Jenkins death?"

She looked at me like, *what are you talking about,* so I said, "Both John and Pop are acting a little strangely this past week. I was just wondering, what all this stress of Glen's family and Molly's death, along with Pop not being able to see his usual doctor friends each morning or John' relationship with Marianne or… I don't know, but what *is* going on with Pop? John seems uptight, too. Haven't you noticed anything amiss with either of them? I've noticed tenseness in both of them, and Pop has sighed several times. I wondered what was going on in his mind. You might want to put your radar up, and see if you can get the same vibes that I have. Taking up farming is the opposite of being a doctor 24/7 for years. Maybe Pop needs to go up to the hospital a couple of times a week and have coffee or something with the other doctors in the doctors' lounge. It would give him a place to ventilate about all that goes on here on the farm… or to maybe brag about us." I chuckled at my own statement.

Mom laughed at that and said, "Lately, it is hard to see things to brag about, huh? I'll do as you say and kind of watch. John may be getting tired of school, and the sameness of his chores and all. Perhaps we need to hire a farm manager of some kind. In a couple of months it'll be time to get the winter wheat harvested and spring planting done. We've all placed ourselves aside to deal with Glen, and that's okay, but there hasn't been time for Pop and Steve to go look for a truck, and that should be done soon. We'll be needing to go get feed for the cattle and chickens very soon, and I would like to eliminate any extra stress coming from any area… no matter how small."

"Mom, tomorrow morning is Molly's funeral. Aunt Susan is experienced at funerals and the aftermath of whatever goes on getting the family stabilized again. Would you do yourself a favor and let some other church women help Aunt Susan and then right after the funeral, John, Pop, Steve and Glen can go look for a truck. I think it would be wise for us to let the Jenkins family have a time of solitude with no outsiders. Is there a meal planned for the family after the funeral, and is it going to be at the church or at the farmhouse?"

"I don't think there is any meal planned at *our* church.

The Jenkins' family were members of the Methodist church in town."

"Well, Mom, I'm just observing things around here, and I know things are not as organized and things aren't flowing like they could and this may all be normal with John and me—not having the same routine as the rest of the family, but with Steve's accident, Paul not being well and my clumsiness, breaking bones in my foot and Glen on board... Mom, there has just been a lot of things to jeopardize the stability of this family. I wonder if it isn't time for you to quit your job and manage the household full time.

I know Paul needs your insurance, but there will be no insurance if you get sick again and die. Besides, we wouldn't have to pay for a teacher or nurse and all those extra expenses, if you were here."

I paused and watched Mom's face for a reaction. Then I thought of something else. "You know, Mom, there's no mortgage on the farm now. If... if we have to take out a loan to cover Paul's expenses or anyone else's, we could do it and meet the payments. We could always go back to the Farmer's Co-op for insurance. Besides that, I think John and I could get insurance through the university. It's something to think about though, isn't it? My feeling is that we are losing some to the routine and continuity around here, and it doesn't make for a relaxed household."

Mom patted my arm and said, "Dennis, you may be right, Pop said something similar a couple of days ago. He was thinking of Glen and Paul though. He said, 'things ought to run smoothly and routinely for the younger boys. So they can find a niche or position in the family and work within it.' Paul did have that, until he got sick. Glen needs it badly and is searching for his place in the family and Chaffee."

I thought about Pop's attitude in the last couple of days and looked at Mom and asked, "Mom were you in complete agreement with Pop to have Glen here and for him to take guardianship of Glen?"

"Well… no… not when he first mentioned it, he didn't say anything to me before he said it to you on the phone. I thought we had all we could handle with Paul's illness and my working. He said to me, 'You could quit' and I said, 'No.' He let it go and said no more about it, but, if you are noticing a strain, perhaps I had better. I know he is retired, and maybe I'm expecting him to run the household and all… when John and I have always been in charge. I don't want Marshall feeling like he doesn't have *his* place around here. This home is *ours*… not just mine."

I thought about what Dr. Lynn had said about building a house between the Jenkins' farm house and this house, and that perhaps John might like to live here when he and Marianne get married, so I said, "You know, Mom, maybe you should start thinking about letting Pop build that house between the Jenkins' house and this place. With John thinking about getting married, and since he will have to find a place to live—maybe, it's time. Build it right next door, so it won't be so far from the barn and the chicken house, fruit trees and your garden space, that we normally use. Or you can plan a big garden and plant more fruit trees right behind the new one.

"I think it would be a good idea. Start your yard about thirty or forty feet on the other side of the twenty feet of space on the other side of our drive. That won't be too close, yet close enough to walk over here."

Mom said, "That is something to think about. Tell you what, how about I hand in a two months' notice, not two weeks, and see how things go. That should make everyone feel better and by then things will be picking up around here."

I frowned. "That's not good enough. Make it four weeks and

that would be better."

John, Steve, Glen, and Pop were back in the kitchen. Steve heard… 'four weeks,' and asked, "Four weeks for what?"

I didn't answer, but just looked at Mom to see what she would say. She didn't say anything. John came in and sat at the other end of the dining room table. He said, "I have about twenty more minutes to spend on one subject, and I'll clean up all my mess here."

Mom said, "No rush."

Steve and Glen came in the dining room. Pop went to check on Paul. I could hear Pop talking to Paul. He said to him as he came out of bedroom and stopped in the kitchen. "Just twenty more minutes and then brush your teeth."

Steve said, "Four weeks? Twenty minutes? What's going on around here?"

Mom said, "Steve, you are listening to two different conversations. Are you going to the funeral home tonight?"

"Should I?"

"It's up to you, Steve. The viewing, as they call it, if you remember, is to give people time to come and talk to the family and tell them how you feel and to encourage them. It's the last time you will be able to look at Molly's face and say good-bye to her."

Pop came in the room and heard what Mom was saying. "Steve, the family has requested that you be a pall-bearer. You need to go to get a feel of the room, and what you will be doing tomorrow. I'll have one of the men on duty at the funeral home explain things to you and the other pall-bearers. However, I suspect it will be similar to what you did for Glen's family."

"Okay. I'll go get changed."

Glen was in the doorway. I wouldn't mind helping, but I'm

afraid I might be crying before it is over. I'm not sure if I should go tonight."

Pop put his hand on Glen's shoulder. "Son, God will bless you for your desire to help, but this time since you just went through such a horrific experience yourself, maybe you had better stay home tonight with Dennis."

Glen said, "But Miss Molly was so good to help me clean my vegetables and get them ready to sell at the stand. She was so jolly and kind to me."

"And… that is how you should always remember her. The next time you see Mr. Jenkins, he would appreciate you telling him that. Kind words like that are helpful. Okay? You run along and get ready for bed and find a book to read, okay?"

Pop then turned to Mom and me. "Now, what was the serious conversation in here and what was in four-weeks? Is it something I don't know about?"

Mom looked at me with a grin on her face and said, "Dennis, here, is doing a mighty good job of convincing me that I should quit my job and start building a house about sixty feet from this one. I said I would think about it and maybe in two months, but he said, 'No, in four weeks.' I'm still not sure, but… if he is noticing some lack of continuity and routine around here with some stress, maybe I should quit and bring some stability to all you helpless guys. I guess you all just need an administrator Mom around here."

Steve yelled, "Rah, Rah, Rah, Mom the administrator. Mom the administrator, Rah, Rah, Rah. Pop, are you ready for an administrator over you?"

He was laughing and we all had a little release of tension and laughed at Steve. Paul came hurrying into the dining room. "What is so funny?"

I laughed and said, "Oh, Steve has always wanted to be a cheerleader, and he found his opportunity."

Mom smiled and looked at Paul, "Paul, how would you feel if I quit my job and stayed home with you instead of a nurse or your school teacher?"

Paul looked around at everyone in the room. "I'm only ten. Am I supposed to make the decision or is this a family conference?"

Mom answered, "It wasn't meant to be, but it sure looks like we are all together... and to decide the fate of my job at that. What do you think... work at the railroad office or quit?"

Paul frowned. "Ah, mom, I don't want you to quit just because of me, even though, Mom, you'd be much better than that other lady who comes in. I don't think she likes our family too much. I think she needs prayer."

I chuckled. "Don't we all? But are you saying, Paul, that you would prefer Mom to a nurse or a home teacher?"

Paul looked at Mom. "I'm sorry, Mom, I would."

He was edging closer to Mom, and she took his arm and pulled him over on her lap, "You aren't too big for Mom hugs are you."

Paul giggled out of embarrassment as we were all looking at him. He laughed and said, "No, not your kisses either."

Pop finally recouped from his shock at me telling Mom to quit her job and he said, "Hey, those lips are mind." We all laughed and it was good to hear it.

"I'm leaving to go to the funeral home in fifteen minutes," Pop added. "Who's going?"

John said, "I'm going,"

Steve looked at Mom and then at Pop, "I guess I will go, too.

I guess that will be four of us—stand up, Paul."

They all took off and left me in the dining room alone, again. I couldn't help thinking, *Man, this family. There is none like us. We are all together and then we scatter. We are like a flock of birds that fly together and then scatter when there is a loud noise. Then we regroup for a minute or two and then scatter.*

———

I had about two hours of good study time with Paul in his room and Glen upstairs reading. I was amazed at Glen's ability to read and retain everything he read. Our farm magazine, Paul's poultry magazine, the new Bible Pop gave him in memory of his family… it didn't matter as long as he had something to read. He even asked Pop if he had a Bible commentary. We all looked at him like *What's a commentary?* Or *you want to read a commentary?* Fortunately, Grandpa had one, and Mom saved it and she had one, also. Pop is so proud of him. He said, "I knew he had good stuff in him. Don't tell me I'm not a good judge of character."

He laughed when he said it. He gave Glen a hug and said, "Son, if there is something in the scripture that I can help you with, just come and ask." Glen took the big book and disappeared to his room.

———

Molly Jenkins had a beautiful funeral service. Mr. Jenkins was so downcast that he looked eighty instead of seventy. He would be missing his wife. With the Jenkins' children so far away, he would be lonely for a while. Aunt Susan would be a good substitute for Molly, but she was uncomfortable being in the same house with Mr. Jenkins since they are both single now, so Brian Lynn is going to stay with him and Aunt Susan is going to come over here. She wants to go back over there every day and make sure the house is kept clean, do the laundry, and fix some meals that the two men can just put in the oven.

We are moving bedrooms around again, to make room for

Aunt Susan. It's a good thing our old farm house is big. We have four bedrooms upstairs and one off the kitchen. Aunt Susan took twin beds out of her storage unit, and we put them in Steve's room as the old ones were down in Grandpa's room. Aunt Susan is taking Kaitlynn's room. Grandpa's old bed is leaning against the wall upstairs waiting for us to have the time to put it somewhere.

Traditionally, as families grow older they get smaller, but ours keeps getting bigger. I don't know how long this will work as Mom did quit her job and is busy working on house plans and building a house. When Dad was living, Mom and Dad were going to build a new house, and they had settled on some house plans. Pop looked at them and thought they were good plans, and he knew just the contractor that could build the house. They hired the man, and he came out to the farm and staked out the house. Fortunately, the man was just finishing up a house near Chaffee. Mom said his foundation crew would be here in another week to stake out where the house would be located.

I looked at the house plans, and Mom said she and Dad wanted to use the plans Dad wanted to build, but then they decided to purchase the farm instead. Pop thought the plans were ideal for our family. It had a huge eat-in kitchen somewhat open to a great room that could have another dining table at the end nearest the kitchen. There would be no formal dining room. The great room or living room would be about thirty-by-thirty feet. It will be large enough for us to congregate for our music practice sessions. The ceiling will be very high and that will be good for the sound from our instruments. I got excited for Mom. I know Kaitlynn and Matthew will be pleased.

John and Marianne finally set a date for their wedding. It is going to be in June. Pop said, "The house construction should be far enough along that they can finish two bedrooms and a bath and move the two younger boys and Mom and I over to the new house."

It sounded like our family continuity and routine was going to be disturbed again. I walked over to where the house was staked out with John and Pop and it looked like they had centered the house right between Jenkins' and our house. It was a little farther than I had expected them to put it. Mom wanted to be closer to the highway, so there wouldn't be a long lane. Pop said, "We'll have to move three project gardens elsewhere or move all of them on the other side of the lane." I agreed that it would be all right.

———— • ————

I had a surprise call last night. Janet called me. She said, "I made up my mind that I would never call you. I would always let you be the gentleman and call me. I haven't seen you except at church, but I need some information on the university and careers available at the Southeast Missouri University, and Robert is working at the Café tonight. He's filling in for someone. Do you have a current catalog? It can be a year old. I'm writing a theme for my English class, and it's due tomorrow on careers available to young women that were not available one hundred years ago."

My heart was pounding the whole time she was talking. There is something about Janet's voice that I can't resist. She turned eighteen the first week in January, and I'm still dragging my feet in dating her. After I broke my foot, and she went to the hospital with me and encountered the man who was not a real doctor, we talked several times on the phone.

So far we have enjoyed talking with one another about many subjects. She came out to the house the night before Molly Jenkins' funeral and we practiced a song for Molly's funeral. It was after the viewing, and everyone was already back home.

With my broken foot, I wasn't supposed to drive for six weeks anyway, and my courses had gotten so difficult at the university, I just didn't feel free to call her... especially with Glen and Paul needing a lot of attention. I wanted to be here for Glen, in case he needed brother-time.

I told Janet, if her mom or dad didn't mind, and I could find a car available, I would bring her a catalog providing she went to the Dairy Hop with me for a shake. She turned and asked her folks and they said (and I could hear them), "With Dennis Moore, certainly, but don't forget to be back in two hours."

I wanted to clap my hands like a little kid because I was so elated, but I couldn't with the phone in my hand. I don't know why I just don't make a standing date with her at least once a week. I think I'll talk to her about that and maybe invite her to sit with me in church. She usually sits with the girls in her Sunday school class, and I don't want to butt in and sit with all the girls. We talked in passing for a couple of minutes when we were at the church, but that's all.

Mom wasn't using her Lincoln, so she said for me to go on and use it. Pop said, "... dating in a Lincoln, that's classy, but you aren't supposed to be driving for two more weeks."

I said, "Well, you are right. I'll use my crutches until I get to the car and use only my right foot. Will that pass to get permission?"

Pop laughed, "Yes, if you don't go to Cape Girardeau... only Chaffee!"

I told Mom I wanted to take Janet to the Dairy Hop, and she frowned... "No eating in my car. If I find a French Fry or a crumb of food, you *won't* date in it anymore!"

"Trust me, Mom. We are going to get a shake. That won't spill like a soda. I'll treat your car like it was my own, and that reminds me, Pop, are you and Steve still looking for trucks?"

"I am, but Steve is enjoying looking at his bank statements

each month and likes the interest he is building up. As soon as the weather starts clearing up, we'll look again."

I was on my way out the door with the university catalog and said, "When you look, keep an eye out for a compact car or small truck for me."

As I went out the back door, I heard Pop say, "That young man is almost twenty and has never had his first car. We need to do something about that."

I wanted to go back in and say, "I heard and I agree," but Janet was all I needed at that moment and I couldn't wait to get to her house.

Janet came out in a parka coat with a hood on it. She looked so much like a doll baby with the fur around her face. No matter what she wears, she looks good to me. I had on Mom's heated seats, so she should be warm enough. When Janet hopped in the car, I hesitated before backing out. She took the catalog off the seat and did a quick flip through it. She said, "I'm ready."

"Me, too, but did you tell your folks I was here."

"Yes, they saw you drive up."

"...and you didn't wait for me to come to the door like a gentleman or does that only apply to phone calls?"

Janet had an expression on her face like I had offended her or she thought she had offended me.

"I'm sorry. Guess my eagerness over-rode my manners. You can walk me to the door when we get back."

"That, I will do." I had a flashback of Marianne and John going in the house and not finding her parents there and Robert and Janet beaten. I will always make sure Janet is safe before leaving her at the house.

We went to the Dairy Hop and I asked Janet if she wanted to go in. She said, "Not really, but if you do, I will go in."

"I prefer to stay out here." I ordered two shakes at the window and went around and parked on the other side of the building.

I said to her, "Janet, I have to tell you that Mom warned me that if she found so much as a crumb in her car, I could not use it again."

She laughed. "Well, shakes don't have crumbs, so we're safe."

"Yeah, that's what I told Mom. I really need to get serious about getting my own car. John has been patient about driving me to and from the university. He waits for Robert and me while we work, and he studies or goes into an empty classroom and writes a letter to Marianne."

Janet said, "I don't know what you guys have said to Robert, but he has been intent on tithing, and he keeps remarking that every week since he started tithing, his tips have been going up—sometimes a dollar and sometimes five dollars. There was a large group in your Cousin Stacy's big room and his tips were good that night. He said, 'I got at least two or three dollars from each person, and there were twenty-six people in the group.'"

"Well, Robert must be half-way to his goal and looking for a car."

"No, he's enjoying counting his cash and going to the bank. He likes looking at that bank statement each month."

I laughed heartily, and Janet said, "What is so funny?"

I told her exactly what Pop said about Steve. That was why he hadn't been too urgent about looking for a truck.

"That's funny. I guess they are really businessmen at heart."

"Speaking of hearts, Janet, in a couple of weeks it will be Valentine's Day. I would love to take you to the Youth Sweetheart Banquet at the church. That's, if you don't have a date yet."

"As a matter of fact, I don't. I didn't know if you would feel out of place going back to something with the youth. I know you're almost twenty."

I smiled my million-dollar smile and looked at her and said, "It's a date." I reached over and took her hand and said, "...and Janet, I'm in reserve for your senior prom, also."

She giggled, "Oh, thank God."

"Oh...?"

Janet frowned, "There's this guy who must have flunked a couple of grades, because he seems way too old to be still in high school. He's been pestering me for a date and told me, 'If you don't go out on a date with me before April or May, you are going to the senior prom with me.'"

She squeezed my hand and said, "I told him I already had a date. I thought if you didn't go with me, I would ask Robert or maybe even my dad or Steve. I was not going without a date, and it certainly wouldn't be him. He scares me a little. Sort of reminds me a little of that awful Officer Blair. He stirs up some feelings in me that take me hours to get over. I get a panic feeling in my stomach."

I put my shake in the holder, and cradled Janet's hand. "Janet, I'm so sorry that there are creeps in this world of my gender. Have you talked to your Mom or anyone else about him and how he makes you feel?"

"No, I don't want to worry them."

I sat there for a minute wondering if I should talk to Robert.

"Janet, anytime you start feeling that way—call me. I know it's been four years, but the assault you had was one that could scar you emotionally for life, and I don't want that to happen to you. This is the reason we wanted you to come to the farm for healing. It had to be with young men or boys in your peer group to help you through your trauma. You needed to know that sin is an awful thing when Satan uses people who don't have the Lord, to help them control themselves. God is first in the Moore family and my life. I need God every day to keep my perspective on life and people… especially in the occupation that I'm going into.

"It's important to realize that God hates evil, but still loves the sinner. It's people like you and me who make the difference in this rotten world.

"Janet, there is always going to be someone like this kid who will remind you of that awful time. Don't let Satan use anything or anyone to undermind you. You are too precious in God's sight and mine. We both will hover over you and protect you.

She looked out her side window and just held her strawberry milkshake. I could feel her hand begin to tremble in mine. I said, "Janet?" She pulled her hand from mine and put her shake in the other drink holder in front of us.

She took her napkin and put it over her mouth and nose and sniffed. She had the biggest tears rolling down her face.

"Janet, what is it? I mean it. I will never harm you and would never intentionally hurt your feelings."

She shook her head *no*. She swallowed hard and said, "You don't know what you are saying?"

I paused for a moment, "I think I do."

She let out a sob, "No, Dennis, you are misunderstanding me. You just don't know what it means to me to hear you express your feelings for me. John was super kind and wonderful that day. Steve was so good to me when we were at the farm, but you… as young as I was and as awful as I tried to sort out my feelings, it was you I was drawn to. You were my dad, my brother, John, Steve, my pastor, my youth pastor every good man I know all rolled up into one person. It was you who made God so real to me."

"Well, Janet, that's a great compliment, but I don't remember what I said or did to get that kind of response."

I couldn't help myself, "Janet, I'm a hugger. I hug Mom. I hug Steve, Paul and anyone who deserves one. Right now, I think

I want to hug you. Would it be okay?" She sobbed and turned toward me. I was glad it was almost dark.

I held her for a couple of minutes and let her cry. I was so overwhelmed with my own feelings that I couldn't say anything. I let a tear fall on her head and she felt it.

She took my napkin and wiped the tears from *my* cheek. "I'm sorry, Janet. I'm sorry that it has taken me so long to let you know how much I care about you. I could have told you when you were sixteen or seventeen, but somehow God wouldn't give me the signal to go-ahead. I wonder why tonight he gave us both the permission.

Janet laughed a nervous laugh. "I don't know, but you have to know that not a boy at school or anyone at church or I've *ever* met has ever measured up to you. When you meet perfection and know it, you pass everything else up. I have prayed about my feelings for you and have asked… why not Steve or why not this one at school or that one, but I have never been able to satisfy myself with an answer, because you have filled my heart and mind to the point that there is no room even to think about any other person."

"Janet, we're both young… what about when you go away to college or to the Southeast Missouri University? Don't you want to wait and see what God has in store for you there?"

"You said that right…*what* God has in store for me… not *who* he has for me. I know it is you. I've talked to Mom about my feelings and she says, 'wait… wait… wait until you are older. You may change your mind.' She has known for two years how I feel about you. All she will say is… 'Dad and I approve.'"

"I just hope you won't throw my feelings to the wind and hope someone else will catch them. God chose a young woman… maybe she was my age to be the mother of Jesus. With that kind of responsibility, why can't I assume responsibility for someone like you?"

"Janet, do you really feel that strongly for me?"

"I have held in in for two years, because I didn't want anyone to think it was a teenage crush or infatuation. I thought perhaps, too, that if it was, I would soon move on to someone else. I have had many opportunities, but I've been faithful to my feelings and commitment to what God has been telling me."

Janet was quiet then for what seem like a long time, as I wasn't prepared for all that she had said. She finally broke the silence by saying, "I think I have spoken too soon, or made a real misjudgment."

My chin was trembling and I couldn't talk. She flipped the light on and looked at my face. I was the one crying like a baby. She reached down and got some tissue out of the box that Mom had left on the floor. She handed it to me.

"I'm sorry, Dennis. I'm sorry."

I swallowed and said, "Janet, have you ever asked why I haven't dated?"

"I wondered. I thought maybe you had too many family responsibilities or wanted to wait until you were further along in school."

"No, Janet, it's because when you came to the farm for those two weeks, I had feelings for you, too. I talked to John about it, and he told me at that time in my life, and yours, I needed to set other priorities, so you would have time to heal and grow up a little. He told me to give you to the Lord, and if you were the one for me He would keep you in reserve for me. Every time I see you or am around you, those feelings have surfaced, and I have had to pray for control and for the Lord's timing. Janet, I love you. It's a love that won't be satisfied. I need you in my life. I am a month away from being twenty, and you are eighteen. Let's make a commitment to get to know each other for the next two years.

Then we'll see when the Lord has a final commitment for us in marriage."

Janet giggled. I couldn't believe she was giggling. "Janet, is there something funny?"

"No, I want to be kissed. I've never kissed anyone but my Dad and brother, and he won't let me do that very often. Have you ever kissed anyone before?"

I was so serious when I had been talking to her, and now I wanted to giggle with her. "Janet, I can honestly say, the Lord held me in check and there has never been anyone besides Mom and female relatives and then it was just a kiss on the cheek. May I kiss you now?"

She scooted over and I put both my hands on her neck and back of her head and we kissed. She started crying again.

"I felt good to me but you are crying again."

"I can't help it. I'm so happy. You had better take me home, before I ask you to kiss me again and again. Oh, Dennis, I love you. I think I know how God must feel loving us and calling the church his bride."

I took Janet home. We hadn't been gone too much more than an hour. I went in the house with Janet. The minute we walked in the door, both Mr. and Mrs. Weber could tell that we had been crying. I let another tear fall. I couldn't help it.

I said, "Mr. and Mrs. Weber, this great big six-foot kid has finally had the nerve to let Janet know that I have loved her from a distance for four years. I have stayed true to my feelings because she was young and I wanted her to heal from the tragedy she had experienced. But tonight, she told me she has loved me, also, and has been waiting for me. God's timing was tonight. I'm young, Mr. Weber, but you have reared two beautiful daughters to be lovely people on the inside, as well as the outside, and I'm relieved that I have finally voiced my feelings for Janet. I hope you know that I will not rush Janet into marriage. She has decisions to make regarding her education and what direction she wants her life to take. I want to be part of that, but I'll wait until she is ready for marriage. I have a priority in my life also, in getting my education. I plan to continue it."

Mrs. Weber said, "Dennis, I knew it was coming. I have been watching and observing you and we have never come up with a reason why you would not be acceptable as a son-in-law."

Mr. Weber said, "Dennis, I'm a hugger… let me give you a hug and welcome you to the Weber family. Two Moore boys… I can't believe we've been so lucky. It's a shame you don't have a sister for Robert."

I laughed through my tears. "I think I have some cousins in St. Louis."

"Well, send them on down."

Mrs. Weber gave me a hug, too, and I asked, "Would it be appropriate, if we held hands and I asked you to pray for us, Mr. Weber?"

"It would not only be appropriate, but it would be right. Thank you for asking."

Mr. Weber asked God for a special blessing for Janet and me and to give us patience during the next few years, and that we would grow closer to the Lord and, as we did, that we grow closer to each other.

"I hope I make it home without going off the road. I'm dizzy with excitement. I must go, though. I'll see you, Janet, and I'll call." I backed out the door and Janet kissed me good-night

CHAPTER 7

It's the end of March. Janet and I started going out one night a week, and we see each other at church. I started singing with Janet and Steve in church, too. She has a beautiful voice and sings the alto part between Steve and me. He sings the melody and I sing the tenor part. Mr. Weber wants to record us as soon as we find the time. He's been coaching us.

A whole level of talent opened up at church since Mr. Weber revealed that he plays a multitude of instruments and used to play in night clubs with his own band. Since giving his life to the Lord, the depth of his commitment to Christ and to our church has been amazing. He spoke at our church on "Men's Day" on Love and Commitment. He told the congregation that it took some sticks of dynamite to wake him up to the importance of God in his life. He told about being tied in the truck of an old car with his wife, and he was wired to the old car trunk lid with a home-made bomb. The following Sunday, there were six couple that committed their marriage to God at the end of the morning service. Mr. and Mrs. Weber were pleased that God used their experience to bring about change in other marriages.

He said, "It is a shame that God had to allow me to go through a near-death experience to bring me closer to my wife and children and to get my priorities right."

After the church service, I heard him telling our pastor that he would be willing to give a testimony anywhere about the blessings

God had given him since that almost fateful day. He said, "The blessing of communication is at the top of the list because my wife and I are no longer arguing over silly things, and the children aren't bickering back and forth. The second blessing is the respect and love that I've had from all three of my children."

He looked over at me and knew that I was within hearing distance, so I did a thumb's up gesture and looked away. He followed up with, "Now, I have the blessing of having my daughters find outstanding Christian young men who will be their life partners. I am praying for Robert to find God's choice of a mate, also. He thinks he has found someone, but we will see."

Janet heard the last part of the conversation and said, "Dad, are you talking about us?"

"I sure am. Why not talk about the people most dear to you. I suspect your girlfriends get an earful talking about that young man of yours."

Janet giggled. "Yeah, I guess they do. But what is this about Robert finding someone? What has he said to you, and who is it Robert *thinks* he has found?"

Janet looked at me. "I found perfection."

Mr. Weber laughed. "Oh-h, my heart breaks. I thought I was the perfect man in this world."

She hit her dad on the arm. "D-a-d… you're the perfect dad."

She gave him a hug and he said, "I have perfect kids, too.

Springtime outdoor work begins soon. March was really cold but the days began to get longer and warmer. Mr. Jenkins began plowing over on his… I mean, Dr. Lynn's farm. The winter wheat is looking good and should bring a good harvest on John's thirty acres and the fifty acres over on Lynn acres. The harvest for the wheat won't be until June when we are out of school. Mr. Jenkins and Pop decided to plow up last year's cornfields and try a different variety. Now that better weather is coming, Mr. Jenkins is adjusting to being without his wife.

After Molly Jenkins died and Aunt Susan moved over with us at our place, Mr. Jenkins was lost for a while. Mr. Jenkins' children tried to have him consider moving to Indianapolis, Indiana, so he would be closer to them but he told them, he was not going to make any decisions for at least three months. He has been on that farm since he and Molly were married, and to move to a large city doesn't hold any appeal to him.

I was talking to Mom one day and she said, "It would be good if Aunt Susan and Mr. Jenkins could find some interest in each other. They are good for each other right now. They both are still young enough to enjoy fifteen or twenty years together. I'm going to pray about that."

I laughed at Mom because Mom is a matchmaker at heart, even though she doesn't say anything to the persons she thinks would be good for each other.

It's been nice having Aunt Susan living with us. Pop and Aunt Susan reminisce about childhood times, and it has made us feel like we have been a part of their entire lives. Usually, though, Aunt Susan stays out of our way, by going to her room and reading, or doing some mending for Mr. Jenkins. She and Mom enjoy each other's company, too.

→ ←

John and I have two more months at SEMO University before summer vacation. I have managed to maintain my B-plus average, and I'm pleased with that. John will have finished his third year. Robert Weber and I will finish our first year.

My job with Dr. Stone will stop at the end of this semester. I won't have time to work at the university and work with the boys in the prevention program and their gardens.

Officer Harrison took my idea of a program for the older boys and developed it into a workable program. He has three boys who will graduate out of the younger group because they turned sixteen, and they will go into the older boys' program with Blake Hegel. Blake was used as a trial person to see how the program would go.

Officer Harrison talked with Wal-Mart, K-Mart, the Food Giant, and Schnuck's Grocery Store and two Farm implement businesses. They all agreed to become part of the program. Blake took a job at Schnuck's Grocery Store for two hours each evening and six hours on Saturday. He is so proud of his job putting groceries on shelves at night from seven till nine. Sometimes when help is needed he sacks groceries or goes to get carts from the parking lot. The jobs don't sound important, but for the store they are very important. The manager is happy with Blake and says he has a good attitude. The older boys will have to turn a copy of their report cards from school to the manager, also. Blake had a B report card the fall semester and the Schnuck's Grocery Store manager, in addition to paying the program twenty-five cents for each hour Blake worked, gave the program a fifty dollar donation. He, also, gave Blake a certificate of appreciation and a twenty-five cent raise. Blake feels like he is a worthwhile person because he has a job and is contributing to his family's well-being.

Officer Harrison and I both wrote a note of thanks to Schnucks and a note to Blake for doing good work as a student and as an employee. I hope all the boys that have worked through the younger boys program do as well as Blake.

Officer Harrison has six boys now ready to go to work in a garden. Since we are moving the gardens to the other side of our lane, we're going to have each boy measure out a section of ground and make the rows again. The strawberries that were planted last year will stay on the other side of the lane. They have spread and made more plants. Mom said when she moves to her new house, she will use that part for her garden and will share the strawberries with the boys. I suspect Mr. Jenkins will want to donate more watermelon and cantaloupe plants. If we can, we will have Glen start his nursery by making bedding plants. He can start by trying to propagate strawberry plants. I'll have Pop talk to him about that.

Janet wants to get a summer job. Mom suggested to Mrs. Weber that Janet learn to make some of the desserts Steve makes for the Café. It would help Cousin Stacy and Mom if she would also make desserts to feed the boys in the prevention program. Steve feels crowded for time, having to keep making the cobblers and cakes. He doesn't complain, but I know that he's graduating in two months from Chaffee high school and will want to turn that job over to someone. However, Mom needs to talk with Steve because Steve takes pride in his cooking and baking. The customers at the Café tell Cousin Stacy, "Your desserts are the best for miles around." Steve has a knack for baking.

It's my personal opinion that with Janet's talents, she would do what Marianne did for several summers and that is to hire on at our Calvary Church and do the summer children's program. Since Marianne is graduating and getting married to John, I suspect she will get a full-time job teaching music in some area school and won't need the job at the church. I have confidence in Janet. I know she can do it.

Janet decided to go to Southeast Missouri University and major in nursing and minor in music. She talked about getting a double major and adding sociology to the nursing. I'm all for that. She will be a good help for Officer Harrison's prevention programs. She can work with the girls' program. I'm afraid with so many classes I won't get to see much of her. Oh. The Lord just reminded me that we were going to give ourselves two years to date and get to know one another.

We will *have* to stay busy to last two years before thinking about marriage. I wish people didn't frown so much on young marriages, I would marry her tomorrow, but then I would have to work to support her, and she wouldn't like that. So, we will continue to see each other on Friday evenings and at church on Sunday, or when we practice to sing some special music for a service.

CHAPTER 8

THIS IS THE THIRD week in May. My last class was of Wednesday. I passed all my exams with flying colors. I am so proud of myself. John did well, also. I will miss working with Dr. Stone, but I will have too much farm work going on.

Besides that, John and Marianne are getting married June 14, and I'm afraid we will be doing a lot toward helping Mom and Pop get their house ready to move into. That has been an interesting project. We have all enjoyed watching the steps the contractors take to build a house from the foundation up. They are doing a rush job on two bedrooms and a bathroom for Mom and Pop to move into. All the interior wall studs are in, and the roof and windows are done. The weather has been perfect during the week, so progress on the house has been going smoothly.

Steve and I are going to stay here in the house with Marianne and John. I am uncomfortable doing that, but there is still work over here to be done. We will just have to stay out of their way. Mom suggested that they take the downstairs bedroom because they would be moving Paul out. John and Marianne would then have their own bathroom, too. Aunt Susan will still be here, also. She is beginning to feel like she needs a place of her own, but doesn't know where or what to do. She loves to go over to the Jenkins' house to do the house work for Brian and Mr. Jenkins. Pop said, "If things continue as they are, he may build her a small house close by... just two bedrooms, a living room, kitchen, bath and a large laundry with a lot of cabinet space to double as a pantry."

I heard them talking one evening, but she wasn't sure yet about that. He said, "Now, Susie, you could use the second bedroom for sewing, crafts, or whatever you wanted."

She just laughed and said, "I appreciate so much you wanting to do this, but I need to find myself a family of my own. I've even thought about being a single mother and taking in some foster children, but at my age, I'm not sure I could get approval from the Division of Family Services."

Pop said, "I think I will look around for a husband with some children who need a mother. Then only the man will have to approve." They laughed together over that and never came to a conclusion about the house.

It's going to be a real time of stress and no schedule or routine when Mom and Pop and the younger boys move over to the new house, and John and I are left here with Steve and one new bride in the house. I think I'll talk to Steve to see if he will carry on in the kitchen until we move out. Marianne can cook if she chooses. When Steve and I are working in the gardens with the kids, Mrs. Weber, Marianne and Janet's mother can come and help Marianne in the kitchen, as she did last year. I'm sure Mom will be over here during that time, also. I suspect Aunt Susan will go over to the Jenkins' house and work as she did during the garden season last year. Maybe Mom can go over there, and Janet can come help Marianne here. That would be nice. Well, we'll see how it all works out. The boys and their gardens are John's and my project. No one else *has* to help.

———

The garden projects are in full swing now. It doesn't seem

possible that weeks have passed. It was a tiring day back in April, when we had the boys out from Cape Girardeau with their notebooks, pencils and Stanley measuring devises. We started the boys at the very beginning again with Mr. Jenkins plowing and explaining how the plows turn the soil over. Then John came along behind him disking the soil with our tractor and disk machine, which broke the dirt into finer soil. The boys were handed a rake and a hoe. There were only two thirteen year-old boys, so they caught on pretty quickly by watching the other four boys. They did a fantastic job getting the soil ready. Then they measured out their plots and the spaces between each plot and the spaces between the rows. The next week they would plant potatoes, tomatoes, and green beans in the morning. In the afternoon, Mr. Jenkins would come over with his watermelon and cantaloupe seeds. The boys in the program were a little distant from Mr. Jenkins last year until they got to know him.

They all seem to respond to him as though he was their grandpa. I enjoyed watching the bonding that went on with the old man and the boys. God was in it. This year, the two new boys fell in with the older boys and bonded with Mr. Jenkins right away.

It was interesting how he applied life situations to the garden and how the boys listened. I think they listened because he was working right along with them. He didn't let them stop to listen. They hoed every weed and pulled others out from between the little seedlings. I heard Mr. Jenkins telling the boys the weeds were like the bad things in life… and they needed to get rid of them any way they could, or they would choke out all the good in their lives.

━━ ━━

Three days ago, I woke up with pain in my head. I don't know if I've ever had a headache. I don't know why. Things around the Moore household have been somewhat stressful, but not enough to give me a headache. When I woke up, I told John, "Something is wrong with me. You'll have to go do the chores by yourself this morning."

He said, "Oh, no... not just before my wedding. You aren't going to be sick, are you?"

I said, "Not if I can help it. See if Mom is downstairs or Pop. I really have a bad headache."

John disappeared. The house was awfully quiet for a Saturday morning. I sat up on the side of the bed, but felt like I was going to pass out. Pop walked in and said, "Dennis, lay back down. You're as white as a sheet."

Mom was behind Pop, and one of them said, "You have a headache?"

"Yes, it hurts from my right temple up over my head and down behind my ear and neck. I feel like someone hit me with a sledgehammer."

Pop asked, "Is it a sharp pain or a dull ache?"

I said, "Neither... excruciating."

He checked my pulse and said, "Your pulse-rate is a little fast."

Mom looked worried. "I wonder what could be wrong."

I couldn't even groan, I just exhaled deeply and said, "I don't know. My head is pounding with my heartbeats."

John said, "I'm headed to the bathroom and then to the barn if you need me."

Pop said, "Wait a minute. Go get Steve and Glen up to do the chores. The boys in the gardens will need you when they get here at eight this morning."

John left the room and the last thing I remember was Pop trying to talk with me and telling Mom, "Go call for an ambulance. This headache isn't normal for Dennis and especially when there is no history of headaches."

⟶ ⟵

It's two weeks later, and I am home under the watchful eye of Pop. I would still be in the hospital, had it not been that Pop is a retired physician and is still very young and remembers the symptoms of diseases.

I asked him to tell me about the day the ambulance came and took me to the hospital, and he said, "Within an hour after you arrived at the hospital, a cat scan found a small aneurysm and it had burst and you were headed to surgery."

Pop was really serious when he was talking to me. I imagine he had thoughts about losing someone else whom he had loved. He said, "The Neurosurgeon thought it was unusual for someone of your age and health, but one never knows. You were rushed into surgery and it was repaired."

I thought I had bricks sitting on my shoulders. My head felt three times as large as it was, and I kept going to sleep and waking up for two minutes and then going back to sleep. Pop was there each time I woke up. Once I remember Janet standing beside the bed, or else I dreamed it. I have never had anything happen to me health-wise. I have always been healthy. Well, I did have a reaction to some bee stings and did break my foot… but that's all. The doctors thought maybe there was a blood clot that formed from all the swelling and bleeding in my ankle and foot and perhaps the blood clot traveled to my brain. It didn't cause a stroke, but did stretch an artery in my head. God must have allowed the clot to break down gradually with the aspirin I took for pain, but the artery wall was weakened. I don't really know anything about those kinds of things; I just know that my life was saved, again.

My family is the greatest. With all the storms life has thrown at my home, it's still a place of refuge and security. I had been reading some scriptures in Proverbs the evening before I woke up with that terrible headache. I was reading Proverbs fourteen and several verses stood out to me. Verse twenty-six say, "The fear of the Lord has a secure fortress and for His children it will be a refuge." We've been in that refuge many times.

I thought about our family and all the illnesses and deaths, yet Mom, Dad's, and even Grandpa's love for God provided a place for us to grow into mature boys. God was Lord of their lives. Dad was always quoting to Mom, "May our sons in their youth be like plants that grow up strong." That was a verse in Psalm one-hundred forty-four, verse twelve.

Dad would look at whichever son was within hearing distance and say, "Young man, "Jesus grew in wisdom and stature, and in favor with God and men." Do you think you can do the same?"

I would always say, "Yes, Sir, with you as my teacher and example, I think so."

Mom would always add in one way or another. "We, as your parents, control you now, but you must be able to control yourself, and you must learn to let God control you."

When I would get out of sorts and do or say something mean to one of my siblings, mom would say, "Let's see now… What stage is my son in? Does he want me to control him or does he think he can have some self-control?"

I always felt guilty and would say, "I'm sorry" to Mom or to John or Steve… whichever brother I was teasing or doing some act of meanness. Now that I am nineteen… almost twenty, I can see the wisdom is what they used to say to us.

People used to say that we were far more mature than most young people our age. I think it was the example of our parents and their trust in God. They certainly had instilled values about family, about money, and dealing with animals reproducing and sex. They taught us we were not animals. We could think and cherish and love the opposite sex. Mom always said, "Fornication is a sin… always has been and always will be according to God." Then she would always add, "There is no honor to God in doing what He does not honor." We all got her message early.

Dad would talk to us about success and failure. I remember when our cows stopped producing milk. He would say, "Son, your cow failed to produce milk, but that does not mean she is a failure. In due time, she will produce milk again and be successful at it."

I learned later about the different stages and things that a cow goes through and why she might not produce milk at times. I remembered that when I failed a test in school. I would tell myself. "I am not a failure… I'm just having a bad day and on the next exam, I will do well and make up for it." Then I would go home with my test and look up all the answers again. On the next test I would do much better.

I don't know why I have been thinking about my family. I guess because I have been thinking about John and Marianne's wedding and about Janet and me. When she was by my side in the hospital the day I was discharged, Janet said, "Dennis, I have definitely decided to become a nurse. If you any objections, I want you to say so right now, and I will reconsider.'

My mind was still not up to thinking straight, but I said, "My personal nurse would be great. My kids will each have their own nurse, too."

Janet is only eighteen, but I can see things in her that will make a good wife, a good mother, *and* a good nurse. I followed up with, "If you have prayed about it and feel being a nurse is what God wants you to do… then go for it."

She quoted another Proverb to me. "Commit to the Lord whatever you do, and your plans will succeed."

"Dennis, I think that I could take up basket weaving or

anything else as long as it is a good and an honorable occupation, and I commit it to the Lord and work to give him honor in it, then God will give me success."

I thought about how God inspired or moved John go into police work very directly. I realized that God does call people into strategic places and occupations and does put them where he wants them. He confirms it to them somehow or someway. But for others, he doesn't get in their face and say, "This is what you are to do."

I think it is because there are so many needs and so many occupations today with all the knowledge God has given to mankind that when a man comes along and wants to honor God with his life, He lets him decide in which occupation he wants to serve Him. I know with Janet's attitude and my thinking, God knows that He is going to use me as a policeman, and He will use Janet as a nurse. Somehow, God always put us in positions where we will automatically do what He wants us to do without any lightning bolts out of the blue sky to say, "Go in this direction." Although I would have to say, being John's brother, God certainly put *him* in a place to lead us into police work. Officer Harrison also was in place to lead us into working with the boys in the crime prevention program.

My mind wanders a lot, and I start thinking about things. Janet was still standing at my bed that day and she leaned over and kissed me and said, "A penny for your thoughts."

I told her I was thinking about the verse she had quoted about committing our plans to God and then we will have success. "Janet, you have my approval to go into nursing, but if you should change your mind, I will still approve."

Mom and Pop walked in about that time and Mom said, "Dennis, the hospital said to get you out of here. They want your bed for some other needy person."

Janet did her funny giggle. "Good, we get to take you home for some good old-fashioned mothering from your mom. And if she will let me, I'll babysit if she has to go somewhere—I mean patient-sit."

Pop laughed and said, "Me first… me first!"

Mom brought me some jeans and a shirt and shoes and socks.

I said, "Do you mean this hospital doesn't let a person walk out in their hospital tux? Well… I'm going to have to talk to Matthew about that."

For some reason I thought about Matthew and Kaitlynn's reception after their wedding and the modeling of what Matthew and Kaitlynn wore to bed and what they *would* be wearing.

I said, "Mom, do you remember how we surprised Matthew and Kaitlynn with what they had been wearing to bed as single people and what they would wear on their wedding night? Let's do something to John and Marianne. It's so close to their wedding time, they won't have time to find out that we will be doing something."

Mom said, "Uncle Al asked me if we were going to do anything. I sent him some pictures of John and Marianne when they were kids, and he is putting them together in a comedy film. I haven't said anything to anyone, because sometimes it's better that the surprise be for everyone."

Janet said, "I'll never tell. I would be glad to model what Marianne wears at the dorm. I know what she wears at home and it's this skimpy old shirt with string straps and it says. 'I'm sleepy, aren't you?' She wears an old pair of pajama shorts with it."

I laughed, "That's perfect. John has several old tee shirts and one says, 'After God made me, He shut out the lights and went home.' I'll look at his tee shirts and pick a good one. He wears old flannel shorts, too."

I looked at Mom, "What happened to the green nightie we bought at the Good-Will store with the feathers on it? The one I modeled at Kaitlynn's wedding reception. Is it still around?"

"I don't know. Let me check with Kaitlynn. If she doesn't have it, we'll find something."

Pop was standing there with an amused look on his face. He finally said, "And I missed that wedding reception. Dennis, Brian will love this. He is a ham at doing comedy routines. Let's see if he can come up with something, too."

━➤ ━

I've been home from the hospital for almost two weeks and tonight's the rehearsal dinner. It was an effort to not walk around with a big grin on my face knowing what Brian planned. John thinks Marianne folks planned everything, but he doesn't know that Mom and Pop did the planning. They met in Cape Girardeau with Marianne's parents, the Webers, and with Pop's son, Brian. Brian came up with a comedy routine for tonight, and he's involving Robert Weber, Steve, Glen, and Paul. They are going to be in a pretend wedding and Pastor Bishop is going to go along with it and be the minister. They asked Cousin Stacy to be the bride and our pastor's wife, Kathy Bishop, is going to be the maid of honor. Cousin Stacy said she has a young-looking wig from years ago and would find another one for Mrs. Bishop. Robert will be the groom and he and Steve are going to walk them down the aisle. Then... Glen is going to walk Brian in the room, dressed as a girl, who keeps adjusting her knee-high stockings and takes her shoes off during the service. She/he will do all sort of things on cue from what Mr. Weber said.

Paul is going to be the ring bearer, and he has a cattle ring that Brian purchased from the hardware store, and it is three or four inches across and will fit like a bracelet.

When Pastor Bishop says, "You may now kiss the bride," we are all supposed to look up at the head table at Marianne and say, "Right now." Then we will act like we are all going to take a step toward the bride, but the pastor will say, "On second thought... I believe that should be the honor of the husband." I'm not sure if we will all remember to do that, or if it will all work out as Brian planned.

Everyone will be giving a toast or saying something, and while they are doing that and finishing up their desserts, we will have the models sneak out. Brian has taken charge of that with Aunt Susan. I just can't wait.

John has acted so casual about everything, but I'm nervous. Since we didn't practice our skit, Brian had said, "You're all on your own. Be the best and most hilarious actors and actresses you can be."

Brian said he told Cousin Stacy to be sure to wear heavy make-up and to make a flower arrangement of carrots with each one tied with a pretty bow and for her to go to the Good-Will store if she had to, and find a wedding dress or something that can be transformed into one.

I was glad when John left the house at four o'clock to go to Marianne's house. The rehearsal dinner was planned for 6 p.m. but we were all supposed to be at the church for rehearsal at five.

The rehearsal went smoothly; everyone seemed to be in a jovial mood. Brian kept quietly telling us what we were supposed to do. I kept telling him not to talk so loud or John or Marianne would suspect something. We left the church and went to the Dexter Bar-B-Q restaurant in Cape Girardeau. I had never been in their big room. Mom and Mrs. Weber planned a menu ahead of time, and they were ready for us when we got there.

When our waiters started clearing off dinner dishes and delivering desserts, we all got up and exited the room at different times. Brian warned ahead of time not to sit together or at least not to get up and leave at the same time. We didn't. Some had left as soon as they were done eating.

Pastor Bishop got up and announced that John and Marianne were not aware of the fact that their wedding had been moved up twenty-four hours. You should have seen the look on their faces, when Pastor Bishop said, "I'm *so* sorry. I have to apologize. It's my error. I'm scheduled for surgery about an hour before your wedding tomorrow and I forgot about it. My wife would not let me change it."

I chuckled to myself as he blamed his wife, but he went on and told a lie in front of God and all of us with a deadpan face. He continued, "Since my wife comes first before anyone, and especially a wedding, I thought if it was okay with the *audience* we would just have a wedding here tonight."

Marianne looked at her mother and she shrugged her shoulders and then she looked at John. They didn't have time to respond to Pastor Bishop and everyone else didn't know what was going to take place because someone immediately turned on the wedding march and the door opened with Mrs. Bishop and Steve. It had been planned ahead of time to leave space between some tables and a platform to the side of the head table with a microphone for the preacher. Steve and Mrs. Bishop started walking down that cleared space. Steve was holding her arm, but she carried a novel she was reading with a flower on the top of it. Everyone laughed as she is a brunette and she had on a long blonde wig and heavy make-up. Her dress was a dark purple and really didn't look too bad for a wedding, but she had on someone's high-top boots. Steve kept the straightest face, as did Mrs. Bishop, while everyone was laughing. When they got to the platform, Steve went to the right and Mrs. Bishop went to the left. She took the flower off her book and tried to pin it on her dress. Steve walked back over to her and was making believe he was helping her.

Then Brian walked in with Glen. Brian was taller than Glen, but not much. Brian had on a dress that that came only to his mid-calf. It was sort of a pink shimmering type material. Mrs. Weber probably loaned it to him. One of his knee-high stockings had fallen to his ankle, and he stopped half-way up the aisle to pull it up. He made motions like he was apologizing to Glen. Glen played the part well and took Brian's arm and put it under his. Paul followed them with his big ring on a little pillow. Someone turned up the music a little louder and Cousin Stacy and Robert walked in. You should have heard the laughter.

Cousin Stacy found enough old curtains to fit over her fifty-inch waist and she had strung ribbon through the hems to make a dress. She had it up to just under her ample sized arms. She made a skirt the same way. There was a wide piece of white satin around her middle for a belt or sash. Her veil was out of a curtain, also, but the ribbon went through the curtain rod's narrow top hem. She tied the ribbon under her chin and it made a ruffle around her face. She smiled all the way up the aisle with a blackened tooth in front.

By the time, she got to the front, Brian was in his bridesmaid position, and he was pulling up his other knee-high stocking, and Mrs. Bishop was turning pages in her book. Brian turned around to Paul and pretended to examine the ring and took it off the pillow. Paul slapped his hand, but he got it anyway. The ring had a hinge on it, and it opened. He put it through his nose and then pulled his stockings up again. He took the ring off his nose and made motions like he was telling Paul not to tell what he had done. Then he turned toward the preacher and tried to act serious.

Pastor Bishop was saying, "Dearly beloved, we are gathered together to unite this bride and groom."

Brian sneezed really loud and looked for something to blow his nose in. He said, "Excuse me," loudly and stepped off the platform and took someone's napkin off a table and blew his nose. Just at the right moment, a waiter walked up with a very large tray on his shoulder and Brian dropped the napkin in the middle of the tray. The waiter turned with a little pivot and walked back through the closed double doors just as he had come in. Brian had planned that, too. He got back in his place and then tapped Steve on the shoulder and politely asked him to move over about a foot, so he could see. All his gestures were slightly exaggerated for emphasis. Pastor Bishop said loudly for the third time, "Dearly Beloved," and Brian gestured for him to go ahead.

It was obvious that Robert was so much younger than Cousin Stacy, and Pastor Bishop began his sermon on May-December love and the beauty and age were not prerequisites for love. He used a certain flower as an example of how it opens up in the dim light of the evening and the Morning Glory flower shines in the morning, yet in a garden together they add beauty to the earth. Then he said, "Mr. May, do you take Miss December as your lawful wedded wife?"

Robert looked at Cousin Stacy and she shook her head, "Yes." So he said real loud, "hu-huh."

The pastor opened his book to another page and said, "Excuse me a moment... No. Those aren't the right names either."

Pastor Bishop was as funny as Brian as he reached inside his jacket pocket and pulled out a piece of paper and showed it to Robert and Cousin Stacy. He asked, "Are these your right names?"

Robert said, "Yes, that's my name."

Cousin Stacy said, "Well, that's not *my* name. That was my name three husbands back. I'm a widow three times over. Oh,

Robert, you are about to make me the happiest bride I have *ever* been."

"Okay, Robert May and Stacy December, are you both willing to be man and wife."

They both shook their head affirmatively, so Pastor Bishop said, "Then I pronounce you man and wife now and *never* more."

Brian cackled loudly with a hilarious laugh. He said in a female voice, "Preacher, don't you mean…now and forever more."

Pastor Bishop looked at Brian and said, "Young lady, I say what I mean. I said, *never* more. This bride will never go before a marriage altar again."

He looked back at Robert and then glanced at Brian but he said, "You may kiss the bride."

Brian said, "Who? Me?"

Robert took his handkerchief out of his breast pocket and began wiping off his lips, and Cousin Stacy pulled hers out of her sleeve and began wiping her mouth and smeared lipstick across her cheek, when Paul yelled, "Preacher, you forgot the ring."

Pastor Bishop looked down at Paul, "Oh, you're right. Bring that ring here."

Paul stepped up right between the couple and handed the pillow and all to Pastor Bishop.

The pastor looked in his notes again and with a serious expression said, "With this ring I thee wed. No, not me… I just married you to Mr. May here… excuse me."

He looked at his paper and read Robert Weber. He said, "Son, have I just married you to someone old enough to be your grandmother."

Robert said, "Yes, but… she's my boss at the Chaffee Café, and I do what my boss says."

Cousin Stacy took the ring with a quick motion and put it in Robert's nose and turned him around to face the audience. She turned to Pastor Bishop and said, "Introduce us quick before I change my mind."

The Pastor said, "I now introduce to you Mr. May and Mrs. December Weber, and you had better greet them quick because January's a' coming!"

The music started with the processional music and we followed Robert and Cousin Stacy out of the room. She was grinning with her toothless grin and he was smiling with a ring in his nose. Brian had to make one last attempt at giving the audience a laugh. He got halfway through the audience and sneezed again and grabbed someone's napkin off a lap and pretended to blow his nose again. Then he said, "Must be the evening flowers or morning glories." He went to the bathroom with the napkin.

The skit all took place in about eight or ten minutes, and by then all the desserts had been placed on the tables. We all changed and came back in. The audience clapped and we sat down and hurriedly ate our dessert. Except for Brian and Cousin Stacy, They had to get some of the make-up off their faces.

Brian decided with Mr. Weber that it would be the time for the audience to give a toast or to wished the bride and groom the best God had in store for them. While everyone was relaxed and listening to the others or still eating their dessert, Brian slipped out one door, and Janet followed in about thirty seconds. About a minute later, I followed out another door and then Kaitlynn left the room, too. Officer Harrison and his wife were waiting with our change of clothes in the rest rooms.

Uncle Al went up to the microphone and said, "When Kaitlynn and Matthew got married they had some models. John Moore and Marianne Weber were those models. They wore what Matthew wore in the dorm at night to sleep in and what Kaitlynn wore at night in her dorm… and then what they would be wearing once they got married. Tonight we are turning the tables and it is their turn to show you what John and Marianne have been wearing to bed and what they will be wearing. May I have model number one, please?"

My sister's husband, Matthew walked in slowly, went up to the platform at the side of the room, and turned around so everyone could read what was printed on the shirt which said, *When God made me, He shut out the lights and went back home.* He had on the old flannel shorts, and a pair of white socks with holes in the heels. Then he stepped aside.

Uncle Al called for model number two, and Brian walked in slowly with the burgundy colored long pajamas with the jacket over his arm. They were the same pajamas we used in Matthew and Kaitlynn's wedding. Brian really changed himself from the last character in the wedding. He looked quite handsome. I spotted Chelsey in the audience, and she was beaming. I could tell Brian had captured her heart. Then Uncle Al called for model number three wearing what Marianne wore at night. Janet came in with a skimpy shirt with the caption, "I'm sleepy, aren't you?" It must have had some other connotations as it had a lot of snickers.

Then Uncle Al called for what Marianne would be wearing, and Steve, at six-foot-four, came walking in with the blond wig on with curlers in it and the pink gown with the sheer robe over it. He carried some pink slippers with big fluffy balls on the toes. He wore white socks, as did all of us. Steve made a point to take curlers out of the wig and brush the wig out when he got to the platform. Steve took Brian's arm and slowly walked out of the room. I took Janet's arm. When we were out of the door, I said, "Janet, will you marry me and walk down the aisle with me for real, next year?"

She looked at me sort of stunned, as we had just performed a bit of silliness. "Janet, you look gorgeous tonight even in that silly night wear of your sister's, but I want it to be us getting married next year. I will be twenty-one and you will be nineteen. I know we are young, but I feel we can make it. What do you say?"

She covered her face for a moment and then said, "Come here." Janet took my hand and we went through the double doors of the restaurant and around the corner. She gave me a powerful hug and kiss, and said, "I was hoping we wouldn't have to wait two years just to consider it as you had said. I must ask, though, do you think that it's all this wedding stuff with John that made you ask me to marry you, tonight?"

I was a little surprised at her question, but I said, "That may be part of it, but the other part is spending a week in the hospital with a narrow death escape. When I die I want to die with you by my side. I want to experience what Pop says about being a completed man because he has a wife. We both have experienced enough of life for two or three lives, and that may be a little sad to say, but it has made us both far more mature than many young people our age. And as you said, "God chose a young maiden to be the mother of his son, Jesus, and I know God planted the love we have for each other in our hearts and for Him.

"If God says *no*, for a wedding next June, he will show us. But then, Janet, you never did answer me, will you marry me?"

Janet smiled, "Yes, how about tomorrow with John and Marianne?"

I chuckled. "That would be nice, but my practical side says no, next June would be best."

I hugged her again and Uncle Al walked up, "Do I hear and see what I think I do? Is there another Moore son going to be married?"

"Uncle Al... Mr. and Mrs. Weber have produced two of the finest daughters and I, for one, am not going to let this one go. God has chosen her for me. She's more than I could ever dream to have as a wife."

Janet looked at Uncle Al. "God told me when I was fourteen that I should marry Dennis someday. I have not dated much or wanted to date anyone because they weren't Dennis. Dennis had been doing the same thing—keeping his love for me hidden because I was young. God somehow finally brought us together. Even though I'm young, by next June, I will be almost twenty. I don't think we need to wait any longer than a year from now."

Janet smiled at me, and I thought, *Wow, What a smile,* but I turned to Uncle Al and said, "Uncle Al, the demands of school will be on both of us. However, the demands of wanting each other and being too busy to date would be more than I could take. It would be nice to sit across the table from this beautiful gal while she is studying and I'm studying and not having to worry about if she is getting enough sleep, or will she have an accident to and from school and all that. And… as my wife, she can work with me with the kids in the crime prevention program. We both have a love for those kids. We both love music. Did you know that she has a lovely voice and plays the piano, too? Our lives have paralleled each other for four years, but I think it is time we walked the same road."

Mom and Pop came out of the rehearsal dinner room and saw us talking. Mom said, "Is this a conference that we can be in on?"

She looked at us in the night wear Janet and I still had on and said, "Son, you two kids really need to change clothes to something more appropriate."

Pop asked, "Was this a serious chat that we need to be in on?"

Janet smiled at him and said, "Yes… Dennis asked me to marry him and have a wedding *next* June."

Mom raised her eyebrows, so I said, "Yes, Mom, I wanted to wait two years, but at the moment, I don't want to go another week without Janet. I want to be practical, but when I was in the hospital, I realized I may not ever have a chance to be the completed man that Pop told John that we men should be, and that is why we need a wife and children. I realize we are young and have our education before us, but I don't feel like I have the time to date and worry about Janet driving back and forth to school and if she will make it safely, or how she is feeling. If we wait until next June, I will be twenty-one, almost twenty-two and Janet will be almost twenty. She will have her first year of college study out of the way, too"

Uncle Al was listening to us as we talked and gave us his blessing. He prayed with us for God to give us wisdom.

I looked at Mom and Uncle Al. "Thanks for your prayer, Uncle Al. Mom, I hope that I have your blessing as well as Pop's."

Uncle Al and Aunt Nancy started to turn to go toward their car, but stopped when I said, "I know there's been some influence because of all that is going on with John's wedding, but I have gone to sleep at night thinking about Janet and asking her to marry me. I don't want to wait two years just to *consider* marriage. That was foolish of me to think like that. I love Janet and want to be with her, to protect her, to cherish her, and to love her. Yes, it will be rough going to school and working, but there would be relief on other levels if we are together. I hope that we have your blessing"

Pop was standing there listening and not saying anything. Mom finally said, "Son, you have my blessing. I know that you will have it hard with both of you going to school at the same time, but I have faith in my teaching and know that you both love the Lord and want His will to be done in your lives, so you have my blessing. We'll work toward next June."

Pop finally said, "I wanted to hear what your mother had to say before I said anything. Dennis, I have been your substitute dad for two years, and I don't know of any more mature young men for your age than you boys are. The fact that you would even consider taking on the responsibility of six boys from poor dysfunctional families, design a program for them, and oversee the work is something beyond my imagination, and then recently designing a new program for older teen-age boys is also beyond my understanding. I know that you assume responsibility for farm work and don't try to shirk any duties. You have assumed responsibility for your family members, too, and I know that you will do equally well as a husband and father, and a policeman. You have my blessing, too. And, if it is okay with your mother, I want you to pick out fifteen acres as a wedding gift. John has the farmhouse and you will need a place of your own. So, that is my gift to you... I mean *our* gift to you."

Janet was so moved she gave Mom and Pop a hug. Mr. and Mrs. Weber walked up and heard the last few sentences of Pop's and said, "Is this some private meeting or a give-away show?"

Janet said, "No, Dad, but I feel like it is. We have just been given Uncle Al's and Aunt Nancy's blessing and Dr. and Mrs. Lynn's blessing. Dennis asked me to marry him this evening and to have a wedding next June."

Both Mr. and Mrs. Weber looked at me, and I knew I had to say something. "I'm sorry I didn't come to you first, and ask you the polite way, if I could have your daughter's hand in marriage, but the opportunity was here to ask Janet to marry me, and I just couldn't wait. I realized that I was not being realistic to ask Janet to wait two years before even considering marriage. I love your daughter dearly and feel incomplete without Janet in my life. I would much rather have her sitting across the table from me studying together, than John."

No offense against John... Janet is just prettier." I laughed, but went on talking like I was already the man of the house.

"I know that I have a lot of responsibilities on the farm and with the youth prevention program and for my family, too, as well as school… but being on the verge of possibly losing my life and finding Janet at my bedside, and family members, also there, when I woke up, I knew… this is what I want. I want Janet by my side and my family and your family as a backup for me. Mom and Dad have already given me a good foundation in life, and a good spiritual foundation, too. Janet knows the Lord and wants His will done in her life, so I can see no reason, why we can't honor and serve the Lord together. We are both young, I realize that, but Janet is the one I want for a wife, and I don't see how I can wait two more years for her. I guess if I were Jacob and had to wait and work for 7 years, I would. That is why I would like to wait one year instead of three or four.

"I do want your blessing, though. Without your blessing, Janet would be very unhappy and I don't want that for her. She loves her family just as I love mine, and you two feel like family, already"

I looked at Mrs. Weber and she said, "Janet, you two really need to go change your clothes and put on something more appropriate."

She sounded just like Mom. She looked at me and said, "Dennis, you are a fine young man, as I said before, I could not have chosen a better person for my daughter than you. You have my blessing."

Mr. Weber said, "Dennis, I wondered why you said you wanted to wait two years before you *considered* marriage. At the time, I thought those two kids really use their heads about things, but then I thought, that was because that was all they used. They didn't consider their feelings—their hearts. I suspected, before two years was up, you would want to get married. I didn't think that the influence of John and Marianne's wedding bring about the decision earlier."

I interrupted and said, "It did influence me, but not to the extent of my recent surprise brush with death and finding the comfort of Janet at my side twice… when I broke the bones in my foot and ankle and the stay in the hospital with the head surgery, I realized Janet is a perfect person to be a nurse, and I will encourage her in that."

Mr. Weber looked at Mrs. Weber. "What do you think, shall we give them our blessing, also?"

She said, "Janet and Dennis already have my blessing."

Mr. Weber stepped up and shook my hand and hugged his daughter. He said, "How about if part of my blessing is a table and chairs?"

Mrs. Weber said, "Plan on taking your bedroom furniture.

My mother added. "…and *your* desk, and dresser are yours, too."

I saw John and Marianne coming out of the dining hall. "I have a favor to ask. Please, don't say anything to John and Marianne. I want these next few days to be all about them—not Janet and me. Our day will come next June. Hopefully, Brian will be out of the country by then."

We all laughed and John and Marianne joined our group. John asked, "What is funny."

I answered quickly. "Oh, I just said, that I hope Brian was out of the country by the time I get married."

Marianne said, "Did any of you have the feeling that Brian has missed his calling?"

Brian walked up and said, "Who missed their calling?"

We all laughed again, and several of us said, *"You!"*

"No, I can support myself with my love for machinery. I can't with a few laughs. But, I am glad to have people laugh. It does something to the soul."

Brian saw Chelsey come out of the dining hall and he quickly excused himself saying. "Hey, there's my girl."

He turned and looked back at us, "Pray for me, I'm about to make my love for her official."

Pop looked at Mom. "Two in one evening... what are we doing... chasing our kids out of the nest?"

Brian caught up with Chelsey and he looked back at us and did a thumbs-up motion and made out like he was praying to remind us pray. Uncle Al said, "Well, let's pray."

I said, "Shall we?"

Uncle Al prayed, "God we ask for your blessing upon Brian and Chelsey and give them wisdom also in the choices and decision they make. Thank you for being their heavenly father and guiding them in your way. Thank you. In your Son's name, Jesus, we pray, Amen"

Everyone said, "Amen."

John looked at his watch, but Marianne said, "We'll be going, too. I'll be back at the house soon."

It was nine-thirty and I said to Mom and Pop, "Do you mind if we go change clothes and spend a little time together?"

I looked at Mrs. Weber. "Is eleven o'clock too late to have Janet home?"

"That would be fine, but remember, Janet, that you have a big day tomorrow. Your sister is getting married."

"Oh, I won't forget, but let me have your cell phone, just in case you need me for anything."

Mom and Mrs. Weber smiled at each other with Janet's last remark.

—▸ ◂—

Janet and I left the restaurant and went back to the Dairy Hop where we first had expressed our love for each other. I was on cloud nine having passed the hurdle of asking Janet to marry me and getting a yes and then getting both parents' blessing and

Uncle Al's, too. Janet and I got a milk shake since we were still in a borrowed car.

We had a lot to discuss and to get our priorities in order. I said, "The first thing on my list of priorities is to get our own set of wheels. I'm committing myself to that."

I asked Janet if she would pray about that. The next hurdle would be money toward housekeeping.

Janet was thinking and not responding. She finally said, "I hope to earn at least fifteen hundred this summer, and that seems like a lot to me, but not with all the incidentals the nursing school requires. I will need to get a stethoscope, my own blood pressure cuff, and uniforms. Dad is planning to pay my tuition this year, but with me being married, I'm not sure he will want to continue that after we are married. So, should I talk to the university about grants and loans?"

I assured her that she would be eligible for grants if she did well her first year. I applied for several, and I'm getting one, and it is going to cut my tuition by a third next semester.

We discussed where we would live and Janet was going to check into married student housing. She wouldn't need to do that until next spring. With four of us going to the university this year and all on different time schedules, it was going to be hectic. We would have to talk with John and Robert to see if we could at least drive only two cars to Cape Girardeau and to the university.

Janet reminded me that Steve is a senior, too, and that would be five people going to the university. There were so many decisions and things to think about that Janet said, "Dennis, it's late and it's foolish to think about all that we are thinking about until the spring semester. Let's concentrate on one thing at a time. First, get a vehicle that will be good enough to last for the next five years."

I agreed with her. I had a lot on my plate at the moment with Mom and Pop moving next door, Paul not quite out of the woods with his leukemia, and Glen still settling in with us as his family. The only person who seemed to have just his own interest to worry about was Steve, but then he helped out with the cooking, filled in for Paul and John and me, and then went to the Café in town to train people for Cousin Stacy. So, even Steve had a lot of responsibility, for a kid who just turned eighteen. I suspected Mom would rely on him a lot when it comes to packing up the house for moving.

I took our milkshake containers and got out of the car and put them in a trash can. I told Janet, "It's getting close to your eleven o'clock curfew, so I'll take you home—lest I get started on the wrong foot with your family.

Janet laughed. "With all the good influence you have had on Robert, you and John are heroes to Dad and Mom. I don't think that will ever happen."

Just the same, I wanted to abide by their wishes, so I took Janet home. It was good to spend time with Janet. I really didn't want to take her home, but common sense and the Lord said, *Take her home.*

This year is going to be so hard on us with all the busy stuff going on. But, the first thing for me is to sit somewhere again and check out the finances and get a car. Steve is ready now to replace his truck. We have to get something for the farm, now that the gardens are in full swing.

—————

This is the big day for John's wedding. He was up early, so I got up and went to the barn to be with him. When I walked into the bar, he was sitting on his milking stool with his head against the cow. His shoulders were shaking and I said, "John, are you okay?

I had this scripture pop into my mind from Proverbs sixteen, verse twenty-one: *The wise in heart are called discerning, and pleasant words promote instruction.*

John didn't answer, and I could tell that he was trying to get his act together. I got my cleaning solution and cleaned the teats of my cow and started milking. I finally said, "Life is one change after another, isn't it? Today is one of the saddest days of your life yet, it's the happiest day, also. It is sort of like what happens when we become the bride of Christ. You leave a life behind and take on a new life in Christ Jesus. You are leaving a family and starting a new one. John, you have been my older brother since the day I was born. You have been a constant presence in my life. Somehow, I think you always will be... whether you are married to Marianne or not.

"Think of this day not just as your wedding day, but 'as the day which the Lord hath made and rejoice and be glad in it.' Marianne is a gift to you from God to be at your side until God sees fit to take one or both of you back to himself. Go and rejoice and be glad for this day. Don't look back at what was, but look to the future and what will be. You both have been so busy, and I know that you have not had the time to make the farmhouse into your own place, but I can assure you that when you get back from your honeymoon, the farmhouse will be yours, and you and Marianne can paint, hang curtains, or do whatever you want with it."

After my speech, I decided I should be quiet and let John think about what I had said, I sat there on my milk stool thinking about the farmhouse, and all the other things, John had not been privy to because he had been so busy.

I didn't tell John that Mom and Pop's new house had the whole upstairs done, and Steve and Aunt Susan were moving over. I'm going to move over to the Jenkins/Lynn house with Brian and Mr. Jenkins. John probably doesn't even know that. It will work out perfectly. It will be a change of living in a different house for all of us except John, and our old house will seem different to him being in the downstairs bedroom and *not* having all the family in it with him.

I'm really getting excited about moving out of the farmhouse and getting it all cleaned up for John and Marianne. Mom told Steve and me that we needed to do something really bad so she could make us wash all the windows. She laughed and said, "No, as soon as John and Marianne leave on their honeymoon, there is going to be a massive move and clean-up. We'll put everything possible from the bedrooms over at the new house and anything we have to wait to move into the new house, we'll store in one room of the old farmhouse out of John's and Marianne's way."

The upstairs in the new house has four bedrooms like the old one, but we will have two bathrooms upstairs instead of one. The master bedroom and bath will be on the first floor and Mom is pushing them to get it done, too."

Mom said, "We can store everything extra in the garage if we have to."

I told her, "Leave the dining room and living room furniture for John to use. That way we wouldn't have to move the furniture, and it would give John a feeling of still being in his old home."

I also said, "I'll empty the kitchen cupboards and pantry. It will be a month or more before the new kitchen is done."

We had already cleaned out Grandpa's room and the bathroom weeks ago. Marianne had been over with Mrs. Weber and had the room all painted and cleaned with new curtains and drapes. Marianne and John had gone shopping and purchased a new queen size bed, two side tables and *him* and *her* dressers. We have been looking in that room for two weeks and wishing Grandpa could see his room now. All their wedding gifts were piled on the bed and on the floor waiting for our things to be moved from the kitchen. I caught John in the bedroom one day with a half-grin on this face looking at the wedding gifts. When he saw me looking at him, I said, "Life can be good, too, right?"

He said, "Yeah, but I'm going to miss the family when they move next door."

I laughed and said, "Well, fill up the house with babies. Mom and the rest of us would be over here constantly, wanting to play with them or baby sit. Then you will want us to leave you alone. Besides, by the time Steve gets around to marrying, he will want a niece and nephew to be his ring bearer and flower girl."

I thought about our big long kitchen table and remembered telling Mom to leave the kitchen table and chairs until John could get his own or… drag out the card tables and chairs and leave one set for John and take the table and chairs.

Mom had said, "Now why didn't I think of that? We have two sets somewhere. We've been using a hot plate, the electric fry pan, the crock pot and a micro-wave oven. They're on some boards on two saw-horses, and we're sitting in four lawn chairs. Where are the folding tables anyway?" I didn't know.

I sat there on my milk stool thinking about so many things about the move. John finally said, "Dennis, I may by your big brother and your hero, but I depend on you for strength. I'm scared again. Honestly, this big body doesn't do me any good when it comes to emotional things. I feel deeply about everything and now I'm wondering if I will be a good husband and father. I feel like I don't deserve Marianne, and I'm afraid I might disappoint her."

I know John reads the Bible and relies more on God than I do, so I said, "John before you leave the house today read Proverbs sixteen, verse twenty and then reread Isaiah forty-one, verses nine and ten and then Isaiah forty, verses twenty-nine, thirty and thirty-one, again. If those verses don't help, read chapter fifty-five. Don't leave the house without doing it. You don't need me to lean on today. You need your God, our Lord. Besides, you are following his guidance aren't you? Why would he abandon you, when you are being obedient to Him?"

John took his full milk bucket to the straining machine and I decided to leave him alone with his thoughts. He went out of the barn, after he put the cow out and mucked out the stall. He checked on Steve's cattle and noticed a new calf already standing. I heard him say, "Well, look out there—a brand new baby bull born on my wedding day. Where is Steve?

John walked on toward the calf and looked over the situation. Steve and Pop came in the barn from the house. I was standing at the back door watching John. Steve and Pop walked over to see what I was looking at. I guess because they heard me saying, "Well, I'll be… What a surprise!"

I turned to Steve and said, "Steve, you had better go out behind the barn and see what John has out there for you."

They both hurried out the back barn door. Pop said, "You mean to say that after that last birth that kept us up all night, we have a new live birth without losing a wink of sleep?"

I remembered that night. "It sure looks like it."

Pop and Steve joined John out in the pasture and I could hear Steve say, "I don't believe it… I don't believe it…" I decided I had better get the milk strained and see what Steve didn't believe.

There were two calves. One of Steve's cows had twins. They were both in fantastic shape. John was checking to make sure one of them didn't belong to another mother, but he couldn't find any that looked like she had just given birth, just the one mother. Pop checked, too, and said, "Well, Steve, it looks like we are twice blessed this morning with twins."

Steve was scratching his head. He smiled and said, "Four months truck payments from each."

I had to laugh. Leave it to Steve to think in terms of profit and loss. I thought about how God deliberately diverted John's thinking to something to rejoice about, and Steve, too.

We all walked back to the house. Glen was coming out of the henhouse with Paul's pink bowl full of eggs. "Guess what? Those hens must have each laid two eggs today. What have they been fed?" He looked down at the bowl and chuckled.

I saw something and said, "Wait a minute!" John started to walk on toward the house with the milk. Pop took the eggs from Glen and Steve took my milk container. I couldn't believe what I was seeing. Paul's new dog had finally grown enough out of his puppy stage to become a valuable asset to the farm. He walked up to us with a wagging tail that said. "Look what I have for you?" The dog had a dead weasel in his mouth. He dropped it at our feet. I couldn't help yelling... *Thank you, God!*" I yelled so loud there was a slight echo way off and down the hill. Glen and I both laughed at hearing the faint *you, God* at a distance.

John looked toward the house and Steve looked toward the barn. They were both smiling big time.

John said, "Perfect! This is perfect. No catching a weasel on this day." He patted the dog and made over him. "We are blessed again."

Steve said, "Thank, God."

"I did." Glen said, as he looked at the dead weasel. He asked, "*What* is that?"

As I turned to go toward the house, I said, "It's a weasel and they kill chickens. I'll tell you the story about weasels someday,"

Pop had already started walking toward the house with John. Their voices sounded like they were really in a good mood. The opposites of what John was when I went in the barn this morning. I shook my head and said as though I were talking only to me, "No one can tell me there's *not* a God and He cares for us."

Glen said, "What? Oh. God is getting more real to me, too."

All I could think to say was, "Glen, that's another blessing for today."

I got emotional and wanted to cry as God proved he exists one more time and he was able to change John's mood with twin calves, more eggs than normal, and the new dog catching a weasel.

Pop was waiting for all the chores to be done so he could take Glen and Steve back over to the new house in the car. The acre of ground between the new house and the old farmhouse was nothing but mud where the contractors had been parking their trucks and equipment. Fortunately they had framed in and poured a cement drive that extended pretty far down the lane and then merged with our hard packed gravel lane. The cement drive was going to be nice. When I walked into the house, Pop was waiting. "Your mother wants you over to the house at noon today. She wants to make sure her boys are all put together in their tuxedoes.

Aunt Barbara and Uncle Charles arrived this morning with several cousins. I think Katie, Trevor, Matthew and Kaitlynn will be in just before lunch. They're all staying at the Drury Suites in Cape Girardeau.

I started getting exited thinking about Mom's biological twin's children, the cousins we didn't know we had until last year—Katie and her brother and sister, Aaron and Michelle. I wanted them to meet Janet. Katie is the one who went to the university in St. Louis with Kaitlynn, my older sister. Because they looked so much alike and had pictures of their mothers in the dorm room that looked identical, they knew they had to be related. Katie knew her mother had an identical twin somewhere, but our Kaitlynn didn't. It was a grand time for Mom and her sister to get acquainted. They each knew they were adopted at birth. All of Mom's biological families were an added blessing to our family when Grandpa died. Mom really needed her new found family because she was a widow for a couple of years.

Katie and Trevor have planned an August wedding and, if I'm not mistaken, I think Brian Lynn and Chelsey will follow soon after. This will be a year for weddings. John will not feel so alone. I think I will suggest a weekend for all of them to get together with Janet and me toward the end of the year.

Marianne is using Kaitlynn, Chelsey, Janet, and Katie as her bridesmaids, and John is using Steve, Brian, Paul and me as groomsmen. Glen will be an usher and will help pass out programs and be a greeter at the front door. It will be a big wedding and a nice one, too.

I need to stop thinking about John's wedding and start concentrating on my own. Pastor Bishop has been so helpful in the planning stage for John and Marianne. I know he will for Janet and me, also.

———◆———

John and Marianne's wedding was beautiful. Even though I am a guy and don't usually think in terms of *pretty* or *beautiful*, the front of the church looked like a garden. Mom and Mrs. Weber must have done some real planning with Marianne and Janet. Janet never gave me a hint of what the church would look like. The reception was in the basement of the church, and I remember Mrs. Weber, Mom, and Aunt Susan's sitting in Aunt Susan's room making white bows. The bows were on the end of the pews and on the corners of the tables with the food and on the cake table, too. I guess for a guy, I'm observant. I think I will tell Janet, if she wants to use anything from Marianne's wedding, I won't mind. It might save some money. I suspect, though, she will say, "My colors are all different." That's okay. Wow, I really need to be earning some money. I need to pray about that. The boys from Cape Girardeau are really getting busy with the gardens now, so I don't know when I will have time to take on another job. I need to spend a lot of time with them. I will pray about that, too. God always comes up with something when my brain gets tired trying to think about something.

At John's reception, Uncle Al had his video all set up to show the lives of Marianne and John from infancy to their wedding day. I don't know how he did it, but he managed to add in the wedding ceremony, too. Uncle Al really put some hilarious shots in the film. He disappeared as soon as the pastor pronounced them man and wife. He probably had his equipment all set up in a Sunday school room and while people were greeting John and Marianne, he was adding the wedding portion to the video. I suspect that Mom gave Uncle Al the video that was done for John's birthday and high school graduation and had gotten some pictures from Mrs. Weber, too.

Last Christmas, we each were given a camera from Mom and Pop. Steve had gotten a video camera and mine was a digital camera. Some of the pictures looked like pictures that Steve had taken with his new camera. The video was good and even hilariously funny in places. We laughed for fifteen minutes—it seemed like.

Anyway, John and Marianne left on their honeymoon and no one seemed to know where they were going except Mom and Pop and Mr. and Mrs. Weber. They kept it a secret, too. John wanted to surprise Marianne. They will be home this next Saturday. Pop said he will come over from the new house to help with the farm chores in John's place. I will miss John, but I know life must move on.

CHAPTER 9

THE FARMHOUSE MOVING DAY started Saturday evening after John and Marianne left on their honeymoon. I didn't tell Mom that I was going to do it, but I went to the hardware store and purchased shelving. I talked with Steve and he said, "Okay... since I'm the only one in my bedroom, set them up in my room."

Mom was tired, but she wanted to pack her dish cupboards, so I told her I would do the pantry while she was doing that. She said, "I just rested at the reception and let everyone else work."

I made a mental note of where Mom kept things and when I had everything packed up I said, "Mom, let me take what you have done over to the new house and I will set them in the hallway upstairs or wherever you want me to put them."

She finished labeling the boxes. I had labeled the stuff from the pantry by which shelf it was on. Mom didn't suspect we were going to make it easy for her and unpack the pantry and put the things on the shelves. Since she had already moved her make-shift kitchen upstairs to one of the bathrooms where she would have water, it worked out perfect to have the foodstuff close by where she could get at everything. Steve helped me. He said, "Let's push my bed against the wall and set up a door for a long table and put the chairs around it."

I had gone over one afternoon and talked with the men about using a half-sheet of one-half-inch thick plywood cut in half. They agreed to do it for me. Mom thought I was just looking at the work progress. I was, but had the ulterior motive of having them fix up a table for us. They did and leaned it again the wall in the garage. I told them to put D.M. on it so I would know that it was the piece that was for the table. Pop had not noticed either.

Steve walked into the kitchen with a box of pictures off the living room wall and said, "I'll take these over when you make the next trip over."

"I'm going right now."

"Steve, it's time for one of us to go get that truck," I said,

Pop walked in the back door and said, "Let's go." I had a box in my hands and Steve had his box."

Steve said, "Monday morning, Pop."

"Pop, would you help us carry these boxes to the car? Steve can go over with them and unload them."

Pop lifted one of the pantry boxes and walked out to the car and put it on the back seat. "I have a feeling you boys are up to something. What is it?"

I know we were looking mischievous. "Pop, we will be delayed over at the house for about forty-five minutes. Have Mom go in the living room and lie down on the couch. She really looks tired."

"I've noticed. Her sister is still at the Drury Suites and is planning to stay over until tomorrow afternoon. I think that I'll have her do just that. She put stew in the crock pot early today, and it should be ready. If I tell her to stop packing she won't do it, but if I tell her I'm hungry and that stew should be about ready, she will stop and feed me."

Steve said, "I'll check it and give you a call. It's already seven and there is something I want done tonight with Dennis's help."

"So, bring Mom back to the house about eight. We'll be home and will finish up the chores by then."

I went back in and got another box from the pantry. Steve

went back in and took a box labeled pantry and dish towels and table cloths. I whispered to Steve, "Do you have a screwdriver and pliers?"

"Yes, I pretended I needed them when I was taking the stuff off the walls in the living room."

When we got to the house, we worked fast. I carried the boxes of shelving upstairs and then went back for the piece of plywood and sawhorses. We set up the table quickly and set the pantry boxes on them. Then we tackled the shelving. Once we got started, and figured out how they were all attached, it went quickly. They weren't the best-looking shelving, but they would do. We set the pantry things on the shelves neatly and in about the same order that Mom had them in her old pantry.

Steve said, "I had better check on that stew."

He went to the bathroom and came back. "It's perfection. Mom is a good cook."

I agreed and asked, "Where are the folding chairs?"

"Mom had Pop take them over when she found them in the attic. Let me run down and see where he put them."

Steve yelled upstairs, "They're down here leaning against the wall. I guess he thought we would set up down here to eat."

I ran downstairs and carried four of them up. Steve grabbed the other four. He chuckled and said, "Dad would have said, 'Now, Dennis and Steve, that's a lazy man's load. Take your time and don't take so many at once.' "

I laughed on the way back upstairs and said, "Yeah, but tonight our time is limited, so we had to carry four at a time—two in each hand."

When we had set the chairs on each side of the plywood table, Steve said, "I wish we had a couple of the Café' table cloths… the long ones."

I remembered the box that was labeled *Dish towels and Table*

Cloths. I said, "We didn't open that box. Maybe there are some in there. Mom kept a couple of old ones when the laundry couldn't get out the stains. But I don't know if she gave them to the Good-Will or had plans to use them for picnics."

I ripped open the box while Steve was looking over my shoulder. He said, "dy-no-mite" like Jimmy Walker and reached around me for a table cloth.

I said, "There are three old ones in here. Quickly, let's use one on the table and find something to put in the center."

He ripped open the box from the living room and pulled out a small flower arrangement that was on top of the piano and put it in the center of the table. We were pushing all the empty boxes out of the way when we heard footsteps on the stairway. It was Glen and Paul first to step into the room, and then Pop.

Mom stopped in the bathroom first and checked the stew. She said "Ah, perfection," just like Steve said. I knew then where Steve had gotten his expression. Pop looked in Steve's bedroom door and grinned from ear to ear.

"Wait until your mother sees this. Her own pantry, dining room and living room all wrapped up in one."

Mom stepped out of the bathroom and said, "What are you talking about?"

Glen and Paul came out their room and one of them said, "What's going on?"

Mom was standing in the doorway with the biggest grin on her face and shaking her head in disbelief. "I didn't need any more than one daughter with boys like my sons. You just seem to know what to do and how to fix things for comfort."

Another car came in the drive. It was Aunt Susan. She came upstairs and said, "Where is everyone?"

Glen yelled, "…in Steve's living room, dining room, and pantry."

She stepped up behind Glen and said, "Well, let me see!"

Aunt Susan smiled and said, "Well, I'll be. Bonnie, why didn't we think of this? It's a good thing we put only one twin bed in here."

Steve said, "Now, Mom, you lie on my bed and give directions and we will do what you say."

"Steve, thank you, I *am* very tired. The first thing we need to do is bring the stew pot in here. "Glen, you and Paul go get the cereal bowls and some silverware out of the bathroom linen closet. I put the bowls and dishes in the linen closet so it would have what we'll need before the kitchen is done. Dennis, you get a big ladle and some plastic glasses with ice in them. The ice chest has fresh ice, and there should be enough."

Aunt Susan said, "I brought the cornbread from over at Mr. Jenkins' I left some for him and Brian. I also brought some sun tea that has been brewing all day long over there. I set it downstairs."

Glen said, "I'll get it."

I told him to bring it to me in the bathroom. Mom had a little refrigerator sitting on the long counter in the bathroom for milk, butter, and juice. I took the butter in and put it on the table. It was eight-thirty and late for us to be eating, but it had been a long day. Mom asked Pop to pray.

Pop prayed a beautiful prayer for John and Marianne and their safety. Then he thanked God for the wisdom and helpfulness of all the boys."

By the time he got done praying, Mom let out a snore. We all laughed and Pop said. "Give her five or ten minutes and she will be as good as new."

Aunt Susan said, "Right now she needs rest more than food."

Pop fixed Mom a bowl of stew and set it aside for Mom and then filled a bowl for each of us, and we passed it around. Aunt

Susan said, "I almost brought over a cherry cobbler, but I figured with all the cake and punch you guys had this afternoon and the lateness of the hour, we should dispense with the dessert. Please watch how much tea you drink… you might be sitting up all night packing again."

I said, "I'll need the tea. I have to get back over to the old house, anyway. I haven't done the chores. Those cows are probably miserable."

Glen chuckled. "You mean chewing their cud and resting is miserable?"

Glen had a look of pride when he said, "Take your time, Dennis. Paul, Pop, and I took care of the chores."

I said, "Oh, thank you all. I really feel better now."

I enjoyed the fact that Glen felt part of the responsibility around here. I relaxed and enjoyed my stew. Aunt Susan went to the bathroom and got the plastic bin that Mom and she had been using to wash dishes in. Glen and Paul got up and put their bowls in the bin first. Pop said, "Brush your teeth and get ready for bed, boys. Tomorrow is going to be another hard day."

Mom rose up quickly and looked at us like… *where am I?*

I said, "Mom did you enjoy your nap?"

"Oh. Um-m, I'm so sorry. Did you get enough to eat?"

Paul said, "Yes, Mom, your stew was good and we chewed our food to the rhythm of your snoring." He mimicked her.

"It was that bad, huh? Hope you don't get indigestion from it."

Paul was still laughing after he had made the snoring sound. "Mom, I was just kidding. You let out a snore only about twice."

Mom put her legs over the edge of the bed while looking at the shelving that we put up. She shook her head again and said, "You, guys, put things just where I had them in the pantry. I have reared some smart boys!"

Glen turned to Mom, "Are you including me?"

Mom looked at him and said, "I didn't have to, your mother and grandmother did a good job all by themselves."

Glen smiled and said, "Thanks."

Pop picked up Mom's stew bowl. "I saved you some stew. I put it back in the crock pot."

"Thanks I am a little hungry. Where is Sister Sue?"

Steve said, "She gathered up our dirty dishes, so you wouldn't rush to do them."

"Well, Aunt Susie is as tired as I am. The dishes could wait until morning."

Aunt Susan walked in the door and said, "Now, except for your mom's, the dishes are done. What do you say we all go to bed early—or just sit here and chat?"

I said, "I'm going home for the night. Where is home for me, anyway, the farmhouse, Mr. Jenkins' or here?"

Mom said, "Oh, Dennis, I see where you are coming from. What would you like to do?"

I sat there and thought for a moment. "Until John comes home, I need to stay at the farmhouse. Who knows how many people know that there are wedding gifts in the house, and you are in the process of moving over here. I think I had better stay at the old homestead until John comes back."

Pop said, "Brian is looking forward to you moving over at the Jenkins.' I think it will be good for you to live away from home for a little while before you are married. What do you think?"

"It really doesn't make any difference to me as long as I have my clothes and a bed to sleep in at night."

I paused and laughed. "I know where the pantry is."

Mom laughed, "...you did a good job of it, too."

We all said, "Goodnight." Glen and Paul had already left the room and Steve's café experience made him do what was natural.

He cleared the table of Mom's stew bowl, straightened the table cloth and then said. Since this is my bedroom, it is now off limits. Pop laughed and said, "Okay. Let's go to our room, too, Bonnie.

The next morning we all were up and ready for church and had our adrenaline set on high for finishing up some of the moving on Sunday afternoon, but Pop told us boys that other than the regular chores, he wanted us to let things go and visit with all the relatives who had stayed over from the wedding."

"I'll buy that," I said. "We don't get to see family that often, and I'll be glad to work hard on Monday to make up for it."

I no sooner said that when the phone rang. Pop had a phone line to the upstairs as soon as we were able to move in upstairs. I was the closest to the hallway, so I answered. It was Officer Harrison. He said, "I didn't want to say anything to you yesterday at the wedding reception, but Blake is having a crisis in his life."

My heart skipped a couple of beats, because the last crisis with one of the boys was with Glen, and his family was murdered. "What kind of crisis?"

Officer Harrison cleared his throat and said, "Well, it seems that some older gang members, not much older than Blake, are feeling some jealousy and are giving him a rough time. On his way to work two nights ago, they roughed him up. He went to the store manager when he got to the store, and the manager called me. I took him to the hospital. He has two broken ribs, a broken nose, and multiple bruises. They kept him in the hospital for observation. His mother has decided to move out of the area and needs a place desperately. We are looking for a place today, but I need you and Steve to go visit Blake and give him some encouragement."

I asked which hospital and the room number. When I asked that, all eyes and ears were upon me. Glen said, "Who... what...?"

"Let me talk to Pop and Steve. It may be this evening before we can get up there."

Officer Harrison said, "Please, pray that we can find a place out of this neighborhood and some kind of vehicle for Blake to drive. He is seventeen and we will see that he gets Driver's Ed. training, even if we have to use some of the money in our budget. Blake's Manager has been extremely pleased with Blake. He says his attitude is good, and he is not lazy… 'always looking for more to do. He's really manager material.'"

I hung up the phone and couldn't talk for a few seconds. I shook my head negatively and Pop asked again, "Who… what happened?"

I was afraid to say anything to Glen, as it had been less than a year since his family was killed, but Pop said, "Am I going to have to ask or are you going to tell us… who and what happened?"

"It's Blake. Some of the hoodlums on the street he lives on made it known that they don't appreciate him. They beat him up on the way to work Friday evening. Jealousy was the word Officer Harrison used. Anyway, he made it to work with two broken ribs, a broken nose, and multiple swollen bruises. Officer Harrison took him took him to the hospital. Officer Harrison would like for me to go visit him and Steve, too, if he can, to encourage him. Blake's in a lot of pain, but his injuries will heal."

Glen was visibly shaken. Blake was his neighbor and in the program with Glen. They encouraged each other. Glen said, "I want to go, but can I wait a couple of days? I'm afraid I will get too upset to encourage Blake."

Pop noticed Glen's reaction, "Son, I think you had best wait more than a week. I'll get a card for you to send to him or perhaps a book or something. I think emotionally you are still very frail. However, we'll leave the decision up to you."

Pop looked at me and asked, "Do you think Janet and Robert would be willing to visit?"

"That's an idea. I'll call Janet when I get home. I mean, back to the farmhouse."

Then I remembered what else he said. "Oh, Officer Harrison said he's looking for a place for Blake's family to move, to get them out of the neighborhood. Pop, do you know of any place?"

Pop sat there for a moment and said, "Where is his mother working now?"

I was pleased to say that Blake said his mother had taken some training and was working at the Lutheran Home as a certified nurses' assistant. She had gone to the Vo-Tech night school and taken the course that it offered.

Everyone went on to their rooms and I sat there for a moment with Pop. He tapped his fingers on the plywood table a couple of times and finally asked, "Dennis, does the program have anything in its budget for emergencies?"

I thought for a moment. "We've had one grant, but it hardly pays very much. We use it for the after school program—school supplies and occasionally a used coat or pair of jeans. Blake and his employer pay into the program less than five dollars a week. The older kids in the program pay into the program a quarter for each hour they work. So each boy's take home pay is twenty-five cents less than minimum wage. If he works only two hours each evening, that's only fifty cents a day or two dollars and fifty cents during the week. On Saturday the boys work six hours and pay in just one dollar, even though they've worked more than four hours. Officer Harrison is going to change the Saturday assessment, but even so we still don't get much paid into the program from the older boys who are working in the program. We've asked the employers to help also, and some of them are generous, but we don't require that much from them. So for emergencies there really isn't that much to work with financially. Maybe a year or two from now, there will be."

There will be three more enter into the senior program next year—assuming we can find jobs for them. Then we will have a little more money come into work with, but the amount will be so small compared to an emergency like Blake has. Besides that, Blake's employer said he would take on one more boy, but he won't do more than two at a time. That's fine. We don't want to lose a good supportive employer."

Pop said, "You know, Dennis. We could spare a quarter of an acre somewhere out of these farm acres. We have more than two-hundred acres. I wonder if we could talk one of those manufactured home dealer's to forego his down payment and set-up one on a quarter of an acre, if Blake's mother can make payments."

I thought about it for a few seconds and said, "You know, Pop, Blake's mother is making rent payments and paying utilities and telephone. Blake buys most all of the groceries. Is a quarter of an acre enough space to put a garden, too?"

"Yes, providing you don't want too much of a yard."

I said, "Pop, Blake's mother did get a little money from insurance or from somewhere when Blake's dad was shot and killed. It's probably all used up now, or else she saved it for emergencies like losing her job."

Pop said, "Uh-huh," and then, "Call Officer Harrison and let me talk to him. I have a couple of questions to ask him."

I put in his number and Officer Harrison answered on the second ring. I handed the phone to Pop and pushed the speaker phone so I could hear, too. He said, "This is Dr. Lynn. Dennis and I are sitting here tossing some ideas around, so I decided we needed to ask you a couple of questions. I know this is personal information that Mrs. Hegel may not want known, but I think I may be able to help, providing I have a few questions answered.

The first question is..., does Mrs. Hegel have a fairly dependable car to get her back and forth to work?

Officer Harrison said, "Yes, we talked a dealer into contributing to the program by giving us a used car that was in good shape. A man died and his wife sold it to someone who traded it in. She has an eight year-old Honda Civic with only sixty-nine thousand miles on it."

Pop cleared his throat. "The next question is—do you know Mrs. Hegel's approximate income?"

"When she was hired on as a nurse's assistant, she started at a little over eight dollars and hour. She has managed to get in forty hours a week, so she brings in a little over three-hundred a week. Why are you asking?"

Pop went on to say, "I thought maybe we could find a quarter of an acre for her to set up a doublewide manufactured home... if she had sufficient income to make payments. I had suggested that perhaps we could get a dealer to forego his ten percent down. There would be set-up fees, but if we could locate the home inside the Chaffee city limits, then we could have her home hooked up to the city without putting in a septic system or a well. It would mean a move out of Cape Girardeau, but it might be worth it for Blake's siblings—to get them away from the risks of the neighborhood they're in. It *is* something to think about. The Food Giant manager here in Chaffee could work Blake in."

Pop paused, "Think about it and call me on Monday, and we can talk further."

Officer Harrison said, "You know Dr. Lynn, I could get very cynical dealing with people whom I'm confronted with every day, but when I meet people like you and Dennis and the rest of your family, it sure is a shot of encouragement. I really needed to hear some kind of an option this evening before I went to bed. I just didn't want Blake released to that same environment or he might get more of the same treatment or worse."

After Pop hung up, I was the one tapping my finger on the table. Steve came in and said, "You guys are going to have to excuse me, but this room ceased to be a living room and is now my bedroom."

He pushed some chairs under the table and straightened out the table cloth again, just like he was at the Café. He looked in his dresser for something to wear to bed. He said, "You know what? This room is about a twelve-by-twelve room."

Pop said, "According to the house plans, it is fifteen-by-eighteen. We made all the rooms larger than average."

"Well... I was just thinking about the early days of our country, when men had to put up shelter for the winter and built rough cabins about this size. Whole families lived in one room like this one. I can see why they made tables that folded up and trundle beds or bunk beds. I suspect they slept two on a bed and quilts on the floor, too. It must have been really rough in those days. We wouldn't be here, though, if they had not had the strength and determination that they had. Right?"

The wheels in my head started spinning. "Steve, you just gave me an idea. When the workers come on Monday, after we have cleared away all the breakfast off this table, let's see if we can get the carpenter working on the kitchen cabinets to cut this table two feet off each end and I will get some hinges and hinge it. Later we can set it up as a picnic table or something else to work on when we need a long table. What do you think?"

Pop said, "Good idea. Cut it in the middle, too. It shouldn't take much time to put six or eight hinges on it. Then it will be easier to store... heavy, but easy to store."

He started laughing, "That's if we don't load up our covered wagon and move on."

He chuckled again. "With that remark, I'm moving on and out of here and going to bed, too. Tomorrow is another day and we have a lot to think about. So, goodnight, guys, I'm out of this bedroom, dining room, and pantry."

I said, "Me, too. Goodnight, Pop."

I left Steve's room as he was climbing into bed. Going downstairs was like walking into a different world. The rooms upstairs were finished with carpet on the floors, but the stairs and all the downstairs were rough with some walls with sheetrock nailed, but not taped.

I thought about what Steve said about our early Americans and realized that those rough log houses must have been cold and dreary. I suspect they had to work together and build a good size log cabin for everyone to be safe during the storms, as many homes would not have been done if they all worked alone. Besides that, they had to build shelters for the animals. While some men were cutting down trees; other men operated a saw mill of sorts and yet, others were doing the building, unless they all cut down trees at the same time, then they all built together. If they traveled alone, the kids and moms had to help with the labor. I suspect it was sometimes both. The women probably sat and made their rag rugs and that sort of thing, and other times had to work right along-side the men. I closed the door to the new house and walked through the garage to go home to the old house.

I could have walked across the field, but chose to take Mom's car and drive on home. I checked the henhouse and barn quickly and went back to the house. The transition of moving was evident everywhere. The house had lost its feel for *home*. I didn't even want to go upstairs. I checked the locks on the doors and went to the living room and flopped on the couch. Mom insisted on leaving a television here for the noon news, and for Paul when he got tired or she did. I turned on the T.V. and the ten o'clock news was just coming on. I listened for a while and the next thing I knew, I woke up cold and with a blank screen on the T.V.

I went upstairs and crawled into my bed with everything but my shoes on. I had forgotten to call Robert and Janet about visiting Blake. I told myself... *I can't do anything about that now, so I might as well sleep.* I lay there for a moment and the house got very noisy. I had never noticed how the slightest breeze would cause a window to rattle and things like that. It started raining, so I snuggled under my blanket and, the next thing I knew, Pop and the boys were waking me up. It was eight o'clock. I shot out of the bed shaking my head. I couldn't believe that I had over-slept. On their way back downstairs, I heard Pop say, "We should have let him sleep. He must have needed it. He probably lay awake half the night worrying about the kids in the prevention program."

I yelled down at them and said, "I'm coming. Let me get my shoes on."

I smelled coffee brewing. Pop must have made some. Steve said, "You know what, Pop? The refrigerator on the back porch has eggs, milk and butter. If you all will go do the chores, I'll throw us together some breakfast. A couple of omelets will go down fine this morning. I walked down to the kitchen and Glen was just coming back in the house. "The chickens are taken care of... here's another dozen eggs. What are we going to do with all these eggs?"

Pop said, "We'll take a dozen back with us for Mr. Jenkins and Brian and a dozen to Mom back at the house. If you have enough cartons we'll see if we can sell a few to the carpenters at the house. Okay?"

I sat down hard in a kitchen chair and it scooted a little. I said, "I need coffee badly. I think stress has finally caught up with me. I came home last night and flopped on the couch and promptly went to sleep. I remember the first five minutes of the news, and that's all I remember until I woke up cold and to a blank television. Steve, omelets sound good. What else do we have?

I got up and went to the freezer on the back porch and looked. Glen was leaning over my shoulder. "What's this? Oh, this is perfect... homemade biscuits!"

Steve or Mom must have made them up for such a time as this morning. I took them back in and said, "Someone must have planned for this day."

Pop asked, "What do we have?" Glen was smiling and said, "Homemade biscuits. They will go good with some milk gravy and scrambled eggs."

Steve said, "Call Mom and tell her that I'm fixing a hot breakfast over here. We will bring her some—for Aunt Susan and Paul, too.

"Steve, have I ever told you that I'm glad you like to cook and you are a good one?"

He laughed and said, "Is that remark how I get my barn chores done?"

I laughed. "Well, give me thirty minutes and I'll be back in here for breakfast."

Pop said, "Let's go, Dennis. Let's both of us milk a cow, and it will be fifteen minutes."

Steve stacked some boxes around the kitchen and made the place look more like home, and I went out of the house with my coffee. Pop stepped out the door behind me, but went back in the house a few feet and yelled, "Steve, I forgot to call your mother."

Steve yelled back, "I'll call her."

Pop and I milked the two cows and strained the milk and put the cows out to pasture. Glen had already checked the water tank, put fresh water in it, and threw out a couple of bales of hay from the loft. He was trying to spread it around as Steve's cattle made their way up to the barn. He looked a little fearful. So, I grabbed a half-bale and threw it farther away and separated it into piles here and there. The cattle stopped there, while we did the same with the rest of the hay off in another direction. I commented that Steve was going to have to send some of them to market or run the risk of not having enough hay for them before the next haying season.

"Well, what about my young calf… the one Steve gave me?"

"Talk to Steve. He knows about the age and when to sell. He watches the market. Remember the calf is yours, and you need to decide ahead of time how much you are going to give to the Lord, and how much you are going to put in the family account. It's a good way to save for whatever you need. That's how I'm going to buy my own car, by saving."

Pop stepped out of the backdoor of the barn and said to us, "Let's go eat! We don't want to be late for whatever this day has in store for us."

Glen laughed, "I hope it's a calm day."

We washed up at the back porch sink and smelled sausage cooking and I was hungry. It was already eight-thirty-five. I asked, "Do you think we will make it to church on time?"

Pop reached for the pepper and salt and looked at the clock, "Oh, sure… we may be a bit late, but we'll make it. Let's eat and you head for a shower."

Steve had sausage and scrambled eggs, biscuits and sausage gravy and orange juice all ready to go. We just had to go to the warming oven and get what we wanted. Mom, Aunt Susan, and Paul walked in when we were ready to sit. They were all ready for church. Steve said, "While we are eating, Dennis, I'm going up and take a shower here. I still have clothes upstairs to move. I ate while fixing breakfast."

Pop said, "Wait a minute… we are all here together, let's pray, shall we?"

Steve stopped in his tracks and Pop asked God for a blessing, thanked Him for the food, and asked God to help us serve and bring glory to Him." We all said, "Amen."

While I was eating, I thanked God for Janet and asked God to bless her and her family. Then I thought *I need to be thanking God for a lot of things.* One thing for sure is that He spared Blake's life. For whatever reason, He did. Then I thought *Blake needs to know that Satan was defeated and God allowed him to live.* I sat quietly with the family and ate breakfast. I took my dishes to the sink and rinsed everything and stacked them with Steve's.

I filled one side of the sink with soapy water and said, "I've started the dishwater. I'm headed upstairs for a shower, too."

Steve wasn't out of the bathroom yet, so I made my bed and got out my clean clothes. It felt strange to sit there for a moment and look at John's bed and realize the he would never be sleeping in that bed again. He had entered into the next phase of his life and would now be sleeping downstairs in a queen-sized bed with a wife. I thought *I can see how some people suffer with depression because I feel sad about this. John and I will never be sleeping in the same room and saying good-night to each other again. I have a little idea what Glen must feel—not having his family at all.* Don't ask me why, but I had tears rolling down my face. I guess underneath *my* big man exterior, I felt deeply, just as John says he did.

"Steve came to the door and started to say, "I'm done in the bathr-o-o-m," but he didn't finish. He said, "Dennis, for Pete's sake, what's the matter?"

"Steve, I just had an overwhelming sense of loss. John and I have been in this room together for years. We have shared most everything, played together, teased each other, and encouraged one another. He will never be sleeping five or six feet away from me again. He has entered the next phase of his life."

Steve looked at me with almost a look of disgust. "So… get over it! You're going to get married, too, and leave *me* behind."

I looked at him while picking up my clean clothes off the bed. I suspected Steve would be feeling just like I am feeling when I marry and leave home. I said, "Steve, every night John said, 'goodnight' to me. Think how Glen must feel never hearing his mother or grandmother or his sisters say goodnight or good morning or ever hear their voices again. I don't know that I could handle it as well as Glen has. I'm having trouble with John just getting married."

Steve sat on John's bed with a pair of socks in his hand and said, "Dennis, we have felt that same loss before, with Dad, Grandma and Grandpa leaving us. That's why we, as Christians, can count on Jesus in our hearts to fill up the empty spaces. I'm eighteen now, and I know that a year from now I'm going to go through the same things you are feeling. I feel it every time I send one of my Angus cattle off to be slaughtered. I have to say, 'Jesus, fill the empty space in my heart,' and you know what? Here comes a new calf and it requires a lot of my attention.

"I don't know what goes on in your head, but I do know God can help you feel better about this whole situation."

Steve got up and headed to his old room, but looked back at me and said, "Brother, you had better head for the shower or everyone is going to be ready except you."

"Okay, Thanks, Steve, I needed what you said."

I went to the shower and cried and prayed the whole time I was in there. I prayed for John and Marianne, for my family, and especially for complete healing for Paul and for mental and emotional healing for Glen in the loss of his family. I thanked God for sparing Janet and Robert's lives four years ago and for sparing Blake's life. I asked God to show us a way to save his whole family and get them out of the environment they were in. It was sort of a healing for me to pray for others.

I shaved and dressed and was out of the bathroom when Glen came knocking at my door. He said, "Pop told me about Blake. I want to go see him after church. He needs me just like I needed him. Pop doesn't think it would be wise, but I have God in my heart now, and I know he will keep me strong for Blake."

I looked at Glen and he had such a serious look on his face that I almost wanted to cry again for this fifteen year-old boy.

"Glen, when did you decide to let God come into your life? Do you accept Jesus as God's son?"

Glen finished my sentence and said, "Yes, and he died for me, so did my family. They all did. Jesus died for me and *my* sin and my family died because of someone else's sin. I find it hard to forgive my stepfather, but because I know there are wicked people in the world and God loves and will forgive them, so I have to forgive my stepfather, too. Besides, my family is enjoying heaven. He has to enjoy living in prison and possibly hell. I have to forgive him."

I had to say, "Glen, you have just given me my first blessing for this day. Pop prayed for a blessing downstairs, and I was feeling so depressed because John would never sleep in the same room with me and would never say good-night to me again. I thought about you and how hard it must be for you. Here you are up here telling me that you want to go see Blake to help *him,* and you have God in your life now, to help you be strong."

I couldn't help it. I had to hug Glen and tell him, "Thank you for sharing with me. Thank you for being my brother—thank you, Glen, for reminding me that I have God in my life to help me be strong. I need to be strong for Blake, also."

"Then you will talk to Pop and see if he will let me go with you to see Blake?"

"Yes," I said, "Yes, I'll talk to him, but if he has any reservations or uncomfortable feelings about you going, then we will honor him like sons should, and not go. Perhaps we can bring Blake here for a few days or over at the new house. We can make room some place for him. Don't you think?"

His face lit up. ""That would be good."

Mom was calling him, so he went on out of the room saying, "See you later...."

I straightened up my desk and decided that it wouldn't hurt to pack up the stuff on the top. I wouldn't be using any of it during the week. I put on my shoes and grabbed my dress jacket and headed downstairs. Mom said, "Dennis! You aren't going anywhere looking like that. Janet will lose all respect for you, or she'll feel that you still need a mother."

"Why—what is the matter?"

Steve and Glen started laughing and said, "Go look in the mirror, Dennis."

"Thanks, everybody, what is wrong?"

I was glad Aunt Susan, Pop and Paul were already outside getting in the car or they would have been laughing at me, too. I ran back upstairs and looked in the full length mirror still hanging in the bedroom. I had not only *not* combed my hair, but I had buttoned my shirt from the bottom up and had two buttons holes above my last button with no buttons. I realized I had done it after Glen left the room, and I was thinking about packing my desk top and I was in a hurry. I stood there looking at myself in the mirror laughing at myself. *Yeah, Janet, this morning I did need a mother. Thanks, Mom.*

I went on downstairs and Steve and Glen were waiting on me. "We decided to wait on you rather than crowd in Pop's car and have Aunt Susan tell us we're sitting on the side of her skirt. We need to leave though."

We piled in Mom's old car and went the five or eight minutes to church. Pastor Bishop was at the side door greeting people. Mom was standing about five feet inside the door and said, "Boys, there are two boxes of bows and other things in the fellowship hall. Would you run down and get them right now and put them in my car trunk? I guess we missed them last night when we were cleaning up."

I looked at Glen and said, "Our work day is just starting, so let's go get those boxes."

Pastor Bishop was standing there smiling. "Mrs. Lynn, you have raised a fine crop of boys."

I looked back, and Mom was just grinning from ear to ear. I thought, *I guess there is a certain amount of pride in rearing or raising good children. I feel sorry for those parents who have willful kids and are constantly pushing at their boundary lines. Like cattle they break out on occasion, and then subject themselves to all kind of danger.*

I told myself to hold those thoughts as I needed to talk to Pastor Bishop about Blake since Blake was the kid that used to go to Calvary Church and Pastor Bishop was always helping him with money for groceries.

I grabbed a box labeled *Moore Wedding* and Glen grabbed the other one. We hurried back up the stairs. I caught Pastor Bishop just as he was leaving to go somewhere, probably to a Sunday school class. I said, "Pastor Bishop, if you are not teaching anywhere, would you mind waiting for just a second."

"I'd be glad to."

I popped the truck and put my box in, and Glen put his in. I said to Glen, "I want to talk to the pastor about Blake. He used to help Blake quite often when they lived in Chaffee."

Glen said, "I want to talk to him, too, about being baptized."

"Glen, that is wonderful. Mom and Pop will be so pleased. We all will be."

Pastor Bishop was still standing on the steps when we got back. I said, "Glen, you go first."

Glen hesitated but said, "Pastor Bishop, I want to be baptized."

Pastor Bishop in his gentle tone said, "Well, Glen, that's wonderful. May I ask, what led you to this decision?"

Glen got a little shy at that point. "Glen, just tell the pastor what you told me in my bedroom this morning."

He was looking at me seriously, but said, "Mom and Pop pray at all our meals and at other times, and I realized that I didn't know how to talk to God, because I didn't know God. I prayed and asked God to tell me about himself. Someway he told me to read about Jesus, His son. I asked Pop and Steve a few questions and they gave me some Bible verses to read, and I thought… I need Jesus to forgive me of my sins, so I asked God to do that and to live in me for all time. I believe Jesus is God's son and He died on that cross for me. He's in heaven now with my family preparing for me to join them some day."

Pastor Bishop looked at me, "Dennis, Glen has the gospel down in its simplest terms." He then explained to Glen why we are baptized and why we respond to the invitation at the end of the service.

Glen said, "I can do that."

The pastor looked at his watch, "Son, you had better go on to class now. I will be talking with you later about a Sunday to be baptized."

Glen said, "Okay." He did a little wave of his hand, "I'll see you later."

He walked off with a big grin, and in my heart, I knew God had filled some empty spaces. The pastor was looking at me like he was thinking, *Well, son, what is on your heart?* I said, "Pastor Bishop, I hate being the bearer of bad news right before the service, but perhaps you can help, or you know someone who can help, someone we both know. Or, perhaps the church benevolent fund can help. It's Blake Hegel, sir. Two nights ago, some jealous boys in his neighborhood got to him, while he was on his way to work. They beat him up and he is in Southeast Hospital. He will survive, but he needs encouragement, and we need to pray for the family and help them somehow to get out of that bad neighborhood. He is doing wonderful in school now and his employer is very pleased with him. Please pray with us for Blake, and if you can visit him, I'm sure he will be glad to see you."

"Dennis, thank you for your concern. Blake's mother called me yesterday, and I went right up to see him. You're right. Something needs to be done about getting the family out of the neighborhood. Let me know if you have any suggestions."

"Well, I do, but Officer Harrison and Pop are talking together. Perhaps you can talk with one of them in a day or two. How is Blake?"

Pastor Bishop opened the door and gestured for me to go on in, and at the same time, he said, "Blake is in a little pain, but he is more worried about his family and what might be done to them next."

"I told Glen, if we had to, we would find a place back in Chaffee to get him out of the neighborhood. At the very least, when he was ready to be released, we would find a place for him alone. Do you have any suggestions? Oh, I asked you that?"

I went right on talking even though Pastor Bishop was walking toward wherever he needed to go. I said, "The only thing I can think of is for the church to take up a collection to help move them somewhere. It is frightening, after what happened to Glen's family, to think there might be a drive-by shooting or some revenge taken out on the younger children, because of the jealousy or resentment for Blake. We need to really pray about the gangs in every city."

Pastor Bishop agreed, but said, "We can talk later about this. Don't miss your entire Sunday Bible Class."

"No, I don't want to, so I'll see you later." I headed to the college and career's class, and he went on to his study.

Mom and Pop were so pleased that Glen went forward in the church service at the invitation time. Mom didn't have any idea that Glen was so close to making a decision for the Lord. Pop and Steve did, but Mom had John and Marianne's wedding on her mind. Uncle Al and Aunt Nancy, Matthew and Kaitlynn, Trevor and Katy, Aunt Bonnie, Uncle John, with Aaron and Michelle all showed up for the worship service. Mom thought some of them had gone back to St. Louis. Our family filled up two pews. Cousin Stacy knew they were staying and had her cooks at the Café ready to give us her large room and prepare extra food, but the highlight of the morning was Glen.

Pastor Bishop asked Glen if he would tell the audience what he had told him outside on the step. Glen gave a testimony of God's love and forgiveness for his sin and how even though his stepfather had killed his two sisters, his mother and grandmother... if God could forgive those that hung his son on the cross and can forgive despicable people like his stepfather than he knew he had to forgive, too. He went on to say that his family was waiting for him in heaven, but while on earth, he was going to do what he could to serve God.

Mom cried, Aunt Susan cried, Uncle Al had big tears rolling down his face. I gulped several times. I couldn't believe what he said next. He said, "Pastor Bishop, I know it's getting late, but I want to say something else. Is it okay?"

Pastor Bishop said, "It's more than okay. Would you like to go up to the microphone?"

Glen said, "No," and then he said, "I believe I will."

Mind you, Glen's fifteenth birthday is in a few weeks, and his voice still cracks on occasion, but no one seemed to notice. Glen talked like a polished speaker who had been in front of audiences a life-time. I prayed, *Lord, speak through him. Take his body and use his tongue for your purpose.* I knew Mom and Pop and others were praying for him, too.

Glen put his hands on both sides of the pulpit, "I feel like I need to say something this morning. You see I have three Saviors in my life. The night that my stepfather killed my sisters, my mother, and grandmother, I heard the shots and ran in the house to see what happened. I faced a gun not more than five feet from me. The gun didn't go off. I ran. I ran next door to a friend's house. His mother told my friend to take me to the Moore's home in Chaffee… that I would be safe there. My friend's mother called 911 and reported what had happened. My friend is almost two years older than I am, and he has no car. He grabbed me by the arm and said, "Let's go. All night we walked or sat down on the ground and rested. I cried and he lifted me up and helped me to stand and them we would walk. We walked again and I would cry. We stopped and he would hug me. At five in the morning, we had walked from our neighborhood in Cape Girardeau to the Moore home. That friend was my Savior that night. He took me to safety. My second Savior was the whole Moore family, especially Pop. He decided that I should be his son and he hurriedly went through the legal system, before we ever buried my family, to make me his son. His influence led me to my next Savior, Jesus Christ."

Glen's adolescent voice would change pitch on him, but he went on to say, "I have to tell you, that every Christian family member should be a Savior to someone and lead them away from the pointed gun of Satan to the safety net that Jesus provided for you and them."

I thought Glen was going to lose it and break down and cry, but he just stood there for a moment. I'm sure God shut his mouth for those seconds or minute to give people time to think about what he just said. I wanted to get up and go stand with him, and I guess Pop felt the same way.

Pop got up and went up to the stage and put his arm around Glen and looked out at the audience. "Glen, let *me* say something."

Glen look up at him, "I want to say something about Blake."

Pop said, "I will."

Pop looked out at the audience and didn't say a word either, for a second or two. The people were waiting... sitting on the edge of their seats as the expression goes. Pop said, "When God looked down on Jesus when he was baptized, there was a voice from heaven, that many people heard, and the voice said, 'This is my son, in whom I am well pleased.'"

Pop looked at Glen and put both arms around him and gave him a big hug. Then he looked out at the audience and said, "This is my son, in whom I am well pleased." He kept his arm around Glen's shoulders and said, "Glen wanted to tell you about his friend, Blake. I just told him that I would tell you. I want to give every one of you the opportunity to be a Savior. Glen's friend that walked with him all the way to safety that long night of his family's death is no other than Blake Hegel. He used to come to this church as a youngster. He had a special fondness for Pastor Bishop, because *he* was a Savior to Blake as a child. Our Pastor gave money to Blake to pick up coffee, milk, and cereal, so the kids could go off to school and his Dad off to work with breakfast. He told one of my boys, that he had to get the coffee so his Dad would come out of his drunken stupor enough to go to work the next morning. Blake has turned into a fine young man.

After the death of her husband, Mrs. Hegel got some training as a nurse's assistant and has a steady job. Blake's mother, sisters and brother have survived with what she earns and Blake's help, but because Blake is doing well in school and working two hours every evening and six hours on Saturday. Satan has stepped up his fury to undermine the family. Walking to work the other night, several hoodlums from the neighborhood, stopped Blake and beat him up. He is in Southeast Hospital. Glen, here, is insisting that he go to the hospital this afternoon. His comment to Dennis was, 'I needed Blake. Now he needs me like I needed him.'

"When God puts love in our hearts for our fellow man… his love, we are supposed to be Saviors for them and for others in need. Glen learned this at an early age. Some of us have never learned it. This morning, I am offering to give one-quarter acre to this family, to set up a doublewide manufactured home. Mrs. Hegel can make the payments, but she will need help in the set-up fees. What do you say… we as a church become a Savior with Glen to get Blake's family back in Chaffee and to our church? If you have any feeling for what Jesus had done for you and after hearing what this young man has said, would you be willing to come up and stand with Glen and be a Savior. Or, if you want God's son, Jesus, in your heart and life as your ultimate Savior would you come up and tell Pastor Bishop."

Pop asked Glen to go back down and stand to the left of the church in the front of the auditorium and Pastor Bishop to stand on the right. Then he did something else that surprised everyone. He said, "I would like for the pianist to stay where she is, and for my son-in-law to come forward and sing, "How Great Thou Art."

Matthew, Kaitlynn's husband, started toward the front. I think Pastor Bishop thought he was in a revival meeting or something with all the sniffing and tears in the audience. I just kept saying, "Thank you, Jesus."

After Matthew was in place behind the pulpit, Pop walked down to the communion table and took a collection plate and dumped the contents into the other one and asked the church financial chairman to come get it. He then walked over to Glen and handed him the empty plate. Pop took several dollars out of his billfold and put them in the plate. I decided I would be next and maybe others would follow. Uncle Al beat me to it. He went up and opened his wallet and took out several bills. He hugged Glen and said, "Welcome to my family, son," I thought Glen might cry, but he said, "Thank you, sir." Several people went by Pastor Bishop and I noticed him call his wife up to get their names. I stayed with Glen and took the plate and held it as several people wanted to hug him, too.

When Matthew had finished the song, Pastor Bishop said, "God is Great! Thank you, Matthew for singing that great song. Thank you, Glen, for sharing your thoughts and feelings with us. Thank you, Dr. Lynn, for your words and I support what Dr. Lynn said. The Hegel family needs us… and I am grateful this morning, and I'm humbled at what God is doing here. He looked at Glen and said, "Young man, God is using you, and I thank you again, for what you shared with us this morning."

He turned back to the audience and said, "We have four people this morning coming to receive Christ as their Savior and for Baptism. I will be talking to them this afternoon. How many of you rejoice at what God has done this morning… say Amen. The audience did… loudly.

And we have some new-comers to our community coming to unite with us as members. Pastor Bishop introduced them all. Then he asked Uncle Al to close the service in prayer. He prayed a wonderful prayer asking God's blessing on each one that had come making a decision for Christ and for the local church.

We were late leaving the church by thirty minutes, but it was the most rewarding thirty minutes that I had witnessed in our local church in a long time. God is going to use Glen's life someway, somewhere, like he did this morning.

Pop told Glen to give the plate of money to the church treasurer and he would hold the money or give us one check for all of it. The people giving the checks, wanted to have a record of their giving for taxes. The treasurer took the money to a back room and counted it.

As we left the church, the church treasurer was walking towards his car in the parking lot. He had the money in a zippered pouch to take to the bank. His car was parked near Mom's old car, so I slipped up behind him and said, "Mr. Patterson, I'm curious. How much came in for the Hegel family? "

"Can you believe eight-hundred and thirty-five dollars?"

All I could think to say was, "Wow, God is good."

Glen and Steve were in the car waiting for me. Matthew was talking to Glen. I got in the driver's seat and heard Matthew say to Glen. "I'll see you at the Café. Man, am I ever proud to have you as my younger brother... even if it is a brother-in-law. You stack right up there with John, Paul, Dennis and Steve."

CHAPTER 10

THE FAMILY HAD A really good time of fellowship at the Café that Sunday afternoon. Pop and Uncle Al enjoyed talking to each other about their former medical practices. Cousin Stacy thought she was in heaven already, with all the relatives in her Café. Since she had grown up alone and then found she was related to my mother, Cousin Stacy has become a real part of the Moore family. I know Mom claims her because she grew up as an adopted child, also. It feels good to have a large family.

All the St. Louis relatives left the Café and headed back north around three o'clock. I went back to the farmhouse. The house was empty now except for me. The dishes and pans that Steve had used for breakfast were all stacked neatly. I heard Steve telling Mom when I was getting dressed that he was going to come over and make up enough biscuits for two weeks and enough pancakes for two weeks and freeze them. It was nice to have biscuits and sausage gravy and the food all came right out of the freezer on such a busy Sunday morning. Except for the eggs and butter and those are fresh all the time anyway.

When I walked in the door of the old farmhouse, I wondered what I could be doing to help the move along. I finally decided to go to each room and check to see what was still in the room and clean it thoroughly. Our living room was all across the front of the farmhouse. Everything had been taken out except the couch, a chair and the small T.V. sitting on a box. Pictures had been taken off the wall and all the knick knacks and plants were gone, too. I said to myself, *Good, I'm going to sweep and dust in this room and then put a note up that says, "Off limits… Room has been cleaned."* I spent about forty-five minutes in the living room, made my sign, and then started on the dining room. Everything was cleared out, except the buffet, table, and china closet and the packed boxes sitting in the corner. I decided to carry the boxes to the car, so they would be ready for taking to Mom's new house in the morning. That was done and then I polished the furniture with lemon oil and swept the floor. I made a bigger sign and said, "Stay out of the dining room. Work has been completed."

I started worrying about where Mom would want all the boxes over at the new house. There were so many. I finally decided I needed to go over there and see if I could find a place in the garage. I thought I should do like everyone else was doing and that was to get my six-foot-three-inch body on my bed and rest like Pop wanted all of us to do. It was about ten minutes after five and I locked up the house and walked to my car. Well, not really my car, but Mom's old car.

On the way down the lane, a car was coming toward me. It was Robert trying out a car. I was surprised that he was able to save enough money to buy a car, but then again, he saved the whole spring semester. Tips at the Café must have been good. We stopped beside each other half-way down the lane. I had to roll down my window, as he did his, and say, "Man… ain't them some hot wheels! Where did you come up with this car?"

Robert was elated. "After what Glen said this morning, Dad came to me after dinner this noon and said, 'Son, I want to be your Savior. You have worked hard for six months and have saved everything except your tithe and I want you to know that I am proud of you. Because of that, I want you to have a car.'"

Robert giggled like Janet does, "I couldn't believe my tight-fisted Dad was finally going to help me buy a car. Dad had this car tucked away in a friend's garage all this time."

I asked, "What is the make? It looks like a Honda Civic."

He said, "It is."

"It has fifty-eight thousand, nine hundred miles on the odometer. Dad says it's just a youngster."

"What does Janet think?"

Robert raised his eyebrows and chuckled. "Oh, Janet is working on Dad by telling him, now that he doesn't have to support Marianne, he should start saving for her car."

I looked off down the road, "Well, Robert, he may not have to support her either after next June. I guess your folks told you that Friday after the rehearsal dinner, I asked Janet to marry me and she accepted. Now the pressure is on to really build up a nest egg. My soybean just won't cover a full year's wages for two people. We're working and praying for one thing at a time. The first priority is our own vehicle."

Robert said, "You're driving one, isn't it good enough?"

"It's fine for now, but it's already pushing one-hundred-thousand miles. Pop is keeping his eye out for a used truck for the farm, so that I can keep this car. He's been keeping the oil changed and generally keeping it in good repair, but come September John' schedule may be different than ours, and I need to work at least twenty-five hours a week, somewhere. John plans to work also, so we may be going in opposite directions. What about you?"

Robert looked out in front of him and said, "Well... I just don't know. I keep thinking perhaps I should hire on at the Red Lobster or somewhere where it is busy and the menu prices are higher. Tips would be greater. Since I have my own car now, I can be more selective about *where* I work. The nice thing about the Café is that I can jog home after a shift or Mom can come after me. It's been nice getting to know the town folk, also.

"I'm hoping to get back on with Officer Harrison at the University for ten hours a week. That job will pay for my car expenses."

"Me, too. My job grading papers and putting the grades in the computer is a no-brainer job. I can handle that again, but I'd like to pick up six hours at least on the days that I don't have classes. You haven't heard of any other jobs around the university have you? Have you looked at the bulletin boards lately?"

Robert didn't answer my question. He started up his engine again and said, "She purrs like a kitten. Don't you think?"

"Nice car! Nice car!" I chuckled and thought, *He's really proud of the car.*

"Where are you headed with all those boxes?"

"Over to Mom's to see if I can find a place out of the carpenters' way, to put all the extra boxes that we keep stacking in corners or carrying upstairs to an empty bedroom."

Robert looked out the other window at Mom and Pop's new house and said… "It looks like to me, that with a three-car garage, the carpenters could work in two. Isn't the smaller one mainly for your lawn mowing equipment and tools and such?"

"Yes, it is… I wonder why Mom or Pop hasn't recommended that. I suspect they have had so many details on their mind with John and Marianne's wedding and all the details of finishing up the upstairs that they've had too much to think about. I'm headed over there now, why don't you come on over. Steve would like to see your car and I'm sure Mom and pop will want to pass their judgment on it."

Robert laughed and said, "Sure. I'm anxious to pass judgment on the house, too. He smiled, "Why is it that I feel like your folks are another set of parents to me or grandparents or something?"

"Probably for the same reason your folks feel like that to me.

Sometimes I feel like your family is biologically related to us. Maybe that's how friends are supposed to be."

Robert revved his engine a little. "I'll go up, turned around in your circle drive by the barn, and then I'll be over. See ya in a few minutes."

I took off down the lane and turned in Mom and Pop's drive. There wasn't a sound coming from the house. I figured this was a day of rest and that's what they were all doing—upstairs resting. I tiptoed upstairs and sure enough, there was a chorus of snores. I wish I had had a recorder. It was funny. Before I got back downstairs and through the garage, Robert drove up and decided to try his horn. He got out and slammed his door and said, "I decided that they might as well all look at the car at the same time. Where is everyone?"

"They *were* all asleep, but I suspect they will be downstairs, now that you've made your grand entrance."

I walked over to the single garage and opened the door and there sat a truck. A magnificent old truck... the same model as the one that was Grandpa's truck. I looked at Robert and I know we must have had our mouths wide open when Pop came out of the house and caught us."

"Pop, what is this? Where did it come from?"

Pop said, "Shhh! This is your Mom's birthday present." He pulled the door down again."

"When we were packing, I found some pictures of your grandfather and grandmother when they bought the truck new. I've had it enlarged. I have been so enraptured with the truck that I decided to check with your security officer and see what he had done with the truck. He invited me to come see it. It hadn't been painted yet, and fortunately I thought to take the colored snapshot with me. He matched the paint and restored the truck to its original color. I offered him more than it was worth and he took it. He said, "I have my eye on another one and this will be more than what I need to restore it. It's a hobby of mine. I love doing it."

All I could say was, "Pop, Wow! You did great. She will like this. John will probably talk her into getting it back, though. Is it drivable?"

"Yes, it has a new motor in it. "That's the only thing that wasn't on the restoration list. The man said people like to get out and drive their old vehicles around and compare notes, so he put a new motor in it."

"Well, Robert came over to show you *his* car and I came over to find a spot to put the boxes out of the dining room. The living room and dining room are cleaned and ready for John and Marianne. Now we need to clear out the kitchen and then the whole downstairs will be ready for them. Is Mom's piano going to stay over there?"

I thought about Janet and how well she plays, "Janet uses your piano... does she not, Robert?

"I suspect someday, Marianne will want a new piano and then it can come back over here, if Mom wants to leave her piano in the house for now."

Robert said, "Janet plays on ours, when she gets up, when she gets tired, when no one is around and when everyone is around. I suspect that she would be lost without Mom's piano."

Pop chuckled, "Well, I guess that settles it. Both girls need a piano, especially with Marianne's degree in music. Bonnie had hers tuned about three months ago, so it should be in good shape for Marianne."

Robert looked at me as though he was thinking about something. He said, "Last night Janet and Mom were talking about a job for Janet after you get married, and Mom suggested that she take on six or eight piano students. Mom called Janet's music teacher, and she said she was getting twelve dollars a student for a thirty-minute lesson. Janet agreed that she could do that on a Saturday morning for three hours and perhaps four or five during the week."

I thought, *That sounds like a workable solution. If she can earn enough to pay the utilities and phone, I think I can do the rest.* Then I thought. *I'll save those thoughts until later.*

I changed the subject, "Pop, do the carpenters need this whole two-car garage?"

He said, "No, they don't. The cabinet maker is the only one using the garage now. Most of the work is interior work. What do you say we stack up all this stuff that is leftover plywood and other scrap wood?"

"Wait a minute. Robert wants you to inspect his car."

Pop said, "I'm sorry, Robert, when I heard the horn and came out and saw the door opened on the single garage... I forgot everything else."

"I'm sorry. It was me who suggested to Dennis that he put boxes in that smaller garage."

"No problem... let me see this car. Pop walked around it and then sat down in it and turned the motor on. He got back out and said, "Looks like you got a good one, son. Do you like it?"

"Yes, I like it even more, now that Dad was willing to help me out on the financing. He gave me a thousand dollars and we are going to the bank and take out a loan. I have to make the payments and insurance. By the time, I transfer money out of my savings; I will have only about twelve hundred dollars left on the loan. I can handle the payments myself."

Pop put his hand on Robert's shoulder, "I'm proud of you, Robert. You have entered the business world. Don't ever miss a payment and always pay before or on time. If you run short some month… come see me. You can really ruin your credit by skipping or paying late."

"Thanks… so you like it?"

Pop said, "…Should last you until you are out of college."

I was just standing there watching and listening to Pop and Robert. I looked over the carpenter's stuff and said, "Pop, let's start stacking boxes on the interior wall. The carpenters are working more to the front of the garage for ventilation. I can get a roll of clear plastic and cover the boxes to keep dust off them. We will be able to see through the plastic to the labels on the boxes."

I got the push-broom that was leaning against the wall and swept out the carpenter's sawdust and cleared away about six feet.

Robert was just watching us work. He finally said, "I need to be leaving."

I looked at him and smiled. "Are you afraid you are going to be asked to go help with the barn chores?"

He laughed, "I told Dad I would be back, but if you need help, I'll call him."

Pop said, "No, we can handle it this evening. You can carry one of the boxes before you leave, though."

Pop took my broom and said, "I'm going to sweep up the rest of this sawdust. No sense in tracking it in the house. The sky looks like it might rain and all this sawdust will make a mess tracked into the house. We moved everything over so we would have a clear path to walk into the house.

Mom came out and said, "What are you all doing? Hey, this looks great. I wondered why those men thought they needed the whole garage. Now I can pull my Lincoln in out of the weather."

I said, "Thanks, Mom. We needed a place to stack boxes from the old farmhouse. You should have heard the chorus of snoring when I came over twenty minutes, ago.

Mom chuckled, "I really feel rested. Better than I have felt for days."

"Mom, you were burning the candle at both ends. Are you going to church this evening?"

"We're planning on it. The youth are meeting at six and we want Steve, Glen, and Paul to be there."

"Then if you don't mind, I'll take care of all the chores. You go to church and come back to your living, dining, pantry, and bedroom. Then sit down with the boys for a good time with a board game or two. You do know six o'clock is only 30 or 40 minutes from now, don't you?"

"Yeah, the boys are getting ready. I'm going to reorganize that room, so Steve doesn't feel cramped. He hasn't complained, but after two more months… he might."

Mom went back in the house after giving me a hug and kiss. I finished unloading the car and went on back to the old house. The sun was setting as a big fiery ball. It reminded me of God creating the universe and wondered how he created something so big and used it to give the little earth light and warmth. It's beyond my imagination… the wonder of it all.

——— ——

I got back to the house void of people noises and worked on the kitchen some more. All the cupboards were empty now except for the eight dishes, glasses, and sets of silverware that we might need before the week was out. I left out the pan Mom uses for vegetables, the one she uses for eggs in the morning, and a couple of cookie sheets. Those I laid on the cleared cabinet with a towel over them, along with the dishes and silverware. I told myself to pack up everything. It's only me over here, and I can go over and eat at the new house. If Steve has everything in the freezer already cooked, we might as well use the micro-wave over at the new house. I'll go over there and eat. I wiped all the cupboards out with Clorox water and the kitchen smelled strong. All the boxes that were packed and stacked in the corner of the kitchen—I put on the back porch. Everything was out of the kitchen except for the things on the counter. I even took Mom's kitchen decorations off the wall and packed them. The U-Haul Company made a killing off us with all the boxes we purchased. I tackled the rest of the stuff in the pantry and wiped it down. Mom could hire me out as a maid… I was so proud of myself.

I looked at my watch and realized the cows were probably begging to be milked. Outside chores had to be done next. I shut up the chicken house and made a mental note that it needed to be hosed out. Paul's pink plastic bowl was full by the time I gathered the eggs. He has to sell some of his chickens, or Steve and I are going to do them in, scald and cut them up for the freezer.

I set the eggs on the back step and went to the barn with Paul's dog following me every step of the way. He sure was good company for me. I took him indoors last night with me, but he heard every creak in the walls and was startled. Tonight, he will be staying on the back porch or in his dog house.

Both cows were milked, the milk run through the strainer, and Steve's cattle taken care of with some hay tossed out the loft window. I went down and clipped the bailing rope and wire and spread it around and put fresh water in the trough. I thought that I heard some voices and looked around the corner of the barn. I couldn't believe what I was seeing.

There were two men with a truck backed up to the back of the house loading the boxes that I had placed on the back porch. I guess they didn't see my car or had looked around and not found anyone. I was up in the loft and I guess when they looked in the barn they didn't hear anyone, or I was out at the back of the barn spreading the hay around. Mom and Dad taught us well. I heard often, "When you leave a room shut off the light!" So, I had done that at the house, except for the back porch light and a light over the kitchen sink.

I went through the barn and was confronted with someone who thought he was big stuff. He said, "Stay where you are buddy."

I walked right up to him and said, "Are you talking to me?" The barn was semi-dark as I had inadvertently turned out the interior light and was going for the light switch to get the milk and feed the cats in the milk room. I guess he heard me, but didn't see me. I was about a foot taller and my class at the university in how to subdue a person came in handy. I flipped him over like a rag doll. He was so surprised and slow at reacting that I had my hand over his mouth and a rag from the strainer machine stuffed in his mouth in less than twenty seconds. I tied him up with the bailing rope I still had sticking out of my pocket. Then I snuck to my car to get my cell phone.

I started to call Pop, but decided to call 911. The police said they were on their way. I ran to the back of Mom's shed, watched a man take out another box, and go back in the house. I ran to the side of the house. I could hear them in Grandpa's bedroom. They were going through John and Marianne's wedding gifts.

I had easy access to their truck and took the keys out and put them in my pocket. I slipped around to the front just in case they saw the police come down our lane and decided to make a run for the front door. I waited out of sight.

Fortunately, I still had the cell phone with me and called the police and told the dispatcher to tell the officers to stop before they got up to the house as I wanted them to be caught in the act. I told them that I was stationed at the front, in case they decided to make a run for it out the front door, and that I had taken their keys.

The whole scene was almost funny. I guess I *am* cut out for police work. I'm fairly calm during a crisis. Some criminals have a mind for stealing and trying not to be caught, but some are dumb, too.

Two officers stopped their car about fifty feet from the house behind a big fir tree. They could see me. I took off running to them and said, "I was able to sneak up and get their truck keys. They are in the bedroom off the kitchen going through wedding gifts. I have one tied up in the barn. They wanted to know if they could get in the house through the front door.

It was locked from the inside. I pulled out my keys... it was the low-down thieves keys. I said, "Here, this is their truck keys. I handed the other officer our house key. He said, "Stay here, Dennis."

The other officer started to go to the back of the house. I said, "No, don't go that way, they are in that bedroom" and pointed to the window. He took off around the house and another back up policeman had arrived and went the other way. The officer at the front of the house opened the door and yelled... "Anybody home?"

I couldn't believe he would announce his presence. I knew the minute he yelled, they would take off out the back door. I was standing where I could see the window and the back of the house. One of them was trying to open the window. I laughed because it was painted shut. He turned away from the window and moved toward the back of the house.

Two shots were fired and I panicked. I decided to wait until I was given permission to move any further. One of the men ran out the back door and headed for the truck, but the waiting policeman was right there. He caught him and had him down in a second. He yelled for the other officer and there was no answer. I decided a third person was needed. I ran around the truck and said, "Give me those" and grabbed the handcuffs and locked them and said, "You'd better go check on your partner."

He ran around the tailgate of the truck and went in the house. I got up and wondered for a second what I should do next. I looked down at the man on the ground and said, "Buddy, your days of thieving are done."

I had some twine in a kitchen box that they put on the back of the truck. I had to reach a little but I had the box opened in a flash and got the twine and put it around the man's ankles. I thought, *God knew this would happen and he planned for that twine to be right where I could reach it.*

I didn't know whether to go in the house or stay out. I called home. The family was home from church, and Pop answered the phone. I said, "Pop, we have a major problem over here. Don't say anything to Mom, but bring Steve over here with you, right away. I can't explain." I hung up and didn't give Pop a change to answer.

There was talking in the house, so I decided to go ahead and go in. One of the no good thieves was on the floor and it looked like he was dead. Officer Glass was on the floor with a bullet hole in his arm. Officer Hume was talking on his radio for an ambulance.

I looked at both of them and shook my head. I said, "I wondered why you announced your entrance."

Officer Glass said, "I figured wrong. I thought maybe they would make a dash for the truck, since I was coming from the front. Too bad for him… he shot me in the arm and was such a poor shot. He missed my vital parts, but I didn't him. I hate pulling a gun on anyone, but this time, it was him or me."

Pop and Steve walked in, "What's going on?

I said, "Well, we have a man in the barn tied up, one outside and this one pulled a gun on Officer Glass. Fortunately, he missed, but got his arm. Officer Glass shot him before he could shoot again. They were loading up our packed boxes and were going through

John and Marianne's wedding gifts and helping themselves to them.

Pop got down on the floor and looked at Officer Glass' arm "Son, I wish I could help you. It looks like the bullet is not in your arm. You have an exit wound. The way you are bleeding, I suspect you have an artery severed. Officer Hume had taken the towel that I had covered the dishes with and wrapped his arm. I was glad it was a clean towel. The detective arrived to get details on the downed man and what all had taken place. The ambulance arrived right behind the detective. I asked, "Officer, what do you want me to do with the one in the barn?"

He said, "Let's go get him."

Steve said, "I'm going, too. My cattle better be in good shape."

"Steve, I fed them and watered them. But I didn't bring in the milk."

Pop asked, "How long has it been sitting out?"

"...About forty-five minutes or an hour."

"Can you afford to dump it?"

I told him yes, so he told Steve to go ahead and dump the milk.

The officer and I went in the barn before Steve, and the man was still on the barn dirt floor. Steve was shaking his head. "Dennis, were you afraid he was going to get away?"

The Officer chuckled and said, "Dennis, you sure did him up good."

"My adrenaline was high, thinking about what they were doing in the house."

The officer undid the gag and I undid his feet. He coughed a little and wouldn't say a word to Officer Hume's questions. He was marched out to the police car and was put in the back seat. The other man was put in another police car. As soon as the detective had taken all the pictures he wanted of the truck and our contents on the back of it, he told us we could unload it. It was dark by then, but we unloaded it on to the back porch. After the police and the ambulance were gone, I just stood outside looking around the yard. It was as though the last hour was just in our imaginations, and we were stunned.

Pop cleared his throat. "Steve, I want you to stay here with Dennis tonight. One of you can sleep on the couch. Let's not take any more chances with anyone else thinking no one is living here and they can come help themselves."

I said, "No, the living room is clean. You can sleep in John's old bed in my room."

I asked, "What are you going to tell Mom? You will have to tell her something. What did you tell her when you left?"

"I just said that was Dennis. He wants Steve and me to come over for something. He didn't say what."

I looked at my watch. With all that went on with the police detective asking questions or taking pictures, I realized two hours had passed. Pop's cell phone started ringing and I said… "I'll bet that's Mom."

When Pop hung up he said, "You were right. It was your mother. The first thing she asked was, "What's going on? I walked out to the garage to see what boxes Dennis had brought over and saw a police car leave, an ambulance and two other vehicles."

He told Mom he would be on home in a few minutes, but Steve was going to stay over here with Dennis tonight. He asked if that was okay with her.

Pop said, "Her voice was shaky, so I had better scoot and explain it all to her. She is almost paranoid when it comes to her man-sized cubs."

He looked at both of us guys, "Shall I tell her about the death?"

"It'll come out in the paper, so you might as well tell her."

I looked at the mess on the kitchen floor and said, "We'll clean up this mess. She'll be over tomorrow and wonder about any blood that we miss, so tell her."

I thought a second or two and said, "Pop, you go on home. I'm going to call her. She will need to hear the story from me and to hear my voice. She needs to know that I'm okay, and I need to make her understand that the training I'm getting as a policeman came in good stead this evening. Otherwise, she will have her emotional radar sky high and wish John and I were going into a different profession. Right now, she needs to only see the positive side."

Pop said, "Well, I'm out of here then. Do you think you can clean up this mess tonight?"

"Pop, I just finished this evening with a lot of Clorox rags that I was using on the cupboards. I'll get them back in here and clean all the blood off the floor and splatters on the walls. If I need any more rags, I'll go check my old clothes. Don't you worry. You just go and keep Mom, Glen, and Paul calm. Aunt Susan is probably over there wringing her hands, too, by now."

Pop left and I called Mom, "Mom, I sure am glad I am staying over here until John and Marianne get back.

"We had some visitors come in and decide they had the perfect place to back up a truck and to load up wedding gifts and other boxes that we had packed. I caught one in the barn looking for the driver of your old car. He was on the ground before he knew what hit him. I stuffed his mouth with a rag from the milk strainer table and tied him up. Fortunately, I had my cell phone and called for back-up. I slipped up to the house and took their truck keys, so the two men in the house weren't going anywhere.

"I'm glad the training I'm getting allowed me to do some quick thinking while staying calm."

I could hear Pop come in the house and say, "Your son is quite a hero." I wished I could say thanks to him right at that moment, but Mom asked, "Well, what were the ambulance and those other cars over there for?"

Pop said, "Because one of the thieves pulled a gun on Officer Glass and he had to protect himself and shoot, too."

Since Mom had the phone on, I added, "The man was a poor shot and got Officer Glass in the arm. The other man wasn't so lucky. Mom, let's thank God that I was over here and that the Lord protected me and all *our* things are still here, as are Marianne and John's wedding gifts.

Steve and I worked until midnight cleaning up the mess on the walls, floor, and outside of some cupboards. We talked the whole time we were working. I guess our adrenalin was still up. It was our first experience with a shooting. Steve commented that tonight's experience wasn't going to be our last. We worried about Glen and hoped that Pop and Mom didn't tell him anything. Although, it might be hard to hide it from him. Glen is very observant.

Steve plans to start next year at the Southeast Missouri University Law Enforcement Academy. He thinks it might be a good thing for Glen to consider, but after his talk in church this morning, God may be calling him to be a minister. We talked about how calm he seemed to be in front of the microphone.

I asked Steve if Glen has said anything to him after the service. He said, "Not really, he did say, 'I'm glad I made the decision to be baptized.'"

I told Steve that I heard Glen later ask Pop if he thought there would be enough money to set up the house for the Hegel. Pop told him we all might have to dig a little into our family account and help again. Dad is not talking to Glen about how much he is worth. He wants Glen to learn to manage money just like the rest of us. The accountants are still trying to work with people in Ireland to track down everything. I suspect when Glen turns eighteen or twenty-one, Pop will sit him down and talk with him, again. Right now, Glen, has to start his own savings account and work toward some goal."

I thought about Glen for a few minutes as I scrubbed at a spot on the floor. Steve said, "Paul told Glen, he would help Blake's family. He thought he could spare some of this egg money. I told Paul, if he couldn't, he could supply Blake's family with eggs once a week or a chicken for chicken nuggets."

I asked, "What was his response to that?"

"He didn't say anything. He plowed into me like a bulldozer and tried to wrestle me to the floor. He's still sensitive about not realizing his chickens could be used for meat, too, when he was younger.

"I had him laughing after a few minutes. Mom got after us and said, 'my living, dining and pantry room is too small for a wrestling ring added to it,' so we quit and laughed at Mom. Did you know she had Pop haul in the small television and put it on my dresser and her favorite rocking chair, too? I'm so glad our rooms are large. I suspect they were thinking about families coming home to visit with children some day in the future. That's probably another reason why they wanted John and Marianne to have the farm house."

Steve and I chatted as we worked and then sat in the living room for a few minutes. We were both so tired. I reminded him that it was just this morning that he chided me for feeling the loss of John and here we were buddies like I was with John He reminded *me* of my lectures about how God always has a blessing for us, if we maintain an attitude of thankfulness in everything.

"Today will be over in... I looked at my watch... exactly one minute and today, we had a wonderful experience in church with Glen. Some people gave their lives to the Lord. We had some new people join our church from other places. We had our St. Louis family here with us until around three. I was able to clean the living room and dining room and kitchen thoroughly and moved boxes over to the new house. We discovered the new truck and I was kept from harm this evening and all of our stuff and Marianne and John's gifts are safe. Thank you, God, for standing by us."

Steve was looking at me with big eyes and raised eyebrows when the clock struck midnight. He said, "Back up a minute in what you said, what new truck?"

I realized that I had let the cat out of the bag and I shook my head and got up off the couch with a chuckle and said, "Oh! I let a secret out."

I flopped back down on the couch. I had to tell the rest of it as Steve has been patiently waiting to replace *his* truck. "Steve, it's not what you are thinking."

"Pop found a picture of Grandpa's old truck when it was brand-new with Grandma and Grandpa standing next to it. The picture was in color, so he had it enlarged for Mom. Then he decided to check on the old truck and the security guard told him to come over and see it. It was all done, except for the paint job. Pop offered to buy it back when it was done. The man took the offer and made a profit. Pop gave him a copy of the snapshot and it was painted in the original color. It's in the smaller garage over there at the house. Mom's birthday is next week and he wants to give it back to her. Steve, it's a beaut!

"I went over this afternoon with some boxes and pulled open the door and Pop came running out of the house quickly to see who opened the door. Robert had come with me to show everyone his newly acquired car. So, we both saw the truck. Pop asked me not to say anything, so I will tell him that you know."

Steve was looking at his watch. "Are you sleeping upstairs?"

I grabbed the afghan off the back of a chair and threw it at Steve and said, "I'm sleeping upstairs in my own bed. Wake me up if I oversleep."

Steve said, "So, Robert finally has his own set of wheels, don't tell me about it. I'll call him tomorrow and let him tell me. Well, that is another blessing today."

I told Steve, "Good night" and went on upstairs. I set my clock and reached for my Bible and turned to Isaiah chapter forty again. I prayed, "Lord, Thank you for this day. Some awful things happened and I know that you are aware of the smallest detail. Please help Mom, Pop, and Steve be at peace with what happened here at our home today. Thank you for the people that came to you today at the church and received you as their ultimate Savior. Thank you for being mine."

I began reading the verses that bring me comfort every time I read them. My thoughts strayed and I wondered if John was reading the same scripture to Marianne because they are his favorite verses, also. The verses starting with verse twenty-eight of Isaiah forty.

Do you not know? Have you not heard? The Lord is the everlasting God, the Creator of the ends of the earth. He will not grow tired or weary, and his understanding no one can fathom.

He gives strength to the weary and increases the power of the weak. Even youths grow tired and weary, and young men stumble and fall; but those who hope in the Lord will renew their strength.

They will soar on wings like eagles; they will run and not grow weary, they will walk and not faint. (NKJV)

I thought about *why* things happened as they did today. I don't understand the *why* of a lot of things. I thought about the strength and courage that God gave to Glen today. I thought about myself and how physically tired I was after all the scrubbing that I had done today, how discouraged I was just this morning. I thought about the way I had memorized the same scripture from the King James version of Isaiah 40 and had learned the words as…*they that wait upon the Lord will renew their strength.* It really doesn't make any difference because I am going to *wait* and *hope* in the Lord.

I closed my Bible and laid it on the floor and started to say, "Goodnight, John, but instead I said, "Goodnight, Lord."

CHAPTER 11

I DON'T KNOW WHAT HAPPENED last night after reading my Bible and praying… but I must have totally lost consciousness. I went to sleep and never knew another thing until the sun was shining in my window. It seemed like yesterday was weeks ago. I thanked God for the good night's rest. I lay there for a few minutes trying to convince myself to open my eyes and get up, when I felt a dripping on my face and shot up like the roof was leaking on my head or was falling in.

Glen and Paul were standing beside my bed with a glass of water snipping wet fingers over my face and the cold droplets brought me to attention very quickly. I said, "Guys, what time is it?"

I reached for my clock and it said, "Eight-thirty." My feet hit the floor, but both boys were laughing.

Paul said, "Your chores are already done. I took care of the chickens, and Glen and Pop took care of the cattle."

"What about the milking? Is Steve up?"

"We were up early, so Pop said, 'Let's go over and help Steve and Dennis with the chores.' We came in and looked at you two lazy-guys and Pop decided to let you both sleep. He said you had a late night working. What kept you up so late? The house looks okay. It's clean, too."

"Thanks… that's what kept us up late."

Paul said, "You must have been tired. Someone left my eggs on the steps outside and Pop dumped out last night's milk."

My mind was scrambling to make order of what happened and when. The boys weren't helping me much. Glen was looking at me like—are you sick or something?

He finally said, "Dennis, are you okay?

I said, "Yes, I think I am, but twenty-four hours ago, I was planning to go to church without my hair combed and my shirt buttoned up two buttons shy of a button-hole. I think my brain is two buttons off from a button-hole. Do I look the same?"

Glen and Paul both laughed and Glen said, "I don't think there is anything wrong with you that a hot shower and a cup of coffee won't cure."

Paul said, "Hot biscuits would be better, but Steve is down in Grandpa's bathroom, and you aren't any better at cooking than I am."

"Thanks, Paul, but I believe I'll start with the hot shower."

"Pop brought over some cereal and juice. It's downstairs. You'll have to go over to the house for coffee. Pop couldn't find a thermos to put some in. Someone packed things good."

"It was probably me, but I'll forgo the coffee right now for that hot shower. Paul, the hen house needs to be cleaned again. Go get the hose and get started and I'll be down to help you as soon as I'm dressed.

Paul did a "Yes…*Sir*," with a salute to it and walked out. Glen was still standing there looking at me as I got my clean clothes out of the dresser. "Dennis, something happened over here late yesterday. I know it did. Would you tell me about it? Pop said, 'Glen, you worry about Blake, right now, okay? I don't think he's being fair. I'm part of this family now, so he should let me share in whatever hurts or bothers someone, or whenever the family needs help. I'm not a dummy. I can think and feel with the rest of you."

"You're right, Glen. Pop just wants to spare you any further emotional pain. For some reason, his protective radar goes up where you are concerned. He fell in love with you… If I may say it like that, from the first time he met you working in the garden. He said a couple of times. 'That Glen is a special kid. I don't know why I feel that way. I just feel a certain communication with him.' Do you suppose God did that?"

Glen looked surprised, "Is that right?"

"Yes, that's right, but that doesn't answer your original question. I will tell you this much. Last night when I was out doing the chores in the barn, we were visited by some brazen thieves. They backed their truck right up to the back door and decided to load up with the boxes we had packed and were planning to load up John's and Marianne's wedding gifts, also. I caught one of them and hog tied him in the barn and called 911. The police came and got the other two. One was not very fortunate though as he pulled a gun on one of the officers and the bullet went through the policeman's arm. The thief wasn't so lucky. He was shot and died on our kitchen floor."

"Well, I won't tell Dad that I know, and I won't tell Paul either."

I said, "Thanks, Glen. You are one step from being twenty years-old in that head of yours."

"No, I'm not. But I *am* a changed person. I have God in my life and *He* knows everything."

I knuckled Glen on the upper arm. "Way to go, Buddy. I'm so proud of you and all my brothers, but I have to go get in that shower."

I walked out of the room leaving Glen standing there. Half-way to the bathroom, I stopped for a second and thought, *Hey... Glen called Pop, 'Dad.'* I smiled and went on to the shower.

———

I had a good feeling as the morning wore on. My chores were done, and the hen house got hosed down. Those who knew about Sunday evening's experience didn't seem overly concerned.

Mom was even in good spirits, though she preferred it never happened. Pop took Glen, Steve, and Paul up to see Blake. I chose to spend the day cleaning every room upstairs, so Mom or Marianne and Mrs. Weber wouldn't have to do it. Believe it or not, I even washed windows. Mom came over to the house to see what cleaning had to be done. I was just finishing up and rinsing my bucket, my rags, and putting my cleaning supplies in a box. I said, "Mom, your timing is perfect. I just finished."

Mom couldn't believe the house was so clean. It was already almost three o'clock in the afternoon. I was tired and my good feelings from the morning were gone. Every room that I cleaned had too many memories all swirling around in my head.

Mom asked me if there was something bothering me or if my working so hard at the old house was an avoidance thing. I said, "Well, yes... I am avoiding something. I'm trying to get everything done, so I can spend some time with Janet. My mind has been so saturated with other things that I can't stay on track about anything. So I decided that I had to concentrate on one thing at a time and right now... this day, it is this house. I'm avoiding all my memories in this house. I'm avoiding having to move over to the Jenkins, so I was cleaning everything over here. I'm avoiding going to Cape Girardeau and visiting Blake, too."

Mom asked, "But why?"

"I don't know why, Mom, I keep having feelings like John used to describe—like I'm a little kid inside a big body. The way I feel right now, I would not be an encouragement to Blake. So many people say we are mature kids in this family, but honestly, Mom, we don't feel like it.

There are times when I long for the times when we were little boys. You and Dad took care of us, and we didn't have any responsibilities. All we had to do were simple chores and play, play, play."

Mom was looking at me so serious. She finally said, "Do you really think and feel this way and did John, also?"

"Yeah, Mom, I'm sure when Dad died and Grandpa came to live with us we felt fairly secure, but you got sick and Grandpa died. I think John and I felt more of a responsibility for everyone and everything than we really needed to, but it just seemed like there was one crisis after another taking place all the time, and we knew it was not fair for you to have full burden of everything, especially when we were capable kids. You know Mom, I think what I really need is to learn to play again. I need some balance in my life."

Mom had tears running down her cheeks and I was feeling so sorry for myself that I wasn't thinking. I was hurting Mom's feelings. Pop was back from seeing Blake. He came in and said, "What's going on?"

I don't think he had ever seen Mom cry. He was visibly upset. I backed off, "Mom, I'm so sorry. I didn't mean to upset you."

Mom came to me and grabbed me in a big bear-hug and said, "Okay, Son, you are going to learn to play again. I think as soon as the boys in the prevention program have their gardens done, and as soon as you have the program for the older boys up and going well, and as soon as we have our house finished, we will take a week and go somewhere away from here for a vacation and you can unwind and learn to play again."

Mom paused. "There always seems to be a *as soon as* time in our life. I'm so sorry, Dennis."

Pop walked over and put his arms around both of us and said, "Mother Moore Lynn, what this boy needs is a vacation from everything and everyone right *now*. He needs to go in town with that pretty little girl of his and spend the rest of this day doing nothing, but sitting in the park, or taking a swim, or looking for a car or whatever comes to his mind to do. For an almost twenty year-old kid, he doesn't need to head up programs that some older person with a couple of college degrees and out of work could do. He needs to have no chores, no responsibility for two weeks. He needs to unwind and rest. Look at what he has done in this house. He burned up all that energy doing something in one day, and it could have been done in three days with three other people.

"Dennis, I want you to sit down here at the kitchen table for five minutes. I have a few phone calls to make and you aren't going to lift a finger while I am making them."

He looked at Mom and asked her to dial the Weber's home. I guess he had forgotten it. Mom dialed and Janet answered. Pop took the phone, "Is this Janet? Dr. Lynn here, known as Pop to Dennis. How much do you love this guy sitting at the table here in the farmhouse at the kitchen table?"

Janet must have asked if he was sitting at the kitchen table because he said, "No, I'm not sitting, I'm standing, but there is a six-foot-three or four inch handsome critter sitting here at the table, and he needs a pretty little gal and an afternoon away from the farm, all the chores, and all the people around him in his family who he worries about."

I knew the way Pop was talking that Janet may get upset and worry about me. I don't know what she said, but Pop went on and said. "Yes, can you have your Mother bring you out here? I'll tell you both what I want you to do and where I want you to go. I won't take *no* for an answer. Okay? Now let me talk to your mother."

Mrs. Weber got on the phone and Pop said, "Rachel, Dr. Lynn here... or whatever my first name is... Yes, Marshall."

He laughed and said, "I've said Dr. Lynn so many times in my life, I still say it to family... sorry 'bout that. Anyway, I don't want to alarm you, but we had some thieves come out to the house last night and try to take our boxes that we had packed off the back porch. They were going through Marianne and John's gifts and things are in disarray. I was wondering if you and my wife might want to get in this bedroom and see if you can put things back together again. The list of gifts should be somewhere in there from the shower, but from the wedding you will have to do the best you can. Okay... second question, I want to send Janet and Dennis into Cape Girardeau for the rest of the day. Do you need her for anything?"

There was a long pause and Pop said, "Okay, we'll see you shortly. Bye!"

Pop sat down, "Okay, Dennis, this is an order and if you don't obey, I will have to have your mother help me and we will take you upstairs for another shower and put some sweet-smelling cologne on you, and dress you, too, like you would if you were going on your first date with Janet."

I laughed, "I'm going... I'm going."

Mom didn't know what to make of Pop or what he had in mind. I grabbed Mom on the way out of the kitchen and said, "Mom, I'm sorry I upset you. Pray for me. Sometimes I need a good spanking like a child, too."

"You are forgiven son, I love you."

"I love you, too, Mom." I hurried upstairs and showered and even shaved closer again. It was sort of nice not having share the bathroom, but I will since Pop is insisting that Steve be back over here until John gets back.

— ◆ —

While I was upstairs, Pop made a few phone calls and wrote an address and a number on a piece of paper. I had no idea where Siemer Drive was in Cape Girardeau or what the number meant. The second number wasn't a phone number.

I came downstairs to find Mr. Weber, Steve and Glen, Mom and Pop and Paul, all standing in the kitchen, grinning sheepishly. I said, "Where's Janet and what is going on?"

Mom said, "Pop told her to go on out and wait for you in the car."

I started to say, that wasn't very nice, but they all had such silly looks on their faces that I knew they had done something and it was going to be a surprise, so I said, "Oh, well, I guess I will be out of here. I don't know where, but I'll try to be home before eleven."

Pop said, "Wait a minute, I need you to pick up something on Siemer Drive for me, if you are going to Cape Girardeau. That's what that note is for."

"I don't remember where that is exactly, but if it is a street we generally go on, I'll find it."

Pop said, "I started to pick it up today, but decided to get on back home."

I noticed Steve walk out laughing about something and said, "Pop, I need to run back over to the house and get a couple of my things, if I'm going to stay here the rest of the week. Do you mind if I borrow your car?"

"Fine, but don't dilly dally around and leave your Mom here to have to walk home."

Mom and Mrs. Weber went in Marianne and John's bedroom.

Mrs. Weber gasped and said, "What a mess! Those skunks! I would like to descend on them, like a vulture."

Pop threw his head back and did a real belly-laugh. Glen and Paul thought it was funny, too.

"Well, Janet has waited long enough. I had better get out of here."

Pop said, "Wait a minute. Dennis, how much cash do you have for a nice dinner?"

I pulled out my billfold and looked. "I have two twenties. That should be enough."

Pop handed me another twenty and said, "Take this. You don't want to embarrass your young lady if it comes a nickel over."

"No, I don't want to do that." I took the twenty and told him I would pay him back.

"Do your mother's errand first, as the place may be closed by the time you get done with dinner."

"I will. Thanks for the twenty."

I hurried out to the car. I climbed in and reached over to Janet and gave her a kiss on the cheek and said, "Do you know what is going on?"

She said, "No, not really. Mom said, 'Dennis is really getting overworked and needs to get away from all the chores, the moving, and what happened here last night.' What happened last night, Dennis? Mom didn't tell me."

I pulled out of the drive and headed down the lane. I knew I was going to have to tell Janet something, but as a policeman's wife someday, I would have to be careful *how* I told her. I was thinking and she said, "Dennis?"

I cleared my throat. "Last night three thieves drove their pick-up truck right up to our back door and proceeded to load it up with all the boxes that we had packed and were about to make off with Marianne's and John's wedding gifts. Fortunately, I was out behind the barn and heard them. I called 911. We caught them red-handed. They didn't get away with anything. Although, my mother and your mother are trying to figure out which gift goes in what box. They made a mess while going through things. They probably thought we had all moved to the new house and knew John and Marianne were on their honeymoon. I've heard there have been some insensitive thieves do the same thing when people are at a funeral service for someone in the family. They must have hearts of stone to do that."

That diverted Janet's attention, but I created another one. She said, "Maybe I should go back and help them."

I didn't say anything for a moment and she came back with, "I'm sorry. My place is with you. You need me more."

I reached over and took her hand and said, "I've needed you for days, but I've been too busy fighting my pity party, by working overtime at getting the house ready for John and Marianne. I don't know, Janet, why I'm fighting this change by moving to the new house and losing John as a roommate and a buddy. We have shared so much over the years with all the responsibilities we've had. Some of them were of our own making—like the gardens and all the boys. God has been good, though. He has used the program to get us acquainted with Glen and Blake and the programs have been great for the communities as well as the boys."

Janet said, "...and look what happened Sunday morning. God changed people's lives and it's all because you let God use yours to make a difference in Glen's life and the other boys' lives, too."

"Yeah, but... I guess I was feeling a little tired and over-worked and out of energy. I hurt Mom's feelings, by saying I wish that I knew how to play. I told her there has been so many crises in our lives that I need to take time out to play-play-play. That's why Pop insisted that I go out with you and get away from everything. He told me I was going out... and no ands, ifs, or buts type excuses.

He picked up the phone and called you. I don't often get depressed, if that was what I was feeling. I know I wanted to sit down in a corner and just cry my eyes out like a child. John used to tell me that he felt like a little boy in a great big body. I understood today, just how he was feeling."

Janet reached over and rubbed my arm. "Dennis, I am so sorry. You're making me feel bad for not giving you more attention."

"It isn't your fault. You would have had to chase me out of the boys' gardens, or from scrubbing down the house, or washing the windows in the house or from carrying boxes to the new house. I guess, Janet, that I am just emotionally and physically tired."

"Dennis, pull over and get out. I'm going to drive. You need to sit over here and let me do the driving and do every decision making thing we have to do the rest of this day."

"Janet, I appreciate that, but Pop wants me to go by Seimer drive and pick up something for Mom. I don't know what it is."

I handed her the slip of paper and she said, "If I'm not mistaken that is the street Wal-Mart is on. Let's check that out first."

We had taken the Dutchtown route into Cape Girardeau and the short-cut down Bloomfield Road. Sure enough, Janet was right. Siemer Drive intersects with Bloomfield Road and goes to the new Highway 74 or the Shawnee Parkway. I asked, "What's the street number on Siemer Drive?'

Janet read the number to me. We couldn't find the number and though it must be up around Staples or someplace in the strip mall. It wasn't. So I called Mom on the cell phone and said, "Did Pop give us the correct number? Is it in the strip mall here, where Target is?'

She said, "No, Pop said he had stopped at the car dealer today and had gotten something, but wouldn't tell me what it was, so check with the numbers on the mailboxes in front of the car dealers."

I hung up. "Pop must be surprising Mom with something else. He has Grandpa's old truck all restored to give to Mom for her birthday and she doesn't know it. So I guess we are on a little scavenger hunt this evening." I checked the first car dealer's mailbox and it wasn't the right number.

The next one was the Bud shell Car Dealer and I thought, *This stands to reason… this place sells many brands. Pop must have found something for the old truck.*

Janet said, "Look at those guys. Business must be slow, and they are either waiting to go home or waiting for another customer."

"Well, I wish we could afford to be their next one, but Pop just wanted me to pick something up here for Mom."

"Dennis, remember faith and hope will get us here for our car someday. God's timing—remember that." I reached over and patted her arm and said, "Thanks, sweetheart, I need to be reminded. I'll be back in a minute."

One of the salesmen came out with a big smile and greeted me and said, "Are you Dennis Moore?"

"Yes," He glanced back at the two men still standing in the window and they were grinning just like the family was smiling when I had left them at the farm.

The salesman said, "I need to ask you to move your car. Would you park it over…." He pointed to another open space. I was taller than the sales man and I looked down at him and said, "I'm sorry, but I won't be spending time here as a customer. I'm here to pick something up for my folks—Bonnie Moore Lynn and Dr. Lynn."

"We have it, but you will have to move your car. We can't have the garage doors blocked."

I climbed back in the car and said, "He wants me to move the car away from the garage doors. He doesn't sound like a patient man."

I moved the car and stepped back out. The salesman was standing two feet from my open door. "Have Janet get out of the car, too."

"Oh, you know Janet?"

"Not, really, I just know who she is."

My jealousy radar perked its head up, but I let it go. I ducked my head back in the car and said, "Janet, he called you by your name, and he wants you to get out of the car, too." I whispered, "Do you know this man?"

Janet looked at me puzzled and whispered, "No-o!" She got out of the car and came around to me.

"Wait right here."

He went in the single door and was in there for what seemed like forever. I looked down at Janet and said," I wonder why he wanted me to move the car. He's a strange sort of person."

"Yeah, and why are we standing here?"

"Oh, here he comes."

"I'm sorry, there must be some mistake. I can't carry it out here to you. You will have to come get it."

"I'd be happy to. Is it that heavy? Maybe I should go back and bring my car closer."

"No, rules are... no blocking the bay doors."

I looked at Janet and she said to the man, "Well, can I help him carry whatever it is?"

He said, "No, you are just a tiny little thing. No way!"

My jealousy radar raised its head again because I didn't like the way he scanned Janet up and down, but he looked the other way as soon as he said it, so I guess he figured what he said wasn't quite appropriate.

"Dennis, how old are you?" I thought that was a strange question and I felt like saying, *Man, we are here to pick up something for my mother... what does my age have to do with anything.*

I realized that I must be in the same bad mood that I had an hour ago and prayed, *Lord, I need your spirit to fill me now and help me to be loving and kind.* I know I must have looked at him for a second or two as I was thinking, but went on to say, "I'll be twenty in just a few weeks, sir."

A mechanic came out the door and said, "Sir, I think this is the box, but I'm supposed to have the young man check it and make sure it is right."

The salesman handed the box to me. It was easily opened with a flap.

I looked inside the box and there was just a set of keys in it. I looked at the man. "I'll have to wait until I get home. The old truck is parked in a garage in Chaffee.

Janet leaned over and looked in the box. "I guess Pop had a second set of keys made for Grandpa's old truck."

It all made sense to me. "What do I owe you for these?"

"They've already been paid for." The man looked toward the building as he said that and then walked toward the building.

I said to Janet quietly, "He's a little strange... he gave us the keys and walked off."

I noticed the other two salesmen coming out of the door and walking toward us. "Well, Janet, I guess we had better be on our way."

One of the salesmen coming out of the door stopped at a car and the other one took the few steps closer to us. He said, "Wouldn't you like to look around? We may have something here you can trade for that car of yours."

I looked at Janet and she said, "Dennis we ought not to put temptation in front of us. I don't think you or I are quite ready to go into any kind of debt."

The other salesman came up beside us and added, "We have a real sweet dear in our garage right now. It just came in yesterday.

The man purchased it last year and only put about five-thousand miles on it, and he promptly died. His wife brought it back in for us to sell. We've checked it over, and it's ready to go."

Janet looked up at me and said, "Temptation, Dennis."

"I guess we had better be going. It's very tempting to just look, but we better not. Let me go home and think about it."

The man said, "It won't be here tomorrow. I have another person who will be here tomorrow, and he will take it."

"You sound awfully sure."

He said, "I am."

The garage bay door went up and there stood Officer Harrison with Blake and Glen, Mom and Pop, Mr. and Mrs. Weber, Robert, Steve and Paul. Another salesman was videoing the whole thing. There was a silver king-cab truck very much like Steve's truck that got wrecked with a big bow on it. Mom and Pop stepped up to me and said, "Happy Birthday, Son."

The salesman said, "The keys are in the box... Try them out."

I looked down at Janet, and she started to cry. I grabbed her and said, "Janet... God has blessed us again."

Then I turned to Mom and gave her a hug. I think I must have hugged everyone standing there, including a salesman. I kept saying, "I can't believe this. Mom, you must have cleaned out the family account."

Pop said, "Son, you had better try those keys out, so these salesmen can go back on the job or go home."

I was still standing there in shock and had a dozen thoughts running through my head, including why they couldn't *carry* it out for me and Janet was *too small*. I looked at Mom and said, "Mom, Pop, I don't have enough in my account to pay for half of this."

"Son, John left me a check and said, 'See that Dennis looks

for a truck. We need one on the farm.' He handed me a check for fifteen-hundred dollars and would not take no for an answer.

"John also said, he thought it was unfair for him to farm fifty acres and you to farm only ten. I told him that I had offered you fifteen acres as a wedding gift and he said, 'Great! That makes me feel a little better. Tell him to take ten more of mine.'"

I had a flash thought about the parable of the ten talents and said, "Well, God expected me to do with my ten acres as well as anyone would with whatever they were given."

Pop said, "That attitude is why you deserve this truck. Now take those keys and try them out."

Steve and Mr. Weber were sitting in the cab and the others were all standing there watching all the discourse. Robert was listening and said, "Now Dennis. If you wait very much longer I'm going to trade my car for your truck."

Officer Harrison said, "Dennis, you deserve this truck. You've done a super job with the boys in my program. I want to help make your first payment." He opened his billfold and handed Pop two one hundred dollar bills.

"If this isn't enough, fill up your gas tank a couple of times."

I shook his hand and said, "Officer Harrison, I really don't deserve everyone's kindness. When did you find out this was going to happen?"

"...From the beginning. This was my uncle's truck. I called your folks and they took the ball from there."

Mom said, "Dennis, the keys."

"Oh...."

I took the keys out of the box and looked toward the truck and realized Blake was standing there. I forgot the truck and hurriedly went to Blake. I said, "Blake, thank you for being here. Can I hug you or are your ribs too sore."

"You hugged me a while ago, but I didn't think you knew who

you were hugging. And yes, I had a touch of your big hands on my ribs, but I'm okay now. I'll forego this hug, though."

We laughed together and he said, "Did you know I'm coming back to Chaffee and I'm going to stay with Mr. Jenkins for a few weeks?"

I looked back at Mom and Pop and Officer Harrison talking. "Thank you, Lord, for your goodness."

Glen had joined Blake and said, "That's what I said."

Mr. Weber got out of the truck. "Well, Dennis, you have a fine truck there. It's safe enough to protect my daughter."

"Thank you, Sir. I can't believe this is happening."

"Well, believe it, son, and enjoy God's blessing. I have to leave this joyous occasion and go back to work for about an hour. You kids enjoy your evening."

Janet hugged her dad. "Thanks for being here, Dad. If I had known it was going to happen, I would have insisted that you be here. I love you, Dad."

He hugged her again and chuckled and said, "Not as much as I love you."

Janet giggled and said, "Ah, Dad."

Steve still had an amused look on his face. "Dennis, the mechanics need you to move the truck on out. Do you want me to move it for you?"

I handed Steve the keys and he moved the truck out of the bay to the parking lot. I walked over to Mom and said, "What am I supposed to do with your car?"

"We were just discussing that and decided that Steve will drive it on home for the moment. Mrs. Weber is thinking it might be one that Janet can purchase. It will be a couple of years before Glen will need to get a car or truck and Paul, too. We'll talk about that when you get home or tomorrow."

Pop said, "There are already temporary dealer's tags posted in the window, so you and Janet are free to go."

Officer Harrison said, "I need to scoot on home, too."

We all walked together toward the truck. I helped Janet in and she said, "This is big!" I got in my side and realized I was panicking and wondered how to get out of the parking lot without hitting one of the other cars. I turned the motor on and then off again. I stepped back out of the truck and said to the salesman, "I think I would be more comfortable, if you would drive the truck to the entrance to the parking lot here."

He said, "Get in and scoot over. I'll do it for you." Everyone got up on the sidewalk in front of the dealer's shop windows and watched us leave. Janet turned and waved.

I pulled on out of the parking lot on to Seimer Drive. "Janet, Let's go to Sikeston, so I can get the feel of this on the highway."

"No, Benton is far enough." I agreed, but was silent, with my mind on everything about the truck. My wildest imagination could never have guessed what I was picking up at the dealer for Pop. Janet finally broke the silence and said, "Well, what do you think?"

"I think God is good."

A week has passed since I worked myself so hard on getting the house ready for John and Marianne. I was really trying to avoid the change in our family and John's and my relationship. I've been driving the truck for a week and love it more each time I get in it. With John's contribution to the truck and with Pop paying some and with what I had saved, I was able to get my payments down to a level that were easy for me.

It's been a week, also, since the thieves broke into the farmhouse. Everything was okay after Mom and Mrs. Weber sorted out all the gifts. They only found two gifts without names on them. We must have caught those men before they got too far, or in their dumbness they didn't take off the cards taped to the boxes. On a personal level, I don't ever want to experience someone breaking or entering *my* home again, but as a policeman, I will have more feeling for others who experience the invasion of their privacy. It really makes me want to go after those kinds of criminals. I hope that the Lord can help me keep from being bitter and love them as He does. It also gave me an experience that I could use to talk to the boys in the crime prevention program.

Since the boys' gardens are beginning to yield some vegetables, it has been a blessing to have the truck. I can carry the tools back and forth and line up the boys produce boxes in the back of the truck. I recommended to Officer Harrison that we buy a big Rubbermaid box-like container that we could lock the tools in. I would save us from carrying them back and forth to the shed several times a week. He thought it was a good idea. Pop bought one the next time he was in the Lowes Home Store and gave the bill to Officer Harrison. It worked perfectly. During the off season, Officer Harrison can take it home with him or we can store it in the barn.

Even though the boys from Cape Girardeau were coming out to work in their gardens, we still managed to get all moved into the new house. The main level was just about completed. A little painting touch-up here and there and the carpeting, and it would be done. Mom insisted that the carpenters work on the kitchen so she could move the pantry and other things out of Steve's bedroom.

She said, Dennis, I decided after your outburst of dreading to move into the Jenkins' farmhouse that we would put Blake over there with Brian and you could move in with Steve."

All I could think to say was, "Mom, I'm sorry about that, but I'm glad I'm here with the family."

So, I moved in with the family, and John and Marianne came home from their honeymoon. They both were very excited to tell about seeing the ocean. John had taken the Buick and driven to Florida through the southern states. He said, "I didn't mind the driving, but on the way back, we decided to go through the Blue Ridge Mountains. The scenery was beautiful, but I'll take the flat land in Chaffee over the mountains. I'll be content to look at pictures of mountains and not drive up and down them.

Marianne agreed. She did say, though, that there were several places that looked interesting and wouldn't mind going back for a visit. Mom told them that since they have had their nose to the grindstone for so long with school and farm responsibilities, that perhaps they really should consider taking a vacation away from everything once a year and travel. There is another whole world out there waiting for all of us.

John agreed that it was good to get away and get a whole new perspective on places and things. He told Mom that perhaps she and Pop should go before the summer was out and take the younger boys.

She said, "Maybe we could… just before school starts.

My nineteenth year came to a close and I had my twentieth birthday. I thought over the past year about the many things that had affected our family. I thought about Paul's relapse with leukemia, my confrontation with the wasps and winding up in the hospital. I thought about my foot and ankle injury that perhaps created the aneurysm and resulted in my head surgery. I thought about Mom and Pop moving out of the farmhouse and leaving John and me to manage the farm. I thought about getting all the fields harvested and getting my job at the university. I thought about Glen and the deaths of his family and Blake's near miss with death. I even thought about how depressed I had gotten and spouted off to Mom. I'm really going to watch that. If I feel like I can't handle any more stress, I will do something first about it, before hurting Mom's feelings again.

Through all the tension of my nineteenth year, it turned out to be a good year. Paul is in remission from his relapse with the leukemia; Blake's wounds have healed and his family is settled back in Chaffee. That is a story that I would like to tell sometime, but I will leave that for Blake to tell. Glen put his past behind him and has moved forward in life. He is learning more about his biological family. Pop is helping him deal with the loss of his sisters, stepmother, and grandmother. Pop learned that Glen is actually a prince, but Pop told him, "A title is no good, unless you are a prince in word and deed."

When God got hold of Glen, the change was dramatic. Glen says, "We are all princes and princesses because, if we believe in Jesus, we are adopted into the king's family. I am a child of the King, and you are, too."

He won't let anyone treat him like he is more than the rest of the family. Glen can't touch any of his wealth until he is twenty-one, but he already has many projects he wants to give money to. Pop told Glen that he could change his mind as often as he wanted to change it, before he is twenty-one years old. Glen wasn't sure what Pop meant until he explained to him different charities change and he might choose something more meaningful to him another time in the future. Pop wouldn't hold him to anything. He was free to change his mind many times.

Glen said, "Oh." He just sat there thinking about what Pop had said.

The two highlights of the year were asking Janet to marry me and having her say, "Yes."

I just can't believe that we had both been interested in the other one for four years and both were afraid that we were just too young, so we didn't say anything. The other highlight was the surprise when the family got the truck for me. I really appreciated that, too. It's great to have a family that looks out for the welfare of the others. I just don't understand why family members don't yield their wants and desires, if it will benefit another one in the family more… or by yielding one's preference it brings about harmony for *all* the family. Mom and Dad taught us right when we were young children.

My first year at the Law Enforcement Academy was a good year. I'm looking forward to my second year. I've learned to count my blessings, and the one thing that was proven to me over and over is *God* is *good*.

I decided to label my journal with the year and sign off. You will see me again in Steve's book…. *Dennis*

P.S. Another blessing was, we did get our new well and the irrigation system is ready to go for the new crop season.